Faking
it

Faking it

BETH REEKLES

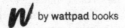 by wattpad books

 by wattpad books

An imprint of Wattpad WEBTOON Book Group

Copyright © 2024 Bethan Reeks

Published in Canada by Wattpad WEBTOON Book Group, a division of Wattpad WEBTOON Studios, Inc.

36 Wellington Street E., Suite 200, Toronto, ON M5E 1C7 Canada

www.wattpad.com

First W by Wattpad Books edition: January 2024

ISBN 978-1-99885-421-9 (Trade Paper original)
ISBN 978-1-99885-422-6 (eBook edition)

Library and Archives Canada Cataloguing in Publication information is available upon request.

Printed and bound in Canada

1 3 5 7 9 10 8 6 4 2

Cover design by Ellen Rockell — LBBG
Author Photo by Bethan Reeks
Typesetting by Delaney Anderson

For Aimee—
here's to all the frogs we've kissed
in the search for Prince Charming.

Sophie, 25
Marketing Assistant at Local Paper

About Me
Let's face it, you've already decided if you're going to swipe right or not just based on my first picture. I promise it's a recent one. I won't promise I roll out of bed looking that put together, so it's best for both of us if you lower your expectations a little now.

Height: 5'7"
Active: Sometimes
Astrological sign: Libra
Education: Undergraduate degree
Drinks: Frequently
Smokes: Never
Looking for: Relationship
My interests: Photography, Burlesque dancing, Museums and galleries, Indie music, City breaks
Perfect first date: Picnic in the park and being a local tourist

A review by a friend:
Sophie, you went to *one* burlesque dance class, that doesn't count. The only dancing you do is when you're hopping around trying to shave the backs of your knees in the shower. What do you mean, this isn't the kind of review you were hoping for? —My Best Friend.

Never have I ever . . .
. . . been in a long-term relationship.

SINGLE, SWIPE, REPEAT

I know it's a commercial fad . . .
but I just want somebody to love.

Views on Valentine's Day from our Dating & Relationships columnist

Published Friday, February 26

Like many single people all over the world this month, I spent Valentine's Day with the people I love most: my friends.

Not in person, of course. Not even over Zoom or FaceTime.

No, I spent Valentine's Day stalking my friends on social media, obsessing over every single loved-up, rosy, romantic post, while my own soul shriveled up with a combination of envy and the looming fear that I'll be alone forever.

A very *real* fear that my happily settled siblings are all too quick to remind me of whenever I see them.

A very real fear that my friends don't *realize* they're reminding me of each time they ask after a recent date of mine, and I am forced to tell them I've been ghosted—again.

My friends, by all accounts, had a spectacular time celebrating Valentine's. One was given a dog—*a dog!*—by her boyfriend. Another was proposed to at the restaurant where she and her S.O. have celebrated many an anniversary. Some enjoyed cozy nights in, though a vase of fresh roses and the glitter of some new jewelry could be spotted not so subtly in the photo. A few went all out with a spontaneous trip to Cornwall, prompting the upload of several sickeningly sweet holiday snaps from the oh-so-happy couple.

Full disclosure, readers: I *love* my friends, and I am happy for their happiness. Any other time of year, I am not so affected by seeing them on social media with their partners that I end up ordering my favorite takeaway, opening a bottle of wine, and wallowing in self-pity that no Netflix binge of *Gilmore Girls* can cure.

But every year, Valentine's Day brings a barrage of successful love lives, making it impossible to ignore the harsh reality that I am entirely alone.

And as much as I tell myself the holiday is a Hallmark gimmick, a commercial fad designed to sell jewelry and chocolates and two-for-one cinema tickets, it also forces me to admit something else I know to be true: I just want somebody to love.

March

Dear Sophie,

You are cordially invited to
celebrate the engagement of

Helena Rose Shelton &
Jonathan Edward Richards

at Eden View Plaza and Hotel
Sunday, March 14, at 11 a.m.

The gift registry can be found at:
http://bit.ly/HandJwedding.

We look forward to seeing you there!

One

"Here on your own?"

The temptation to look around in surprise and say, *What do you know? So I am!* right in her face is almost too hard to ignore, but given that I've only just arrived it feels far too early to make a prat of myself.

I would at least like a couple of mimosas before I do that, so I have something to blame it on afterward.

"Oh, yes," I say, smiling politely at Lena's mum. I've met her twice: once at graduation and the second time a few months ago when I went to visit Lena after her heart surgery.

I guess she must know about me, the same way as I know about her—through secondhand stories and the occasional appearance on Lena's social media. I wonder *what* she knows about me, and decide that I'll give her a pass for asking me if I'm here alone.

Until, that is, she clicks her tongue and pats my arm with sympathy I never asked for.

"Helena did mention you've had a hard time meeting someone. Such a shame."

A muscle twitches in my face, my smile becoming strained.

Hard time meeting someone? Is that what my friend said about me, or is that just what her mum took away from the conversation?

I doubt it's what Lena *actually* said; in all fairness, she loves hearing stories about my dating antics as much as I enjoy telling them.

"Not like my Lena," Mrs. Shelton goes on, with one of those *I'm such a proud mum but if I smile demurely enough we can both pretend I'm not bragging* smiles. "Gosh, she got so very lucky with Johnny, didn't she! Meeting on the first day of university and now engaged! Just wonderful, isn't it? Oh, is that your gift?"

Her eyes drop to the card in my hand, barely giving me time to recover from the emotional whiplash. And, because Lena's mum is apparently That Kind of Person, she looks a little bit insulted at the fact I'm only holding a card and have not shown up wielding the outdoor pizza oven that was on the registry.

(And, honestly, a *registry* for an engagement party! Is this a thing now? Is this really the same Lena who adopted us donkeys for our twenty-first birthdays?)

Mrs. Shelton blinks, and then the disdain really settles into her features when she gives my outfit a very slow, very critical once-over. I shuffle from one foot to the other. Even without yet having entered the party, I know I've made a mistake: my swishy green midi skirt and white T-shirt are way too casual compared to the cocktail dresses and casual suits everybody else is wearing. I left my dark, shoulder-length hair natural today and wonder if *that* was a mistake too. Maybe I should've made the effort to curl it or attempted some classy updo? Mrs. Shelton's gaze lingers for a while on the scuff on the toe of my ankle boot, and I clear my throat to get her attention. Better hand over my gift and get this whole thing over with, I think.

I keep the smile plastered on my face as I hand her the card to be placed on the small table, which she appears to be guarding.

I mean, I guess "guarding" *might* be a little harsh, but Mrs. Shelton does somewhat remind me of a dragon guarding its haul, not least because of the garish burgundy two-piece she's wearing with its crocodile-scale effect.

"It's a gift voucher for a manicure," I find myself explaining. "I thought it might come in handy for the wedding. Or just, you know, as a bit of a treat. So she can really show off that engagement ring."

"Oh!" Suddenly her face splits with a wide smile. "Gosh, that is thoughtful! Well done, you! Oh, just a moment, Sophie, that's Johnny's great-aunt and great-uncle arriving, I'd better—"

She's off before she even finishes her sentence, leaving me to breathe a sigh of relief and grab a mimosa off a passing tray.

It's a challenge not to down it all in one.

Instead, I take a very reserved (but very long) sip, and scan the party.

It's a helluva venue. The Eden View Plaza is one of those fancy boutique hotels in the town center, and it's got a lovely conservatory area. There are tasteful arrangements of bouquets, a few sets of tables and chairs, and waiters milling around the room with trays of canapés or drinks. It looks posh and *beautiful*. The only (literal) dampener on the party is the fact that it can't extend outside, since it's currently pouring rain.

It's a bigger event than I'd imagined. Not that I've been to very many engagement parties—three, I think? Maybe two?—but this all feels a bit above and beyond. Actually, it feels a *lot* above and beyond. When my stepsister Jessica got engaged last year, we just had a family trip to our favorite restaurant. And she *definitely* didn't have a gift registry for the occasion.

Then again, maybe Lena and Johnny are the kind of couple who go above and beyond for everything now. He did take her on a spontaneous weekend away for Valentine's Day—a holiday she always pooh-poohed as pointless before now. But I suppose that's bound to change when your boyfriend uses the day as the perfect opportunity to propose.

It seems like Lena and Johnny have invited all their family as well as plenty of friends to celebrate their engagement. I recognize a few faces from their Instagram accounts, and a few more of our mutual friends.

Finally, I spot the happy couple themselves.

I make a beeline for them just as they wrap up a conversation with some other guests I don't recognize, and wave my free hand to get their attention before someone else can steal it.

"Lena!" I call.

They both turn—as do a few other people—and Lena grins her gap-toothed smile at me, bouncing on the balls of her feet and throwing her arms around me once I'm close enough to be hugged.

"I'm so glad you made it!"

I hug Johnny, too, and tell them both, "Congratulations! I'm so excited for you both. And thanks for the invite today."

It's not like I haven't spoken to them since he proposed a month ago, so I'm not totally sure what else to say. Do I repeat all the things I said over WhatsApp or in the comments of her Instagram and Facebook posts?

I settle for grabbing Lena's hand and saying, "Let's see it, then!" like I've seen people do in films.

She giggles, letting me, and then twisting her fingers this way and that to show off the sparkling diamond on her left hand. It really is a beautiful ring; Johnny knows her taste well. It shines so brightly that the photographs she sent of it are only a paltry imitation.

Johnny wanders off to greet some of his own friends while Lena tells me all about the ring and the Valentine's weekend away, gushing about how surprised she was, and then she hugs me tight again and says, "Oh, it's *so* good to see you, Soph! You didn't have to be up too early to get the train here?"

"I would've traveled all night to get here in time," I joke, although I'm actually quite serious. When did meeting up with friends become so difficult and require so much advance planning? I swear if I want to see more than one friend at a time we need at least five months' notice to align our schedules. It makes me miss the impromptu afternoons mooching around the shops at uni or the summers where we'd just say, "Hey, I'm on my way to you! Let's hang out!"

I say as much to Lena and she laughs.

"Maybe we all need to get engaged more often—give us a good excuse to meet up!"

Even though I laugh along with her, even though I smile, something prickles uncomfortably along my skin and sits heavy on my chest. It's only a moment later that I realize what's wrong: it's panic. It's the realization that my friends might not make the effort to come and see me without "a good excuse" like getting engaged, which is something that's not looking likely anytime soon.

But obviously I don't say that out loud, because it's Lena's day and I'm not going to be that girl who's so upset about not having a boyfriend that she has to bring everyone else down too.

I think Lena must sense something is a little off with me because she changes the subject quickly. She grabs lightly at my arm and leans in close, cringing.

"I saw you got cornered by my mum. I keep telling her not to verbally attack everyone who walks in, but—" She rolls her eyes. "She didn't have a go about your outfit, did she?"

Oof, *ouch.*

But I know Lena means well, and she wouldn't have cared if I'd shown up in grubby old pajamas so long as I was here to celebrate with her, so I laugh and grab her hand to squeeze it. "Honestly, you don't have anything to worry about. She's just welcoming people to the party. It's keeping her out of trouble, right?"

"Hmm." She purses her lips long enough to give me a withering, unconvinced look, but then starts laughing again, beaming. And she *is* beaming; she's so bright and sparkling even without that diamond ring on her finger. She is someone who is so obviously happy, so completely in love, so utterly content with everything in her life right now that it's impossible not to notice.

I want that.

It's a small but familiar flare of jealousy, the same kind I get when I see someone post about their promotion at work or that they're on some fabulous, sunny holiday while I'm stuck in the office.

I want what you have. I want to feel like I have everything too.

It's just so bloody *miserable*, being single. Watching my friends settle down, get engaged, get mortgages, even start thinking about having kids or getting a pet with their significant other . . . I'm happy for them, obviously, *obviously*, but each time they share good news I feel a little more alienated. Pushed aside, forgotten about—a little less important in their lives.

It's lonely. I can see why nobody wants to be single.

I wish I had what they all have. I wish I had a boyfriend—and trust me, it's not for lack of trying on my part. I just wish that whenever other people asked how my dating life was going or if I'd found myself a partner yet, they didn't always look so sorry for me.

Like I don't feel sorry enough for myself already.

Lena looks across the room at Johnny, where he's now talking to some older family members, and I think, *I want that too. I want that feeling, and I want someone to share it with.* It doesn't matter that he's oblivious to her in this moment, because he's hers, and she knows that if she needs him, he's there, and their lives are so intertwined by now they know each other as well as they know themselves.

I hate feeling jealous of my friends. I don't want to be.

"I'm so happy for you, Lena," I say, and I really do mean it. I clink my mimosa gently against her glass of champagne in a "cheers" and take a drink.

"Thanks. But—"

But? There's a but! Thank god. Looks like the grass is not always greener and—

"But do you mind not calling me Lena? It's just that, well, Johnny's family are . . . they're very traditional, and they don't like nicknames very much."

I almost spew my mimosa all over her.

I catch myself at the last second, clamping a hand over my mouth and trying to choke it down, but I'm coughing so hard that some dribbles down my chin and Lena has to pat me on the back while all of her guests stare at me for making such a scene.

Well done, Sophie. A veritable model of poise and grace.

Lena manages to acquire a few paper napkins (so posh that, at first, I think they're made of cloth, but it turns out they're just ten-ply and disposable) and dabs at my chin and neck like I'm a child. Somehow this feels more embarrassing than when I had to help her take a bath after her surgery because Johnny was away for work for a week and her parents were off on holiday. My cheeks are on fire, and dozens of pairs of eyes are burning into me.

"I didn't get any on you, did I?"

Lena doesn't even look at her pretty white tea dress to check, only waves a hand dismissively. She beckons a waiter over, switching the napkins for a glass of water, which she hands to me. "It's fine. You all right?"

"Yeah, yeah, I'm—sorry, you just . . . are you serious?"

"About what?"

"Don't call you Lena? Because Johnny's family don't like nicknames?"

She blinks at me, startled, too surprised to say anything at all.

"*Johnny's* family," I repeat.

"Yes."

"*Johnny's.*"

She huffs, pulling a face that's somewhere between embarrassed and exasperated, although I'm not sure if that's aimed at me or her soon-to-be in-laws. "Well, it's just, you know. They're very posh."

I do know. *Johnny* comes from old money. *Johnny* was a university student who was baffled by the idea of an overdraft, and whose parents own property. As in, multiple. Including holiday homes—again, plural. There were rumors one of *Johnny's* aunts knew Prince William and Kate. *Johnny* has a family crest with a Latin motto.

That's not why I'm confused, though.

"Johnny is a fucking nickname, Lena."

She pauses. "Oh. I guess so."

She can't be serious. This cannot be the first time this thought has occurred to her.

Except it obviously is, which means I shouldn't have said it.

While I'm at it, I may as well also point out that the link they made for their gift registry says *HandJ*, which looks a bit too close to hand job.

"Lena's quite modern, though, I suppose," she says, her tone shifting to something prickly and defensive. "And I go by Helena at work. It's not like *everyone* calls me Lena."

"Oh, yeah. Yeah, I know." *Shit, shit, shit.* Where is the Ctrl+Z for real life? "No, I get you. Helena. I'll remember."

Helena smiles at me, but it's a bit strained and a clear indicator that it's time to wrap this up before I inadvertently insult her and the groom any further. I give her another hug and tell her congratulations again, because that feels like the way you're supposed to wrap up a conversation with the bride-to-be at her engagement party, and she makes an excuse about seeing her cousins and needing to go and speak to them, which suits me just fine.

I cannot get away fast enough.

Two

The Right Honorable Lady Helena might have escaped my mimosa incident unscathed, but as I quickly discover in the ladies' room, I haven't. My top is stained with orange juice and my face and neck and hands are sticky from it. There's also a large wet patch on the end of my sleeve where I'd covered my mouth with my hand.

I spend a while in the bathroom scrubbing my sleeve with soap and water, and then sticking it under the hand dryer. At least it's a good excuse to hide out for a bit.

This is the problem with my friends achieving things in their lives and hitting all those conventional success milestones. I'm always worried about saying the wrong thing. I'm terrified of the first friend who has a baby, because I don't know anybody with babies, so I don't know what "the done thing" is. I don't know how much to drink—or not drink—at weddings, and if I'm supposed to mingle or stick with the handful of other people I know. When someone buys a house, do you give them mugs and candles—or not, because that's what everyone else is probably buying them, but then again can you ever have too many mugs or candles? And are you supposed to *ask* them if you can visit so you can see the house or is that rude? Is it ruder still to not ask about visiting and then risk looking totally disinterested and like a terrible friend?

I learned the hard way that, when it comes to a friend's relationships, I should never bad-mouth their significant other. At least, not to their face. Magda, my work bestie at my first job out of uni, was having a tough time with her boyfriend, so I thought I'd have her back and cuss him out, but then they got back together and all of a sudden she "didn't feel like she could talk to me if I had such a low opinion of him," and that was the end of *that* friendship.

I *do* like Johnny. For the record.

But come on, it's *her* name! If she wants to go by Lena, what does it matter to them? And if they're going to be interfering with a simple thing like that, what about the rest of her life? And what does Johnny think about it—does he let his family walk all over him? Does he support her on the things that matter to her, because he bloody well *should*. Is she really sure about this?

Except obviously you can't say that to someone, even one of your closest friends, and especially not at their engagement party.

But, you know, also, it's just a name, and if it doesn't bother her, why should it bother me? Who am I to get on my soapbox when she hasn't even asked for my opinion?

With the vague intention of distracting myself (and half a mind to message someone who's not here, so I can vent) I get my phone out. Distraction wins out, if only because I have some notifications to catch up on.

The family group chat is going off, from the looks of it. My stepsister Jessica's been at the florist today with her big sister, Nadine, but since their mum—my ex-stepmother, Camilla—couldn't make it, they've been flooding the chat with photos and comments. Dad's pitched in a few times, but it looks like all he's said is "that's nice" about basically everything. I snort quietly, imagining how worked up Jessica is probably getting. She's taking wedding planning *very* seriously. I don't think I've seen her this serious since A-Level results day, or that morning she was trying to get tickets to the Jonas Brothers' tour.

There are so many messages that I just skim through the notifications. I notice one from Camilla about a bridesmaids' dress fitting next weekend, if that works for everybody.

And I notice a reply from Nadine, that she'll call to book it in because I'll definitely be free.

I bristle, glowering at the notification.

I mean, I *am* free. But it feels a bit rich for them to assume. Is it because I don't have a boyfriend to make plans with? No wedding of my own to plan?

I *could* have plans.

Defeat sinks in, and I sigh. Well, I definitely have plans now, I suppose.

There's a message from Duncan too. My best friend at my job at the local newspaper, and fellow pathetic perpetual singleton. He's sent a screenshot of some rave comments on my anonymous (and admittedly somewhat snarky) Valentine's article, accompanied by an *I told you so* message about how he knew I'd do a great job of it, and congrats again on it being made into a regular monthly feature on the paper's website instead of just a one-off. I roll my eyes but can't keep the smile off my face. I was so scared of the article tanking that I didn't tell anybody outside of work.

Now I'm scared it was a little bit *too* honest. I know that if my friends and family knew it was me I'd have to bite my tongue and watch what I say in future editions of the column, which is the exact opposite of what my editor is looking for. I've only published one so far; I can't afford to fall at the first hurdle.

I stay in the bathroom long enough to realize that no amount of posh hotel soap will fix my outfit. It will only make me smell very strongly of peonies.

By the time I get back, the party is in full swing. Lena's mum has left her post by the now-full gift table, the drinks are flowing a little quicker, and Johnny's dad is calling for quiet to give a toast. Even the rain that was thundering against the glass roof has let up a little bit.

With the toasts beginning, this is not the moment to go looking for my friends. Everyone stands around in a crowd, clustered in the center of the conservatory to listen, so I can't start barging through. I'll find them later. They'll be here somewhere.

I loiter near the back of the crowd and fidget awkwardly. I have to crane my neck to see Mr. Richards, but his voice carries well enough over our heads as he talks about how thrilled they all are to have "Helena" cemented as a member of the family, even though, of course, she already is after seven years of dating Johnny, ha-ha! And when Johnny came to talk to him a few months ago to ask for his advice on proposing . . .

A throat clears right by my ear.

I jump, knocking against someone, my right shoulder and arm brushing against them. I open my mouth, ready to whisper a hasty apology to whatever relative I've just bumped into, only to find a glass of champagne being pushed into my hand and a brown-haired guy in a crisp gray suit standing *very close* beside me.

"You're looking a little bit lost. And I'm not sure if you've just walked into the wrong party or not but, if you have, it's too late to leave now—and either way, you can't make it through the toasts without one of these," he murmurs, gesturing with his own drink.

"Thanks."

I rack my brain, trying to remember who he is. He looks about my age, but he's definitely not one of our crowd of uni friends. Someone Johnny knows through work? A cousin? I must've seen his face once or twice on Instagram but can't for the life of me place him.

"Bride or groom?" I whisper to him.

"Bride. I'm Hel's friend. Family friend, from our school days. Sorry, I mean—"

"*Helena,*" we chorus at the same time, loud enough to earn a glare from an elderly couple just in front. I smother a giggle, and the guy rolls his eyes, clearly sharing my exact sentiments about the whole nickname nonsense.

Finally, someone sane at this party.

"What about you?"

"Bride," I say. "We lived together through uni."

"Ah! Yeah, I think I've seen you on her Facebook and stuff. It's, uh . . . ?"

"Sophie."

"Sophie. That's right."

He smiles at me, and my stomach does that weird flip-flopping thing that usually means trouble. The suit is the kind that obviously costs *a lot* of money, and he looks like he spent too much time on his hair, but he's quite good looking. A little bit shorter than me in my heels. His suit must be tailored judging by the way it shows off a toned body that looks like it's spent a lot of time in the gym. Plus, he's doing that weird smiling-but-not-really thing where one corner of his mouth is quirked up and his eyes crinkle a little at the corners, but it also looks a bit aloof and very casual, and damn him, but it's *working.*

"Mitch," he introduces himself quietly.

A noise ripples through the crowd in front of us; a titter of laughter at whatever anecdote Johnny's dad has just shared.

And all due respect to Mr. Richards, I'm sure it's a great speech, but right now it's sexy Mitch and our whispered conversation taking my full attention.

Johnny's dad wraps up his speech, everyone claps, and Mitch and I interrupt ourselves to chime in, "To Johnny and Helena!" only to pick it right back up when Lena's dad takes over with his speech.

"God, this is going to go on forever, isn't it?" Mitch whispers, so close that his lips actually brush the shell of my ear. I shiver. Bold move but, hey, I'm not complaining. "Her sister's got one prepared too."

"Bloody hell," I say, although I'm actually looking forward to Lena's sister's speech, if only because I know she'll embarrass Lena at least a little and it'll be a bit of a laugh.

We lapse into quiet for a moment until Mitch says in a casual murmur, "Do you want to nip to the loos for a quick shag?"

Prince Charming, I have found you at last.

Three

And then he slid into my LinkedIn DMs.

An alternative to dating apps from our
Dating & Relationships columnist

On the bright side, Lena's engagement party dissolves into something a bit more fun and carefree after a light lunch is served and music starts to play—a careful balance of upbeat pop music and catchy '80s tunes that has everyone bobbing their heads, and most people up dancing.

Mitch, I wasn't sorry to see, had to leave before lunch.

Honestly. Who asks someone for a quickie in the toilets like that?

If I didn't think it'd be a great story for my next column, I'd be way more pissed off about it. As it is, I sit at one of the tables making notes on my phone, half engaged in conversation with some of the uni crowd.

The music shifts into another pop song that makes a couple of women shriek with laughter.

I don't notice what it is at first.

It's only when Lena rushes over, cheeks flushed and eyes bright, calling, "Sophie! Soph, come on!" that I realize what song is playing.

It's by Beyoncé.

Lena's sweaty hands grab mine. She puts my phone down for me and pulls me to my feet. "Come on! It's your song!"

That's right, you've guessed it—it's "Single Ladies"! Come on down and claim your prize!

Fuck.

I don't care if this is her engagement party. She could have just been named queen for all I care, I still wouldn't have to oblige her.

But Christ, I forget how bloody strong she is.

Lena ignores my frantic, hushed protests and the way I'm digging my heels into the floor. My other best friend, Tally, whom I've hardly seen all day in all the party madness, is suddenly there too—but not to rescue me, only to grab me by the waist and push me along, laughing with Lena and oblivious to my panic.

A few feet ahead of me on the dance floor, a circle has formed of seven or eight other women dancing around. A couple look mortified but put on brave smiles as if to say, *Ha-ha! Great joke! I'm totally in on it! This is so much fun!* Another person on the floor is Lena's great-grandmother, shimmying like there's no tomorrow and waving her walking stick in the air, having the time of her life. There are two girls who look about thirteen, and even though their faces scream reluctance, they pull off some ubercoordinated dance I guess they learned on TikTok, absolutely showing off.

I shouldn't be so caught off guard.

Like, I *knew* this was going to happen at some point. Everyone loves the "Single Ladies" song, and is it even a party if you haven't played some Beyoncé? I've heard about this exact thing happening at weddings and stuff, but I really, honestly didn't think my friends would do it to *me*.

But they did.

They're shoving me forward into this newfound circle of hell for me to dance as one of the few single women at the party, while they all dance half-heartedly around us. Everyone in the room is singing and thrusting their hand in the air on the chorus, and they clap and cheer along.

One of Lena's cousins is dancing near me. She's not a very good dancer, nor is she enthusiastic, but sort of juts her hips from side to side and tosses her hair and pushes her face up, pouting. One of Johnny's mates is nearby, though, watching her avidly, so I guess she's doing a good job of looking sexy.

I wiggle and shimmy my way over to Lena's great-grandma to dance with her. I throw in a few moves I learned from TikTok, as well as some old favorites from my uni days—probably making a fool of myself, but at least I do it with confidence. Grandma gives me a big smile, trying to copy me, and by now the teens have come over to teach us some arm-wiggle move, and before I know it, the DJ has moved into the "Macarena" and the floor is full of arms jabbing at the air and people jumping ninety degrees to the right, and the nightmare is over.

I give Grandma a high five and leave her learning a new dance with the teens, and storm off to grab my friends, who are Macarena-ing their hearts out. They both beam at me, laughing, and do not stop dancing.

"Brilliant!" Tally cries. "OMG, loved it."

"So funny," Lena echoes.

And I level her with the most ruthless, deadly serious glare I can muster, take her by the shoulders, and vow, "If you play 'Single Ladies' at your wedding reception, I will kill you with my bare hands."

• • •

Later that night, once I'm home from the party, still reeling from having been propositioned during the speeches and having my single status flaunted for the entire party to see, I cannot believe that I also have to explain to my friends in the group chat that no, I did not disappear from the engagement party to have sex with one of Lena's old school friends in the toilets; that is categorically untrue.

Yes, I'm sure I didn't.

Well, it's not my fault if nobody saw me during the speeches, I was there.

Lena, at least, thinks it's hilarious. She knows it isn't true and that an overheard snippet of conversation has gotten wildly out of hand, but she messages our group saying she wouldn't blame me if I did do it.

You've got to have a doubly exciting single life now so we can all live vicariously through you, ha-ha!

Yeah, ha-bloody-ha.

If you need to live vicariously through me, maybe don't get married, Lena. How about that?

My actual reply in the group chat is a photograph of how I'm spending my Sunday evening now I'm back at home: in faded fleece pajamas and fluffy socks, curled up on the sofa watching old episodes of *Call the Midwife*, one of my go-to comfort shows.

Does that mean you get to be doubly boring too?

I joke in the chat because it's too exhausting to even think about picking a fight. Then I immediately read my message back and cringe because it sounds like I *am* picking a fight.

I promise myself I'm not mad at Lena, it's just . . . it's hard, isn't it? Things will change when she gets married, they're bound to, and she'll start thinking about having a family, and that changes things, too, and it's just that I miss how easy and effortless our friendship used to be. It's not that I'm upset that she's engaged; I'm upset we have to grow up. Grow *apart*.

Yes, that is the mature way to think about it.

I don't think it's necessarily true, but I would like to convince myself it is.

The cherry on the cake is when I get a notification that evening: Mitch has added me . . . on LinkedIn.

What?

Has he seriously just added me on a professional networking platform like I didn't (very quietly and calmly) just a few hours ago threaten to pour my drink over his suede loafers if he didn't back the hell off and leave me to listen to Lena's sister's speech in peace?

What a tool.

While the familiar drama of a *Call the Midwife* episode plays out on the television, I flip between apps on my phone. Twitter, Instagram, back to Twitter, no new messages from anyone on WhatsApp or Messenger . . .

Switching between apps to scroll mindlessly feels automatic, second nature. It's also automatic at this point to add a dating app into the mix. Tonight, it's my new favorite one, Hookd. I click on the icon of the red fishing rod, hooking a heart on the end of the line, and the app explodes to life on my screen.

I wonder if my new and hopefully improved profile will have secured me any more matches. I haven't really used any dating apps since my last breakup just before Christmas, so a few weeks ago Tally and I decided to revamp my profile a bit: swap out some photographs, write a new bio, use some different prompts.

No man, new me, and all that.

Not that it was exactly *heartbreaking*, as breakups go. We only dated for a couple of weeks and we were still in the getting to know each other stage. But, you know. It's not exactly *nice* to be broken up with on Christmas Eve when you thought you were meeting up to exchange presents.

In spite of that—and in spite of Mitch's very chivalrous offer of a quickie in the toilets—I'm back on the horse when it comes to dating.

Although I'm not really sure I've ever been "off" it.

Hi, my name is Sophie, and I've been single for . . . ever.

Cue the Greek chorus: *"Hi, Sophie."* Because honestly, I'm pretty sure my love life counts as a tragedy in anybody's book.

I mean, I've basically been single forever. I don't count the "boyfriend" I had when I was thirteen, when the extent of our relationship was holding hands in the cinema on a trip out with all our friends, and every relationship I've had since then has never been, well, serious.

Part of that is my fault, I'm sure, or I wouldn't still be single.

But part of it isn't. The guys who, after nine weeks of stringing you along, say, "We're just talking. We're not *exclusive*, are we?" or, my personal favorite, "I'm not ready for commitment," and then the next thing you know they're on Facebook announcing they're having a baby with their ex or something.

(Which happened *once*. But that is one time too many, right?)

It's a fun story to tell my friends about now, obviously, and since so many of them are in relationships, they thrive off tales of my dating life—or so they claim, like Lena just did—but honestly?

It's exhausting.

Why can't it be that easy for me? Meet a guy, start dating, *keep* dating, probably end up married one day. Like all my friends seem to be doing.

Sometimes—or, fine, basically *all the time*—I wish I was like them. That I had what they've got. Not just someone to kiss good morning or go on dates with, but *someone*. A person who's mine, and I'm theirs, and we're an "us," and it's nice, and good, and comfortable, and it's the whole rest of our lives.

I wish I had someone, so I could build a future like everybody else is instead of being faced only with a panic that, because I'm alone, I must therefore be a failure. I won't get to throw big parties that all my friends have to go to, and I won't be able to buy a house and make a home with someone, or even have someone to split a bottle of wine with on a Friday night!

I wish I didn't always have to feel so alone and left behind.

I catch myself quickly; that is not a thought spiral I want to give in to, not today. It's a Sunday night, for god's sake. I have work tomorrow. Now is not the time for a self-pity party and a *why can't I get a boyfriend* existential crisis.

My phone screen lights up, like it knows my attention is somewhere else and I am in desperate need of a distraction.

You have a new match!

That tiny five-word message on my screen sends a little thrill through me. It's a feeling I relish. Whether it's someone I really fancy or someone I just swiped right on because I was bored and/or drunk, it's that rush of *Someone likes me! Someone thinks I'm attractive! I have been deemed worthy!*

It's shallow, I know.

I open the app back up to take a look at the person who's matched with me. His name is Joseph. He has three sisters and likes to travel. His first photograph is him sporting a great tan and a pair of rainbow-pattern swim shorts, posing on a pile of rocks near some exotic waterfall. He has a group photo with some friends outside a pub at a stag do, and one with what I assume are his sisters at one of their weddings.

He says very little about himself on his profile so I don't have an awful lot to go on, but he looks nice and I'm flattered he likes me back, so I message him.

> Joseph and his technicolor swim shorts, how you doing?

The reply is almost instantaneous, which gives me another spike of dopamine.

> Haha, that's a great one! I'm doing good thanks. How about yourself?

> All cozied up with some Sunday night telly, so pretty good.
> What're you watching?

> *Call the Midwife*. (Don't judge, I promise I'm not catfishing and actually like a middle-aged woman with eight cats, or something.)
> Haha, sounds good.

Hmm.

Maybe he's not the chattiest of guys, or maybe it's just that he's a bit shy and needs to talk more before coming out of his shell.

Still. He looks cute, and he looks nice, and he's liked me back, so I'm willing to see how this goes.

I spend most of the next hour messaging Joseph, teasing more out of him about his job (technical engineer for some company I've never heard of), his hobbies (weight lifting, travel, horror movies), and rewriting my own messages in my head before I type them, trying to match his shorter sentences so the conversation feels more balanced.

Not to be a total bore, but I think I'm gonna turn in
for the night. It's been kind of A Day!
Been great to chat to you though :)

Now for the moment of truth. Three little dots appear and disappear and reappear and disappear several times as he painstakingly types his reply. I watch them with a tight feeling in my chest and a sinking feeling in my stomach, bracing myself . . .

Talk tomorrow? Xx

And he gives me his number.

Four

"What happened to that guy you were talking to?" Tally asks me a week later while she's busy perusing the menu in Costa, like we both don't already know she'll get a medium skinny caramel mocha, because that's what she always gets if there are no seasonal drinks available. (In the peak of summer, it's a skinny caramel frappé. She likes to mix things up.)

I look up from my phone. "Rainbow Joe? We're going for drinks again tonight."

"Huh? Oh, no, the, um . . . what's his name? You know the one I mean. Charlie Weasley."

Charlie Weasley—not the fictional character studying dragons in Romania but the redheaded thirty-year-old who worked at the zoo and had a pet lizard. His real name was Daniel. We matched just after I'd updated my profile and I met him for dinner once, about two weeks ago.

I shake my head. "Fizzled out."

Tally turns away from the menu behind the counter, the look in her dark-green eyes something a little too much like sympathy. "Did he ghost you?"

If she wasn't my best friend, I'd try not to roll my eyes. But I do roll my eyes and I huff for good measure. "*No.* It just, you know, fizzled. Mutually."

"But I thought you liked him!"

"I—well, I did, I suppose, but . . . "

But, yes, he ghosted me. *Fine*, Tally wins. But it hurts to admit, and I hate how it makes me question every word, every action, wondering what I did to mess it up so bad that he can't even let me know he's no longer interested.

Tally's face creases with a little more pity, and I hate her feeling sorry for my singledom as much as I hate being ghosted, so I barrel on. "I don't think I'm what he was looking for. He was very reserved and introverted, and we just didn't have the same sense of humor. That's okay. We gave it a shot."

"His loss," she says firmly, the sympathy in her face vanishing. "So what about Rainbow Joe? Sorry, I promise I do read your messages, it's just . . . "

To be fair to Tally, I know it's not her fault. She's in the middle of some huge project at work with a looming deadline *and* they've just announced mass redundancies *and* she's in the midst of trying to buy an apartment with her boyfriend, Sam, so she's got a lot on her plate. Meeting up for coffee before work, midway between both our offices, was her idea, so we could catch up properly. We never really got the chance to hang out much at Lena's engagement party.

After we order our drinks, I fill her in on Rainbow Joe—Joseph, with the rainbow swimming trunks. His messages are supershort and he never double messages, so sometimes I feel like the conversation is a bit stilted, which means I don't like to send him small essays asking more about his life or telling him stuff about me.

But I don't think he's being *intentionally* curt.

Tally nods wisely. "He's just being a guy. Yeah, I get you."

I tell her about how much better the conversation flowed when I met him last Thursday night for a drink, after we'd been talking for a few days; how he asked me about myself and seemed genuinely interested and had wanted to see some of my photography when I mentioned it was a casual hobby of mine; that he had a dry sense of humor and kissed me on the cheek at the end of the night before I got an Uber home.

Tally scrunches up her face. "Oh."

"What?"

"Just a kiss on the cheek?"

"He just got out of a long-term relationship not too long ago. I think he wants to take things a bit slowly. That was the vibe I got, anyway."

"How long is not too long ago, though?"

"Like three months."

She pulls a face and makes a *hmmm*ing noise, skeptical, but quickly smiles at me again. "That's good, though, that you're seeing him again tonight! Are you going for dinner?"

"No, just drinks again. Keep it casual, I guess. Then back home since it's a work night."

She makes the *hmmm*ing noise again before she can help herself.

"What?"

"Nothing."

"*What?*"

She sighs, fidgeting with her napkin. "It just seems a bit non-committal? I don't know. Like, what's wrong with just going out for a meal? Why does it have to be *drinks* again?"

"You're overthinking this," I tell her, because I have to, because it's exactly what crossed my mind and if I give in to it, I'll just over-analyze the whole thing and ruin it before I've even given Joseph a real chance.

Drinks are nice, casual. Too casual? And on a weeknight where it's only two, maybe three drinks at a push, then the bus home? *Hmm.* It does limit our time together, and it's not as intimate as dinner. More conducive to a conversation than going to the cinema or a club, so bonus points for that. Did he suggest drinks again because he thought that was what I wanted, after I said how much fun it was last week? Or is it because he's saving the expense and effort of a weekend dinner date for a girl he's more interested in and I'm just a midweek ego boost and a way to kill some time?

See? Overthinking it.

So if Joseph wants to meet for drinks on a Tuesday night, that's fine. I'm happy that he wants to see me again.

"I just don't like seeing you get hurt," Tally tells me. Her heart-shaped face scrunches up, full lips pursing into a pout.

I feel a pang of something I can't quite identify—I don't know if it's panic because she's right somehow, or offense, or sadness; I just know it doesn't feel good, so I tamp it down quickly and give a dismissive snort. "I don't think I ever manage to date a guy long enough to get hurt."

"Maybe not hurt, exactly, then. But you're disappointed whenever it doesn't work out. And you took a *break*," she points out, "after The Gareth Who Stole Christmas."

The Gareth Who Stole Christmas, code name for plain ol' Gareth, who broke up with me on Christmas Eve.

"You came over with a bottle of Baileys and cried over him. You had *two* of your emergency cigarettes."

"Because it was Christmas Eve! The season of goodwill! Not a day you break up with people on! It's like, in the top five worst days of the year to dump someone. Right up there with Valentine's and your birthday."

"And you said, 'Tally, I'm not doing this again. I can't keep wasting my time and energy on these losers who string me along.'"

"That was then. I'm over it now."

"You've said things like that before, though, Soph."

"And?"

Tally sighs, and it's a sigh I know well after being friends for ten years. She's not the only person from school I still talk to, but she is the only one I'd invite to my wedding (if I ever manage to find a partner to have one). She's my oldest friend, and my closest—both emotionally and geographically. Anyway, it's the kind of sigh she does when something seems glaringly obvious to her and she doesn't know how else to explain it to me. A bit like when she used to help me study for my maths GCSE, or that time she talked me through how to cook asparagus.

"Wait," she says suddenly, reaching for her phone. "Here, I think there's something you should read . . . Hang on, I know I liked it on Twitter . . . there!" She clicks a link on her phone and then places it in front of me.

SINGLE, SWIPE, REPEAT: I know it's a commercial fad but I just want somebody to love.

My own anonymous article about being sad and single stares up at me from her phone, and I'm not sure whether to laugh or cry.

The column started out completely by accident. A few times, as part of my bid for extra responsibilities as a marketing assistant, I've written up pieces for advertisements—usually when companies want it to read as an organic part of the paper, not a paid ad.

Local news isn't, generally, the most exciting of circles to move in. Dog shelter adoption days, school fairs, a stay-at-home dad who's gone viral online for his crochet creations on Etsy. Once we did actually have a major drug bust that involved snipers and everything, but that was two years ago now.

The marketing department is only marginally more exciting, because we're owned by some media company with a bunch of other local papers across the country, so we get pretty decent marketing links.

Like last December, just before New Year's. We had a fully comped night in a spa hotel, and I begged my boss, Jenny, to let me do the write-up. It was supposed to be a romantic couples' getaway, and because they were pushing for me to take a guy and Gareth had just dumped me, and my go-to guy friend Frankie said he wasn't sure his girlfriend would like it if I took *him*, I ended up taking my work bestie, Duncan, who's more like a brother figure in my life than anything else. The two of us got hammered on the complimentary champagne. He slept in the luxury claw-foot bathtub and declared it the best night's sleep of his life.

But since it was supposed to be a romantic getaway—the hotel gave us a complimentary couples' massage, champagne, a tasting menu, the lot—I wrote it up like it *was* one. Nobody needed to know we went as friends or that I was newly single, and so what if I made up a romantic kiss with my unnamed "boyfriend" that Duncan and I laughed about when I sent him my draft of the article? It was just a little white lie, and only for the sake of a story. I didn't lie about the *hotel*.

It did better than anybody expected. The editor, Duncan's boss, Andy, said the traction it got on the website was good enough that the company who owns the paper took an interest, and suddenly I was agreeing to write a monthly column about relationships and promising Jenny that it wouldn't affect my work on her team.

My only condition was that it be anonymous. Both Andy and the team in legal encouraged me to change names, dates, any identifying factors and all that jazz, which suited me just fine; I didn't want my friends or family knowing I was behind it.

Should I tell Tally, now that I'm faced with it?

Part of me would love to, to prove that I'm doing something with my life, that there's something *worthwhile*, something successful about me, especially since things with my normal day-to-day role at work have been a bit bumpy lately.

Before I can make up my mind, she's already resumed talking.

"I think," Tally says, "you put a lot of pressure on—"

Her phone rings. It's not her usual ringtone; it's the one she set up for people from work.

Tally swears under her breath and scrabbles to grab her phone back from me, moving it to her ear with both hands so abruptly she knocks her glasses askew. "Hello? What's . . . no, I haven't seen . . . oh shit, really? Bollocks. Right, no, it's fine, I'll— He's what? Okay. Okay, no. Yeah. I'll be in soon. Okay."

"What were you saying?"

"Oh, nothing, it's just—" She swaps her phone for her coffee, chugging it like a first-year uni student would a pint. She gasps when she's done and swipes her hand across the back of her mouth, smudging her lipstick. I grab her bag for her, rooting around inside for her lipstick and holding up a compact mirror so she can fix it. "Someone signing off on things they shouldn't be. Which is exactly what I need to deal with today when we've got a last-minute drop-in from the higher-ups wanting a full presentation updating them on progress. *Like we've got the time.* The usual crisis. Ugh."

"No, about me. I put a lot of pressure on what?"

Tally's mind is racing a hundred miles an hour, though, and

it's already at work. She's mentally drafting emails and scripting conversations she needs to have. Her brain has moved on from our conversation and it's clear from the brief, wide-eyed look she gives me that she's already forgotten.

"It doesn't matter," I say, even though it does. "Don't worry."

"Text me later? Let me know how it goes with Rainbow Joe?"

"Will do."

Tally finishes her lipstick, tosses it into her bag, and starts wrestling herself into her coat.

"Do you want to hang out this weekend?" I ask.

"Huh? Uh, I think we might be going to Sam's parents' this weekend, and we've got another couple of viewings. I'm sorry, babe, I know I'm being a pain."

"No, no, honestly, it's fine! I know you're busy. We'll sort something out some other time."

She blows me a kiss and squeezes my arm as she walks past, calling goodbye over her shoulder and leaving me by myself to finish my tea.

Which is fine. It's the same with pretty much all my friends: they have things to do, people to see, houses to buy, and whatever else. Half the time, it's a logistical nightmare to meet up.

So I open up Hookd to see if I have any new matches.

April

FRANKIE AND FRANKIE'S HOUSEWARMING PARTY

APR
17
Come celebrate F&F's new home!
Francis Donnelly invited you

Going   **Maybe**   **Can't Go**

Details

23 people are going, including Tallulah King and Helena Shelton

Event by Francesca Collins

16 Kenton Drive, York

Hi, everybody! Now we've finally moved into the new house (yay!) we wanted to invite you all for a bit of a get-together! We'll provide the nibbles and booze so please don't worry about bringing anything. There's limited room for any sleepovers, so if you do need somewhere to stay, there is a Travelodge at the nearest motorway junction and the air beds/sofas here will be first come, first served! We really hope you can come to celebrate this next chapter in our lives with us! xxx

Five

Seriously, can we stop asking someone how long they've been single? Especially on a first date.

Views on a dating minefield from our
Dating & Relationships columnist

"So how long have you been single, then?"

Oh wonderful. We're starting out strong.

I take a sip of my Diet Coke to buy me a little time and assess the guy in front of me. It's a Friday night and I'm out for dinner at a local Jamaican place I've never heard of. His name is Sebastian ("Like the lobster in *The Little Mermaid*," he said, ignoring me when I pointed out that Sebastian is actually a crab).

Sebastian (not the crab version) is twenty-eight and works in corporate finance. His profile says he's six foot, but he looks more like five-ten on a good day. He has too much gel in his hair, but he's wearing nice cologne and has nailed the smart-casual dress code for a dinner date. He likes mountain biking, the Batman movies, and while he did *not* once meet Barack Obama, he *did* break his arm in a high-school production of *Grease* and is a partially qualified sommelier.

Also, he suggested dinner instead of drinks for our first date.

Things with Rainbow Joe didn't work out. He canceled our third date at the last minute, canceled the rearranged-for-Sunday third date, and then never replied when I messaged to see if he still wanted to grab a drink.

I haven't told Tally, and she hasn't asked. I haven't told anyone, actually.

One, because it's not a big deal, it was only a couple of dates. And two, because then they'll ask *What happened? I thought your first two dates went so well!* and *I don't know what happened*, but if I try too hard to answer I'll just think of all the ways I might have messed up and go right back to feeling miserable about being single for the rest of my life. Which is a lot of emotional turmoil to deal with, considering it was only two dates and a few bland text conversations.

Tonight, I'm back on the proverbial horse once again.

We've only just got our drinks and already we're diving in at the deep end.

The question "How long have you been single?" might seem harmless and ordinary enough for a first date, but it's a minefield, and you have to adjust your answer based on the kind of guy you're talking to.

For instance: Do you want to be the girl who took some time to "find herself"? Did you put your career first and dating went on the back burner? Have you just been enjoying single life and are only looking for something casual? Do you refer instead to the last time you were in at least a sort-of relationship so it doesn't seem like you're a pathetic loser who can't get a man or else like someone hideously uptight that people prefer to steer clear of?

It's not about lying, of course. It's just about the way you frame it.

I look at Sebastian's expensive shirt, the arrogance of the way he's sitting—one elbow hooked over the back of his chair, legs sprawled wide, one hand loosely around the twist-top wine he actually insisted on tasting before letting the waiter pour him a glass.

"A while," I say, in my breeziest tone. "My job can be pretty demanding."

"You're a journalist, right?"

"Not exactly. I work in marketing for the local newspaper. Managing some of our advertising accounts, the social media, our website. But I do some writing, too, sometimes! In December I wrote a column featuring a local spa hotel."

It's a bit of a stretch but it's also not untrue. It's best foot forward, the sort of positive spin I'd put on it if this was a job interview.

But Sebastian nods, like I have said something important and meaningful. "Yeah. Yeah, for sure. Working in media, can imagine that gets pretty hectic. Lots going on."

"Mm-hmm."

I'm about to ask him about his job, but apparently I don't need to. He launches into talking about it—but, to his credit, he does ask me a few questions in the middle of it, and when our food arrives he turns the conversation back to me and, picking off the list of first-date conversation starters, asks, "So have you got any nice plans coming up? Holidays or anything?"

"Actually, I'm going up to York soon, visiting some friends. Not exactly a holiday, ha-ha, but I'll make a bit of a weekend of it. They've just bought a house together, so—"

"Oh, brilliant! The market's really strong right now. First-time buyers?"

"Yeah, they're—"

"Mm," he says, nodding and chewing his food. "Great time

to invest. And the returns you can get on the rental market right now—"

"No," I interrupt. "They're living there."

Sebastian looks surprised, which is baffling to me. He's only a few years older but how can he possibly know *that* many people buying a place with the intention of renting it out rather than living there? Aren't all his friends scrabbling to balance rent and bills while saving what they can every month in the blind hope that they'll eventually pull enough together for a deposit on a place somewhere?

"Do *you* own property?" I blurt, and cringe at the way I've phrased it, how accusatory it sounds.

"I've got a two-bed flat in the city center," he tells me, like this is no big deal at all.

Something triggers in the back of my mind: I'm sure he mentioned something about his commute to work, which doesn't make sense if he lives so close to where he works. I say, "But you're not living in the city center."

"What? Oh, no. I rent it out. Much more lucrative. I live with my parents."

"Oh! Right. Fair enough. So I guess the plan is to put the profit back in to get yourself somewhere?"

Sebastian gives me a strange look and then laughs. "The profit is what pays for my BMW."

Well, hey. To each their own.

I don't really want to keep talking about our personal finances—it feels like a risky topic for a first date anyway, but there's something off about his attitude. I can't determine if it's more arrogant or defensive, but either way, I think I'd rather steer the conversation back to some kind of neutral middle ground or next thing I know he'll ask me how I voted in the last election.

And since I never got the chance to ask him earlier tonight, I say, "So how long have you been single, Sebastian?"

He shrugs. "About six, seven years. I'm just looking for something casual, though."

• • •

At work the next day, I really want to tell Duncan about my date. Tally and Lena never replied to my messages last night—actually, they never replied to my messages that I *had* a date, let alone asked how it went—but I know if I tell Duncan, he'll see the funny side. And then *I'll* see the funny side, and things won't look so bleak.

But he's not in the office, having gone out to do some research for an article, and soon enough I'm swamped with my own work.

My week ends up going from a bit rocky to an earthquake that's nice and high on the Richter scale. Maybe with a tornado thrown in for good measure.

Basically, a complete fucking disaster.

I spend the morning working through a backlog of emails and some notes on my next article from Andy in the editorial department, when an email sent by Satan himself lands in my inbox.

Technically, it's from *Steffan*, my contact at the chain of local pubs I've been managing our advertising contract with. With a dozen pubs scattered across the city and nearby, they've been advertising with our paper for the last three years. Jenny let me have the responsibility of renewing their contract. I've been taking on more tasks like that over the last year or so, hoping it'll help me work my way up from marketing assistant to marketing executive one day, and this one felt like a big coup.

Plus, I really needed to prove I could do it, especially after the graffiti disaster. (Like it was *my* fault the artist we hired defaced a shop front with our ad campaign back in January. It wasn't like I *told* him to do that specifically. But since we had to pay the shop owner damages, I'm sure that particular project landed me with a big black mark next to my name.)

A mark I was hoping this pub contract would help get rid of.

Hi, Sophie, hope you're doing well . . . Steffan's email begins.

And then, ensuring I feel the exact opposite of "well," he informs me that they feel the cost to renew the contract is too high, and the team did not agree with my pitch to move from twice-weekly half-page ads in the physical newspaper to monthly physical ads with regular online slots to better suit their audience.

As if they know *anything* about their audience, I want to reply. As if they have their own stack of statistics somewhere that brought them to that decision.

. . . wish to inform you that we will be terminating our contract with you in June this year . . .

Shit. What am I going to do?

This was my chance to redeem myself, and I've messed up royally.

My eyes drift to Isaac, the marketing assistant who sits at the desk opposite mine. I glance over at Karl and Oscar, the execs on our team at the next bank of desks, and then over at Jenny's office, where she's in a meeting with a couple of people from the finance team.

I barely manage not to scream or groan or cry out loud. The *finance* team. Yeah, this will be great, let me just go to her office, interrupt her meeting, and have *them* know I've just lost the paper a considerable sum of money.

Again.

Shaking, I reach for my phone and make an escape to the

bathroom. I message my friends to see if they're free, telling them something bad has happened at work and I need their help, but none of them reply.

I call Mum, but it rings out—and then I remember she's in New Zealand and it's the middle of the night.

What am I going to do?

Several slow, deep breaths later, and no calmer, I emerge from the toilets and wait nervously at my desk until Jenny's meeting is over. I knock on the glass door and she looks up, her warm smile making me all the more nervous, and try not to vomit all over her office as I tell her just how badly I've messed up, and what a mistake she made in trusting me.

Six

Francis, affectionately dubbed Frankie One, is my internet friend, despite the fact we have been IRL friends for years now. We met on Twitter, bonding over a shared love of photography. It was the sort of friendship where we'd just send each other links we thought the other would appreciate, and it evolved from there, though it never even nudged into flirtatious territory—and for once in my single life, that hadn't left me gutted and disappointed; I was just happy to have a new friend. The first time we met up, I took Tally and Lena with me, and he brought a mate along as well. We all ended up getting drunk and going to karaoke, and then staying up until four in the morning eating pizza on the floor of the Premier Inn room we'd booked.

I don't see Frankie very often but he's one of those fail-safe friends who are always there when you need them. Even if he didn't see my recent *help, I messed up at work* message until the next day, he still *tried* to help after the fact.

We've hung out a bunch since meeting, usually staying with each other for a weekend or so, which means we know a lot of each other's friends. I met his girlfriend Francesca (aka Frankie Two) twice, and Lena has gotten quite friendly with her—it turns out they have mutual friends, having both grown up in Nottingham—so the invite to their housewarming extended to Lena and Tally too.

The three of us have booked a hotel for the night and we'll go out for brunch on Sunday morning, which takes the pressure off for the party itself. I'm not convinced Francesca likes me very much, so I'm relieved to have the girls there as a buffer.

I'm glad for the invite to the housewarming, full stop. The girls have been too busy to hang out and I was too embarrassed about how much I messed up the pub contract at work to tell my family, so I really need this weekend.

Lena, though, is stressing out. I've been parked outside, idling, for twenty-eight minutes now as she runs back and forth between the house and my car.

The first crisis was over what to wear (Tally has opted for jeans and a nice top whereas I've got a going-out dress, so we were no help between us for an indecisive Lena). The second one was because I said she could sign my new-home card, only to realize I'd left it behind, so she went hunting for a spare she was sure she had. I'd turn around, but I'm already more than an hour away from home.

As the only one of us who knows how to change a tire and check the oil in my car, and since Tally shares a car with her boyfriend, Sam, it's been an unspoken rule for years that if ever the three of us take a little road trip somewhere, I'm the driver.

Now Lena leans through the passenger window where Tally is sitting and asks us, "What are you bringing?"

"What?"

"Do I need to bring something as well?"

"Like what?"

"Well, wine or something."

I blink, and stare at her.

"I've gone for red," Tally says without missing a beat. "A nice cabernet; it's a brand Frankie Two likes. I've seen it on her Instagram."

"Shall I bring white, then? I bought them a nice box of chocolates too. What've you got, Soph?"

"I haven't—" I look between the two of them, nerves scratching at my throat. "She said on the invite we didn't need to bring anything!"

"You've got to bring *something*. You can't show up empty-handed."

"Says the girl who had a pizza oven on her engagement registry. Says the girl who has an *engagement registry*."

Lena blushes, mumbling something about her and Johnny's mums getting carried away, but Tally gasps, scandalized, and smacks my arm. "Sophie! You can't go to their housewarming party without anything!"

"I got them a card! Or I did, until I left it at home. What? Don't look at me like that! She *said*, don't bring anything! Why would you say that if you didn't mean it?"

They both roll their eyes, and I get that pang. Like I'm out of the loop, like I've missed the obvious social cue that *they* know.

Eventually, Lena gets in the car, and we stop off at the nearest supermarket. She buys them a bottle of midrange prosecco to match the box of chocolates she's already bought. I choose some spiced rum. Tally meets us at the till with a basket full of snacks and sweets for our little road trip.

• • •

My mouth falls open and I whisper, "Shiiiiit," as our taxi draws up outside 16 Kenton Drive, home of the Frankies. It's an estate of newly built houses, and even though Frankie sent me the link to the show home on the website when they put in the offer a few months ago, I was not expecting this. There's a small, immaculate lawn on either side of a paved pathway leading to the front door. It's three bedrooms, but I'm realizing now that it's a *large* three-bedroom. There are hanging baskets, bright and vibrant, either side of the door.

Tally whistles. "I need to move up north. Bet our deposit would get us something like this up here."

The three of us swallow our awe (and jealousy). Lena pays the taxi driver, since she's the only one smart enough to bring cash, and we make our way to the front door.

Frankie Two answers—bloody hell, she looks elegant. Black midi skirt, floaty white top, sparkly diamond necklace . . . has she had her hair blow-dried? I bet she hasn't. I bet she can get it to look that good all by herself.

Her outfit isn't miles away from what I wore to Lena's engagement party, and yet it's so much nicer. So much prettier and more sophisticated.

She should be one of Lena's bridesmaids, I think, *not me.*

She's like a perfectly curated Instagram profile, except in real life.

Francesca Collins isn't the kind of person who would show up empty-handed to a housewarming party after being told not to bring anything.

She smiles brightly, holding the glass of wine in her right hand out of the way to hug us one by one with her left arm, kissing us each on the cheek. "You made it!"

"Are we late?" I ask. It's only three minutes past eight.

"Oh, pretty much everyone's already here. Don't worry, I made sure to keep some nibbles back. I know you like your food, Soph! Have you lost weight, Tallulah? You're looking fantastic."

Tally says she's actually put a few pounds on lately, but she beams, flattered. I fidget with my dress until Lena bats my hand away.

She clears her throat and lifts her gift bag with the wine and chocolates, handing it over. Tally and I follow suit. "Just a little something!" Lena says, as we're ushered into the house, adding our shoes to a pile by the door and handing Frankie Two our coats to put on a sofa so she can take our housewarming gifts. The place looks clean, crisp, and a little sterile.

"Gorgeous house," I say.

Listening to Francesca's "please don't worry about bringing anything" was obviously not my only faux pas. She looks less than impressed with the rum, if the way her nose wrinkles when she sees it is anything to go by.

They say it always comes in threes, and I quickly find out what my third screwup of the night is.

I'm way overdressed.

Or, maybe not *over*dressed, but incorrectly dressed (again), at least. We all go through to the kitchen-dinner-lounge (a second lounge area! What!) and it's immediately clear that this is a jeans or skirt and a nice top kind of party, which is how Lena and Tally have decided to dress for the night—the traitors. My black knee-length dress with the short puffy sleeves and V-neck suddenly feels ready for a night out at a bar instead of a night in with nibbles and a glass of merlot. I'm relieved Frankie Two made us take off our shoes, because I don't think my gold-studded boots with the chunky heels would have made this outfit any more casual. I itch to rub off my bright-red lipstick.

I'm just wondering if I should go to the bathroom and wash it off when Frankie One makes his way over, a beer in hand and great big smile on his face. "Finally! We were starting to think you guys weren't going to show up!"

He hugs me tight, leaning back to lift me off the ground, which makes me laugh through my awkwardness.

"The Facebook event says eight!"

"Oh, pshaw," he says, sounding out every letter of "pshaw," turning to give Tally and Lena quick hugs hello. "Didn't you get the reminder, Soph? Grown-up parties start early, so we can all get home in time for the ten-o'clock news."

Tally laughs so hard at that she snorts.

"Have you seen what the girls brought us, babe?" Frankie Two says, gesturing with the collection of bottles she's holding.

"Ah, thanks, gals. You really didn't have to—" He stops dead, his hand flinging out to grasp my shoulder, eyes bugging wide and a smile stretching wide across his face. "Is that what I think it is?"

"Oh yes, it is."

"Fuck off, did you?"

"I absolutely did."

The rum is a pretty expensive brand and although it's not hard to come by, it's the one we all drank at karaoke the first time Frankie and I met in person. It's what we order every time we meet up now, practically tradition. Much as I'd intended to grab a bottle of whatever wine looked nice but was on sale, I couldn't just leave it there when I saw it in the supermarket earlier.

Frankie laughs, wrestling me into another hug and then grabbing the bottle. "We've gotta have a shot, for old time's sake. Come on, girls. Jordan's somewhere round here, too, where'd he . . . Jordan! Hey! Come look what Soph brought!"

He leads us across the kitchen to get some shot glasses (and bloody hell, we must be getting grown-up if he owns actual proper *glasses* for shots instead of those crappy plastic ones) and his buddy Jordan, who came with him when we first all met up, peels away from a conversation to come over.

Oh no.

Oh, *no.*

I don't know what's happened since the last time I saw him, but . . .

Tally whistles quietly near my ear, just like she did when we pulled up outside and saw the house.

And Lena whispers, "When did Jordan get fit?"

Seven

I'm a couple of drinks down and press my hand to Jordan's shoulder. It's firm, strong. I push it again for good measure, like I have to confirm to my slightly sluggish senses that it's real. I don't think he's more toned than the last time I saw him, but the way he's dressed certainly makes him look like it.

"Last time I saw you," I'm saying before I can stop myself, "you had that silly man bun, that massive beard you never looked after, you wore flip-flops and tank tops everywhere, and now you're . . . "

"Pretty good looking, huh?" He rubs his clean-shaven jaw, turning his head this way and that like he's only pretending to show off but we both know he's actually enjoying showing off a bit, and he laughs.

"Was it an intervention?" I say, mock serious, and then gasp. "Was it the Fab Five? Are you going to be on a UK edition of *Queer Eye*?"

He tells me quite proudly, and earnestly, he had an epiphany about how the way he was dressing was only feeding his depressive cycles. It didn't make him feel good about himself, he realized, so he decided it was time for a change—the first of many proactive, productive changes he's made to his lifestyle lately now he's weaning off his meds, he explains.

"An epiphany," I repeat, nodding along. "Thanks to therapy?"

"No," he tells me. "A girl."

"Ah. That ol' chestnut. So? Tell me about her. Is she here? Is she one of Frankie Two's friends?"

Oops. We're not supposed to call them Frankie One and Frankie Two to anyone else. I mean, I do with my Frankie sometimes, because it's him and he's my mate, but I don't think Francesca would see the funny side if she overheard.

Jordan doesn't even seem to notice my slip—maybe he calls them that too. "We're not together now. She, uh . . . god, this is going to make me sound really pathetic, but *fine*. If you're gonna be pushy, Soph. She broke up with me because I embarrassed her and always looked like a dirty layabout."

"Her words?"

He pulls a face and laughs again. "A more polite, concise version of her exact words. She broke up with me because I didn't look like I cared about myself, and while my therapist did help me work through all of *that* stuff, I did think, you know what? I'll change. And then I'll get her back. And she'll see she was wrong and that I do care and I can scrub up well, and she'll realize how much she loved me and she'll take me back."

"And?" I say, leaning in, eyes bulging wide. I'm hooked. "What happened?"

Jordan smirks, but there's no humor in it this time. He takes a long swig of his beer. "By the time I'd got my shit together, she'd moved on. She said maybe I should focus on *working on myself* for a while."

"Ouch."

"Tell me about it."

"Well." I lift my wine. "Here's to being single and having your shit together."

At least for one of us, I think, hiding a wince when I remember about work.

"Cheers to that."

A heavy arm lands around my shoulder, and a second jostles Jordan forward slightly. It's Frankie One, leaning on both of us to get our attention. He drops his arms and straightens up again, smiling at us. "All right, guys? What're we talking about?"

"Being single," I say.

"Sophie reckons she's got her shit together," Jordan says.

"Ha! Barefaced lie, if ever I heard one."

"Oi!" I glare at them both, but they're laughing, only teasing. So I plant one hand on my hip, half a power pose, and jut my chin out. "I will have you know that in my last annual review, I got a pay rise *and* had the second-best feedback in my team."

"Aren't you a team of five?" says Jordan.

"Didn't your boss just have to take some stuff back off you because you lost that massive advertising contract?" says Frankie.

"And," I say, ignoring both of them, "I have my own apartment." (Which I rent, but still.) "And I have my own car." (Leased, but I never default on the payments.) "And I have a gym membership I use maybe like five times a month, which is much more than I used it last year. Just because I'm single and don't have weddings and babies on the cards and things are a bit rough at work, doesn't mean—"

"Oh, Soph, come on, we're only teasing," Frankie says gently, which is when I realize the way my voice was climbing, turning high and wobbly. I pause, sucking in a deep breath. There's a lump in my throat and I have to gulp it down. It won't go, so I swallow some wine in the hopes that will get rid of it.

"Who wants to be tied down at our age, anyway?" Jordan says.

"You don't have a body clock that everyone likes to remind you is tick-tick-ticking," I mumble.

"Pshaw," Frankie says. "You're twenty-five! You've got bags of time!"

"*Bags*," Jordan agrees gravely, nodding. "Anyway, look at him—Mr. Boring, with his girlfriend and his mortgage. Ew."

"Aye, all right. Listen," Frankie adds, in a low whisper. "I'm off out the back for a smoke."

"Not me, mate."

"Talk about Mr. Boring." Frankie laughs, clapping Jordan on the shoulder. "Your body is a temple now, eh? Soph, you coming?"

My Hookd profile says that I never smoke. I like photography and museums, and I don't smoke.

Which I don't. Most of the time. Like, a solid 90 percent of the time, which is basically the same as never.

I mean, I also haven't been to a museum for months, so . . .

"Sure," I say, and follow Frankie outside.

It's dark out, but a little motion-activated light snaps on near us. The back garden is small and square, surrounded by a tall fence that backs onto the neighboring gardens. There's a small patio area near the house, and a few steps down to the grass. Frankie takes a seat on the steps and I follow suit. The ground is damp with cold, and I shiver.

"Think we've missed the ten-o'clock news," I say.

He laughs. "Damn. Might as well stay up till the six-o'clock one tomorrow morning now, eh?"

"Only reasonable solution."

He takes out a packet of cigarettes and a lighter, lighting one up for us to share.

"I thought you said you quit, that Francesca doesn't like it?"

"I am quitting. This is my first in four days."

"Good for you."

"She hates the smell of those e-cigarettes and vapes," he tells me. "And doesn't want me using them in the house. Which I get. We didn't spend three grand on sofas just for them to stink."

"Three grand?"

He shrugs. "We got them on finance."

"All right, Mr. Boring. God, when did our lives get like this? Revolving around sofas on finance and—"

"And your womb going tick-tick-tick?"

I nudge him with my shoulder, taking the cigarette off him for a drag. The smoke tastes bitter in my mouth, feels heavy in my lungs. I don't like it, and that's what makes it exactly what I want right now. I always thought the concept of social smoking was a weird one. For me, it's always been *anti*social. It's a vice, so that I can say "this is the thing making me feel crappy," so I don't have to focus on what actually *is* making me feel crappy.

The last time I had a cigarette was Christmas Eve after getting dumped.

"No luck with the dating, then?"

"Nope."

"You and Jordan seemed to be getting on well."

I give Frankie a long, amused look. Jordan's fun to hang out with, and he is looking very attractive these days, but—"You mean your mate Jordan who lives all the way up here in Yorkshire, ages away from where I live?"

"Long-distance might suit you."

"Trying to say I'm impossible to live with?"

He laughs. "Well, you make your long-distance friendships

work. Tallulah's the only one you actually live in the same city as. And that guy from work. But you've got loads of friends. You're always doing something, off meeting people, seeing your mates, going to parties."

Scoffing, I tell him, "Maybe you've cracked the code. Maybe that's why I can't get a boyfriend. Or *maybe* it's because the last guy I went on a date with lied on his profile."

"Oh. Catfish?"

"He told me he was only looking for something casual. But he put on his profile he was looking for a relationship."

"Right . . . "

"Well, it's just rude, you know?"

"Luring you to dinner under a false impression. I get it."

"Don't be a dick, Frankie."

"I'm not. I'm being sympathetic."

"Likely bloody story." But I lean against him for a moment, head tilted to rest on his shoulder, and let out a long sigh. He passes me the cigarette again.

"You'll find someone soon, Soph. Any guy would be lucky to have you."

So why haven't I found someone yet?

I don't want to ask him that, though, because it feels too real, so I inhale deeply, pass him back the cigarette and say, "Speaking of lucky, what about you? Congrats, mate. This place is fantastic. Francesca gave us the grand tour. All the 'room to grow.'" Space for you to have an office for your photography work. You've really got it all, haven't you?"

"All that glitters, Soph. All that glitters."

"Oh, come on. What can you possibly be missing?"

He gives a long and weary sigh, staring off into the night that only stretches as far as the end of the garden, and then turns to me, deadly serious.

"A dog."

I burst out laughing, and so does Frankie. We lean against each other, laughing, and smoking that one cigarette between us, and even though I get the sneaking suspicion that he's covering up by saying "a dog," I don't push him, because maybe he's right.

Maybe his life glitters, but maybe it's not gold either.

I wonder if that's what my life looks like from the other side.

Eight

It isn't a good end to the night.

At first it's fine. Frankie and I go inside when the cigarette burns out; there's music playing in the kitchen, plates of mini brownies and slices of rocky road have been assembled on the breakfast bar. Everyone's chatting and laughing and having a great time.

I head to the swanky gray corner sofa across the room where Lena and Tally are chatting to some people, tagging onto their group and a conversation about the latest celebrity scandal and the politics of it all.

I don't notice Frankies One and Two arguing in the corner of the kitchen until one of the girls nudges someone else, and then heads start turning and voices start dropping, a unanimous and unspoken group effort to eavesdrop. Francesca notices and stalks into the hallway, head held high, face composed. Frankie dithers around the kitchen for a minute before rushing after her.

Now the kitchen is almost silent. Someone turns the music down a bit.

"We talked about this, Fran—"

". . . asked you not to invite her!"

"It was *one cigarette.*"

"With *her!*"

"So next time I step out with Jordan or Lewis for a smoke, it's secretly to shag them? Babe, I've *told* you—"

"She shows up here looking like some cheap tart. A few drinks and nibbles, we said! You'd think she just walked out of an audition for *Love Island*, and you're—"

Dread prickles across my skin, uneasiness settling like a stone in the pit of my stomach. A hot flush creeps up my neck and over my cheeks. A few heads turn to look at me, which only makes me cringe even more. I fidget with the neckline of my dress, trying to pull it up higher, only noticing now that the edge of the lace on my bra is peeking through on one side.

Great. I'm sure that's really going to help my case.

Except it's not my case, is it, not my side that needs defending? It's Frankie's, because he's the one with a girlfriend; he's the one with something to lose, something at stake.

I remember when he met Francesca. He said she was a bit of a jealous type, but I'd thought that was normal. People got jealous, didn't they, at least early on in relationships? He'd not really mentioned it since, so I hadn't thought about it. I definitely never assumed it was anything personal about *me*.

But I guess it'd explain why I never felt like she liked me very much. Why, whenever I see her, she always makes a point of asking me if I have a boyfriend yet while she puts her arm around Frankie.

Because in her eyes, I'm a single girl who's a bit too close to her boyfriend. I date a lot, Francis and I are affectionate people—both huggers—sneaking off at her party . . . yeah, I see how that could look.

But Francesca can go screw herself. At least I don't look like I just walked out of an audition for *The Apprentice* at my own housewarming party. If anything, I'll take being compared to someone off *Love Island* as a compliment.

"Do you think we should go?" Tally whispers.

"I need the toilet," I mumble back.

I don't, but it's an easy excuse to leave the room. In the hallway, Frankies One and Two stop sniping at each other to look at me. There's a long, horrible moment where nobody says anything. The silence threatens to suffocate me.

"I think you should go," Francesca tells me with a sniff, clenching her jaw.

I want to snipe at her. Say something cruel and cutting and *nasty*. I want to ask her why she can't just accept that Frankie and I are friends, or why she has such a problem with me.

But Frankie looks wrecked, and angry, and so does his girlfriend, and I know I haven't done anything wrong and it isn't my job to fix this, but I also know that he's my friend and I feel bad that he's in this position.

So I say quietly, "We really are just friends, you know. All he does when we hang out is talk about you."

Francesca's visibly startled—she knows me at least well enough to have expected me to snap back a bit. But she gulps, looking ashamed, and that look isn't directed at me, but at Frankie.

It's a good job I like him so much, or I would be much angrier about his girlfriend sidelining my feelings like this.

"I'll call us a taxi. You're right. I should go," I say, and go into the bathroom. I don't really need to pee, but I need an excuse to hide for a minute or two.

Nothing like being accused of being the other woman to ruin your mood and remind you just how lonely and left behind you actually are.

Frankie One hugs me when we go and he mumbles, "Thanks," in my ear instead of *Sorry*, but I get it. She's his girlfriend. She comes first.

I'm used to that.

Lena and Tally are sympathetic on the drive back to the hotel. Even though Lena's friendly with Frankie Two, I was her friend first, and, honestly, it is nice to feel like someone is putting me first for a change. I'm too exhausted to say very much, but I appreciate the way both of them rant on my behalf—how bang out of order it was for Francesca to go off like that, to say those things about me, to *think* those things about me, and, god, what does it say about her relationship with Frankie if she doesn't trust him?

"You're so lucky, Soph," Tally tells me. "You don't have to put up with any of this drama, being single."

"Yeah. Yeah, I feel really *lucky* right now, Talls."

All that glitters, indeed.

● ● ●

By the morning, at least, I don't feel so shitty. It's not my fault that Francesca is so insecure; it's not a reflection on me that she can't get her head around the idea of Frankie being friends with a girl. And my dress was party, not tarty. If anything, *I* feel sorry for *her*.

(And a bit angry that she thinks I'm some kind of man-eater who's out to steal her boyfriend just because I don't have a boyfriend of my own, but I'm trying my best not to think about that. And a bit scared that Frankie One will stop being so friendly with me just to appease Frankie Two, but I'm also trying not to think about that.)

The girls read my mood and don't bring up last night's disaster ending. Instead, we get dressed up for brunch and a mooch around a few shops in York, talking about how nice it is to spend time with each other.

"Yeah," Lena teases, nudging me as we share the hotel-room mirror, her doing her eyeliner and me trying to fix my bedhead with the straightener. "Especially after you disappeared at my engagement party."

Tally snorts from where she's getting dressed in the bathroom.

"I cannot *believe* you all actually thought that happened. Do you really think it's the sort of thing I'd do?"

"I dunno," Tally says. "He might've been really fit. He might've been a regular Timothée Chalamet."

"Don't blame Mitch," Lena says, trying to take the middle ground. "He just got out of an eight-year relationship. I think he's taken the whole 'sowing his wild oats' thing a little too seriously."

"Vom," Tally shouts. "I hate that phrase. So gross."

'"You can tell him I might've agreed to go on a date with him if he hadn't been so gross," I tell Lena.

She waves her eyeliner at me. "Oh, way ahead of you. I already read him the riot act. Told him he'll be disinvited from the wedding if he tries to shack up with every girl who gets up to dance to 'Single Ladies.'"

"Vom," Tally says again.

"Think one of Johnny's groomsmen is single, though." Lena catches my eye in the mirror. "He's quite good looking."

I swear, any time you ask your friends to set you up with someone they draw a blank. But the second you're not asking—bam, they've got them lined up for you. And as helpful and well meaning as they want to be, they've lined up a guy with a combover who wears Crocs and socks out in public, or a guy who seems normal until you go to his place and discover his extensive collection of

Sylvanian Families covering every surface, which somehow *nobody mentioned until now.*

I make a noncommittal noise. Maybe, if I'm feeling lonely enough on the day, or he's charming enough. "So long as he's not like Mitch. *Helena.*"

It's nasty of me, but it's out of my mouth before I can stop myself.

She sighs, and Tally jumps on board too. "Do we really have to stop calling you Lena?"

"Just around Johnny's lot," she says, her tone more dejected than the defensive one I got at the wedding, which only makes me feel worse for taking the swipe. "His sister told me his mum thinks it sounds *common.*"

"Wow," Tally says.

I opt for, "What a cow!"

"Johnny can't apologize enough about it, though. And it's not like I mind going by Helena anyway. And she's—she's all right, just . . . she's a bit snobbish, that's all. Everything's got to be just so. You get used to it."

I really want to ask if she's sure she wants to tie herself to these people, but then Tally's saying, "I know what you mean. Paul, you know, Sam's brother, he's an absolute tool. I have never seen him lift a finger to do anything around the house. Not so much as make a cup of tea. And me and Sam have been together for four years now! He's just *rude* too."

"Ugh," Lena says.

"Yeah. But I'm not dating him, am I? I'm not buying a place with him or thinking about having kids with him one day. And I really bloody love Sam."

I wonder what that feels like, to love someone so much and so deeply that you're not just loving them in spite of or including *their* faults, but their family's too. I mean, it's one thing when it's your own family, but you're *choosing* these other people and you can't call them out if they're mean to you without risking offending the person you're so in love with.

I mean, I love Lena, but, god, I don't think I could put up with her mum for an extended amount of time. And as her friend, not her partner, I don't have to. And I love Tally, but Sam's hardly my favorite person; personally, I think *he's* kind of a tool too. But I don't have to love Sam. I just have to be nice to him and not pick a fight when he says something I disagree with.

I make all the right noises as the girls carry on talking to make it sound like I'm listening and engaged in the conversation, but I don't really have anything to contribute. It's not something I understand, and honestly?

Sometimes I'm scared I never will.

Nine

"So, Sophie, how's the love life? Are you seeing anyone right now?" my ex-stepmother, Camilla, asks, just as I take a massive bite of my burger.

I love my family, even if we are a little bit dysfunctional at times. Since we're fairly close in age, Jessica feels like an actual sister, while Nadine . . . well, even if we've never quite connected the way Jessica and I have, I know she's there if I ever need her, and I think of her as family. And even though my dad and Camilla divorced years ago, they're still on good terms, and I like that Camilla treats me as one of her own, just the way Dad does with her daughters.

But my god, would I love it if, just *once*, I could get through seeing them without being asked about my dating life.

Everyone looks at me expectantly, waiting for an answer.

I chew my burger slowly to buy myself time.

As much as I enjoy rehashing my tragic dating stories to my friends, my family are another matter. I'd tell Jessica, but she'd only tell Nadine, and then our parents would end up inevitably finding out.

With my friends it's funny; it's a good story to tell, even if it's my only story. Usually, the most exciting thing to happen to me is that I treated myself to a takeaway and watched *Emily in Paris* for the umpteenth time. So I tell them about my dates, even when they're awful or I have such high hopes only to have them dashed later.

With my family it's different. It's not funny; it's just sad. It's not like I keep it a secret, I just . . . don't tell them about it.

Which is a totally different thing, right?

It's bad enough that I get my own hopes up every time I match with a guy on a dating app—I don't need to get my family's hopes up only to disappoint them too.

I don't need them to be disappointed in me.

Usually, when they ask about my love life—which they do *constantly*—I manage to give fairly evasive, noncommittal answers, then swiftly move on to talking about work or my friends instead. Lately, I've been able to switch the topic to Jessica's wedding and the upcoming bachelorette weekend or the fact Nadine is pregnant— both of which overshadow anything I have to say by a wide mile.

I finally swallow my food and try that exact tactic.

"Oh, you know, same old, same old. Nothing new, really!" I give it a beat so it's not glaringly obvious what I'm doing before barreling on. "Oh my gosh, Jess, I still cannot get over your dress! It's so gorgeous. I bet you anything Dad cries when he sees you all dressed up for the wedding."

Camilla scoffs. "Of course he will. You know what he's like."

Jessica isn't so easily deterred, though, saying, "What about your plus-one for the wedding?"

"What? What about it?"

"Haven't you found one yet? I'm running out of time to confirm things with the caterers."

Nadine pulls a face. "Oh god, Soph, please don't bring some random guy from Hookd. *No way.* What if it doesn't work out? Then he'll be in all the pictures, spoiling it."

"*And* he could be a Pisces," Jessica says, nose wrinkling.

"That's rich, coming from a Capricorn," I shoot back.

"Oh, that's a good point," my ex-stepmother says diplomatically, nodding along with Nadine's point, ignoring me and Jess. "Yes, Sophie, who are you going to bring? We really need to get it locked in. The table plan—"

Table and *plan* are the activation words that turn Jessica into a bridal Winter Soldier. Immediately, she throws her fork down, groaning, exclaiming about how she *cannot* change the table plan again, she's already had to adjust it half a dozen times and don't I *know* how long it takes, and she's already got a thousand other things to think about, and they have to confirm within the next fortnight so the calligraphy artist can get it all written up, and . . .

There's a mania and a fury to my stepsister that makes me equal parts terrified and in awe. Organization has always been one of her strong suits, and her ability to be laser focused on something serves her well in her job as an accountant, but the wedding has taken it to another level.

If there's one thing I've learned from this experience, it's to rock the boat as little as possible.

Don't point out that the lilies might leave pollen stains everywhere.

Don't say I think the color of the bridesmaid dresses might make us all look a bit washed out.

Don't bring up the fact I haven't pinned down a plus-one because everyone assumed I would—*should*—have a boyfriend to bring with me by now.

Jessica spirals and Camilla has to rub her back in small, smoothing circles, an act that's so second nature I don't think she even realizes she's doing it. Nadine skewers me with an accusatory look, like this is my fault.

"I told you at the time not to worry about a plus-one for me," I mumble down at my lap, half hoping they don't hear.

"You might've at least made an effort to *try* and put yourself out there and find someone," Jessica tells me, her voice uneven. She's one wrong reply away from wailing, but I can't blame her. The wedding planning has been a lot of work.

And, really, it shouldn't be so hard to find a partner. Everyone else has managed it, haven't they? So, clearly, the problem must be me.

It's on the tip of my tongue to tell her, actually, I *have* been trying. Fuck, have I been trying. Doesn't she know how many guys I've swiped for, started messaging? What about Rainbow Joe who ghosted me so inexplicably, or Sebastian "like from *The Little Mermaid*" whose profile was so misleading? Mitch, who, maybe if I gave him a chance after rejecting the quickie in the loos, might have actually been a decent guy after all?

But it's so much to explain, so much I haven't told them—too much for a casual meal out after a dress fitting. And rallied around a stressed-out Jessica, the three of them look like such a united front, and I don't know when I became the villain here but I *do* know I need them to back off, back down, and that, somehow, it's on *me* to fix this.

Before I know what I'm doing I jut my chin out and my chest puffs up as I declare, "Actually, I *do* have someone. A . . . a guy I've been seeing for a little while."

Nadine and Camilla exchange a look, and Jessica falls silent, her mouth gaping open.

Nadine fixes me with a glare. "Don't say that if you don't mean it."

"I do mean it. I just didn't want to say anything because we've been taking things quite slow. But you don't need to worry. I'll ask him when I see him next. He's, um, he's away at the minute, but once he's back, I'll ask him."

Oh god, what am I doing? Where is this coming from?

Stupid question. I know exactly where it's coming from. Pride. Panic. Both.

When Jessica first told me that of course I'd have a plus-one for her wedding, I hoped I would find someone to bring with me. Her fiancé, Conor, proposed well over a year ago and I thought that would be plenty of time to find a boyfriend, to find myself in a nice, steady, settled relationship, just like everybody else.

I wasn't supposed to still be single at this point.

Things haven't exactly gone well with my attempts at dating lately, but things have got to turn around soon, haven't they? The next guy I match with will be a total catch, I'm sure.

Four hundredth time's the charm.

It's not like it'd be a big deal to come to Jessica's wedding with me. It's free food, some drinks. It's basically like any old party. What guy would turn that down for a date?

Jessica throws her head back dramatically. "Well, *thank you* for not telling me and making me stress out over nothing!"

"I *knew* you were hiding something from us!" Camilla squeals, reaching over to jab my arm playfully. "Oh, I knew it! Always so cagey any time we ask you about your love life!"

Well, *yeah*, because these days it's both a total shambles and the subject of an increasingly popular anonymous online column I still haven't told anybody about.

"What's his name? What does he do? How did you meet?" they ask me.

Shit.

I *definitely* did not think this through enough. (Or, you know. At all.)

"No!" I say as coyly as I can manage, forcing a laugh. "No details! Not until I ask him. I don't want to jinx anything."

I give a strained smile and look around my family. Who look *happy* for me. For once.

There's no eye rolling, no pity, no *Oh, poor Sophie, still alone— how sad and pathetic her life must be, with nobody to share it with.*

They look *excited.*

They look relieved, too, which is more than a little bit insulting.

I'll give Jessica a pass on that, since she's probably only thinking about the table plan, but seeing the relief on Camilla's and Nadine's faces grates on me. My blood starts to boil, my chest tightens. My fingers, trembling, clench into a fist around my knife and fork.

Why does it matter? Why does it make any difference?

Isn't it supposed to be something I want for myself, not what everybody else wants for me? Isn't that supposed to count for something?

Maybe it should, but that's not the reality right now.

My anger blows away quickly, and I find myself wanting to lean into this. I want them to be happy for me. I want them not to worry. I want them to think I'm not a complete failure and a disappointment.

I want, just for a little while, to pretend like I have it all too. Just like everybody else. I want them all to look at me and not see some-one whose life is made incomplete by the absence of somebody to share it with.

So I grin and say, "I can't wait for you guys to meet him at the wedding! I'll ask him soon, I promise."

And Jessica says, "This mystery man's not got any nut allergies, has he?"

May

JESSICA'S HEN DO

Jessica Cox
Hi, everyone! Really looking forward to seeing you all tomorrow! Just wanted to drop a note to remind everyone of the details, but please give me a shout if you have any questions!
- Accommodation (Coral Cottage—full address in the email Nadine sent around last week!) will be available from 11:30 a.m. so please arrive PROMPTLY so we can start on activities!
- Friday night will be pizza party with manicures
- Saturday we have paintballing (leaving at 10 a.m.!) so PLEASE remember to bring some sensible clothes and shoes!!! Minibus is booked for 1:30 p.m. to take us into town for afternoon tea and then a cocktail-making class. Dinner is booked for 8 p.m. so PLEASE remember to also bring your party clothes and shoes, lol!
- Checkout on Sunday is 10 a.m. so mind your hangovers!
- Nadine has also emailed each of you a small shopping list to make sure we have plenty of supplies to see us through the weekend. Relying on everyone here to pull together so PLEASE don't forget!!
Love you all lots, can't wait for a brilliant weekend! xxxxxx

Lydia Smith
Thanks, Jess, can't wait! Got my supplies from your shopping list all ready to go, SO excited! Do we need anything in particular for paintballing? (Shoes/ clothes . . . ?)

Nadine Cox-Dawes
@Lydia probably trainers and leggings are a safe bet for paintball. More details in the message just above from @Jessica and the email I sent last week x

Nadine Cox-Dawes
@Ola, @Eden, please make sure you send me the money for your share. Have texted you both my bank details a few times but let me know if you need them again x

Georgina Spurrs
Thanks, gang, excited to see/meet you all! Just to flag, can we make sure there's some dairy-free stuff on the pizza order and at afternoon tea? Let me know if you want me to bring any goodies or drinks or anything :) x

Eden Rose O'Leary
Hi, Nadine, did send you an Instagram DM to explain. Would be good if you read it. @Jess, SO sorry, babe, but as I told you the other week, can't make it. Gutted to be missing out but hope you all have a brill time! Take pics at go-karting for me!

Lydia Smith
Wait did I miss something? Are we go-karting as well now?

Nadine Cox-Dawes
@Eden, have replied to you privately. @Lydia, no go-karting, that was one idea we had a while ago but the majority vote was paintball instead x

Sunita Reddy
Thanks, Jess. See you all soon! Xxx

Sunita Reddy
PS. What time do you want us all tomorrow? I finish work around 4 p.m. so can make it for about 6 p.m. but idk if that's too early?

Sophie Barker
Sent a screenshot
Here's Nadine's email with the schedule if anybody missed it. See you all bright and early tomorrow!

Looking forward to it!

Ten

Are hen parties just the wake at the funeral of your single life?

Views on popular prewedding traditions from our
Dating & Relationships columnist

Normally, I'd be much more concerned about what to wear on a first date, what kind of impression I want to make, especially now that I need my date tonight to go well so I can convince him to come to my sister's wedding. But quite honestly, I have much more immediate things to worry about.

Namely, Jessica's hen do this weekend.

Does celebrating really need to be a weekend away featuring no fewer than *five* activities? Hen parties are going to bleed me dry. I just hope to god that Lena does something a little (read: a *lot*) more understated when it's her turn.

It's not Jessica's fault, really. I mean, it is, but she's a people pleaser. She wants to make sure everyone's having a good time. If it was up to Jess, she'd be doing paintball and go-karting, and it would be vodka and cranberry juice on my shopping list instead of prosecco to go with the pizza party. But paintballing, although it proved the more popular choice than go-karting, isn't everyone's thing, and we have to do afternoon tea because Nadine is pregnant so she can't drink and Sunita doesn't drink, but *everyone* is doing a cocktail class so she can't *not*, and we have to have a nice dinner out because that's also the done thing and before I know it I've spent the equivalent of half my monthly rent for a long weekend with people I've mostly never even met before.

Eden, a girl from Jessica's work, has apparently been really pissy with Nadine and refused to come along, purely because of the cost of it all. And honestly, I don't blame her.

It's no wonder everyone my age who's buying a house or whatever is doing it *with* someone else, because wedding season is bankrupting me and it's barely even started. How am I supposed to save up for a deposit on an apartment when I'm obligated to spend hundreds of pounds at the drop of a hat *and then* still have the wedding itself to consider?

Although I think the worst part as far as I'm concerned is that we're doing this on a bank holiday weekend. *And yet* I'm having to take Friday off work, and we're not even going to be there on the bank holiday Monday.

I have ninety-nine problems and this weekend is all of them.

But it's fine. It'll be a nice weekend. This is what people do.

This is what they'll do for me when it's my turn. Right?

I don't want to sound like I'm complaining on a purely financial basis, because I'm terrified of sounding superficial and miserly. I don't want to sound like I'm complaining *at all* so I avoid talking about it with any of my friends. Obviously, I can't sit there and call Lena to whine about all this when *she'll* be inviting me to this sort of stuff soon enough. I don't want her to feel bad for enjoying her moment, or like she can't invite me because I'll resent her for it.

Plus, you know, while I'm on the money thing, at least they get to split the cost of everything with someone else. Of course they can afford engagement presents and rent and all these other things so easily, because they're bloody sharing it! But I refuse to be that person who half arses it just on principle. They're my friends. I love them. I'm going to show them that in the same way everyone else is, with an orange Le Creuset casserole dish.

Anyway. This is not something I can talk to my friends about, since us singletons seem few and far between, and I'm sure the loved-up ones won't understand. Which is why, for better or worse (and let's face it, it's probably for worse), I end up complaining about it all to my date tonight.

I don't *mean* to. But he asked what I was doing this weekend, and I said I was going to a hen party. And he asked what we were doing for it. And then he laughed and said, "Blimey, would've been easier to ask what you *aren't* doing! That must be costing a pretty penny."

And here we are, one long, frustrated rant giving away just how deeply, desperately single I am later.

So much for making a great first impression and convincing this guy to agree to be my plus-one for Jessica's wedding. He won't even want to stay for dessert, at this rate.

"Sorry," I say quickly, cringing. I grimace at him, my shoulders hunching, my hands curling into claws on top of the table. I snatch my wine and take a gulp. "You only asked what I was up to this weekend! I swear I'm not normally like this."

My date laughs. "Don't apologize, I completely understand. I had three stag dos last year and they were all abroad. Big drinking sesh every time. All *lads, lads, lads!* sort of thing. I need a loyalty card for Budapest at this point—I swear I'm single-handedly funding their tourist industry."

I relax a little bit as he carries on, although rather than ranting like I did, he tells me a funny story about how after putting two of those events on his credit card in close succession, he forgot to pay the bill, and when it was his turn to buy a round in some restaurant, his card got rejected—with a dead phone battery and no cash on hand, he'd been completely broke for the night, leaving the soon-to-be groom to pick up the tab.

My date tonight is Jaxon. There was a moment when I was channeling Lena's future mother-in-law and almost swiped left because I thought his name was spelled weirdly, but he had such a big, lovely smile in that first profile photo—and in all his others, actually. One of those big, toothy grins that made his eyes crinkle around the corners. It was a refreshing change from all the profile photos of chin-tilted, pouting, actually pretty sullen-looking faces. He has a dog too; a big fluffy Labrador crossbreed he was quick to disclose in his bio would "come before any girlfriend, sorry not sorry."

We matched two days ago. I was in a bad mood about this weekend so I asked him if he wanted to go for dinner, thinking it would cheer me up before I had to gird my loins and set off for a weekend of nonstop, precisely scheduled fun.

I'm glad I asked him out. He's a good date. He's asked me about myself, he's cracked a few jokes, he's been polite, he's obviously made an effort with his appearance and he looks good. Jaxon's twenty-seven but looks younger now I'm meeting him in person: his face is round and soft, the beard from his first profile picture apparently a thing of the past, and he's wearing brown-rimmed round glasses, but it's a cute look, and it works on him. I don't know that I would have swiped for him if he'd looked like this in his photograph, but I guess that's the beauty (er, literally) of meeting up with someone in person, not just talking to them on an app.

We finish our desserts and conversation is still on our not-single friends.

"So how long have you been single?" I ask, and then cringe. "God, sorry. I hate when people ask me that on a first date."

"No, no, it's fine." He smiles at me. "About two years, two and a half? Something like that. How about you? I know you said on your profile you've never been in a serious relationship. But, honestly, I wasn't sure if that was just some, uh . . . like a bit of a joke?"

"Oh," I say. "No, it's serious. I mean, I *date*, but . . . ugh, see this is why I hate being asked this question on a first date. I promise there's nothing so completely horribly wrong with me that I don't end up dating guys for very long. Ha-ha!"

"Maybe you've just not met the right guy," Jaxon says, winking at me and reaching across the table to brush his thumb across the back of my hand, sending a little shiver down my spine. Warmth creeps across my cheeks the longer he holds my gaze.

"Maybe," I murmur. I'm not so sure Jaxon's the right guy—nothing against him, only that it's too soon to tell—but he's certainly saying all the right things, and I have to hand it to him, it's working.

And, hey, who am I to say after only one date that he's *not* the right guy?

Jaxon ramps up the smooth talk as we decide to have one last drink. I'm enjoying his company enough that I don't mind staying out a bit longer, and, hell, it's not like I have to be at work tomorrow, is it? As dates go, I've definitely been on much worse, and objectively speaking I don't think there's much I could ask for to make it a better date.

When the bill arrives, he reaches for his wallet and I grab my purse, and he says, "No, no, no, put that away! I've got this."

"Excellent," I say, deadpan. "That whole rant about wedding

season being too expensive was all a ploy to make you feel sorry for me and foot the bill."

Jaxon laughs. "Well, it worked a treat. Honestly, no, it's all right. Please."

"We'll go halves."

He shakes his head, though, and then gives me a cheeky smile and says, "You can get the drinks next Friday."

"Drinks next Friday?"

"Sounds like a great idea. Thanks for asking, Sophie, I'd really like to go on a second date and get drinks with you next Friday."

Oh, he's smooth.

We gather up our things and put on our coats. "I guess I should call an Uber," I say, all too aware of what I'm doing when I say it. I'm not stalling or hinting for us to go for another drink somewhere else.

"I guess so."

"Which way are you going? Maybe we could share."

Nope, not trying to prolong the date, exactly. I'm angling for him to come home with me.

I don't stop to wonder if it's a good idea or not. I know from experience there are mixed results from sleeping with a guy on the first date. Sometimes that's all they're interested in and that's okay, because sometimes it's all I'm interested in too. I think I would like to see Jaxon again; I don't think sleeping with him will screw that up. Besides, it's not as though after one date I'd be left heartbroken if it does.

Mostly it might not be such a great idea because I left my bedroom in an absolute state between the date prep and packing for the weekend, and because I haven't waxed.

But Jaxon raises his eyebrows slightly, gives me a small smile, and says, "I could be going the same way as you, Sophie, if you like."

It's not like you could cut the sexual tension with a knife, but he is fairly good looking, and, based on our brief conversations online and tonight's date, I like him.

Plus, you know, it's been a couple of months.

I smile at him and take his hand as we go outside to wait for an Uber. "Yeah. I'd like that."

Eleven

I wake up a little groggy and disoriented, comfortable in such a way that makes me want to curl up against the warm body next to me and snuggle back into the pillow to rest a while longer. Jaxon's arm is wrapped around my shoulders and my face is nuzzled against the coarse dark hair on his chest. One of his legs is hooked around mine. We're both still naked.

He stirs beneath me, sensing I'm also awake. "Hey," he murmurs, voice thick with sleep. I lift my head, turning around to face him and smile.

"Morning."

I lean up to kiss him. His hand trails from between my shoulders down my spine. I think he's going to take it a little further, and after last night I'm not objecting, but then he says, "Didn't you say you had to leave early for your sister's party?"

"Hmm?"

Oh, fuck.

I jolt upright, scrambling away and accidentally kneeing him in the thigh as I lurch across the bed to check my phone.

Yup. This was definitely a bad idea. A terrible one. I got so caught up last night I didn't set any alarms and shit, shit, *shit*, I should've been on the road over an hour ago!

I still haven't been to the supermarket with Nadine's shopping list.

I fly out of bed, kicking the covers away from me, cursing to myself and hopping into a clean pair of knickers and some jeans. Do I need to shower? I probably need to shower. I think I definitely need to shower. But I don't have time.

So much for arriving "PROMPTLY."

And so much for me telling him between kisses, "But you can't stay, I have to leave early tomorrow," last night while I was straddling his lap and we were peeling each other's clothes off.

Amazing work. Well done, Soph, you've ballsed up the *one thing* you were supposed to do today, for sex. Great job.

Jaxon is checking his watch, then his phone, and while I'm snatching up some clothes to get myself dressed and throwing a few last pieces into my open suitcase on the floor, he gets into his own clothes.

"I think I'd better be off too," he says. "I have to be at work soon."

I pause, straightening up to give him an apologetic grimace.

"Yeah. Sure. God, I'm—I'm really sorry. I promise I'm not normally this much of a mess."

I say it with a gesture at the carnage around me: the unmade bed, the upturned jewelry box on my dresser, the pile of handbags on the floor by the wardrobe from when I couldn't pick which one to take for our date last night, but I don't mean the mess in my bedroom. I'm thinking about my accidental rant last night, and the way I'm running so late now.

Either way, Jaxon tells me with a laugh, "I don't know. Ask me again after a couple more dates and I'll get back to you."

So smooth.

I allow myself a small break from the stress of being so late to kiss him goodbye, tell him that I'm looking forward to drinks next week, kiss him once more, and by then his Uber has arrived.

Jaxon kisses my cheek when I see him to the door. "Have fun this weekend."

"Thanks. I will."

If Jessica and Nadine don't kill me first, that is.

• • •

Jessica and Nadine will definitely want to kill me.

I'm already late enough leaving for this Airbnb cottage Nadine booked for everyone, but then there's the added delay because I have to stop by a supermarket and pick up my share of the shopping for the weekend. I know they're going to be annoyed with me and that this is stress they don't need, that I'm spoiling the weekend by letting them down—so much so that I'm almost tempted to turn around, go home, and tell them I'm not well, because I hate the idea of ruining this for Jessica somehow.

It's not so bad at first: Nadine phones me when I'm back on the road. I answer over the car's Bluetooth.

Instead of *hello, Sophie*, she hisses, "Where are you? You were meant to be here at ten thirty!"

"What? Jess said half past eleven on the group chat yesterday!"

"And *I* texted you the other day to remind you we were going to tell everyone else a bit later so we had chance to get there and set up. You're supposed to be here to help decorate! Jess shouldn't be blowing up her own balloons, Soph!"

Shit.

Yeah, to be fair to Nadine, she did text me. This is absolutely on me.

Not that it would have made much of a difference the way this morning's going, but still.

She sighs. Nadine is ten years older than me and Jessica, so had already moved out by the time our parents got married, and so wasn't really around the house very much when we were growing up. She and Jessica have always been really close, but the two of us? Not so much. Not that I dislike her or anything, but I wouldn't say I love her like a sister the way I do with Jess—at least, not in the moments where she's telling me off and making me feel bad. Although I guess that's maybe exactly what I should expect from a big sister, in all fairness.

"How far away are you?"

"Uh . . . a while." I am still two hours away. "I don't think I'll be too much longer."

It's a barefaced lie, but she's obviously stressed out enough as it is.

"Did you remember the shopping?"

"Of course I did!"

"And you got my email this morning asking you to pick up some nail polish and face masks and things? You didn't text me back to say you'd seen it. Honestly, it's *so* bloody rude. I can't believe they canceled on us. Last time I book an at-home spa experience."

It takes all my willpower not to sigh or swear out loud. Gritting my teeth, I flip on my indicator to move lanes so I can get off at the next exit and find another shop and buy whatever's on Nadine's updated shopping list.

"Yes, I saw your email. Sorry, Nads, it was just all systems go this morning. Bit hectic so I forgot to message you back. Don't worry, I've got it sorted."

I *will* have it sorted, at any rate.

An hour later there's a bag of nail polish and ninety-nine pence face masks in the back of my car and Jessica is on the phone.

I am officially late.

"Are you on your way?"

"Yes! Yes, I just, um, there's a bit of traffic, and—"

"Okay. Well, get here soon, all right? You've got all the prosecco."

Finally, at Coral Cottage, aptly named for its bright pink-orange front door and colorful flower boxes around the windows, all eleven of Jessica's closest friends and a few family members are lined up on the big gravel driveway to applaud and cheer my arrival at long last—a full two hours late. Three, if you're counting the fact I was meant to get there early to help set things up.

While I'm sure this welcome party is well-intentioned and all in good fun, it sets my teeth on edge.

But I can't be late *and* a bad sport, so I get out of the car with a flourish, holding my arms above my head and closing my eyes as though basking in glory, and then I curtsy.

"Not to fear, ladies, the cavalry has arrived!" I call. Nadine is already storming toward my car to open the boot and grab the supplies. Their cousin Lilly and some friend I don't really recognize help her out while I rush over to Jessica to envelop her in a big hug.

"I am so, so sorry," I tell her.

"There wasn't traffic, was there?" she says when I draw away. She keeps hold of my arms and raises one eyebrow, looking remarkably like Nadine for a second, but a smile plays at her mouth. She glances at her sister then whispers to me, "Lydia and Chrissy were coming from your way too; they said it was a clear run. *And*," she goes on, looking very triumphant over her detective skills, "you smell like a man."

"Oh, gee, thanks."

Jessica laughs. "Like men's cologne, I mean. Go on," she says, forgetting to whisper now, grabbing my hands, "were you with that guy, your mystery plus-one?"

"Are you seriously late because you were busy having morning sex?" Nadine asks me abruptly, overhearing, and *she* definitely speaks loudly enough so that all the rest of the group can hear too.

"We didn't have morning sex," is all I can say.

Jessica gasps, acting scandalized, but it's obvious she's enjoying the gossip.

"Ooh! I can't believe you've been keeping him secret from us all this time. I can't wait to meet him properly. Prove he's real, ha-ha! Well, anyway, it doesn't *quite* excuse you from missing half of the weekend, so you're going to be sleeping on the sofa bed. Sorry. First come, first served. And Nadine's claimed a whole double bed to herself. Back's killing her," Jessica says sympathetically of her pregnant sister.

I'm sympathetic, too, but I'm not convinced it's the only reason I've been relegated to the sofa.

Still. "I deserve that."

"Damn right you do. Now come on! Come in! We were just setting up pin the veil on the bride! And you can tell us all about your fabulous new love life!"

• • •

As much as I've complained about this hen do, I'll be the first to admit that I'm having a good time. Our Friday afternoon is chilled out—there are a few alcoholic drinks and many cups of tea, a few silly party games, plenty of snacks, and lots of gossiping, understandably mainly about the wedding.

It's the gossip that lets me know I am one of only three single people here. The second is Jessica and Nadine's cousin, Lilly, whose relationship recently broke down after her boyfriend decided he wanted to move to Singapore permanently for work; the third is Jessica's friend Siobhan from the school where she works. Siobhan is (according to her Instagram, because I had a little stalk) a forty-three-year-old aro ace woman who is passionate about education, and whose feed is filled with photographs of her out doing things with different sets of friends or walking her labradoodles. She has bright-purple hair, ears full of piercings, and is easily the coolest person here.

Not because of the purple hair or anything. She just seems so completely comfortable and confident. While the rest of us are forcing laughs over jokes we don't really get or being overly polite to relative strangers we're suddenly sharing a space with, she seems totally at ease.

I can see why Jessica likes her. She's the sort of person who makes you feel good when she's around; her positivity and easy-going demeanor are infectious. I quickly decide to stick near her throughout the evening. If she's unlucky, I'll decide to glue myself to her side all weekend.

Our huge order of pizzas arrives and someone sets up *13 Going on 30* on the television. Drinks are refilled and we all make ourselves as comfortable as we can in the lounge. It's a large space with three big sofas, but a few people end up on the floor regardless.

I'm one of them.

Lilly lets out a loud sigh as the movie plays and a young Jenna wishes to turn thirty. "Someone should've told her it's not this glamorous. It's more like thirty and in debt and wondering what you've wasted the last five years for."

I look over at Nadine, thinking maybe her cousin has over-indulged on the prosecco, but she only rolls her eyes and shrugs: *Let her have this.*

Some of the others jump in immediately—there's a chorus of "No, don't say that! Don't think like that! He doesn't know what he's given up, babes! You've got your whole life still ahead of you! Who needs him, anyway? You're *much* better off without him."

And then Jessica says, "It's not like single life is that bad, Lilly! Look at Soph! She seems to be enjoying it plenty. Or, you know, she has been. You were single for ages, weren't you, Soph? You've always had fun going on dates and stuff."

That's the first I've heard of any of my family thinking I've been having "fun" being single. Where's the pity? The embarrassment on my behalf?

Heads turn toward me.

"Actually—"

Nadine kicks me in the leg.

I clear my throat and beam at Lilly. "Actually, she's so right. It's brilliant. Plus, there are tons of great guys out there. I mean, look at it this way: you get to go out for dinner with some really interesting people, and most of the time they even pay."

Thankfully, Lilly hasn't drunk so much that the prospect of being suddenly single has her breaking down, sobbing over her slice of Mighty Meaty. Instead, she gives a forced laugh and says, "I guess you're right."

"Isn't it a bit miserable, though?" one of Jessica's old college mates asks me. "All this effort to try and meet guys, go on dates, and it never working out?"

She's lucky she's sat all the way across the room and can't get a kick in the side from Nadine.

"No!" I have to say. "No, not at all! Honestly, Lilly, you'll love it. It's so much fun."

"And you'll meet someone else eventually," Nadine adds. "Sophie has."

Ah. *There's* the unwitting insult I'm so used to.

Jessica gushes, "I still can't believe you've been keeping this guy a secret from us, Soph! Come on, tell us everything! Have you got a picture?"

They all turn to look at me expectantly, excitedly. Like they're all so happy and hopeful for me; like I've achieved so much just by finding someone to bring to the wedding and go to the cinema with and stuff.

And like at lunch the other week, I don't hate how it makes me feel. Like I'm finally included, somehow. Like I'm finally doing something *right*.

"I'm sure I told you," I lie, busying myself with my phone to buy time. Maybe I should just pretend it's Jaxon? Last night did go well, after all, and if it doesn't work out, there's still weeks before the wedding, so I could meet somebody else by then.

I try to bring up Jaxon's profile on Hookd to show everyone, but the app keeps crashing and won't load anything. Maybe it's for the best—I'd probably jinx it after only one date.

"Don't you have a screenshot?" Lydia-from-uni asks me.

I shake my head. "The app notifies you if someone screenshots your profile."

"Oh god, I'd *hate* that."

"You'll just have to take my word for it that he's very handsome," I crow, the delirium of being part of the group for once getting to me a little.

"All right for some," Lilly mutters to herself. "God, I'm going to be single and alone forever. I'm so jealous."

"No, you won't!" Jessica exclaims. "Tell you what, we'll all be your wingwomen tomorrow! Try and find you some fit paintball instructor or someone to give your number to!"

This starts up a whole new line of conversation, about how most of them have been in a relationship for so long they've almost forgotten how to flirt, *ha-ha*! And gosh, they could *never* imagine being the one to approach a man or give out their number; how confident you must have to be!

"Nice one," Nadine tells me, giving me a smile and a nod. "Will you do me a favor, keep a bit of an eye on her tomorrow? I think Jess might be serious about this wingwoman thing."

"Sure."

I don't know if looking out for Lilly will involve reining her in if she gets too carried away or consoling her if she starts getting upset about being single, or if Nadine means that I should actively take up position as wingwoman to set her up with someone, but we can figure that out tomorrow.

If it's the latter, I can only apologize to Lilly. How am I supposed to be a decent wingwoman when I can barely manage to date someone myself?

Twelve

I only forgot my sensible bloody shoes for paintball, didn't I?

I cannot believe it. I mean, really. I can picture them; I know exactly where they are! They were the big walking boots I bought that year it snowed really badly, but they're bulky and wouldn't fit in my little suitcase so I put them next to my suitcase in my bedroom so that I wouldn't forget them and *obviously I forgot them*, didn't I?

Never mind my stepsisters, I'm sure a good 80 to 90 percent of the gang don't believe me and think I just willfully ignored both the final email and Jessica's reminder in the WhatsApp group chat, in spite of the fact I was the one who sent the screenshot of it when the others started asking questions we already had the answers to.

I wonder what I look like to them. Especially to those who've never met me before. Scatterbrained and helpless, barely functioning as an independent adult, and just really bloody useless. I wonder if any of them are whispering to each other, *It's no wonder she's been single for so long*, and I wonder if the ones who do know me, like Lilly, are saying, *Oh, you know, that's just Sophie. She's a bit of a hot mess.*

We carpool; I offer to be one of the drivers in a pointless effort to make up for my shortcomings so far. I get stuck driving Jessica's mates from university: Lydia, Chrissy, Ola, and Sunita. The four of them talk nonstop among themselves, chattering excitedly, their voices overlapping and their laughter filling the car.

On the one hand, this is awful, because they're so busy "catching up IRL" that they barely even think to draw me into the conversation. I may as well be their taxi driver, except I'm not getting paid at the end.

On the other, this is perfect, because I don't have to pretend to be much more put together or cooler than I really am, or have to make up any lies about the plus-one I've promised I have for the wedding.

It's a half-hour drive to the paintball place, the last ten minutes of which are down dirt roads carved into a forest, before we finally stop at a set of small huts and a large log cabin. A serious-looking man in a khaki coveralls and giant boots is waiting for us, hands on his hips.

We pour out of the cars, everyone in leggings and T-shirts or some kind of sportswear, hair tied back in ponytails and French braids. Nadine's in jeans and a pretty white blouse—exempt as a mum-to-be—and evening out our party of thirteen to twelve.

The serious man introduces himself as Kyle. He begins to divide us into two groups before Jessica stops him and says we all already know our groups (she's even had this part of the weekend planned for weeks), so he directs us to one of the huts to pick up our own coveralls. One team in blue, the other in red.

I start to follow everyone else when he stops me, holding a hand almost in front of my face and saying, "Whoa, there, missy. Someone missed the message about appropriate footwear."

I look down at my sandals like it's the first time I'm seeing them.

"Oh. Yes. Um."

"There's always one." He rolls his eyes. "We've got some spares. What size are you? Get yourself a suit; I'll find you a pair."

While he goes to find me some shoes, I hurry into the hut with the other girls to get my coveralls. The material is coarse and stiff, and we're all dressed in a onesie that's either too big or a bit too snug, all looking equally ridiculous (except Siobhan, who somehow has managed to make it look effortlessly chic by finding one that mostly fits and rolling up the too-long trouser legs to just above her ankles. Hers is even splattered in paint that matches her purple hair).

Once we're all suited up, Kyle demonstrates how the paintball guns work, tells us how the session will go, and lays out a few rules. Big goggles like we used to have to wear in science class at school get passed around, and I'm also provided with a pair of giant, heavy, ugly boots. I sit down on a bench to put them on and it's only when I take off my sandals that I realize I don't have any socks with me.

I'm on an absolute roll this weekend.

Nadine, god bless her, seems to have been expecting me to do exactly this, because no sooner do I realize I don't have socks than she's standing next to me holding out a clean pair of socks, looking a little bit fed up but saying, "Have fun, Soph. And make sure you beat Jess's team, yeah? She was driving me nuts in the car on the way here talking about how she was going to win."

I grin at her and take the socks. "You got it, sis."

• • •

My team does beat Jessica's at paintball, but it's not because of me. I'm complete rubbish, as it turns out. But it is fun, and even the losing team don't seem to mind very much. I'll happily admit we're all having great fun.

Until we realize that, by the time we're back at the cottage, there is only an hour and a half for twelve girls to use the three bathrooms, scrub the paint and sweat and mud off ourselves, and get ready for afternoon tea then cocktails then dinner.

There's an almost manic energy as we all hurry to get ready. Although the minivan is kept waiting a mere eighteen minutes longer than Jessica's originally scheduled departure time, we end up late for afternoon tea too.

I do find it a bit hilarious that everyone has such a mix of out-fits. The gang from university are the most coordinated, all having opted for minidresses and high heels, ready for the idea of a night out. A couple of people, like one of Jessica's workmates, Nadine, and Lilly, have all opted for cute floaty skirts or blouses that are more in keeping with the afternoon tea part of the day. Meanwhile, Siobhan is in a floor-length smart-casual black dress that wouldn't look out of place at a corporate event and somehow blends into both groups, and I am wearing a red leather miniskirt and a white T-shirt that says in tiny print IF YOU'RE READING THIS YOU'RE TOO CLOSE, an outfit I now think is equally inappropriate for afternoon tea, a cocktail class, and a sit-down dinner.

We all get a few odd looks as we pour out of the minibus and trek a street or two over to the café, but I think that has nothing to do with the cheap veil and BRIDE-TO-BE sash we've put Jessica in. To be fair, I would look at us pretty weirdly too. It's not at all obvious that we're even all together.

I end up sitting at the end of the table, opposite Siobhan, and I couldn't be more relieved about it. Jessica, of course, is smack in the middle, but everyone else has fallen naturally into their little groups. Nadine and Lilly are at the opposite end of the table, with Jessica's other friends from work. I'm relieved because I'm not stuck alone with in-jokes and references I don't get, and because Siobhan is by far the easiest person here to talk to.

She also seems completely nonplussed by the mad rush to get ready after paintball. Everyone else seems a bit harried, a bit tense; the "fun" atmosphere at the café feels a bit too forced, especially with everyone dividing themselves up to stick by the people they already know.

Unlike yesterday, when we all threw ourselves into the start of the weekend, and unlike earlier when we were too busy paintballing or being paintballed to get cliquey.

At some point, Nadine declares we have to leave: the cocktail class is a fifteen-minute walk away—or twenty, for some people, in their heels, she says—and we don't want to be late because if we're late to *that* we'll end up late to dinner and then we'll lose our reservation. There's a scramble as half of us do the undignified thing and shove the last French macarons or cucumber sandwiches or tiny slices of Victoria sponge into our mouths before we're rushed out of the door.

The groups divvy up a little more during the cocktail-making class (which includes mocktails for Sunita and Nadine), with Jessica's friend groups mixing a little now that we're all more comfortable around each other.

The class does get pretty exciting at one point, when some of the girls decide that they want to try to set Lilly up with the guy running our class. Max. Max the Mixologist. He's the kind of tall, broad, manscaped guy you'd see on *Love Island*, with an East London accent and a crooked smile that gives him a certain kind of charm it looks like *everyone* is falling for.

"I can't wait to be married," Jessica says, loudly, pointedly. "Are *you* married?"

"Me?" He laughs. "No."

"Girlfriend?" Ola presses, leaning almost all the way across the table, her eyes bugging and a giant grin on her face.

Lilly is sat beside her and giggles, flushed from drink and embarrassment, hands flapping at Ola as she says, "Shhhhh!"

"No girlfriend," Max says affably.

"Boyfriend?"

"Nope."

"I don't believe it," says one of Jessica's work friends, Georgina. "A guy like you? You must be taken! *So* fit. Isn't he, Lilly?"

Lilly squeals, shrinking in her seat, and Max gives a polite laugh. Poor guy, I think. How many of these things must he sit through with women trying to flirt with him? Especially since, as Jessica says, *everyone* is doing these kinds of classes at their hen parties now.

"But obviously," he says smoothly, all charm, "you lovely ladies are all taken."

"Unfortunately for us," laments Lydia, to another chorus of giggles. "But not *Lilly*."

"Oh, now, I don't believe *that*." Max plays along gamely, I'll give him that.

"Maybe you should give her some tips," says someone, though I'm not exactly sure who. "Go on, what's your best chat-up line?"

"How much does a polar bear weigh?" he answers immediately.

"Enough to break the ice!" shriek a few of the girls, dissolving into peals of laughter.

I say, "Do you know that the etymology of *Arctic* comes from like, the ancient Greek or something for *bear*? Because that's where the polar bears are. So *Ant*arctic is kind of like, 'no bears.'" I think that's so cool. Isn't that cool?"

"Isn't anything about a polar bear arguably 'cool'?" Siobhan jokes, making me snort with laughter.

"Is that true?" Max asks me, looking me right in the eye with a curious tilt of his head. The sudden, undivided attention from a charming, attractive man makes my heart do a little stutter against my ribs.

"Listen, when enough guys use the polar bear chat-up line, you start looking up the *actual* answer, and then you end up down the internet rabbit hole and it's three in the morning and you're looking up things like Ursa Major and how people were too afraid to say the word for bear so actually we just call it 'brown,' that's what bear means, and then . . . Arctic, Antarctic."

They're all looking at me. Max and a couple of the girls (Nadine included) look genuinely quite interested in my useless bear knowledge, with Max leaning a bit closer, like he wants to ask me more, but most of them are looking at me like *I've* just turned into a bear. Or like I've lost my mind. Either, or. I notice Ola roll her eyes and then see Lilly frowning at me, looking distinctly put out, which is when I realize my real faux pas here.

A faux paws, if you will.

I can feel an all-too-familiar sense of panic rising in my throat and flick a piece of mint on the table next to my drink, laughing in the most offhand way I can manage and announcing, "What can I say? When you've spent years being as single as I am, you have a *lot* of free time on your hands to end up in a Wikipedia wormhole."

They laugh at my expense, and I laugh, too, and Ola tries to egg Lilly on to try to flirt with Max, but then he's announcing that we should finish our drinks as the next class will be due in soon, and Nadine does her thing again, calling up Maps on her phone to dictate a route for us and corral the tipsy party out the door. I wonder if I can make Max, the flirty, attractive bartender, part of the story in my next column. I'm sure there's a sex on the beach joke in there somewhere.

I fall into step at the back of the group with Siobhan, who seems to hang back purposely to speak to me. She loops her arm through mine. Ahead of us, some of the girls have Jessica cackling over some joke, and they start dancing down the street singing some Taylor Swift song noisily, and badly. I watch with a strange sense of detachment and an ache in my chest.

"Don't you think it's weird?" I blurt.

"What?"

"This. Hen parties, stag dos. The idea that you need to, like, mourn the end of your single life before you have the wedding and celebrate being married. It's like . . . it's like a funeral for your single self. It's just a glorified wake."

Siobhan lets out a loud hoot of laughter. "A wake! Oh god. I mean, I suppose that's one way to look at it."

I bite my tongue rather than try to explain myself. I sound so mean, so bitchy, so *jealous*. And I think I probably am, but for the most part, I just feel sad.

"So aside from the occasional Wikipedia wormhole," Siobhan says, "how's single life been treating you?"

"Oh! Well. You know. It's like I said yesterday to Lilly and everyone. It's great. The dates. Meeting new people, going out and doing new things or . . . I love it. Well, like. You know. I don't *love it*, or I wouldn't be trying to not be single by going on dates and things, but—"

Despite the slight sway in her step, Siobhan fixes me with a very steady, serious look, head cocked slightly to one side. Her eyeliner is winged, a sparkly gold. It's really pretty. I wish I could get mine to look like that.

"You don't sound very happy about dating."

The laugh that leaves my mouth is short lived and obnoxious. "Is anybody? All the rejections or the guys that are just . . . god, really bloody awful at worst, and boring or stuck-up at best? It's—" *Exhausting*, I want to say, like I wanted to say last night, but I clamp my mouth shut quickly. Single life is supposed to be so much fun! It is fun!

I open my mouth again, and a hiccup comes out.

So I say, "It's a bit draining sometimes, that's all. But it has its upsides too! For sure. Tons of them. And—" And *shit*, I'm supposed to be dating someone. "And obviously it's working out now, because I'm with a really lovely guy! He's my plus-one to the wedding, you know? And that's . . . that's obviously going really well. Really great."

"Yeah. Yeah, of course. But—"

"Shiv!" Georgina, one of the work buddies, shouts over, running toward us. "Sorry, Soph. Siobhan, mate, I was just telling Chrissy and whatshername with the red hair about your uncle in New Zealand and how he met Orlando Bloom that time and thought he was Paul Rudd, but I don't tell it right."

"Your New Zealand accent *is* horrible." Siobhan laughs and lets Georgina drag her away. For a minute, I'm left lagging at the back on my own, thinking about how much I *don't* want to think about dating and being single and other people's relationships—which is unavoidable, really, when this whole night is about celebrating my stepsister's impending wedding and Nadine's expecting me to do a speech at dinner about how happy I am for Jessica and her fiancé.

Dating is exhausting, but this . . . so is this.

I am so, so tired.

But tonight's not about me and this is not my pity party, so I gather myself up and run on ahead to walk with Lilly and gush about how cute Max the Mixologist was and did she think he was flirting with her? He was definitely a bit flirty. Maybe there'll be a cute waiter or someone at dinner; I'll be sitting by her and we can be on the lookout all the rest of tonight. We can look up cheesy chat-up lines to use on them.

"You all right?" she asks me, after she stops giggling over the mere idea of flirting with someone. "You look a bit . . . "

Gee, thanks.

"I'm fine," I tell her, and smile. "Just a bit tired."

June

Dear Sophie Barker & Guest

You are cordially invited to
celebrate the engagement of

*Conor Fellowes &
Jessica Cox*

Request the honor of your presence at their marriage

*On Saturday the nineteenth of June
at two thirty p.m.*

*At The Regent Terrace Hotel
Castle Combe*

With dinner and reception to follow

NOTE TO SELF: PLANS FOR JESSICA'S WEDDING
Last updated 10 June

Family dinner at hotel on Fri 18—table booked for 7:30 p.m. but BE THERE FOR SEVEN, everyone else will be early!!!

Hair and makeup in Nadine's room from 8 a.m., remember to go with hair wet!!

Ask Nadine what we're doing for breakfast???

And also lunch!!!!!

Ceremony starts 2:30 p.m., PEE BEFOREHAND

Ask Nadine if I need to have money with me for the bar??

Remember to bring snacks to leave in room in case dinner is late because photos

Pack portable charger!!

WEAR. IN. THE. SHOES.

Pack Band-Aids.

Don't let Camilla start on brandy

Ask Dad for a copy of his speech—promised Jess to vet for super-embarrassing stories and dad jokes. DO NOT FORGET.

Ask Duncan to be my backup date, just in case.

Thirteen

Marriage is a huge commitment—so why does asking someone to be your plus-one for what is essentially dinner and free drinks seem just as big a leap?

Views on inviting someone to a wedding (and when to avoid the bouquet toss) from our Dating & Relationships columnist

The week of the wedding I have my fifth date with Jaxon. It's been almost a month since we've matched, and so far things are . . .

I don't want to jinx it, but things are *kind of going really well*.

The week after Jessica's hen party, we spent the entire weekend together. He invited me to a pub quiz with his mates last week—which, more importantly, meant he wanted to introduce me to his friends! Which is a big deal! Tally has her opinions on weeknight dates, I know, but after a couple of weeks of dating, I don't think it's weird to see him on a Monday night for dinner, especially when he's offered to cook for me at his place.

Jaxon's house share is minimalist, clean, and tidy. Much tidier than my place, at any rate. The only clutter I notice is a newspaper left on the coffee table in the living room.

I help him cook, preparing some salad while he checks on the lasagna.

Jaxon is nice. He's sweet, easy to talk to, always asks about my day, and he texts regularly. Recently, he's started signing off with *Goodnight, beautiful xxx*, which I think is a very good sign.

So, in the most offhand way I can manage, while he slides the lasagna back into the oven and sets the timer for another five minutes, I say, "I don't suppose you'd fancy coming to my sister's wedding with me this weekend?"

He stands up so fast he smacks his shoulder on the kitchen countertop, wincing as he rubs it. He pushes his glasses back up his nose, staring at me. I carry on cutting up some cucumber, smiling, pretending like this is no big deal.

"Pardon?"

"Oh, well, you know, it's Jessica's wedding this weekend. And obviously I have a plus-one, so I thought . . . maybe you'd like to come with me? I have a hotel room booked already, so really it's just a bit of an all-expenses-paid weekend away."

During which he will undoubtedly face polite but intense interrogation from my family, and I'll of course have to try to circumvent the fact that we started dating *after* I told my family I was seeing a guy who'd be my plus-one, but—

"Um, that's . . . wow, uh . . . thanks, Sophie, that's very generous of you. It sounds great—"

"So you'll come with me?" I blurt, a little too quickly and a lot too enthusiastically, with way too much relief in my tone. I look away, unable to bear any potential (and probable) judgment of how clingy I sound.

"I have plans this weekend," he says, not quite meeting my eyes. "I'm sorry."

"Oh."

I can't ask what his plans are. That really will sound clingy. And

I refuse to be the needy girlfriend when we haven't even established if we *are* boyfriend and girlfriend yet. I know that inviting him as my date to a family wedding is a big step; I have to suck it up and take the rejection.

So I tell him, "That's okay!" in a voice that makes it very, very clear it's not.

And after dinner, Jaxon yawns, and apologizes but he needs to get an early night, he's really sorry. I get the message and after he kisses me goodbye and thanks me for a lovely evening, even apologizing again for not being able to come with me this weekend, I head home to my own bed, alone and terrified.

Have I screwed things up by asking him to meet my family? He's invited me out with his friends; this isn't *really* that much different, is it? And I wasn't even really asking him to *meet* them anyway, just . . . hang out at the same event as them.

The bigger problem—at least for spiraling, self-centered me tonight—is what I'm going to do about my plus-one for the wedding.

There's nothing left for it. I'll have to ask Duncan. He can schmooze anybody, and he's a good enough friend that he'll help me save face just this once, I'm sure. He'll be a great plus-one.

We can dance to "Single Ladies" together.

It's going to be fine. I'm sure of it.

Helena Shelton
Saw this article about single girls and dating—made me think of you, Soph! It's hilarious, last month she ACTUALLY hooked up with a mixologist in a cupboard at a hen party! Can you believe?! "I'd choose sex in a stockroom over Sex on the Beach any day," lol!

Tallulah King
OMG! I love this series. It's my new obsession.

Helena Shelton
Tell me about it! @Sophie have you read them???

Sophie Barker
Lol yes, have seen them going round on Twitter. If
only my dating life was that exciting!

Helena Shelton
If only!

Tallulah King:
Can't wait for the "wake to the funeral of your single
life" Lena! We'll have to make sure there's a sexy
mixologist on hand for Sophie!

Helena Shelton:
Well, she does LOVE to sneak off to hook up with
some rando at a party, lol! Mitch 2.0 coming up!

Something cold and unpleasant prickles across my skin and settles into my bones as Tally and Lena carry on chatting, the notifications sliding onto my phone screen one by one.

That's my article. They're talking about my column, about me.

All the things I can't say to their faces, would never say to their faces because it could ruin our friendship . . . Coming from some anonymous stranger online—they're lapping it up.

Lately, the column has been getting more and more views each month. And now even my own friends are sending it to me.

I should probably feel proud. I should be ecstatic that at least that part of my job here is going so well, even when I'm floundering to recover from losing the pub contract and the graffiti incident.

But all I feel is sick.

I stare at the messages on my phone, which are still pinging through—now chatting about what Lena might like to do for her bachelorette—and wonder what would happen if I just told them. If I said, *Hey, not to interrupt, but that article? I wrote that.*

Something tells me they wouldn't find it half as interesting or funny then.

And I'm willing to bet any conversations about Lena's hen party would take place outside of our group chat and no longer involve me, especially after my fairly scathing article ripping apart how extravagant and expensive they are, which I wrote with no holds barred.

Yeah, that's just what I need this morning. To alienate my friends as well as the guy I've been dating. Wouldn't that just be the cherry on the cake?

"Someone got up on the wrong side of the bed today."

I jump. I hadn't noticed Duncan approach until he was right next to me. Isaac, sitting across from me, pipes up, "She's been like this all day."

"I have not," I argue, but it only comes out sounding petulant, not helped by my scowl. Isaac smirks to himself, ignoring us and going back to his work as I say hello to Duncan. He usually drops by my desk when he's in the office, with some excuse to chat.

Usually the excuse is that he's bored.

I shove Lena's and Tally's messages out of my mind, not wanting to bring it up in front of Isaac and not really in the mood to talk about it even to Duncan. I'm not sure I'm in the mood to chat at all, really, but needs must, and since Jaxon turned me down for the wedding last night, I don't have much choice.

I give him my biggest, sweetest smile. "Duncan . . . "

"If you're going to ask me to bring you a cup of tea, the answer's no."

"No! I was actually going to ask for a favor. Although, really, I'll be the one doing you a favor."

He pulls a face, skeptical but intrigued. "Is that so?"

"How would you like to be my plus-one for Jessica's wedding? You'll love it. I know you love a party. Come on, it'll be great fun—free food, I'll buy your drinks all night . . . "

And without hesitation, he says, "Yeah, go on then. When is it?"

"Yes! Thank you! I bloody love you! You're a lifesaver. It's this weekend, and—"

"Oof. Uh . . . this weekend as in, *this weekend*?"

"That is what 'this weekend' means. You can come, right? You don't have plans? You don't have plans," I repeat, more authoritatively, as if simply by eliminating the question from my voice, I can make it true.

"I'm visiting my brother in Dublin this weekend," he explains, sounding genuinely apologetic. "I haven't been back since his kid was born, and a couple of our cousins are visiting, too, so I thought why not?"

"But—but you can't! It's the wedding! I need a plus-one!" I shriek, each word shriller and more frantic than the last.

The irony isn't lost on me that I'm always mad at people for assuming I never have plans because I'm single, when I've done the exact same thing to Duncan when thinking of him as my backup plan for the wedding.

"I'm sorry, Soph. I would've come if I could, you know that. It's not a big deal, though, right? I mean, you'll find someone else to go with, so there's no more stress over the table plan, right?"

Who? Tally is on holiday this weekend—a getaway with her boyfriend before prices spike during the school holidays. Lena's seeing venues and trying on dresses and stuff this weekend. There's Frankie, but I immediately remember how angry his girlfriend was about us nipping out for a cigarette at their housewarming, and I know that even if he did agree to come, it probably wouldn't end too well.

I mumble under my breath, getting my phone out. There's Frankie's friend Jordan, the one who's quite fit now, and I know it's a bit of a weird request but . . .

I find his Instagram quickly so I can DM him to ask but stop in my tracks. There are a couple of posts at the top of his profile with a girl. I check the date and caption of the most recent one—posted only this weekend, and clearly his girlfriend.

Shit.

Who else do I know?

Desperately, I look up at Duncan.

His smile stretches wider, but his nose and forehead scrunch up so he's cringing. It's not a very reassuring expression. "Well," he says. "I mean, it doesn't matter anyway, right? So long as you're there."

In theory, yes. In practice . . .

I can already hear all the *Here by yourself?* and *Oh no, we thought you were bringing a boyfriend, Sophie! What a shame it didn't work out*, and *You know, sweetheart, my nephew's a doctor* comments I'm bound to get. Especially because I'm sure none of my family made a secret about how I was bringing someone. A romantic interest someone, at that.

I can already picture the empty seat beside me throughout dinner, the pitiful looks I'll get as people start to whisper among themselves that *Poor Sophie, she's just been dumped, and at her sister's wedding too! How sad.*

I knew it was silly to go along with the whole *of course I'm seeing someone* thing just to shut my family up, but . . .

I just . . .

I was really banking on this one, that's all.

For once, it felt like something was finally going my way. That after being single my whole life, I was finally going to be, well, not on the outside. I was going to be one of those girls at someone else's wedding, happy and smiling and with a guy's arm around her shoulder. And nobody would be looking at me like they felt so sorry for me or like I failed, or wondering what was so fundamentally wrong with me that I was all by myself—again.

I should have known that the idea that, finally, I was going to be doing it all right, that for just one weekend, I would be one of those people who had it all, was too good to be true.

. . .

Alone in my flat later that evening—as usual—I decide to chalk today up as one of the worst days of my life. It even beats being broken up with on Christmas Eve, and I end up huddled by my bedroom window, wrapped in my dressing gown, fidgeting with a cigarette I promise myself I'm not going to light.

My friends like my anonymous article—love it, even—but I know they'd hate *me* if they found out I was the one behind it. They'd think I resent them. They'd think I was jealous and catty, and they'd be hurt I hid everything from them all this time—not just the column but how I *actually* feel about stuff going on in their lives. I've written about all the money I'm expected to spend on celebrating their lives, talked about how neglected I feel by my friends as they put their partners first . . .

They'll hate me, I know it.

Throw in having to tell my family that my mystery boyfriend isn't coming to the wedding—worse, that he never existed in the first place—and I want to be sick. I want to crawl underneath my duvet and not come back out until the whole wedding is over and done with. I wonder if I could bail, claim a stomach bug. It's drastic, and it's awful of me, but not as awful as the well-intentioned, actually very hurtful treatment I'll face from everybody at the wedding when I show up alone.

Oh, and Jaxon's barely replied to my texts all day.

Faking It

Talk about hitting rock bottom.

My phone pings, lighting up from its spot on the windowsill.

Meet new singles in your area!

Hookd encourages me, the little fishing rod–and–heart icon doing they best to tempt me.

I stare at it until the screen goes dark, then toss my unlit cigarette to the floor and snatch up my phone instead.

If this is rock bottom, I think, I might as well revel in it.

EDIT PROFILE

Sophie, 25
NEEDS PLUS-ONE FOR WEDDING

About Me
So it's my sister's wedding this Fri./Sat. and I'm suddenly stuck without a plus-one. Can't bear the humiliation of going alone so here's the offer: dinner, dancing, drinks, I'll drive, accommodation is on me.

Also I need you to pretend to be my boyfriend. Don't actually have one, but sort of told my family I do lol.

Would also be really great if you own a gray or navy suit.

NO VEGETARIANS/DIETARY RESTRICTIONS.

Height: 5'7"

Active: Sometimes

Astrological sign: Libra

Education: Undergraduate degree

Drinks: Frequently

Smokes: Occasionally

Looking for: Something Casual

My interests: Photography, Documentaries, Museums and galleries, Indie music, City breaks

Perfect first date: At my sister's wedding pretending we're already dating

A review by a friend:
She's an absolute loser who can't keep a man, but she's chill. Who wouldn't want a fake date with a funny, pretty girl for a weekend?" —my mate Duncan, who is a terrible friend who made plans with his family so can't go to the wedding with me either.

Never have I ever . . .
. . . been so bloody desperate to not look single.

Fourteen

After updating my dating profile on Hookd, by Wednesday night I have a couple of matches. I've altered my usual age range from twenty-four to twenty-eight to include guys well into their thirties—I need all the possible matches I can get. I just need someone normal and nice to get through this weekend, and then afterward . . .

Well, that'll be afterward, won't it?

That's a problem for Future Sophie, and Future Sophie can just say she didn't want to cause any extra stress for the bride or anybody else and looking back, isn't it just so funny? What a laugh! Such a brilliant, harmless little prank, ha-ha!

I mean, Jaxon won't come with me, and I can't show up *telling them* I've brought some random guy, can I? That's even worse. Nadine said as much. They'll wonder why I brought a total stranger to the wedding. This is just . . . cleaner. Simpler. Less stressful for everybody involved. Except maybe me, but you know. What's a little collateral damage in the form of my stress levels compared to the wedding running smoothly?

I end up discarding a couple of the matches pretty quickly. I get a weird vibe or just have second thoughts after being a little too swipe-right happy in my earlier desperation, but there are two

I talk to a little more, explaining the situation a bit. One of them unmatches me less than a minute later.

I don't really blame him.

Thursday morning, Duncan comes over to ask me how it's going, and when my manager Jenny huffs at him to go back to his own desk and let me work, he blurts the whole thing out to her.

Which is why I'm now sitting with Jenny and Duncan both leaning over my shoulder as we swipe through Hookd, while my colleague Isaac, sitting opposite me, tries to act all haughty and like he's above it, but we all know he's listening in and keeps trying to peek around his monitor to look.

"So, hey, Isaac, got any plans this weekend?" Duncan says, pushing his chair back to look around.

Before I can stop him, or before Duncan gets out another word, Isaac says flatly, "Not a chance." Quickly, he adds, "Sorry, Sophie, I'm sure . . . um . . . your family are very nice, and it'll be a lovely wedding, and . . . you're, um—" He clears his throat, and I repress a giggle at how pink his face is turning.

"Ignore him," I tell Isaac. "And no offense, but also, no, thank you."

He cracks a smile at me, a little relieved.

"Last thing I need is you two getting in on this harebrained scheme together," Jenny says. "As your manager, I categorically cannot support it. If only because I'm ninety-eight percent sure this is how all the best Hallmark movies start."

"There are good Hallmark movies?" Isaac mutters, none too quietly.

"Ooh!" Jenny says then, ignoring him. "Look, a match!"

Isaac gives in, now coming over to ogle the profile with us.

Harry, thirty-three, a production exec at "Local TV studio" has matched with me. He's six foot one, a Pisces (sorry, Jessica), likes hiking and camping . . .

But more importantly, he's actually really bloody fit, and he's matched with me.

I message him quickly—saying hi, and is he sure he wants in on this "harebrained scheme" with me? Jenny gives an excited little squeal when three dots pop up as he types his reply, covering her mouth with her hands.

And I get not just one, but three messages. He's in.

> Are you kidding? This sounds hilarious
>
> I just got out of a long-term relationship and could do with a laugh
>
> Drinks tonight? You can fill me in on the whole shebang then

• • •

After work, with Duncan in tow (because, you know, this guy could be a total weirdo), I meet my new match at a popular bar in town. It's happy hour, but still a little early so the place is well lit and fairly empty, and five minutes after we grab seats near the window, Harry shows up.

Oh god, he's even more attractive in person.

He's tall—as in, genuinely as tall as he claims on his profile, for once—and wearing a plain white T-shirt with chinos and loafers, along with an expensive watch. His dark hair is coiffed in that way that makes him look like he cares about his appearance but not too much. He's sporting a tan that gives his skin a bronze glow, and his gray eyes crinkle at the corners when he gives me a wide smile, raising a hand in hello.

He's a regular modern-day Adonis.

"Harry?" I say, like I don't already know.

"Yeah. It's Sophie, right? And—" He laughs, and oh god, that laugh will be the cause of my death because it's enough to make all my insides turn to jelly and make me melt right here on the floor. It's a low, warm sound that seems to reverberate in my chest. He grins at Duncan, sticking out a hand. "I'm going to take a wild guess you're the friend from her bio who can't make it to the wedding?"

"Just here to make sure you're not a serial killer," Duncan says jovially.

"Nah, I leave the axe murdering until after the summer. Bodies decompose too quickly in this heat."

I snort with laughter so suddenly I can't catch it, which I really wish I had because it's not an attractive sound at all, and, in case I haven't mentioned, this guy is *really fit*.

"So," Duncan says in a grand voice, "before I leave you two lovebirds to it, what's the deal here? Why'd you swipe right?"

"Is it really sad if I say it's so I can have something to put on Instagram to show my ex I've moved on too? But also, I mean, this sounds hilarious. I work in TV and this kind of thing—I can't promise I won't steal it to pitch to our writers . . . but I could really do with a good laugh and some no-strings-attached fun."

"Well," I say, "I can promise the fun and the Instagram revenge, but this is strictly business."

Harry raises an eyebrow, which, honestly, should be a crime, because it's unbearably sexy and makes my heart give a little somersault and my brain stall for a second. He says, "Yes, ma'am."

Get it together, Sophie.

"I'm talking kiss-on-the-cheek, hand-around-my-waist, act-like-I'm-the-greatest-thing-in-your-life, impress-my-family, never-see-each-other-again-after-Sunday-morning kind of business." I press on. "The hotel for the wedding is fully booked but I'll see if I can get a twin room, or worst-case scenario you can have my room and I'll pretend we had a fight or something and bunk with someone else."

Harry looks at Duncan. "I feel like Christian Grey had fewer stipulations in his contract."

"Yeah," Duncan says, nodding gravely. "She's into some really kinky stuff. Watch yourself or she'll want you to slow dance with her."

Both Harry and I laugh at that. There's a little moment when he catches my eye as we laugh, and I feel heat creep over my cheeks.

Duncan sticks around a few more minutes before leaving. Harry and I order a cocktail each (since it's two-for-one) and we're still there three hours later, having ordered some food and a couple more drinks during that time.

Unashamedly, I tell him about how I'm just straight-up sick of being single at this endless parade of celebrating how much everyone else has their life together, which is why I'm recruiting a fake boyfriend rather than just doing the ordinary thing and going alone. Harry tells me it's not all it's cracked up to be on the other side of things. He explains that he was with his ex for seven years and the last year had been pretty rocky, and, in some last-ditch attempt to fix it, he proposed on Valentine's Day, both of them rushing through a summer wedding, only for things to get steadily worse—culminating in her becoming cold and snappy, and him cheating.

"I'm really glad I'm not interested in dating you for real," I tell him. "The cheating would be an instant deal-breaker."

He doesn't disagree, only shrugs affably, and says, "I screwed up. That's on me. But I can't be sorry we broke up."

"Why do you have to show her that *you* moved on, though?" I want to know. "If you're the one who cheated?"

"Oh," he says mildly. "Because then she slept with my brother."

"Yeah . . . yeah, this is *way* too much baggage."

I laugh at my own joke even though, really, I was serious, and notice his smile twitch—but after a beat, Harry joins in with a self-deprecating roll of his eyes.

"Right? But for the sake of this weekend, I'll be the perfect, noncheating boyfriend who's a model of perfection for your family, and we'll both pretend like our love lives aren't colossal fuckups."

"Cheers to that."

Fifteen

Friday afternoon, the sun is shining brightly, and the air is pleasantly warm with a gentle breeze. With my car windows down, I could almost pretend like I'm Bridget Jones off for a romantic weekend getaway with her sexy boyfriend. I'm only missing the silk headscarf.

Well, and the boyfriend, I guess, but that's only a minor technicality.

Harry is undeniably sexy, though. He might be a nefarious cheater and a bit of a weirdo for going along with this whole thing, but he's got a killer smile and a jawline that could cut glass, and he smells incredible.

Since I made the mistake of asking Jaxon to come to the wedding with me, I've barely heard from him. The *Goodnight, beautiful xxx* texts are still there, but we only exchange four or five messages during the day at best, which is in stark contrast to how chatty he was before. I'm not sure if the whiplash is purely emotional or from whipping my head around to look at my phone every time it buzzes in case it's him.

Even with the relative radio silence, I feel kind of guilty for being out with another guy, even if Harry isn't a *proper* date.

The guilt doesn't last very long, though. I'm having too much of a good time.

Harry proves easy to chat to on the drive out to the fancy hotel where Jessica's wedding is taking place, but I think that has a good deal to do with how much we—ironically enough—don't have to pretend around each other. I don't have to pretend to be perfect and put my best foot forward in the hopes that this guy will like me enough to ask for a second date or act like I'm someone who never gets jealous of her friends and isn't plagued by loneliness; he doesn't have to pretend like he didn't cheat on his ex-wife or like he's not a workaholic who gambles maybe a little bit too much and is absolutely terrified at the idea of getting back out there to date seriously when he always expected to be settled down and starting a family by now.

He's funny, too, in a quippy, snarky sort of way that I enjoy.

And I kind of can't wait to see him in a suit. I bet he's the kind of guy who manages to look swoonworthy in a suit.

Not that I plan to swoon or anything, but . . .

Well, I can't deny I like the idea of pretending *that* kind of guy is my boyfriend in front of all these people who would be full of pity and disappointment if I showed up single.

As we get nearer to the hotel, we run through the game plan again one more time.

"And you told them you and this imaginary boyfriend started dating in March, you said, right?"

"Yes, but maybe"—I swallow, hesitating as I think it through—"maybe don't act too lovey-dovey. If Jaxon ever texts me back and I decide to introduce my family to him, I'd need to pretend break up with you, so my family can't go thinking we're totally perfect for each other or anything."

"Gotcha."

I'm glad one of us sounds so convinced.

The wedding venue is breathtaking, which is saying something as I've already visited a handful of times with Jessica. The hotel is a great sandstone building with three stories and an impressive staircase leading up to the front doors. There are arched windows and statues that look vaguely Roman, of cupids or women draped in fabric looking pensive and pretty. A neat lawn sprawls on either side of the hotel and I know that at the back of the building, there are some impressive rosebushes and topiaries, and a stunning gazebo.

It looks pretty and romantic in the early evening light as the sun dips just behind the trees at the back of the hotel, casting light shadows and a golden glow over everything. It's the sort of place you could almost imagine Keira Knightley running down the stairs in some period drama.

Harry and I grab our things from the back of the car. His overnight bag is one of those small, sturdy suitcases that fits in overhead luggage even on cheap flights, well-worn and covered in scratches, but he carries his suit in a separate bag that reads HUGO BOSS. He offers to carry my garment bag with my bridesmaid's dress, but I tell him I've got it.

"Save the chivalry for tomorrow," I joke.

Check-in is a painless experience. I forked out for a second room for Harry for tonight, but, with the place fully booked with Jessica's wedding guests tomorrow night, I had to use my *I'm in the bridal party* authority when I phoned ahead to make sure my room is a twin, so we'll have separate beds tomorrow.

In my room I dump my things and get changed quickly from my jeans and T-shirt into a floaty summer dress, swapping the trainers I drove here in for a pair of heeled sandals, and freshen up my makeup quickly.

When I meet Harry back down in the lobby, he gives a cheeky whistle and says, "You don't scrub up too bad, do you?"

Not that the outfit change was for his benefit, but I blush.

"Shut it," I say, trying and failing at hiding my smile.

Maybe it's a *tiny* bit for his benefit.

So sue me. He's attractive. I'm only human.

I'm early to dinner but by my family's standards I'm still late. They're all standing around the bar in the hotel restaurant having drinks and chattering away when Harry and I join them at quarter past seven. There's Dad dressed up in a suit. Camilla's bought a second fascinator just for dinner tonight, but at least this one is small and unobtrusive, a dainty turquoise one nestled in her blond curls. Nadine's stomach is protruding more noticeably now; she's wearing a casual cotton maxi dress and sweating buckets, fanning herself with a drinks menu. Her husband, David, and Jess's fiancé, Conor, are dressed looking a bit like they've come from the office, each with a beer in hand, talking animatedly about something that makes Dad roll his eyes and disagree. Conor's parents are busy talking to Nadine; his younger brother is off to one side with AirPods in, attention fully on his phone.

Jessica is glowing.

I mean, she should be, but she really is. Her cheeks are flushed and there's a huge, beaming smile on her face, almost as bright as the diamond in her engagement ring.

And she notices us first, eyes skirting past her mum as they're talking and lighting on us. Her eyes go wide, and she bounces up on the balls of her feet, waving us over excitedly. "Sophie! Soph, you made it!"

I'm not even that late . . . I'm not even late, period!

As we reach my family, I give her a hug and tell her how great she looks. I say hi to Conor and then, not sure what else to say, tell them both, "Congrats again. This is so exciting! You guys must be so *excited*."

Maybe I could turn this into a drinking game. Take a shot every time I use the word *excited*.

"Why don't you introduce us to your friend, Soph?" Camilla says in a sly, teasing sort of voice.

"Oh, uh, yeah, um . . . "

All right, here we go.

"Everyone, this is Harry, my . . . boyfriend."

There are a couple of not-at-all-surreptitious looks exchanged, in which my family make it very clear they're sizing us up as a couple, but Harry gamely ignores them and just smiles broadly at everyone, saying hello, and then directly to Jessica and Conor, "You must be the bride and groom, then. Congrats, both. And thanks for letting me tag along. Brilliant venue."

He shakes Conor's hand. Jessica gives me a bit of a look, which I take to mean, *Damn! Look at him!*

I can't disagree.

I make a quick round of introductions. Conor's brother looks up just enough to give us a half-hearted wave and say, "Hey, Soph," when his mother snaps at him. To be fair to him, if I were a sixteen-year-old boy, this wouldn't exactly be my idea of a fun Friday night either.

Dad reaches over to shake Harry's hand. "I wish I could say we've heard a lot about you, but Sophie's been keeping you very secret."

"Oh dear." Harry laughs, and grins at me. "I hope that doesn't mean there's nothing good to say about me, Soph?"

"No, of course not. I just thought . . . you make such a good first impression, that's all."

"You know me," he says, and has the audacity to wink at me, which should also be a criminal offense, for the record. "I aim to please."

. . .

In hindsight, a fake boyfriend is not just a stretch too far, but absolutely fucking crazy and more than a bit ridiculous.

But by some miracle (or more likely, by sheer luck) we get away with it.

Harry goes down a storm. He's charming and funny and bull-shits his way smoothly through our supposed relationship when asked. He talks about politics with Conor's dad, some popular superhero show with Conor's brother (apparently he met the lead actress in it once at a function and supplies a funny story about how she stepped back, not seeing him, standing on his toes and spilling her champagne all over him). He talks to Nadine about her pregnancy and Jessica about the wedding, and asks Dad and Camilla for embarrassing stories about me.

He's a perfect date.

Shit. No, he's not. He's just—he's a perfect *fake* date.

And definitely not a real date, either way.

He makes up a couple of embarrassing stories about me too.

"You should've seen her at the pub quiz a bunch of us went to a while ago," he says. "Arguing with the guy running the night about the correct lyrics to a Harry Styles song. I thought she was going to start doing karaoke right there in front of everybody. We still lost the music round, though."

He says, "Do you know, our second date only happened because she used me as a parachute call? You know, like when you're on a date and it's not going well, and you need someone to phone and give you an excuse to leave? Do you want to tell them why, Soph, or shall I? It was because they went to this bar with old arcade games and the guy beat her at pinball. Well, I mean, it did sound like he was getting a bit obsessive about beating the high score, but you know Sophie. Total sore loser. Poor guy never stood a chance, did he? I guess I should've known then you wanted any excuse to see me again, eh, even if you were too proud to *actually* be the one to ask me out."

It's all I can do to not gawp at him as he shares these made-up stories about me. Not because I would never do these things (I absolutely did make Tally my parachute call once, and given enough drinks I might argue with a quizmaster over Harry Styles) but because he works them in to conversation so seamlessly.

I know he said he signed up for improv classes after his breakup for a bit of a laugh, but, bloody hell, he is *good*.

He makes it too easy to relax, to have fun. I forget all about my half-baked plan to act like things aren't going so great in our pretend relationship.

Now he slings an arm over the back of my chair with a cocksure smile when Camilla gushes about what a sweet couple we make, and playfully scolds me for keeping him secret from them all this time.

"It's not been that long," I mumble, trying not to squirm in my seat.

"Tell me about it," Harry says. "It feels like we met just yesterday."

I scoff and shrug at his arm, which is now around my shoulders rather than the back of my chair, but my cavalier reaction loses all effect when he gives me a crooked grin and another wink, and my face positively burns with the heat of a blush. *Damn him*. I try to write it off with a laugh as everyone else laughs, too, and I steal a bite of his dessert with my fork to feel like I've had the final word, even when I'm a little bit speechless.

Sixteen

Weddings, I think, are stressful enough, but being a bridesmaid is a thousand times worse. I go down to breakfast to meet Harry, wanting to thank him for being such a good sport last night and being a perfect fake date, but Nadine collars me on my way to his table, eyes bulging and lips in a tight line.

"What are you doing?"

For a horrible second, I think she knows. Somehow, I've been caught out.

"Getting breakfast?" I reply, as nonchalantly as I can.

"You haven't even been in the shower yet! The hairdresser is going to be here in fifteen minutes!"

Crap. *Show up with hair wet.* I forgot.

"It'll only take me two minutes," I say, shaving off a generous thirteen minutes at best. But, hey, that takes me up to a round fifteen, exactly when we're supposed to sit down with the hairdresser, and . . .

And leaves me no time for breakfast.

Nadine huffs at me and flaps a hand. "I don't have time to deal with this today, Sophie, I really don't. Mum and I have already had to deal with Nan dropping coffee all over her outfit at the service station, and Conor's got a hangover—"

"How? He had, like, one beer with dinner!"

She rolls her eyes. "Ask your boyfriend—he ended up with Conor and the groomsmen for more than a few pints last night in the hotel bar. Bloody hell. Just be upstairs in fifteen minutes and *take a shower*."

I don't argue and resist the urge to salute and stand to attention, but I do hurry over to Harry, whose hair is rumpled and who gives me a sleepy smile over his coffee and full English breakfast. It's not fair of me to cause any extra stress today, so I don't waste time asking him about drinks with Conor and the groomsmen last night; I barely manage a thank-you, leaving Harry with my room key so he can bring his things by after checking out from his room. I grab a couple of pains au chocolat, wrapping them clumsily in a napkin and all but running back to the elevators to go take a shower.

I totally *did* have time for breakfast as it turns out—I have to sit there in a hotel robe with my hair sopping wet for almost half an hour before one of the two hairdressers is free to do my hair for me, blow-drying and styling it into a pretty updo. Despite the indigestion I'm sure I gave myself, I'm glad I shoveled down the pastries beforehand, because there are some mimosas that Camilla organized for us—and no sign of lunch plans before the ceremony starts.

With the hairdressers, photographer and photographer's assistant, and Camilla, the room is a hive of activity and chatter. Jess's bridal party consists of me and Nadine, her best friend from university, Sunita, and her friend since primary school, Isobel, who couldn't make it to the hen party.

Jessica is a far cry from the relaxed, excited person she was last night. Now it's all systems go. She checks her phone every thirty seconds, as if expecting some apocalyptic disaster, and dealing with people asking just once more for the address or double-checking the time for the ceremony. Her cousins have been sent to fix her nan's wardrobe malfunction and she seems blessedly unaware of Conor's hangover (which I'm sure is nothing a good, greasy breakfast won't solve; Nadine's husband is in charge of sorting him out, though, saving us the trouble).

Nadine and Camilla have obviously been through the whole getting married thing themselves; they can fully empathize with everything Jessica is going through right now, whatever she's going through. Sunita is hoping her boyfriend will propose soon; Isobel is getting married in October.

All I can think as my stepsister cycles between a giddy excitement and stress so intense I think it might bring on a full panic attack, is that I'm glad it's not me.

For once, I'm so glad it's not me.

There's no jealousy today, not even a hint of wistfulness as I sit here single and alone and facing this romantic day that most people dream about. There's no pressure weighing on my chest, threatening to crush me because this feels like something I might never have, and no grating irritation at feeling so left out.

Instead there's just *relief*.

Normally I hate feeling like I'm on the outside of this happy, loved-up lifestyle but, at least for this morning, I embrace it gladly. I don't envy Jessica whatever she's going through right now, even if it's overall good. I don't wish this on myself. I don't have any desire at all to be on the other side, like they are, to understand this. Far from a glowing, loved-up bubble of perfection, it looks like terror and stress and fear and panic. It looks like a lifetime tied to one other person, and maybe losing myself a bit in the process. It looks—

I'm suddenly thrown back to Frankie's housewarming in February, and him telling me all that glitters isn't necessarily gold.

Nadine, furiously messaging her husband to check in on the groom. Jessica, hyperventilating as she declares with shrill pseudo-excitement that "her whole life is about to change!" Even Sunita, worrying if her boyfriend will ever "truly commit," doesn't seem very gold, or even very glittery.

Things are pretty good from where I'm standing, thank you very much.

We get into our outfits: Sunita, Isobel, Nadine, and me in pale-purple bridesmaid dresses—which Jessica *now* thinks wasn't quite the right color choice (it takes all my willpower to hold my tongue, because I wanted to tell her as much so many times); Camilla in a lavender two-piece and her (quite large) fascinator; and Jessica in her wedding gown, with its wide skirt and off-the-shoulder straps that are more for decoration than any kind of support. Getting Jessica ready is a whole thing because the photographer is supposed to capture the moments, and we have to stop and help her out of it and then do it all again because she realizes with a hysterical, sort of manic laugh that she forgot to do a wee first.

We have to go downstairs in groups. Jessica needs two people in the elevator to help with her dress and the veil, making sure nothing gets stuck in the door or creased too badly; the photographer has tons of equipment; and Nadine is quite pregnant. Figuring out how we all get downstairs in the "so small they're cute but really just horribly impractical" elevators is like that riddle about getting the fox, the chicken, and the grain across the river.

But eventually everyone is downstairs, and we make our way around to the back of the hotel. The room where the ceremony will be looks out onto the gardens, so we can (and by *can*, I mean *are obligated to*) take a bunch of photos on the stone steps at the rear of the hotel before actually going in.

I'm starting to see why Jessica has been taking all the planning so seriously. This is a military operation.

It's only on the trek there that I wince, my shoes rubbing, and realize that I never got around to wearing them in, and the Band-Aids I threw in my suitcase are still in my suitcase, and no good to me now. If I'm lucky, I'll be able to grab them before dinner, at least.

Dad's waiting for us, and I watch the emotions play out over his face: the way his face crumples and his eyes fill when he sees Jessica in her wedding dress, and then the hasty stoic look as he tries so hard not to cry, and then the big smile he just can't hide.

It's sweet to see, though. Jessica and Nadine's dad is around here, somewhere, but he's not really been "in the picture" or "on the scene," or however else you want to say it, for about the last fifteen years. They speak to him a bit more now they're grown up, and he's invited today, just as he was for Nadine's wedding, but it's my dad Jessica asked to walk her down the aisle. I'm so used to thinking of him as *our* dad that I guess I never really notice it, because he's just our dad, but it's nice, now, recognizing what this moment must mean to both of them.

Dad gives her a big hug and she laughs, saying something about not making her cry again.

He looks so proud of her.

I can't quite figure out why, because I genuinely believe it's a lovely moment, but something about it feels bruising.

I don't even get a chance to say hello to him before the photographer is corralling us with a speed and a finesse that equal parts impresses and terrifies me.

Posing for photos, I let my mind drift.

I should probably be thinking about Jessica and what a wonderful day this will be for her and how lucky we are that it's such beautiful weather without being too hot, but instead I wonder how Harry's getting on. Is the whole boyfriend ruse still going strong, or has it worn thin? Maybe he's having regrets about the whole thing. I hope he isn't too bored, sitting around waiting for a wedding where he knows absolutely nobody—not even me, his date. Maybe he's texting his friends to complain about what an idiot he is for getting suckered into my reckless plan and telling them how much he regrets it. Maybe he's even setting up a parachute call.

I hope he isn't.

I know he's not here as my *actual* date, but it's been fun hanging out with him. Regardless of *why* I needed a fake boyfriend for today, I'd be genuinely disappointed if he did leave.

It's warm standing out in the sun and my cheeks begin to ache after long enough smiling for the camera. I think about how I don't know how Jess will manage today, but she can't seem to stop beaming now. She keeps glancing toward the door where she'll make her grand entrance, where her guests and the love of her life are all waiting, moving agitatedly like she can't wait to be in there.

Neither can I, but that's only because I hope there's air-conditioning.

And my shoes are really starting to hurt.

Camilla goes inside before the rest of us and suddenly the groomsmen have come out; they all hug Jessica and tell her how beautiful she looks, how happy they are for her, but then some staff member is urging us inside and I realize the music has started playing. It's a sweet, pretty, piano version of an Olly Murs song, since Jessica and Conor had their first date at one of his concerts.

The whole thing becomes one weird out-of-body experience. I don't really know how I get from posing on the steps arranging Jessica's veil with the other bridesmaids as instructed by the photographer to walking down the aisle with Conor's brother, but I'm suddenly aware of all the faces staring at me. Some of them I know. Lots I don't. And I know they're not looking at *me*, because I don't matter today. I'm an accessory. But they're staring and I'm sweating and I'm sure the skin on the back of my right ankle is already raw and red, and . . .

And I'm at the altar, and nobody is looking at me.

Conor throws me a fleeting smile before his eyes dart to the door again, neck twisting so he can look over his shoulder. His hands are clasped in front of him but his fingers fidget and the muscles in his face twitch, like he doesn't know whether to be calm or smile or cry. I've never seen him looking like this—wearing anything other than his usual slightly bored expression—and get the sudden urge to squeeze his shoulder and tell him it'll be okay.

In the front row I spy Camilla, already tearing up. She fumbles through her bag for tissues she apparently forgot to bring. Nadine's husband is sitting near, and after him is Harry, with seats left empty in the row for Dad, me, and Nadine. I try to catch Harry's eye but he's too busy getting up, bent over so as not to attract attention, and he shuffles over to Camilla, offering her a handkerchief.

He catches my eye on his way back to his seat and gives me a little wave and mouths "Hi." I wave my bouquet back at him.

Shit, but he looks good. I was right: he's the kind of guy that once you put him in a suit, he just looks absolutely irresistible. I don't think I've ever wanted to describe a man as delicious before, but . . . yeah. Harry looks pretty delicious. His suit must be tailored, I think. It seems to accentuate his long legs and his toned arms.

The navy fabric really pops against his tan and his gray eyes look silver in the sunlight. I thought he looked good with a bit of stubble yesterday, but now he's clean-shaven and somehow that looks just as good on him.

The whole effect is devastatingly handsome.

The music swells.

The other bridesmaids have taken their places next to me; the groomsmen are lined up on the other side with Conor.

I sort of want to see his reaction, so rarely seeing this weird, vulnerable side of him, but I forget all about it when Jessica catches my attention. It's ridiculous, really, because I've seen her in the dress a hundred times. I was there when she picked it out in the shop. I've just spent an hour with her helping her dress and take photos.

But there's something about the light spilling in from the high windows and the doorway behind her, the way she's gripping Dad's arm so tightly, the way she looks a bit like she wants to hike up her skirt to run at Conor because this walk is already taking too long. She looks beautiful. She looks so happy.

And there it is, at last.

That flare of jealousy.

Why doesn't that get to be me?

• • •

"You," I declare, "are a saint."

Harry laughs as I take the Band-Aids from him. "Not sure my ex-wife would agree with you there."

"Eh." I grab his shoulder, using him for purchase as I wrench my poor, mangled foot from my shoe in the middle of the gardens to start putting them on. My left foot has, somehow, got away pretty unscathed, but my right is another matter entirely. I can't believe I forgot to wear in the shoes. I've only had them sitting in a shoebox in my wardrobe for months.

Harry helps me keep my balance and when I'm done, easing my foot tentatively back into the offending shoe while he holds a handful of my discarded wrappers, he says, "You know, this isn't how I think the story was supposed to go."

"What story's that?"

"The one with the handsome prince, the pretty girl at the ball who loses her shoe . . . "

"Hilarious," I tell him, although it does make me laugh.

Right now it's drinks and canapés in the garden before we go into dinner. I can't escape because every so often I'm summoned for photographs, but this also turns out to be a blessing because it means my conversations with extended family keep getting cut short. They can barely get out a "So when's it going to be your turn?" before I'm having to excuse myself.

It *does* make me glad I came up with the whole fake-boyfriend charade. (Or, you know, got sort of press-ganged into it.) I don't miss a few aunts and cousins, seeing Harry and looking quite impressed, saying, "Oh, Sophie, is this your boyfriend, then?" And there's a part of me that really relishes saying, "Yes, yes, he is," and wiping that sad and sorry look off their faces.

"Shall we go get some more drinks?" Harry suggests, nodding in the direction of the crowd of guests in their bright outfits and sharp suits, but I shake my head.

"There's only so much I can handle. I need to pace myself if I want to make it through the whole day."

"You lightweight," he jokes, and I laugh, even though I was talking about the mingling, not the drinks. We chat for a while about the guests—people-watching and joking remarks, for the most part, and Harry pitching in with some of his favorite stories from his friends' weddings over the years, and I'm relieved for the break from having to be "on" and play the role of bridesmaid for a little while.

Plus, my foot is wrecked from these damn shoes, so the break from hobbling around is pretty welcome too.

Camilla, Nadine, and David come over at some point to chat and after they filter away just as we're ushered back inside for dinner, Harry tells me, "It's nice you're all so close, still."

"Yeah. I mean, Dad and Camilla ended things on pretty good terms, but they were so involved with us kids by that time it would've been hard to cut ties completely anyway. And it's nice, you know? Having siblings. I didn't have that when I was little."

"Well," he says with a wry smile that, for once, doesn't reach his eyes. "Just don't sleep with their husbands if you want things to stay 'nice.'"

"Duly noted." My mouth is suddenly dry, and I hesitate, not sure whether to ask him more about his brother and the whole mess with his ex-wife. I know we've been getting on well, but we've only known each other a couple of days, and it's really not my place. So instead, I just babble on about how great Camilla and my mum get on, how I still send Camilla a Mother's Day card, and that it's sweet my dad got to walk Jessica down the aisle.

But as I say that I remember all too vividly Dad's reaction just before the ceremony, and something settles like lead in the pit of my stomach.

I trail off, and Harry gives me a funny look. "What? What's that face for?"

"It's just," I whisper, conscious I don't want to be overheard even with all the joyful hubbub around the room, "he looked really proud of Jessica. And I'm not saying he shouldn't be, you know, but—"

"But he shouldn't be?"

"She fell in love! That's luck of the draw! She met a decent guy she's compatible with and you'd think she just won Star Baker and got a handshake during Bread Week on *Bake Off* or something. She didn't have to do anything."

I hate how much of a bitch that makes me sound, but it feels so fucking good to say it out loud.

Harry, for his part, only laughs and reaches into the middle of the table to pour us each a glass of wine. "Yes," he says to me. "You're such a disappointment for not putting up with guys you don't like or have no connection with just because you don't want to be single anymore. Joke's on you for having some self-respect, Soph. And now look at you—your date is a thirtysomething cheating divorcé pretending to be your boyfriend just so he can brag about it on his Instagram later."

He hands me my glass of wine, one eyebrow slightly raised and a smirk on his lips. His long fingers brush against mine as I take the glass and my stomach flip-flops. My knee grazes his leg beneath the table and I find myself biting my lip just a little as we maintain eye contact.

"Yeah," I say. "Sucks to be me."

Seventeen

I'll be the first to say it: inviting Harry to be my pretend boyfriend I'll pretend break up with shortly after the wedding was a terrible idea.

If only because I'm hideously, hopelessly attracted to him.

And, I'm guessing, the feeling is mutual. It's not like I've been keeping a diary of all the little moments between us throughout the day, but I *do* find myself replaying some of them after dinner winds down and we have a couple of hours to mingle again before the reception kicks off this evening. The way we were both in helpless fits of giggles over some silly joke waiting for the main course and leaned against each other as we gasped for breath and tried to get a grip. The compliments he so casually gave about me when talking to the rest of our table. The way my leg pushed into his when I turned in my chair to get a better view of the speeches and instead of scooting away or pushing me back, he put his hand on my leg instead.

Not that I'm thinking about it.

But I'm definitely thinking about it.

My fake boyfriend is everything I needed him to be. He's handsome and funny and charming and polite and a good conversationalist and interesting to talk to and honestly, how dare he? It's grossly unfair.

It's a good job he's like, almost ten years older than me and not the kind of guy I'd usually go for, or I'd be seriously thinking about asking him on a real date after all this.

I mean, for one, his work schedule is superbusy. He works long hours; he travels a lot; and recently, with how much I miss my friends, I'm starting to think I might be quite needy when it comes to relationships. Plus, you know, he's *technically still married*, so I'm not sure he's exactly looking to jump into another relationship right now. Or if he even likes me—*could* like me—that way.

Which he probably doesn't. Because he's playing a part. And we won't see each other after this weekend anyway. And besides, given my dating history, it's not bloody likely, is it?

I spot a few of the girls from the hen do who weren't in the bridal party nearby and excuse myself from Harry to go say hello to them. I didn't exactly make any new besties that weekend, but it'll be nice to have a chat with them—plus, I figure, it's only the polite thing to do.

The day has felt like one huge blur of "Oh, hi! Hello, how are you! How are things? Gosh, yes, no, I'm doing great, thanks" and then when you add going through all the rigmarole of the cere-mony and the dinner and the cake-cutting . . . I don't know how I've managed to talk to so many people and yet hardly to anyone I really care about talking to. Isobel and her girlfriend were at our table for dinner, and so were my cousin Lilly, her parents and her brothers, and some great-aunt I don't really know, but even so. I've barely spoken to Jessica since this morning, and only had a chance to speak to the rest of my family when we were all in photos together. I can only imagine how much of a whirlwind the day has been for Jessica.

I said as much to Harry at one point, adding, "I know I moan about being single and how much I want all this, but . . . I'm starting to think maybe I *don't*. At least, not the big white wedding part."

"Don't," he deadpans in return. "If I wanted to waste fifteen grand on a single day, I'd rather do it in Vegas."

Now Ola and Lydia from Jessica's uni days are talking to Lilly and the work friends from the hen do, Georgina and Siobhan; they're clustered together with drinks and phones and clutch bags in hand, all chattering and giggling about something.

"Hiya."

"Sophie!" they say, and we all take turns hugging—because it's a wedding, of course we do. "Oh my god, isn't it such a lovely day? Jessie got so lucky with the weather, didn't she? She looks absolutely *gorgeous*. You all look so lovely in your bridesmaid dresses; that purple is such a . . . lovely color, very . . . interesting choice, isn't it? But such a flattering style for you all!"

We churn through all the pleasantries about the day, and I let myself get swept up in the excitement. Even if I am feeling a few fleeting moments of jealousy or annoyance, it really is a good day and I am having a good time. The girls' enthusiasm is infectious, though, and it's easy to let myself fall into it as though they're my own close friends as we dissect everything from the way Conor looked at Jessica when they exchanged rings to the slightly disappointing parsnips at dinner and the cringey-but-hilarious anecdotes the best man shared in his speech.

So much for being a bitter old hag of a spinster.

"And who's your friend?" Ola asks me then, making a great show of leering over my shoulder to ogle in what I can only assume is Harry's direction; he's talking to a petite, pretty brunet woman I don't know. "Is this the mystery boyfriend you were so tight-lipped about at the hen party?"

Okay, Sophie, now's the perfect opportunity to lay some ground-work for the fake breakup later down the line.

"Harry. He's, um, we're . . . I mean, yes, we're together, but, um . . . it's still early days, you know? Really, he's doing me a favor by coming along."

"He can do me a favor anytime," Lydia mumbles into her drink, sending a peal of laughter through the group.

"You guys aren't serious, then?" Ola asks me.

"Well, um, we're . . . I mean, he's here with me, so . . . Wait, I thought you had a boyfriend? Wasn't he supposed to be coming with you today?"

Before I can look around for him, Ola's face hardens and she rolls her eyes in a way that I think is supposed to look effortless, but I can tell it's taking her a *lot* of effort to appear composed right now. She clicks her tongue and sighs, and eventually says, "We had to call it a day. It just got . . . well. We were fighting about the most ridiculous stuff all the time, and you know how it is."

The others nod, sympathetic. This is my chance to claim I do know, that things with Harry and me are a bit tense at the minute too. But for some reason I can't bring myself to now that I'm suddenly confronted with what that might mean.

Ola gives me a piercing look and says again, "You guys aren't serious, though, right?"

Georgina gives a scandalized cry, shoving at her friend with a loud laugh. "Ola! Babe, I know you're on the rebound, but you can't just steal someone else's boyfriend like that! You've been reading too much of that column."

"Column?" I repeat, hoping they don't notice how strangled my voice sounds.

"You know, *Single, Swipe, Repeat.* Everyone's talking about it.

It's all over social media." Georgina whips out her phone and a few taps later, holds it up so I can see my article about dating apps and LinkedIn. I force a smile and a nod, giving a noncommittal noise as if to say *Yes, I've seen it too.*

"She's *so* brilliant. God, I'd love to be her." Ola sighs wistfully, bitterly. A scowl slips onto her face and she takes a very, very long sip of her lemonade. I'm willing to bet there's a shot (or two) of gin in there. Most of the others all nod in agreement, even though they're all in relationships—even Lilly, who bounced back quick after her brutal dumping.

Siobhan looks at me and raises one eyebrow, mouth twisted up to one side. Her lipstick is deep mauve, and her hair today is pink. "Who wouldn't want to be her, right, Sophie?"

And in that instant, I realize—

She knows.

Siobhan knows.

Fuck.

The others disperse over the next few minutes. Siobhan and I end up sitting on a wall talking about some blog, and it's only when I lose my train of thought midconversation for the fourth time that she calls me out on it.

"Right, you," she says, in an almost mumsy tone. "Shall we stop beating around the bush? This is about the column, isn't it?"

"The column."

My column.

All I can do is look at her plaintively and whisper, "Please don't tell anyone. Oh my god, please don't tell anyone."

She gives me such a wide, warm smile that my panic disappears in an instant. I hardly know her, but something about her makes me trust her with this secret. I breathe a sigh of relief.

"You gave yourself away a little bit after calling a hen party a 'wake at the funeral of your single life.' You said it to me at Jessica's and then used it for your article. She and Georgina were reading it in the staff room in fits of giggles, and I just couldn't *believe* she had no idea you were the one behind it. I did like your little fantasy about the mixologist, though. That was a fun read."

I blush. "It wasn't a fantasy. Just . . . my editor says people are responding to that stuff, so I should write about it. Like in my March article, I said I went back to that guy's hotel room in the middle of a friend's wedding, and he slid into my LinkedIn DMs later that night. In reality, it was an engagement party, and some arsehole suggested a quickie in the toilets, and I told him where to go. Although the LinkedIn bit was sort of true—he added me on there later that night."

"Ah. A little embellishment of the truth. I see."

"Only for stuff like that, though. Which is part of why *nobody* can find out! I mean, imagine if Jessica was reading that stuff about being fingered in a stock room and she thought it was me? I think I'd die."

Siobhan laughs again. "So what about your new beau? You two look quite loved up."

"Uh . . . "

I remember why I like Siobhan so much: she has such self-confidence and self-assurance and it's comforting to be around, especially when coupled with what I'm sure is a relentless optimism.

Maybe that's why I blurt out the whole mortifying truth.

Or maybe it's just because I am way out of my depth here and she seems like the kind of person who could tell me firmly what the ever-loving fuck to do *and* keep my secrets at the same time, but either way, I spill it all. That I was too embarrassed to show up alone, that I didn't want to look like I'd let Jessica down by having an empty chair next to me at the wedding, how I liked it when they thought I *did* have a boyfriend, how the guy I'm *actually* sort of dating is sort of ghosting me since I asked him to be my plus-one and how it was arguably *worse* to bring a complete stranger to the wedding with me at the very last minute, and, *worse* again, that I think I actually sort of like him, that the chemistry is—at least in my opinion—undeniable.

As I talk, I steal a few glances Harry's way. It doesn't escape my notice that the pretty brunet has been replaced by Ola, who is shamelessly flirting with him. Something unpleasant lurches in my stomach when she says something and he laughs, and she lays a hand on his bicep while tossing her hair.

Siobhan distracts me from it by laughing so hard she gives herself a stitch and sits clutching her side, wheezing, tears at the corners of her eyes.

"It's not funny," I insist in a hiss.

"Mate, it's not just funny, it's *hysterical*. I mean, honestly. When was the last time you heard about somebody pulling a stunt like this? You're off your rocker. I bloody love it. No need to embellish the truth for your column there! If anything, you'll have to *unem*-bellish. Nobody would ever believe this."

"You *cannot* tell anyone about this. Especially Jessica."

She mimes zipping her lips shut. "You're going to tell them, though."

"Actually . . . actually, I thought we would just 'break up.' Make up something about us not really working out or being too differ-ent. And we are quite different, to be fair. They never have to know."

"Oh, Sophie," she sighs.

But before she can tell me what a bad idea it is (like I don't already know) or give me any kind of advice or maybe even a pep talk, Siobhan's attention is caught by someone behind me. Mischief steals over her face instantly. Her tongue pokes out over her teeth as she breaks into a grin and calls, "Harry! How funny, we were just talking about you!"

Kill me now.

Possessed by the fruitless notion that I might somehow be able to make a run for it before he notices me, I make to stand up, only to have Siobhan grab my elbow and yank me back down. Her arm loops through mine to keep me in place. I'm sure the mortification is burning all over my face and I'm sure Harry can see it, that he knows exactly what we were talking about somehow and . . .

"All right, ladies?" he says, flashing us both a smile. "I was starting to think you'd been avoiding me, Soph. Everyone's just starting to make their way back inside for the reception."

"You seemed a bit preoccupied mingling," I reply. It sounds a bit curt—the kind of thing Frankie Two might say—and I regret it instantly. Quickly, I add, "This is my sister's friend from work, Siobhan."

"We've only met the once before this," Siobhan tells him, cocking her head to one side with a mischievous grin. "How about you, *Harry*? You must know Sophie very well. I bet you know her favorite color, her birthday, her obsession with true crime documentaries about men who catfish not just a woman but her *entire family*, pretending to be something they're not . . . "

He starts to laugh but catches himself, smile frozen in place as his eyes flit between the two of us. "Uh . . . "

I meet his eye. "I do actually really love true crime documentaries."

"Your secret's safe with me, darling, don't worry." Siobhan gestures for him to sit down, which he does, on my other side. Close. Not close like he's sitting *right* next to me, but close enough that his elbow and knee shift lightly against mine as he leans forward to see Siobhan better.

He reaches a hand across to shake. "Good to meet you, Siobhan. I'm Harry, stand-in boyfriend and stand-up guy who is hopefully not the subject of a future true crime documentary."

"Lovely to meet you too. So, what did you think of the lovely Ola? She was bending your ear for long enough."

He pulls a face at the two of us, so melodramatically bamboozled I have to laugh.

"Yeah, I mean, she's lovely and all, but it's *really* weird to have someone try to flirt with you when you just *know* they think you're someone else. Like, I said I moved recently, and she asked about my old place and what am I meant to say? That I agreed my wife could keep it while we sort out the divorce? I felt awful. I don't know how catfishes do it—it's horrible. Besides, she's a bit young for me. I'm sure I should be flattered but I just feel *old*."

Siobhan laughs. "I'll say. Just can't keep up with these young whippersnappers, what with their mad fake-wedding-date shenanigans . . . "

I roll my eyes at her but say to Harry, "She's only a bit younger than me."

"So?"

"*So*, you had your Hookd filters set to pick up girls in their twenties."

He blinks at me, my words sinking in.

"Well, now I feel like an absolute creep. Thanks, Soph."

"*Now* you feel like a creep?" Siobhan echoes, laughing. "Not when you were pretending to be someone else at a wedding where you don't know anyone?"

Harry doesn't respond to her, but shrugs with an awkward, embarrassed smile. Undeniably bashful now, his cheeks turn a faint shade of pink and it makes me grin; I don't think I've ever seen such a confident kind of guy *blush*. Instead of answering Siobhan, he just stands up and offers us each a hand off the wall. "Shall we go inside for the reception, then?"

We do, joining the groups filtering inside. There's a nagging feeling in the back of my mind like there's some bridesmaid's duty I should currently be fulfilling, but running through my mental list of today's schedule, I come up blank.

I'm sure someone will come fetch me if I'm wrong.

The three of us order drinks from the bar (soft drinks; we're all pacing ourselves before the party and parched from spending so long out in the summer sunshine) and mill around the room like most everyone else is doing.

Before long, the DJ has started and the group shifts, forming a circle near the dance floor: it's time for the first dance.

I haven't seen Jessica or Conor for maybe a couple of hours now, but they're clearly enjoying this whole thing. It looks like Jessica has touched up her makeup—the mascara smudged by sweat I noticed earlier has gone—and Conor's suit looks a good deal less crisp than it was first thing this morning, but they're still the most beautiful couple in the world right now. They're grinning from ear to ear, tearing their eyes away from each other every few seconds to look around at their guests. I think they've been holding hands for hours now.

It's probably a sickening display, but the bitter old hag of a spinster in me is nowhere to be found right now—all I can think about is how happy I am for them, how wonderful all of this is and how much I love them. Even Conor and his resting bored face.

They sway tenderly back and forth for their first dance, another Olly Murs song, of course, oblivious to the rest of us. It's so blindingly obvious that despite the dozens and dozens of people they've invited to share this day, this moment, with them, none of us exist for them right now. It's just the two of them, and Olly Murs.

We all watch and coo and take photos on our phones and applaud when the song ends, and then another starts, and they dance again with that same gentle sway that's not really dancing but as good as. Dad asks Camilla to dance; Nadine and her husband David are up for a bit of a dance along with some of the other bridesmaids and groomsmen.

I don't really think much of it until I feel Harry shifting beside me.

He stands in front of me, offering his hand.

His smile is small, almost daring me.

"Well?" is all he says, and I take his hand.

He whisks me onto the dance floor, into the circle formed around the bride and groom, his hand staying clasped lightly in mine while his other settles on my waist and he brings me in close. My free hand rests on his shoulder, and, after a moment, so does my head.

And for just a little while, I let myself enjoy it: the feeling of being held by someone like this, of sharing this moment, this intimacy and tenderness, the sway of the music carrying us side to side and my heart giving an erratic pitter-patter at the feel of his hand on my waist.

It's nothing, really. It's not even real. I know that. But it's nice.

That slow dance isn't my only one with Harry. We throw ourselves into the party as the evening draws in and dusk falls. The drinks are flowing and we're no exception, doing a round of shots with the groomsmen and another with Dad and Conor and some of his family later. Harry and I stick together through the night, alternating between getting up on the dance floor and mingling or taking a little break at a table for a few minutes with another drink; we hardly stop talking the whole time. We've both let our guard down; not because of the alcohol but just because this is such low stakes—there's no bar to try and meet, there's no good impression to be made. We can just be honest and ourselves—and it's *fun*.

At some point in the evening, it's grown dark outside and the music has become a scooch louder and Camilla's definitely had a brandy or two (I was supposed to be on the lookout and stop this happening, but it's too late now; her voice has risen a full octave and she's sharing baby stories about Jessica, her cheeks ruddy underneath her makeup and her fascinator askew). The party is in full swing.

Before long, the music slows down again.

Couples filter out to dance. Conor's dad goes up with some niece who can't be more than about seven years old; she stands on his feet. Harry and I are already up, having been half dancing and half chatting (or half flirting . . . just a little bit) and now, without the need for either of us to say anything, we rearrange ourselves to sway along with everyone else. My arms hook around his shoulders and his hands rest on either side of my waist. Like this, he's tall enough that I need to crane my neck to look up at his face, and when I do, he gives me a little half smile, mouth quirking up on one side, his eyes dark, and butterflies erupt in my stomach.

His breath ghosts over my face, tickling along my neck, and my own hitches in my throat. I'm acutely aware of every place our bodies are touching—his touch searing my waist and lower back through the fabric of my dress, the tickle of his hair at the nape of his neck where my hands are resting, the way my chest brushes against his as we rock side to side and how one of his legs has slotted just ever so slightly between mine, so they knock together each time we move.

I'm also acutely aware of every place our bodies are not touching, and how badly I want them to be.

How badly I want to kiss him.

Somehow, I've leaned in closer, arching that little bit farther into Harry's embrace, and one of his hands has slipped low on the small of my back. I can hear his breathing turn shallow, but only barely, over the sound of my own pulse thrumming in my ears. I pull my gaze up to his, but it seems to take an age; my eyes move from looking somewhere over his shoulder at the rest of the dancers to the open collar of his shirt where his tie is now hanging loose around his neck, up to his jaw where a hint of stubble is showing, his lips, up to his eyes, which have turned from liquid silver in the sunlight to a stormy dark gray that pierces right through me like a bolt of lightning. It's a look that makes every inch of my skin tingle, like my body is made of live wires, and I let myself get lost in it, in the way it makes me feel and the way I want him and the way the air seems thick and charged around us now, and—

The music changes and we're yanked apart. The girls from the hen do have a hold of me, all shrieking and squealing about how "it's our song!"—some Queen one we all ended up singing at some point on the night out, and I'm swept up in the crowd, Harry disappearing in a blur of brilliance and bridesmaids.

• • •

It's only a little while later as I'm on my way back from the bathroom that I see him again.

I'm guessing he was just on his way to the bathroom when he sees me, but we meet halfway in the hallway, our steps slowing as we get nearer, and even though we never actually kissed and even though neither of us has even said anything, it feels like the hallway suddenly floods with tension again. It hangs heavy around us and there's something about the look on his face that makes me sure he feels it too—whatever it is.

"Hey, sorry—"

"So, uh—"

We both start talking at the same time, and both stop at the same time too. I give an awkward laugh and he shrugs one shoulder as if to say *you first*, but neither of us bothers trying to say another word.

Because the next thing I know, his lips are on mine and my back is against the wall and my hands are grabbing his jacket to pull him closer and I was absolutely right: he is delicious.

It's the kind of kiss that leaves me breathless, that makes the rest of the world cease to exist, the kind that makes my foot pop in a *Princess Diaries* moment (or it would, if I wasn't right up against a wall). It's hungry and relentless and it makes me dizzy, but I don't want it to ever end.

But I do end it, because I'm all too conscious of the fact this is a very public place. And I would like very much to rip his clothes off right now.

Harry pulls back, looking dazed and breathing hard, and then he gives a quiet, dry chuckle and runs a hand through his hair. Between the heat, the long day, the booze and the dancing, it's not the carefully coiffed look it was this morning.

I'm dying to run my fingers through it.

I place my hands over my mouth instead, which is still tingling with the imprint of his kisses, to restrain myself.

Harry gives me an uncertain, crooked sort of grin. He's blushing again.

"That was a really bad idea, wasn't it? Ah, shit. Sophie, I'm really sorry, I didn't—"

"No! No, that's not . . . it wasn't . . . I mean—" I glance back toward the room where the wedding reception is. I can see the pink and green and blue and white lights flashing, spilling into the rest of the hotel where someone's left the door ajar, and the music pulses out, carrying the sound of chatter and laughter with it.

"I should—I should probably get back, is all, before I'm missed."

"Right. Yes. Yeah."

"But I'm sure nobody will mind if I duck out and call it a night in about half an hour or something."

The hesitation on Harry's face disappears, and I realize he thought I pushed him away because I thought this was a mistake, not because I want it to go further. But judging by the smile that lights up his eyes and the way he looks at my lips again, he's pretty happy for it to go further too.

The next half hour is the longest of my life.

The couple of hours after that might be some of the best.

• • •

Somewhere around three a.m. I flop breathlessly, bonelessly, onto the bed beside Harry, one arm flung over my head and the other resting on my stomach as he gets up to go and get rid of the condom. He comes back, hair sticking out at all angles, and slips back into the tangle of sheets with me. He kisses his way up from my hips to my collarbone before lying beside me, wrapping me in his arms.

"I was just thinking—" he says, and I stop him with a laugh.

"Oh no, this isn't the part where you declare your undying love for me, is it?"

"Next best thing. You know how we said this was going to be a one-off?"

"This *is* a one-off. I mean—I mean *this* was . . ." I wriggle away slightly, propping myself up on one elbow. "I'm just . . . sort of, maybe seeing someone at the moment. A little bit. Remember, that guy I told you wouldn't come with me? Jaxon."

I've never been the kind of girl to be interested in more than one guy at a time. When I meet guys on Hookd, there's no overlap in dates. If one doesn't work out, then I move on to the next one.

One bound-to-fail, never-quite-a-relationship at a time is all I have the energy for.

It feels weird, to say Jaxon's name when I'm in bed with Harry.

Harry, meanwhile, rolls his eyes. "The *Goodnight, beautiful* guy, who's half ghosting you?"

"I'm more interested in dating him than *you*," I bite back, with no idea why I'm suddenly defensive of him, or so nasty to Harry. I wince, but Harry gives a good-natured scoff and tucks me back into his side.

"I'm not talking about dating, you muppet. Freshly single out of a terrible marriage, remember?"

"Well," I interrupt, "you *are* on Hookd."

He gives me a deadpan look, like it's so obvious. I guess maybe it is. "Yeah, because I don't know how to be single. Alone. *By myself*, you know? It's been like a month since I officially moved out, and I'm already sick to death of my own company and desperate for a rebound."

I nod, understanding—mostly. "And someone to make you look good on Instagram."

"That's exactly what I'm talking about. Maybe we could carry on a little. Use this to our mutual advantage. I can be your fake boyfriend to get your family off your back and you can be my fake girlfriend as far as *my* friends and family are concerned. Really drive home the midlife crisis for them."

He says it with a self-deprecating laugh, but I glance at his face before he can hide the weary, sad look on his face. One that I know all too well. I hug him a little tighter, pressing a kiss to his shoulder before looking back up at him.

"Okay. Yeah. Yeah! Why not? And if things get serious with Jaxon, we call it off."

Harry's eyes light up, glittering through the darkness. A slow smile tugs at the corners of his mouth, making me want to kiss him again.

"Really?"

"Really. And no tagging each other in stuff on Instagram, or else they'll find out we haven't actually been dating since March."

"Obviously."

We don't shake on it, but lie quietly together. Harry kisses the side of my head and my hand splays over his chest, feeling the rise and fall of it become slower, steadier, as my own eyelids become heavier. Harry reaches down to pull the covers up over us.

Just before I can doze off, I murmur his name.

"Yeah?"

"You're a pretty great fake boyfriend. I just want you to know that."

"You're not too bad yourself, as pretend girlfriends go," he mumbles back with a sleepy chuckle that gets swallowed in a yawn.

Yeah, I think, something uneasy and unending coiling in the pit of my stomach and spreading through me. If only someone would give me the chance to be a *real* girlfriend.

July

Oh, Baby!

Join us to celebrate Baby Rigby!

An afternoon of tea and tipples, cakes and party games

92 Church Lane, Kenilworth
Saturday, July 17
1–4 p.m.

Gifts are welcome but not expected!

Registry at http://ba.by/rigbyoctober

See you there!
Dawn & Janice Rigby

Eighteen

Stop making people justify their singledom.

Views on the pressure to partner up from our
Dating & Relationships columnist

"So what's the latest with that boy you're seeing? Not going too well?"

"What? No. Why would you say that?"

I'm immediately on the defensive, my hands clutching tighter around my phone.

Harry, his clothes drenched in leaking toilet water, tosses me an insufferably superior look that *should* be undermined by the plunger in his hands and the fact he's kneeling on my bathroom floor, but somehow that only accentuates it.

"Because you've been writing and rewriting a reply to that text you just got for the last ten minutes. I can hear the keyboard clacking, which, by the way, I bet if I had the sound on my phone like that, you'd tell me it was giving you the ick. So I'm guessing things aren't going so great if you have to agonize that much over a text message. Unless—oh-ho, *Sophie*," he gloats, laughing. "Don't tell me you're breaking up with the poor sap over text?"

"Of course I'm not! And it's not Jaxon, anyway. *And* his name is Jaxon, which you full well know, not 'that boy.' 'That boy' makes you sound like an old man. Watch yourself down there, you might pop a hip out."

Harry raises one eyebrow at me, mouth pulling into a crooked, good-natured smile as he gestures toward the toilet and jokes, "And to think, this *old man* is here doing you a favor out of the goodness of his heart. Not even expecting a blow job in exchange."

"Now you sound gross *and* creepy. Just shut up and fix this, will you?"

I don't mean to sound so snippy, and immediately feel bad, shrinking into the edge of the doorway, phone pulled close to my chest. My irritable mood curdles, thickening, clouding the air around me like something tangible and poisonous, and I hate it.

I look at Harry on the sodden floor of my bathroom, fixing my broken toilet for me at nine o'clock on a Friday night, having bailed on a night out with his friends to be *here*, helping me, because I called him in a panic not knowing how to deal with this. (Are plumbers even around at this time of night? How do I find a good one versus an overpriced one? What if it's something supersimple I should be able to fix myself and a plumber would laugh in my face about?)

I think about my desperate phone call to Harry, me on the verge of tears and him yelling down the phone, struggling to hear me in a busy bar while his mates jeered playfully at him in the background, and the fact that he's here at all.

It's a massive fucking favor—I know that.

The words are thick and heavy on my tongue but somehow, I manage to say them anyway: "I'm sorry. I didn't mean that."

"It's okay."

BETH REEKLES

"No, it's not. You're a lifesaver, and I'm a heinous bitch." And for some godforsaken reason, my eyes well up and I sniffle—and the last thing I want is to look like I'm throwing myself a pity party when I'm genuinely trying to apologize.

"You're definitely not a heinous bitch," Harry tells me, digging the plunger into the toilet firmly. The muscles on his arms flex, and my eyes are drawn to the way his long fingers curl around the handle, the ripple of his shoulders as he moves, the way his butt looks in his jeans as he's kneeling down. (Maybe those cheesy porn videos were actually onto something after all? Who knew.)

He carries on, "If you were actually being a bitch, you would've screamed bloody murder down the phone at me and insisted I abandon my night out to come help you, rather than what you *actually* did, which was apologize profusely for interrupting my plans and try to insist I didn't need to come over."

"Well, I obviously didn't insist hard enough."

I smile, though, and he smiles back, telling me archly, "You did sound *very* pathetic. I could hardly leave you to fend for yourself. It's not in my dashing, knight-in-shining-armor nature."

"Like I said—you're a lifesaver."

"So how *are* things going with that boy?" he asks, deliberately not using Jaxon's name, all casualness, all the while very determinedly looking back at my leaky toilet. I'm not sure if it's on purpose, but he tosses his head to move some loose strands of chestnut-brown hair out of his face, then uses his shoulder to brush them away. It's definitely on purpose, actually, because it has the intended effect: making butterflies erupt in my stomach, firmly reminding me exactly *how* attractive he is.

"Um, okay. Good, I think? We're talking again, so it's pretty much back to how it was. We're going to another pub quiz next week

160

with some of his friends. I think he's over the whole awkwardness of me asking him to Jessica's wedding."

I hope things are good between us. I hope he's over it and that we're back on track. We haven't actually talked about it; it's sort of been swept under the rug and we've moved on, trying to fall back into our normal rhythm of texting about how our days are going and setting up dates. I'm nervous to mention the wedding around him, but I think that has as much to do with Harry as it does the fact that Jaxon almost ghosted me over the last-minute invite.

It's abundantly clear that Jaxon still wants fun Soph, not serious Soph. He hasn't delved into anything more serious than asking me if I prefer barbecue or tomato sauce on a bacon sandwich (promptly declaring, "It'll tell me a lot about you, Sophie, so choose wisely!") so I don't want to be the first one to change the dynamic. And that's okay. We're just taking it slow. Figuring each other out. That's fine. It's very normal.

"Obviously not good enough that I decided to call you first in a crisis rather than him," I say, trying to make a joke about it before I sound *too* serious. It's weird to talk about Jaxon with Harry. "I thought maybe that was too much of a 'girlfriend' thing. Didn't want to risk him ghosting me again, lol."

Oh god. I've just said *lol* out loud.

I mean, I do it with Tally and Jessica and stuff, but never around boys.

If Harry finds my *lol* totally cringeworthy, he doesn't show it. Instead all he says is, "Please tell me this isn't what dating is *actually* like."

"Plunging girls' toilets and not even getting a blow job as a thank-you?"

"*Ha-ha.* The ghosting thing. I mean, I know it's a thing, so don't 'old man' me again or anything, but . . . I just think it doesn't sound like a great start to a relationship if you're doing everything you can just to *not* get ghosted every time it looks like they're losing interest. Why would you want to be with someone like that? It sounds exhausting."

It is, I almost say. *Oh god, it really is.*

It's so exhausting I could cry, but this whole night has stressed me out enough that I think I will actually cry if I admit it out loud, and I don't want to do that.

"It's not that bad. And Jaxon's not that bad either. I get where he's coming from, that's all. When you're still getting to know someone, trying to work out if you're compatible, if you want to get into a serious relationship with them, that's a big commitment, you know? And when you've been single for a while, you have standards, you know? Or things you *know* you're looking for. And you start to spot the red flags. So I'm sure that's all it was, that he thought maybe I was looking for something too serious too soon, and he didn't want to mislead me, so that's why he backed off."

It's definitely that.

It's also complete bullshit, and not the deep-down-honest kind I put into my articles.

Harry must hear the defensiveness that's crept back into my voice because he only nods and says lightly, "Go on, then, what are your red flags?"

"Cheating."

Not that I'm one to talk, I guess, since I slept with him while I'm still seeing Jaxon. But he smirks and nods for me to carry on, moving now from the plunger to the toilet cistern, which has been steadily trickling this whole time.

"Guys who say they never read, like it's a good thing."

"Mm. I do love a good sports biography, to be fair."

"That's *worse*. Also, guys who say they're looking for someone who can 'match their banter' and 'doesn't take themselves too seriously.' Guys who put in their bio that they're interested in cryptocurrency but put the little diamond emoji next to it. I thought it was code for some sex thing for *ages*, you know. Turns out, no, it's just that the guys who do that turn out to be self-righteous pigs half the time."

"Understandable."

"Cat people."

Harry stops fiddling with things inside the cistern very abruptly and fixes me with a determined stare and a small scowl. "You're a *dog person*?"

"Isn't everybody?"

He pulls such a horrified, disgusted face that I almost want to laugh, but instead I point out indignantly, "That's *exactly* how I feel about cats. Ugh. They're *horrible*."

"They're better than dogs. Much more self-sufficient."

"They'd kill you, soon as look at you."

"I'm not denying that they can't be little devils," he says, but there's some affection in it. "But they're certainly better than dogs. Even if they *do* take the wife's side all the time, or are sick in your shoes or leave a dead mouse in your spot on the sofa."

I blink at him, somehow stunned by this revelation. "You have a cat?"

"Yeah. Well. *Had*, I suppose. Obviously, she stayed in the house with my ex. My new place wouldn't take pets anyway."

It's like the ground has shifted under my feet, like I'm seeing Harry for the first time. I try to picture him on a sofa with a cat on his lap, or changing out a litter tray, and grimace.

"What else don't I know about you?" I ask, and can't keep the disgust from my voice.

He laughs. "Like you're such a peach yourself?"

And while he fixes my toilet and helps me clean up the mess on the floor and bundle soggy towels into the washing machine, we share all our little habits and worst qualities.

I'm really bad with spicy food and will tear up if I eat anything stronger than a korma—it's the lemon-and-herb part of the Nando's spice scale for me all the way. I don't get to the airport until I absolutely have to be there, I'm quite strict with keeping a monthly budget, I put the jam on scones and then the cream, and I think *The Lord of the Rings* is wildly overrated.

Harry only listens to boring businessy podcasts related to his industry, likes to have a physical pen and notepad on his desk at all times, and thinks sustainable fashion brands are a scam. He once campaigned as a local Lib Dem councilor (and lost, badly) even though he voted Tory his whole life until then. He makes his bed every morning, tracks his meals and workouts in an app, and has a retainer he never wears.

His idea of a dream holiday is a road trip across America. I can't think of anything more nightmarish than being stuck in a car for hours—*days*—on end, except maybe having to *drive* all that time.

He thinks it's shameful I don't separate my laundry properly, and I accuse him of being a snob when he looks down his nose at my wonky IKEA television stand—although that might just be because it looks like it might collapse in on itself at any second, to be fair to him.

Over the next hour or so—and a bottle of wine—we find out a thousand tiny ways we aren't compatible, joking the whole while that it's just as well we're not dating for real when each of us have a dozen deal-breakers that the other is recklessly flaunting.

"I could never get over the gambling and the attitude to money," I tell him.

"I'd never cope with being late to everything," he shoots back and shudders for dramatic effect. "The *stress*. So unnecessary."

The two of us end up slumped side by side on the sofa. My legs are tucked up beside me and one of my hands rests on Harry's thigh, indecently high up. One of his arms is slung around my shoulders, his fingers absently toying with the ends of my hair.

I really *wasn't* going to have sex with him again. I wasn't even going to kiss him again. I wanted to give Jaxon my full effort and attention, and not get distracted by something as base and ordinary as a bit of sexual chemistry with a good-looking fake boyfriend.

But it's not ordinary. It's anything but. The air feels electric; I am consumed with the way it feels to have his body so close to mine and how much I want something more—how much I need to feel the skin of his chest under my hands or hear him groan a curse word into my mouth while we kiss, bodies tangled together.

Somehow, no amount of deal-breakers can subdue my racing pulse or the heat pooling in the pit of my stomach. He's saying something but the words are lost on me. All I comprehend is the slow, low cadence of his voice, which lures me in like a siren song, until I swallow his sentence in a lazy, wine-hazed kiss, climbing onto his lap and sighing when his hands settle against my back to anchor me close to him.

Unlike at the hotel after Jessica's wedding, this time the sex is slow. Tender, almost, which feels new and strange; it feels like it *means* something, like we mean something to each other, and I don't remember the last time it felt like that—if it ever did.

I don't want to think about what, exactly, it means. I don't want to think about the fact it feels like it means anything at all.

But I do know it feels good to be close to someone like this. Not just physically—it feels good to not have to pretend or stand on ceremony. It feels good to be *honest*. Be myself. Even if it turns out we're grossly incompatible and absolutely not the other's idea of someone they'd ever actually want to date, there's *something*, and I like the intimacy it brings. I like the fact I don't have to seek it out, or invent it, or fool myself into hoping it's there just to feel like I have someone in my life the way everybody else does.

Harry spends the night, and even though we've been talking for hours already he's obviously not done. He links his fingers through mine and brushes a kiss on my knuckles before asking, "So what was the text you were trying to reply to earlier, that got you so worked up? If it wasn't from that guy."

A flicker of guilt lights up in my chest, his words conjuring up Jaxon's smiley face in my mind. Trying to distract myself from that, I groan and bury my face in Harry's chest, declaring, "And you'd done such a good job of making me forget all about that."

He waits, though, curious—*nosy*, the bastard—and I find some of the tension in my chest unspooling as I tell him, reaching for my phone to show him the offending text.

Dawn Rigby
Hey, kiddo! Can't wait to see you next Saturday for the baby shower! Don't forget it starts at 1 but only going to be serving finger food/snacks so you might want to have a big brekkie! Going to be such a lovely day. Your mum said you're staying with her afterward, does that mean we'll see you at Granny's for Sunday roast? Hope so!!! Been WAY too long since we got to have you for a whole weekend but suppose that's what happens when you hide a secret boyfriend from us lol! <3 See you soon! Auntie Dawn xxxxx

It's a nice text. It's a well-intentioned text.

And I don't want to reply. I know she didn't mean it, but the implication is that a relationship is the only acceptable excuse for me not making the trip to see my family basically *every weekend*. Or, you know, more than once every couple of months.

I have to give Harry the backstory, of course, so it all makes sense. How Mum was young when she had me, at twenty-two. She'd been an only child until she was fifteen years old, so my auntie Dawn is closer in age to me than my mum, which my mum *hates* because it means sometimes she gets asked if she's Dawn's mum, too, which is something she swears has added to her gradually growing collection of gray hairs and wrinkles, which make her look even more like she could be Dawn's mum.

If you add that to my dad's two divorces and my two ex-stepsisters, my family tree is about as easy to explain as something in *EastEnders*, but Harry takes it in stride and I can practically see him filing away the information for later reference, building up a mental picture of my family tree in his mind. It makes me realize how little I know of his family, beyond the existence of a brother who slept with Harry's wife, and how Harry seems to go out of his way to avoid talking about them at all.

Maybe I'll ask him about it, sometime.

I explain that I love Dawn and her wife, my auntie Janine, and that I hate Janine's mother, Laura, who I think is a snide, uppity cow.

Apart from Laura, I'm sure the baby shower itself will be all right. A few silly games and a round of present opening, a couple of Auntie Dawn and Auntie Janine's mates and some extended family all gushing about tiny booties and the merits of different strollers and talking about their own kids. It won't be conversation I can really join in on, but it'll be cute, and I can coo over babies as much as the next person.

It's more the . . . everything else. The *It'll be your turn next!* comments when a baby is pretty far off my radar right now. When I haven't even decided if I *want* one. Harry's sympathetic about that—he's used to the *So are you two trying for a baby yet?* comments from his marriage. He mentions, offhandedly, how he'd love to be a dad, but there's an undercurrent to it that suggests it's a whole other, bigger issue, and he doesn't volunteer so I don't push.

Plus, I explain instead, my mum will be there, and she can be . . . well, as my dad would put it, *A bit of a headache or a bit of a whirlwind, depending on the day.*

To hear Mum tell it, her relationship with my dad was all fire and passion (ew), which meant there was plenty of good in it, but also meant they were awful as life partners.

Dad doesn't tell a different story, exactly, but where Mum looks at it as another chapter in her life, he'll sigh and shake his head and say, "Honestly, Soph, your mother . . . good luck to the man who tries to tame her."

Flighty is too strong a word, but my mum definitely likes adventure, or at least likes chasing the idea of it. She's worked on research projects at the Great Barrier Reef, Yellowstone, conservation parks in Africa and Thailand; I lived with Dad when he got remarried, and Mum would go away for months at a time on these kinds of trips for work. I used to love it. I felt like my favorite childhood fictional character, Tracy Beaker, with this superstar, glamorous mum doing all these incredible things and having exciting stories to tell every time she video called with some exotic new backdrop.

I have a great relationship with both of my parents, but sometimes my mum is a lot to keep up with.

In a small voice, comforted by the darkness blanketing my

bedroom, I murmur, "I don't know if maybe I'm a bit jealous or resentful but I do know it makes me feel a bit *less*, somehow."

Harry nods, like he understands. I don't think he does, but I like that he doesn't pick my comment apart trying to understand, making me feel all the more foolish for saying it in the first place.

"Which is silly," I press on, "because it's my mum, and she's got this whole life of her own, and it's not like I want to be off doing those kinds of things, but—"

Auntie Dawn never understood. She's a homebody. She likes her week away once a year in Spain or maybe Greece, a long weekend in the Lake District or West Wales, and that's plenty of adventure for her. She always loves Mum's stories, and they don't drag her down, not the way they do me these days. I tried to explain to her once, and she just suggested I take a delayed gap year if I wanted to travel, which wasn't really the point, but I could see she wasn't ever going to get it.

I don't think I really get it either, in all fairness.

It's a really crappy feeling sometimes, is all.

Normally, this is the sort of thing I would have vented to Tally about, but when I asked her earlier if she could meet me soon for a coffee or maybe even dinner, she said this week wasn't so great, and I guess she was too busy to even ask me what's up.

It's not even family drama, is the problem. It's my own personal drama, that I've created, all for myself and to my own detriment.

It feels weird to talk about this stuff out loud to a relative stranger, but at the same time, it doesn't feel weird at all. The words spill out of me easily, Harry's nonjudgment and infrequent but reassuring responses encouraging me to keep talking.

It's a stark contrast to how I've talked about my mum to Jaxon: I entertained him with some of her best stories, starting with the time a wombat got into her car and she accidentally took it halfway home with her before noticing it, then transitioning seamlessly into that time she ran into Cate Blanchett, who went to lunch with her, and that was when my mum met the guy she dated for the next four months.

A life that, for a number of reasons, even I can't wrap my head around.

"And there's me, single and struggling at work, and I don't want to *tell* them about the stuff going on at work because it's not like I have anything else going for me, and I love them, but it just feels lately like every conversation I have with my family is so *draining*. Like they've worn me down and I just feel so small and useless all the time. And Tally was meant to be coming to the shower with me as a buffer, but she canceled on me because something came up with her boyfriend, and—"

And . . .

I sit up, twisting around to face Harry, his eyes shining silver in the shadows.

"Will you come to my aunt's baby shower next week with me?"

I watch as his lips quirk up into a grin he tries to fight off, the mock-serious expression he can't maintain longer than about two seconds. "Are you cashing in on our little fake-dating agreement?"

"Yes."

"All right, then."

"And also dinner with my mum and a Sunday roast with my grandparents," I blurt quickly, although now that I say it out loud, I realize that Harry is the perfect excuse to bail on those things.

I don't *want* to bail, though. I do want to see my family and spend time with them. Just, preferably, in a less baby-focused setting.

He's quiet for a minute, face so serious that I cringe. It's too much. Like it wasn't enough I paraded him out in front of my family last month, now I'm dragging him to *another* weekend with the other half of my family, the poor guy. Now he's going to start to ghost me like Jaxon did after I asked him to the wedding, and I've just ruined everything, and—

But then he says, still deadly serious, "Sophie, I will *never* turn down a roast dinner."

I'm so relieved, I almost tell him I love him.

Nineteen

"Sophie, sweetheart! Hello! Ooh, how are you? How was the train?"

Mum envelops me in a big hug. A floral scent fills my nostrils and I realize she's changed her perfume. I like this one; it suits her. She's wearing a pair of black cigarette jeans, which makes me wonder if I'm overdressed in a pink midi skirt.

My mum is one of those petite, waify blond women I feel jealous of sometimes—the kind who can wear a potato sack and look stylish. I got stuck with my dad's genes: taller, darker, the very idea of a thigh gap a physical impossibility.

I know it's not all about looks and that a lot of it, for people like my mum but especially when it comes to my mum, is attitude.

I just wish I had that, sometimes.

I hug her back and let her take my overnight bag from me. "Hi, Mum. Yeah, it was fine. Do you think I should change before we go to Auntie Dawn's?"

"No! No, don't be silly. You look lovely." She pauses, though, plucking open my jacket to scrutinize my top, with a face that says, *I'm not too sure about that*. She adds quickly, "It's fine, it's only a little do at her house, anyway."

Then Mum turns to Harry—I say *turns*, but in reality she has to take half a step back and tilt her head up to see his face properly.

She gives him a warm smile and looks so genuinely excited to meet him—that same relief in her face that I saw on Camilla's and Nadine's before Jessica's wedding—that I flinch.

"And you must be the lovely Harry we've heard so much about! It's so nice to meet you at last. Sophie's only been keeping you secret from us for the last few months!"

Mum gives a light laugh, punctuating the point with an admonishing but affectionate look my way. While I grimace, Harry places an arm around my shoulder.

"Oh, you know Sophie! She's got more secrets than an MI6 agent."

Mum laughs again, like the very idea is ludicrous, like I did such a bad job of keeping Harry a secret all this time.

Little does she know.

We all head to the car with Mum and Harry exchanging polite small talk, Harry once again proving he's a model fake boyfriend. When we're all buckled in and on the road—straight to Dawn's, I realize—there's only one thing on my mind.

"What are we doing about lunch, though?" I ask, talking over Harry.

"There's food at the shower, darling."

"Only like, canapé things, though."

"It's only Auntie Dawn," Mum says, waving a hand. "She won't mind if you go make a sandwich or something. We'll be there a bit early anyway."

"You'd better be right," I grumble. Harry starts to chuckle, and I cut him a look that only makes him laugh a little more. The other good thing about not having to stand on ceremony for a guy who's only my pretend boyfriend: I don't have to pretend I'm not hangry when I absolutely am.

And after last Friday night, when Harry literally plunged my toilet and then I told him all my worst and most particular qualities, being a bit hangry around him is definitely the least of my concerns.

"I'm your mother," Mum tells me brightly. "I'm always right."

Last time I saw my mum in person was just before Lena's engagement party: a flying visit for Sunday lunch at Granny and Granddad's. We FaceTime a lot and text most days but lately when she's been home and reached out to see if I'm free, I've already had plans in place—like Frankie's housewarming or rare plans to see a film with Tally. Mum's been consulting with some team in Germany for a while, which means she's close enough that she can nip home to see the family for a weekend, no problem. I think this job has something to do with electric vehicles but, honestly, every time she gets into the details, it starts to get fuzzy. It's like my brain tries to translate it into something I can understand but all I end up getting is radio static.

Still, I ask her about the project anyway, and she starts rattling off a story about how she ended up going from a research trip to a test-drive circuit to going out to some Michelin-starred restaurant with a guy who made some kind of breakthrough for Formula 1 engine designs, which piques Harry's interest and has the two of them chattering away for the rest of the drive.

As we walk up the front path to Auntie Dawn's end-of-terrace house, Mum wraps up her story, saying, "Anyway, he's moving back to Ecuador before I get back to Munich, but it was nice while it lasted. But enough about that! What about—" She cuts off as the door opens. "Dawn! Ooh, hi! Hello! So lovely to see you! Gosh, aren't you big!"

The door opens and Mum pulls Auntie Dawn into a tight hug like the one she gave me, beaming and touching her sister's protruding stomach before stepping aside so I can have my turn to hug Dawn hello too.

Am I supposed to touch her belly as well, or is that annoying? Is it rude to agree with Mum and say how big she looks? I have no idea what the baby protocol is.

Auntie Dawn gets there first anyway, saying, "Let me take your coat, sweetheart. Love that skirt. Come in, come in! Pop your shoes off, just—yeah, just by there, that's it. Sorry, I know it's silly, everything will get messy when baby arrives anyway, but—come on through! Janine and I were just pulling together the platters. Granny's here too! And Janine's mum, Laura, you remember her."

As if I could forget her. Laura could give Lena's mum a run for her money in her ability to undermine you with a single look.

"And you must be Harry!" Dawn announces to him, much like Mum did. They even look alike, although Dawn is a little taller and a little softer than Mum. "You are spoiling us, Sophie, we get you for a whole weekend *and* get to meet your new man! Well, *old* man, I suppose, since—"

"Oh my *god*, he's not *old*," I blurt immediately. Even if I tease him about our age gap all the time, I'm mortified on his behalf for the way he hasn't even managed to say hello before being insulted.

Dawn scoffs. "I should bloody hope not, or you'll be calling me old too! I just meant you two have been together a while."

"And yet it feels like just last month," Harry jokes; even I manage a bit of a laugh at that. Then he hands over a gift bag and says, "Lovely to meet you, too, Dawn, I've heard nothing but good things. Here, just a little something from us two."

He really is the perfect boyfriend. Perfect *fake* boyfriend, I mean. I'd sent him a photo of the baby shower invite and told him which train I'd booked this morning so he could meet me at the station, and he showed up having ordered a gift from their registry. He'd wrapped it and everything.

I hadn't bought anything because, obviously not. The invite made it sound like gifts were only a *suggestion*, and besides, I'd only end up buying something else once the baby was *actually* born. But obviously, I insisted on paying Harry back for it—like he hadn't already gone above and beyond without buying a gift for a total stranger too.

As for only hearing "good" things about Dawn—well, he's heard *everything*, as of last Friday night. Honestly, if he doesn't make a career as a fake boyfriend, he could totally be a therapist.

Dawn takes the gift bag. "Oh, aren't you sweet! Come on, this way. So, how's things, Soph? Feels like ages since we saw you!"

"Sorry," I say automatically, even though last time we were meant to meet up, *they* were meant to come to see me, but it fell through. "Yeah, I'm good, but shouldn't I be asking you that? You're glowing."

I think she's glowing. Her skin looks fresh, her cheeks rosy, but that's the sort of thing they say about pregnant women, isn't it?

Safer than saying *You're huge!* anyway.

"I don't feel it." Auntie Dawn laughs, but she's obviously flattered so I breathe a small sigh of relief at having said the right thing. "I haven't slept properly in ages, and just *look* at these!" She waggles one of her feet at me, showing off a purple Croc. "These are the only things that fit me right now."

"They do look quite bad," Mum tells her. "Mine were never that swollen with Soph."

"And the *farting* . . . "

The two of them wander down the hall into the kitchen, swapping pregnancy stories. I exchange a glance with Harry, who seems unfazed by it, and then wander along after them. There are yellow and silver balloons strung up everywhere and a pin-the-nappy-on-the-baby board leaning up against a wall. The table and counters in the kitchen are covered in different foil platters of snacks and finger foods: mini salmon and cucumber sandwiches, tiny sausage rolls, grapes and melon cubes, and little brownie bites. Auntie Dawn and Mum head outside, where a large picnic table has been set up for the shower. In the kitchen, Granny is fussing over bowls of Doritos and it sounds like I've interrupted Auntie Janine and her mum bickering about drinks.

"It's a *baby shower*," Laura huffs.

"Exactly! We're celebrating!"

"You don't need to have alcohol to celebrate. Look, Dawn won't be drinking, or your friend whatshername with the nose ring, or anyone who's driving."

"Oh, bloody hell, Mum, I'm *not* having this conversation again. It's hardly a piss-up, is it? It's afternoon tea. Look, I bet Sophie wants a drink. Soph, do you want some champagne?"

"Uh, I mean—"

Sorry, Laura.

"Yes, please. If it's not too much trouble."

"See? Told you. It's in the fridge, love, help yourself."

Granny catches my eye and pulls a face like she's trying not to laugh before rolling her eyes and giving a little shrug. I go give Auntie Janine a hug and a kiss on the cheek, which she returns warmly, and introduce her swiftly to Harry, then I say hi to Laura but that goes unacknowledged because by then they're bickering over having only decaffeinated tea and coffee in the house right now.

Granny leaves the bowls of crisps to get me a champagne glass. Being petite like Mum, she has to half climb up on the counter to reach them on the top shelf of a cabinet; I catch the back of Harry's coat to yank him back when he moves to help, because Granny is *always* determined to do things for herself. She puts down a couple more glasses and whispers to me, "Although I think Janine probably needs a vodka, but she'll have to make do. Been like this *all* morning. Should've heard Laura going on about not having pink balloons up."

"Oh." I look around. "I like them. They're pretty. Match the décor."

"They're balloons," Granny says in a flat voice. "Not like the baby's even here to see them either way."

I snort and try to smother a laugh.

"Anyway, hello, you. And it's Harry, isn't it? Hello. How was the train?"

"Yeah, fine." I finish pouring the champagne, pass one to Janine, and say, "Can I make some toast or something? I'm starving."

Laura huffs, pursing her lips. She didn't hear my hello, but she sure as hell heard *that*. "Didn't you know it was going to be a bit of a buffet?"

"I meant to grab some food at the station, but—" But I got a bit distracted with Harry showing up with the gift and was still sort of astonished he'd shown up *at all*, and I thought I'd have time to have something quick at Mum's before coming here . . .

"Go ahead, Soph, help yourself. And you, Harry, make yourself at home. Mum, *honestly*, it's just some friends and family, I don't know *why* you're getting so worked up."

"Well, excuse me for wanting everything to be perfect for my first grandchild—"

Luckily for us, the two of them storm off to argue somewhere else.

Auntie Dawn almost immediately pops her head back into the

kitchen. "Oh my god, are they still going on? Been like that all *week*. As bad as each other. I'd say we're not always like this, Harry, but I'd hate to lure you into the family under false pretenses." She sighs and rolls her eyes, looking exactly like Granny. She eyes my drink with open envy. "God, I'd love a champagne."

"If it helps," Granny says, "I only picked up the cheap stuff."

"Oh, good," I say. "That means nobody will mind if I drink a whole bottle, right?"

"Sort yourself out some lunch first, maybe," Mum says. "Here, I'll make you something."

Auntie Dawn takes up Janine's empty chair at the breakfast bar with a bit of a puff, leaning back and rubbing her belly, and says, "So how are things with you two lovebirds? Tell me everything. I need all the gossip you've been hiding from us."

Granny winks at me and, with a very obvious nod in Harry's direction, loudly stage-whispers, "And we do mean *all* the gossip, Sophie! You've bagged yourself a handsome one there!"

"Uh," is all I can manage. Harry smothers a laugh by clearing his throat, and does nothing to help me out, apparently too entertained watching me flounder.

"What *I* want to know," Mum says, "is why I had to hear about it from your ex-stepmother and not *you*."

The funny thing is, Mum and Camilla get on really well. They've been on day trips to spas and gone shopping together and stuff. And since Camilla and my dad ended things on such good terms, all the parents even have this big group chat together. The WhatsApp grapevine works furiously fast sometimes. It could give Vin Diesel a run for his money.

"Well," I manage eventually, "we were just, um, you know, taking things slow. Seeing how it went, before telling everyone."

"You kids these days," Granny says. "You know, when your granddad was courting me—"

"Courting! You weren't born in the eighteen hundreds, Mum." Auntie Dawn laughs. "Who do you think you are, someone out of *Bridgerton*? Your first date was at the cinema, don't be silly. Talking like he signed your dance card for a bloody quadrille!"

Finally taking pity and coming to my rescue, Harry says, "Well, we got there in the end. Didn't we, Soph? I'm surprised you're not sick of the sight of me already, what with all the 'courting.'"

He winks at me, and my stomach fills with butterflies. Granny levels a finger at him and announces to nobody in particular, "I like this one," and Mum picks up on the comment about work to ask me how that's going.

I almost wish she hadn't asked; I mumble, fumbling over my words, trying to make it sound better than it is and like I'm not terrified of how I seem to constantly mess up. I obviously can't mention the column, but, unluckily for me, Dawn suddenly remembers the promotion I talked about wanting in January that I never got, and I have to pretend like I'm still working toward it rather than just trying my hardest to keep my head above water.

But for a change, it's not a topic I have to talk about for long. It's not the only thing I've got going for me: now, of course, I have a boyfriend, and I can push the conversation in his direction instead for a while. So I do, and it works.

I've always felt like I've had to rely on my job to justify myself, somehow. Like it's not so bad that I'm single, because work's going great. I'm a Career Girl, I could say. People tend to give you a little more leeway with a failed dating life if they think you're just "focusing on your career right now."

That's part of why spending time with this half of my family, and particularly my mum, stresses me out. Mum has *passion*—in spades. She's built her career around her passion to make a difference in the world and protect the environment. Dawn is into music, playing in an orchestra in her spare time, a passion she shares with Granddad. Granny enjoys painting, and since retiring took up pottery too. Janine is a teacher, the kind who runs after-school clubs and volunteers to coach a local girls' football team.

I've always been in awe of them for that.

I've always resented that it seemed to skip a generation, in me. My career isn't as glamorous as Mum's, my spare time filled now with catching up on errands or Netflix, an occasional bit of photography when I'm in the mood, or traipsing around celebrating how my friends' lives are moving on so spectacularly.

But at least, now, I don't have to justify myself. I don't have to pretend to be the career girl, or anything else. In their eyes, now, everything is fine: my life is great.

I have a boyfriend. My life must feel so complete now.

What more could I want?

Twenty

All things considered, it's not a bad baby shower.

Not that I have anything to really compare it to, but Auntie Dawn and Auntie Janine seem happy, so that's the main thing. The other guests are their friends or people from work they're close with, or one of Janine's cousins. Two of the guests are also pregnant; many already have kids of their own. Everyone seems to be having a good time; they drink the champagne (or don't, and nobody really cares either way), enough of the food is eaten that you know they enjoyed it but weren't left wanting more, they howl with laughter over a couple of games and some stories people swap, and they coo over the gifts they've brought as they get unwrapped.

"What about you?" a guy from Janine's work asks me at one point.

"Oh, um, I'm, uh—" I look around for help, but Auntie Dawn is currently busy unwrapping some elephant-print onesies and gushing over the tiny matching hat. I laugh, maybe a bit too loudly, and sip my champagne. "I think I'm a little bit young to think about having kids myself, yet."

Unfortunately, Auntie Dawn *does* overhear that because she says, "I wouldn't be so sure, Soph! You'll be my age before you know it."

"I'd already enrolled you in school by the time I was your age!" Mum adds.

"I had my first at about your age," agrees some old uni friend. "What are you now, Sophie? Twenty-three?"

"Almost twenty-six," I mumble, shrinking in my seat.

"Time's a-ticking," someone else says with a laugh. "You don't want to be leaving it too late, after all!"

And someone, some absolute villain, pins Harry and me with a look and asks, "Haven't you two talked about having kids yet?"

Which is, objectively, funny, because we aren't a couple. But they don't know that, and I choke on the cheap champagne I've just taken a sip of. We've never been a religious family but I find myself praying frantically now. *Please, God, or whoever's up there, if anyone's listening, please just get me out of this conversation somehow.*

There's no divine intervention, though, so I'm left coughing, sputtering attempts at an answer, relieved when Harry gives my thigh a gentle squeeze and takes over.

"Yes. We're on the same page, which always bodes well, doesn't it?"

He says it so cheerfully, with such a charming smile, that all the others can do is smile back and nod along, Janine saying something about good communication being the key to any relationship. A few people are obviously expecting more of an answer—a bit rich when it's none of their business.

Would they like to hear when my next period's due, and what my preferred type of tampon is, too, while we're at it?

But apart from that, it's not a bad baby shower.

I assume that Mum and I (and, by extension, Harry) are sticking around to help clean up after the other guests leave as the afternoon wears on, but only a minute or two after the last one is out of the door, Mum's grabbing her coat and pushing mine at me too; Harry is distracted by an ambush from my grandmother, though they look like they're laughing about something. I wonder if it's at my expense.

"I've got us a table booked at that new Greek place across town," Mum explains, more to Dawn than me and without any apology. "Dmitri, you remember Dmitri? Put us up in that lovely hotel in Brazil that weekend you came to visit me in São Paulo. Anyway, his friend is an investor, so he's pulled a few strings. They're normally booked up weeks in advance, especially on a Saturday! See you tomorrow for lunch? Sophie, sweetheart, did you want to change first? Shall I grab your bag from the car?"

"What's wrong with this?"

"I've got a blouse you can borrow, if you need," Janine offers and oh my god, what is *wrong* with the one I'm wearing? Seriously? Is it the off-the-shoulder style? The frill along the neckline? Is it covered in stains I haven't noticed? I look down but find nothing objectively wrong with it. I guess it's just not their style. I didn't think it looked that bad. I look at Harry for help now that he's finally approaching to put his coat on, too, but he merely shrugs, as confused as I am.

"She looks fine," Granny says, and thank god for Granny, because she shoos us out of the house so that they can crack on with tidying up, citing the early-evening traffic as another excuse to boot us out.

Mum had obviously planned for this to be a little mother-daughter evening, but that's exactly why I roped Harry in as a buffer. As we climb into the car, I'm relegated to the back seat and we fall automatically into discussing the baby shower: the guests and their presents, Janine's overbearing, pernickety mother, and the ghastly neon-yellow dress one of Dawn's friends was wearing keep us busy all the way into town, into the Greek restaurant, and as far as ordering some drinks.

It's not difficult to see why Mum had to pull some strings to get us a table.

I mean, I'm sure the place is fancy, and the food is going to be great, but it's also, most importantly, *tiny*. It's a hole-in-the-wall restaurant with maybe fifteen tables, max, all clustered so tightly on top of each other I think maybe all the waiters here are really skinny for a reason, because if they weren't they'd never be able to get around. There's music, like it compensates for the fact you could easily eavesdrop on about five different conversations at any one time, and the ceiling is high with all these exposed wood beams and long trailing plants hanging from them, which I guess is supposed to make up for the lack of square footage.

Although I have to hand it to Mum's friend Dmitri and his investor friend because the food is excellent, so I'm glad of our table. Even if the man behind me keeps bumping his chair into mine and knocking me with his elbow whenever he turns to summon a waiter.

And, actually, it's a nice evening. The conversation is easy and light, and for once, I don't feel any pressure; I don't feel quite so inadequate when I've got Harry's leg pressed against mine beneath the table, his eyes twinkling in the candlelight every time he catches my gaze. Which is often.

Like, *all the time* often.

But when he excuses himself to the bathroom and I'm left alone with Mum, she pounces.

"He seems very nice."

"He is."

"And things must be going well. Quite serious," she clarifies, with a pointed tone I don't quite understand but know I don't appreciate. It feels patronizing, somehow, and my jaw clenches in response.

"And you liked him enough to invite him to Jessica's wedding," Mum presses.

Shit. *Shit.* The fake-boyfriend gimmick was all well and good, but I keep forgetting that it can't be *too* good or it'll make it harder to break the news at some point that we called it quits, decided we were better as friends.

Skirting around it, I say, "I—I mean, yeah, I guess. It's not a big deal."

Mum purses her lips, but like she's trying not to smile. Her eyebrows go up and her whole face seems to say, *Well, it seems like a pretty big deal.*

Irritated, feeling backed into a corner, I suddenly regret bringing Harry along with me at all, and wishing I could just, *for once*, not feel less than because I'm single, I bite out, "Just because you don't date men with any idea of how long they'll stick around—"

"Oh, please, don't make this about me. You're deflecting, don't think I don't know what you're doing. I just wanted to talk to my daughter about her relationship, that's all."

"*Now* who's deflecting?" I mumble back, shrinking down in my seat.

Mum sighs but indulges me. "Sophie, I tried the whole 'relationship' thing with your dad, and it didn't work out. No amount of chemistry could make up for being fundamentally incompatible," she says, with such sureness that it strikes me square in the gut, and all I can think of is the long list of reasons why Harry and I don't match up we discovered last week.

Mum, thankfully, doesn't notice my reaction.

"And anyway, even if that was the sort of thing I was looking for, with my sort of career—the consulting, the research projects, traveling all over the place for months at a time . . . "

"Oh, so it's all right for *you* to focus on your career, but whenever I try to do it, it's always still, 'How's the love life going?' Like *my* job isn't good enough as it is," I drawl. I scoff, stabbing my fork into the dainty, deconstructed, and actually very delicious moussaka on my plate, glowering down at it. "Right, yeah. Got it."

"Sophie," she says, serious; and great, she's *worried* now too. Brilliant. Mum frowns, leaning a bit closer, which isn't difficult, considering how small and cramped our table is. The guy behind me bumps his chair into mine again.

"Sophie," she says again. "Is this about work? That promotion you got turned down for after Christmas? You know, I told you, if—"

"I didn't get—! Mum, I went for that job *months* ago. That was in, like, January. And I did really well in my annual review. They just went for someone else with more experience, so . . . "

And someone who doesn't cost the paper pretty hefty sums of money every time they ask for more responsibility and subsequently ruin *everything*.

"I know. But I remember you were quite upset you got turned down for it. You were talking to your dad at the time about maybe leaving the newspaper, going for a new job somewhere else . . . You sent me your CV to look at, remember? And then you didn't apply for anything new."

"Well, yeah. I mean. I was upset, but it was just a knee-jerk reaction." Plus, just after that, I was offered a regular column, so . . . "I like it at the paper. Anyway, Jenny, my manager, she's just let slip to everyone she's pregnant, so they'll have to recruit for her maternity cover in a few months and I might be able to apply for that."

I stun myself with the declaration, even if I keep a poker face when Mum raises her eyebrows thoughtfully. Put myself forward for Jenny's maternity cover? Where did that even *come* from?

There's no way they'd let me do that. Is there?

Although Oscar has only been with us since January, and Karl never puts himself up for promotions, and I've been with the paper longer than Isaac. And people at work *like* me, and leadership roles are quite people focused, aren't they? And I do manage to do *some* good stuff, sometimes, like that online photography campaign I helped organize that got the community involved in a big scavenger hunt. It's not always a cataclysmic disaster. It's not *totally* outside the realms of possibility that I might be able to be Jenny's maternity cover.

"Mm-hmm. Well, maybe it's worth thinking about. Looking for a new job somewhere else, I mean."

"What? Why? I *just* said—"

"Then what were those snarky remarks about focusing on my career, missy? Your job not being good enough? And don't think I didn't hear you avoiding talking too much about your job at the shower earlier. You got quite grumpy about it a couple of times."

Well, *yeah*, I want to say. Of course I did. Because apparently the only good reason for me to be single is to have some amazing, high-flying, supersuccessful, hashtag-girlboss career. Like I should be running my own advertising agency focusing on inclusivity and donating half my profits to charity and then campaigning against period poverty in my spare time and throwing some luxe ribbon-cutting ceremony for the new office I just signed the lease for.

(Which is only a *slight* exaggeration. Or at least, a combination of things I've seen some girls from uni or school posting on their social media.)

Maybe I don't *love* my job, but I like it well enough. I like it at least most of the time, and it's basically the sort of thing I want to do, even if sometimes I'd like a bigger salary or some more responsibility and authority. But it just feels like a normal job. The kind anybody could have. It's not special. It's not jealousy inducing or awe inspiring. It's just a job.

Which is A-okay with me, because my ambitions in life include having someone senior to me to ask questions of and help fix any mistakes I make, then going home to scroll through social media and maybe read a few chapters of a book before I go to bed then do it all again the next day.

It's not that I'm unsatisfied with my career, I want to explain, it's just that other people seem to be expecting *more*, and it's frustrating as all hell. Like not having a boyfriend means there is this great, gaping void in my life, and I must fill it somehow and surely, surely, that void must then be filled with success at work or money in the bank? And if that's not the case, then why am I not putting more effort and energy into finding myself a boyfriend? My life is never just *enough* for anybody, never okay as it is—to the point where for the most part, I agree with them because I've heard it enough times.

I don't know how to phrase that, though, and I don't know if Mum will even understand.

Because even if she doesn't go looking for relationships, they always find her, and she's got *everything*. This great, amazing, totally fulfilling career that she absolutely loves and ultimately even does some good in the world, men she can enjoy casually dating for three weeks or maybe eight months, and time at home to see her family.

She's got it all in the same way as Lena or Frankie Two have it all.

So I just *know*, if I try to tell her how small my life feels sometimes, she's never going to get it, and the best I can hope for is pity, which I could really do without.

Plus, you know, she thinks I have a boyfriend.

I settle for saying, "I didn't mean to be snappy. You're right, I guess I'm just worried if I go up for Jenny's maternity cover I won't get it, like the promotion. It's been stressing me out a little bit. I didn't want to get into it at the baby shower."

Mum sighs, all sympathy, gentle and caring and just so completely my mum in that moment, but before she can try to offer advice or make me feel better, Harry's back, easing awkwardly into his squashed-in seat and dropping a kiss on my cheek before saying, "What're we talking about?"

And I say, "Nothing."

And Mum doesn't contradict me.

• • •

The rest of the weekend is easy, pleasant. Or it would be if I could shake off my bad mood.

At the apartment that Mum keeps for her irregular visits home I'm on an air bed and Harry's on the sofa, meaning I don't sleep well—and Jaxon's ignored the text I sent him Saturday morning, which doesn't do much to cheer me up as I enter twenty-four hours of radio silence from him, officially verging on ghosting territory once more.

We all head to Granny and Granddad's for Sunday lunch, Dawn and Janine included, and maybe they notice I'm not feeling too chatty, or maybe Mum told them I'm stressing out about a promotion I've just made up for myself last night, or maybe they're so distracted by my shiny new boyfriend, but by some miracle I fade into the background. I pitch in to the conversation, of course, but I know how brief my answers are, how much I don't feel like myself.

Before we leave, when I hug each of my family goodbye, they all tell me how much they like Harry; I don't feel the smug glow of pride over it like I did at Jessica's wedding.

I don't even talk much to Harry on the train home. I doze a little, and pretend to doze most of the rest of the time.

When we disembark at the station back home, Harry stands in front of me, brow furrowed and a serious look on his face.

I get the familiar, sneaking suspicion I'm about to be dumped. The *this was great but it's just not going to work out* talk. And honestly, I couldn't blame him: I've been a terrible fake girlfriend. The poor guy's been saddled with Serious Sophie, not Fun Sophie—all the bad stuff of being in a relationship without any *actual* feelings to make up for it. Roast dinners and casual sex can only go so far, I suppose.

But instead he simply says, "Do you want to go see a film?"

I blink at him, dazed, sure I'm hallucinating.

"You look really crappy," he says, like that explains it.

"Gee, and here I thought you were such a charmer."

Harry lifts his backpack with his change of clothes onto his shoulder and takes my overnight bag from me, then takes my hand in his free one. His palm is warm, a pleasant weight around mine.

"Come on. We'll find a bad action film or a boring documentary or something and just zone out for a couple of hours." Then he gives me a smile that I can only describe as shy before adding, "I don't have any plans for the rest of the evening, and you look like you're only going to go home and wallow in a pint of ice cream. Come on, it might cheer you up a little."

Oh, god.

That's really sweet. Like, properly, genuinely sweet.

So much so that it takes all my willpower not to tear up as I wonder if this is what it's like to have a boyfriend, a partner, someone you share your life with. Someone who tunes in to your emotions, tries to help you through them. Someone who wallows with you, even if it's over popcorn and not ice cream.

"I actually really like documentaries," I tell him.

"Really? Huh."

"It's on my Hookd profile. One of my interests, you know."

"I remember. You said at the wedding you like true crime stuff, but I thought that was a joke. I just . . . guess I just thought it was one of those things you put up on your profile to make yourself sound more interesting."

It draws the first real laugh out of me since we left for the baby shower. I lean into his side as he leads us into town. Ironic that he'd assume that, when it's one of the few consistently honest things on my profile—no exaggeration, no little white lie, no best foot forward.

The only movie about to start when we arrive is a thriller, so Harry buys the tickets and I buy us some snacks, and we sit in the dark together with a few dozen other couples, and for a while, I get to feel like one of them. I hold the popcorn in my lap and rest my head on Harry's shoulder, and at least for those couple of hours, it doesn't feel quite so fake.

August

LUCY'S WEDDING

Wednesday, August 11

Lucy Edmonds
Hey, Soph! So glad you and the girls can make it to the wedding this weekend, can't wait to see you all! Told Tally and Lena as well but just wanted to say, really sorry again about the plus-one sitch, we're trying to keep costs down—but SO lovely to see you've got yourself a boyfriend now (at last, lol!). I saw your photos on Facebook from your sister's wedding of the two of you, supercute! See you Saturday, when I become Mrs. Williams!

Sent 12:36 p.m.

ANNABELLE AND PATRICK'S WEDDING

To Harry Chapman and guest,

Michael & Carol Walker
Request the pleasure of your company
at the marriage of their daughter

Annabelle
to
Patrick

Saturday the Twenty–First of August
at two o'clock
Marshall Oak Farms
Cotswolds

Twenty-one

If you're not supposed to "settle" for someone, why do they call it "settling down" anyway?

Views on settling from our Dating & Relationships columnist

"You're too good for him anyway, Barker."

I jump, dropping my phone on my desk with such a noisy clatter a couple of people in the office turn around to look. I hunch in my seat and twist my head to look up at Duncan, scowling. He's standing over my shoulder, where he has snuck up and has obviously just seen me checking Jaxon's WhatsApp—as if by opening our conversation, a message from Jaxon will suddenly, miraculously appear, and by some strange glitch I just missed the notification I've been on high alert waiting for.

Everyone goes back to work, all limp and sweaty and tired from the mid-August heat the office's AC is doing nothing to combat. It's making everyone else listless; it's made me irksome. Duncan moves from lurking behind me, dragging over an empty seat and leaning an elbow on the half of my desk that's taken up by a precarious mountain of miscellaneous freebies. And to think we (meaning, *I*) just cleared it at the end of July.

We *really* need to get another intern.

I refuse to make tidying up the merchandise my job. At least, not all the time. Not when I've been here a whole year longer than our other marketing assistant, Isaac, who keeps making a point of dumping the stuff on *my* desk like it's *my* problem.

Not that it's Isaac I'm annoyed with right now, or the merch pile stressing me out, or even the sweltering heat, but they're as good an outlet as any until Jaxon texts me back.

Duncan nods in the direction of my phone, which is now lying facedown on my keyboard. I move it out of the way and turn it face-up, so I'll see the notification if it buzzes.

"How long's he been ghosting you?"

"He's not *ghosting* me," I snap, but then relent and mumble, "He said yesterday he's not sure if he can see me for our date tonight, and he just . . . he keeps blowing hot and cold, you know? One minute he's sending a string of kisses and telling me he can't wait to see me again and then I barely hear from him for a few days."

"Ouch."

"No," I insist, plastering on a smile like maybe if I can convince Duncan, I'll convince myself too. "It's fine. I mean, he's just busy with work. And so what if he has to cancel our Friday-night plans? It's not a big deal. Stuff comes up all the time. It's not even that last-minute."

"Oh, yeah, no, for sure." One side of Duncan's mouth quirks up into a smirk, though, and he raises his eyebrows at me. "And that's why you've sent *five* messages since that he hasn't replied to all day?"

"Maybe he's busy. *Some* people have to actually *do work* at their job, you know."

He laughs. "All right, boss, calm down. I'm waiting for some editorial notes to come back. At least I'm not too busy mooning around over my phone to work. So he canceled date night, huh? Why don't you just call it quits if he's getting on your nerves and won't commit? Do you like him that much?"

I open my mouth to give some haughty response and then tell Duncan to go away and leave me alone, but . . . I've got nothing. When Harry asked me something similar last time Jaxon was sort of almost ghosting me, I could claim he just wasn't used to the dating world since he was only just out of a long-term relationship, but Duncan's another matter. He's as woefully single and desperately dating as I am. He knows how this goes. He knows when to cut his losses and when it's not working out.

Is it not working out, with Jaxon?

Because actually, now I *really* think about it, the only reason I've carried on seeing Jaxon is because it's convenient. Because on paper, he ticks all the right boxes—and he certainly ticks the boxes Harry doesn't, like being a dog person and not gambling on football matches while paying his rent that month on his credit card. He's what I'm supposed to want in a boyfriend: someone kind, with a solid, steady job; someone capable of cleaning the bathroom and keeping a houseplant alive; someone I get on with and who also wants to find someone to settle down with.

I like Jaxon because he's exactly the kind of boy I'm supposed to like. And I *do* actually enjoy spending time with him. I like him as a person—but as a boyfriend I think, maybe, I want to like him a lot more than I do. I think I'm expecting to just decide one day that I'm falling for him, like it's that easy.

But isn't that basically how it works? More or less? It's not like all the couples I know fell in love straightaway. Jessica didn't even *like* Conor for the first few months she knew him, and now they're married.

Duncan sits quietly while I run through a small existential crisis over Jaxon, and then he says, "Maybe he's got a date with someone else."

"What?"

"Tonight. You know, he canceled on you, no real explanation. You guys have kept things pretty casual for ages now—maybe he's seeing someone else."

"But he's seeing *me*."

He looks at me, like, *So what?*

Worst of all, he's got a point. Jaxon and I have never had that "exclusive" conversation.

"This is why you're single," I grumble at Duncan instead, not daring to acknowledge he might be right. I elbow his knee as a sign for him to go away, then turn back to my computer to continue my very hard day's work of not focusing on my inbox and not proofreading a couple of local business adverts. Low-stakes work that even I can't mess up too badly—perfect for a day where I'm so distracted and where everyone else is too drowsy to care.

Duncan, of course, doesn't go anywhere.

"I just mean," he says, more gently this time, "that maybe he doesn't think it's very serious just yet. Could be worth the conversation if you *do* actually like him. And besides, you can't talk. You're seeing Harry."

"I'm not 'seeing' Harry! We just—we text."

"Didn't he come to your place for dinner on the weekend? Didn't he invite you to go to his friend's wedding next weekend?"

I huff, not dignifying that with an answer. Only because we were both bored. Only because neither of us had anything better to do, and when I reached out to Tally and Duncan and even Jessica and Nadine, everyone had plans already. And as for the wedding, well, that's our deal, isn't it? We go to events together to make each other look good.

And besides, he made it abundantly clear at Jessica's wedding that he was only after a casual intimacy to take the edge off the all-consuming loneliness of his abrupt singledom. So. There's that.

"I didn't even sleep with Harry last weekend. We just hung out. Because I'm *seeing Jaxon*. And Jaxon isn't like that. He doesn't need to be told not to cheat on the girl he's been dating for more than two months. He's just—it's *nothing*."

"You're looking awful stressed out over nothing," Duncan points out. "Even Jenny and Isaac noticed. I heard them saying so in the kitchen when I was getting coffee earlier."

Bloody Isaac.

I should've known he'd be too busy gossiping about me to tidy the merch pile.

"Look, Barker, a few of us are going for drinks tonight after work. Come with. Some of the finance and IT lot are coming too. Maybe it'll take your mind off this loser for a bit." He snatches my phone, puts it in front of my startled face to unlock it, and then taps away a couple of times before putting it back down. "There! Muted your WhatsApp with him. So now you don't have to lose it every time your phone goes off and can forget about him for a while."

"That's not—"

"Five thirty, yeah?" he says, getting up. "We're all meeting down in the foyer; we'll head out somewhere from there, find a beer garden, and make the most of this sunshine. A couple of pints and then on home."

"I don't—"

Laughing, he rattles my chair, shaking me, and says, "Ah, *come onnnnnn*, it'll do you good!"

"What, like this conversation did? I hate to break it to you, but I wasn't even worried he was seeing someone else until *you* put that idea in my head, so, thanks for that."

"You're too good for him anyway, Soph."

"You don't even know him," I point out.

"True," Duncan says, shoving my shoulder and grinning affably. "But I know you."

And then he strides off, calling over his shoulder, "Five thirty! Don't be late!"

• • •

Sometimes when I talk to my friends I can't help but think that their lives completely revolve around their partners. Or maybe not "revolve around" so much as "are completely tangled up with," because they *are*. They're each a part of a couple. They're building lives with their partners and that means so much of their everyday is inextricably linked with them.

And I guess that makes sense. You know, you can't think about taking the bins out without factoring in someone else, or whatever. You need their opinion to pick out crockery from IKEA or have to wait for them to replace a toilet seat. (Which I did for Lena, when I was staying with her after her heart surgery, and because Johnny had been "meaning" to do it for weeks but hadn't gotten around to it. And Tally actually called me over once when Sam was away to deal with the mouse trap and accompanying dead mouse under the sink.)

That's just how it is, for all of them.

And sometimes that *baffles* me. The fact they'll have to consider this other person in every part of their decision-making about something as simple as hanging out on a weekend: Will they be able to pick them up? What will they both do about dinner that day, then? Will it interfere with some housework rota they've got going?

It all seems so much, and so unnecessary, and sometimes I sit there staring at messages from my friends where they've so casually mentioned their significant others when I didn't even realize they were relevant to whatever we were talking about, and I think: How can you live like this? How can this be what I want? How can you all be so utterly obsessed, *consumed*, by these other people?

And yet, here I am, having thought about hardly anything other than Jaxon for about, oh, forty-eight hours now, since his radio silence throughout Thursday and Friday and the date he bailed on. Here I am, unable to talk to the girls about anything but Jaxon, especially since they still don't know about Harry and I'm too scared to talk to them about work much in case I accidentally tell them about my column.

(They still think the guy with me at Jessica's wedding was Jaxon. I haven't corrected them. It's fine. It's all totally fine. It's too late to set the record straight now, anyway. I haven't told them about my occasional hangouts—and, okay, hookups—with Harry, so it's not like I'm really *lying*.)

But, yeah, more fool me for being so utterly obsessed by this other person when *he isn't even my boyfriend*, and *I'm not even sure I want him to be my boyfriend.*

I'd like to think I'm not boy crazy, but the evidence to the contrary is pretty damning. I was never that girl in school who always put on lip gloss and tossed her hair around boys and had a new crush every other week, and I was never that girl who would see a guy she liked around campus at uni and suddenly stalk Facebook groups looking for him and then track down his Instagram to see if he had a girlfriend or if she could slide into his DMs.

What I *am* is that girl who thinks too much and too often about a guy she's dated more than once or twice—something I know from experience, in my thus far unsuccessful dating life.

Personally, I don't think I'm that out of order on this particular occasion.

I mean, just look at the facts: I've been seeing this guy for just over *two months*, and now he hasn't replied to any of my messages since Thursday, and then I finally got a curt reply about how he was "busy with some stuff" and would "catch up with me soon."

"*Catch up with me soon*," I snarl now at Tally, wrestling with the buckle on my shoe. We're at some tiny B and B above a country pub in the middle of nowhere in the Cotswolds, getting ready for the wedding of our friend Lucy. "Like I'm his goddamn colleague or something, not like I'm—well, maybe not his girlfriend, but I'm as good as! Aren't I?"

"It is very weird," she agrees. "And you're sure nothing happened last time you saw him? He didn't say anything, or . . . ?"

Or you didn't screw everything up somehow? goes unsaid.

"Yes!" I give up on my shoe for now and twist around on the bed to face her. "I'm sure! It was totally normal. He came over Monday night, we ordered Chinese food, watched a few episodes of that superhero show on Prime, had sex, went to work the next morning. He kissed me goodbye and everything, said he'd see me Thursday night, and then just—"

"Didn't," Tally finishes for me. She swipes on some lipstick and then, after blotting, pouts at me, frowning, her head cocked to one side. "That *is* weird."

"You don't . . . I mean, you don't think he's—" I swallow the lump in my throat. My palms have started to sweat; I wipe them on the duvet.

Bloody Duncan, getting in my head.

I ask, "You don't think he's seeing another girl, do you?"

"Oh, sweetie, no!" Tally exclaims, face stricken, horrified at the mere idea—and giving away that, actually, it's crossed her mind too. I know her a little too well for her to get away with it, but even as I raise a skeptical eyebrow she barrels on. "Absolutely not! You said he'd deleted his Hookd profile ages ago"—a little white lie, actually, so I could avoid showing it to her during one of our rare morning coffee catch-ups and having her realize Jaxon and Harry are, in fact, not one and the same, because we didn't have time that day to get into all that—"and he told you he didn't use any of the other apps anyway so . . . and you'd have noticed if he was seeing someone else! Who'd have the audacity to start dating another person *three months* into a relationship?"

I think about my trip to the cinema with Harry after Dawn's baby shower, the sex after he came over to help me fix the toilet, how easy it was to hang out with him for dinner last weekend . . .

Oblivious to my blush, Tally continues, "I know it's still a bit casual and early on but even so! No, of course he isn't seeing some-one else. He'll just—maybe he's got something else going on."

"Like what? What's going on that he can't even text me *Have fun at your friend's wedding*, or whatever?"

Tally doesn't have as quick a reply this time, but as we finish getting ready she shares her theories: maybe he's under a lot of stress at work and is just so run-down he hasn't got the energy to text me, or maybe he's in trouble, or maybe there's some family drama and we're "not quite there yet" for him to involve me. Maybe it's a lot of other things.

Or maybe it's the age-old classic: he's met someone else.

That's worse than any outright rejection. It's the insult of being replaced. It's the slap in the face of sorry, but you're just not *good enough*.

And, even from a guy I'm not sure I truly like anymore, that stings.

Twenty-two

Lucy is one of our friends from university. She's the kind of friend where our relationship these days mostly consists of commenting "Looking gorge!" on each other's Instagram photos or whatever. We used to be quite close at uni. She was in the house share with me and Tally in second and third year, and she's how we met Lena; they were in the same course. Except now Lena is one of our best friends, and Lucy . . .

Lucy has a *lot* of other friends, though, as is made clear by the volume of guests at the wedding.

If I was going to be a bitch, I'd say it's less that she's close to so many people and more that she just likes to show off and have everyone fawn over her.

But it's her big day, and my special gift to her on this occasion is to not be a bitch. And the silverware set that Tally, Lena, and I went in on together.

Lena takes up the mantle of bitch quick enough, though, because we've barely entered the cavernous barn where the ceremony is being held before she says quietly, grabbing us both by the arm, "Oh my god, is she serious? All that bullshit about 'sorry, we're keeping costs down and it's just close friends and family so no plus-ones,' when *this* is what she calls close friends and family? I bet you anything this venue cost upward of five grand alone, I'm telling you. The cheek of it!"

Tally joins in, harrumphing, the three of us surveying the packed rows of seats and taking turns spotting other old friends from uni, and I can't say I blame them for being so annoyed. I know it's not that they can't be without their boyfriends for ten minutes but the "low cost" excuse for none of us getting a plus-one.

For once, I get to join them in their righteous anger because I, too, could have brought a plus-one.

I, too, could have flaunted the fact I have a significant other in my life, and therefore must have it all. I remember Lucy's text from a few days ago and her "at last" comment about me having a boyfriend; it makes me grind my teeth just to think about it.

Although, maybe it's for the best. I suppose if Harry had been able to come along, I would have actually had to explain the whole fake-boyfriend thing to the girls and wouldn't have been able to vent to them about how things are actually going with actual Jaxon right now.

I'll explain it at some point. They'll understand. And it'll be fine.

Another day, though. *Any* other day.

"I knew we should have just got her the salt and pepper mills and been done with it," Lena grumbles, adding our expensive silverware set to the large pile on the gifts table. The three of us shuffle away to find some seats.

Despite the fact I'm attending two weddings this month, I can't claim to have been to very many. This is maybe the fourth or fifth I've been to in my whole life. But even I know how overboard it is: Lucy's brother sings, of all things, "My Heart Will Go On" during the ceremony, the vows take a lifetime, there are *three* poetry readings, and the officiant has a novel's worth of lines to read out.

The whole thing is painful, but we plaster on smiles and clap along with everyone else when they're finally pronounced married. For once, I know the girls are as sick of the whole wedding schtick as I am; Tally all but leads the charge from the barn to the field outside where drinks and canapés are being served.

Drinks in hand, the three of us gravitate back to some of our old university friends. There are maybe ten of us, total. Conversation is stilted for the first several minutes because we're all hyperaware of the fact that we used to hang out day-to-day, squeeze into bathroom cubicles together on a night out at a club, argue over someone throwing a rowdy party while some of us still had exams . . . and now we barely talk at all.

But the peach-flavored cocktails making the rounds do a great job of greasing the wheels and after talking about how lovely the ceremony was and reminiscing awkwardly over a few "fond memories" that we force ourselves to remember because it's the only common ground we have right now, the *So what are you up to now!* begins.

On the one hand, this is perfect because everyone loves talking about themselves, and occasionally one of us gets to say, *Oh, and congrats! I saw you just got engaged a few weeks ago!* or, *OMG, I live for your Instagram stories of your pug. So cute!* or, *Lena, god, I saw you had heart surgery a few months ago, that must have been so scary! I remember all those tutor groups you used to miss for doctor's appointments. I'm so glad you're doing all right now!*

On the other, it's a circle of hell.

Three are already married. Another two (counting Lena) are engaged. Four (counting Tally) are living with or in the process of moving in with their significant other, maybe even buying a place together.

There is one single guy, Leon.

"And what about you?" Tally asks him. "Are you seeing anybody right now?"

"No," he says, like it's that easy. "I'm not with anyone at the moment."

I vaguely remember Leon as someone from Lucy and Lena's classes. I say "vaguely" because most of our interactions were on nights out, during which a lot of booze was involved and so the memories are pretty hazy. I remember him being a good dancer and trying to teach me how to swear in Korean after I found out he lived in Seoul until he was like, five or six. I remember him being a great guy, and he seems it now, so I'm surprised that he's single.

I wait for everyone else to grill him about why, or when his last relationship was, or if he's "putting himself out there" like they will inexplicably be comforted by the knowledge that he's at least *trying* to find someone, but they don't. Something about it sets my teeth on edge; I big up my relationship with Jaxon, making it sound much more serious than it is and not mentioning the fact he might be sort of ghosting me right now.

Tally and Lena don't call me out, but I see them exchange a couple of looks, and I staunchly ignore them.

The ten of us end up sitting together for dinner too—all still busy updating everyone on our wonderful, brilliant, successful lives. Everything I say about myself has the same positive spin I'd give it on a first date—unsurprising since these people have become relative strangers, but I still want to impress them, much like meeting a guy after matching on Hookd and exchanging a few messages.

It's exhausting and, worst of all, I don't even know why I'm trying so hard. It's not like I'm going to see them again until Lena's wedding, if then.

Luckily for me, though, Tally and Lena aren't having the best time either. Although in their case, they're more annoyed that Lucy barely gives us more than a "Hello, thanks for coming, isn't my dress gorgeous, have you tried the cake yet!" before flitting off to talk to other people.

"I don't know why she bothered inviting us at all," I say, listening to my best friends bitch quietly about it.

Tally snorts. "Because she can't help but show off. It's all Lucy's world, the rest of us are just living in it. Remember?"

She's not wrong. Now she mentions it, Lucy *was* always kind of like that. It used to annoy us, but we put up with it because she was fun on a night out, always had spare flash cards to lend you, and would volunteer to take the bins out.

In the end, the three of us make an early exit, find a chip shop open late, and pile onto the bed in Lena's room to stuff our faces with greasy food and watch old episodes of *Friends* on an iPad. We're all too irritable and exhausted from the day to talk much, but I don't mind.

Even sitting quietly like this, it just makes me think about how badly I miss spending time with my friends, and how much I love them.

Twenty-three

The morning after Lucy's wedding, I finally hear from Jaxon—apologizing for not talking much lately, hoping I had fun at the wedding, asking if we can reschedule last Thursday's date for later this week. He adds some smiley faces and a few kisses to the text.

"See!" Tally says when I show her. "I knew everything would be fine. You overthink this stuff way too much, Soph. You had nothing to worry about. Maybe you've been a bit off with him, so he's worried about seeming too keen if he's not getting the right vibes from you. You can do that, you know."

"Do what?" I ask, not sure if I'm more surprised or offended.

Tally shrugs, like it's no big deal. "You can be a bit demanding of people sometimes. Set your expectations too high, I mean. Expect it all to be perfect right away."

I can only stare at her, too stunned to speak.

How can I be the one demanding perfection of other people—of the guys I date—when I'm the one who . . .

When *I'm* the one demanding perfection of myself, whatever that looks like in the situation.

But that's not just my fault, I want to scream. It's not like I do it voluntarily. It's only because it feels like everybody *else* always expects so much, expects more, and I'm always pushing to meet *their* expectations: namely, to not be single anymore.

I don't say any of that to Tally, though, and I avoid the topic when we meet up with Lena for breakfast before I drive us all home. Tally must know I don't really want to talk about it, but, later that evening, she sends me a link to an article she thinks might help me gain some new perspective.

It's my most recent column: a scathing, witty takedown of the need to justify your singledom.

Ain't that a kick in the teeth, I think, and don't reply to her. Instead, I channel my energy into assessing the situation with Jaxon, trying to decide if this actually is all my fault. Maybe it's not that I don't like him enough to be in a relationship; maybe I just haven't given him a real chance.

He deserves that, doesn't he? Or at least for me to put in a little bit more effort.

Things with Jaxon *do* get a little better over the next week— better enough that I think Tally's right: I've been overreacting and making it all up. He was busy with work. He went home to see his family on the weekend, which is why I didn't hear from him much. At his suggestion, we go to dinner on Tuesday night at a nice restaurant I mentioned I wanted to try; he's obviously making an effort and making *me* feel like a fool for thinking he wasn't invested.

I wish he hadn't made the effort. It makes it harder for me to figure out if *I'm* invested or not.

Things fizzle into quiet again by the end of the week, his texts once more few and far between. It's work, again, maybe, or his family, that's all.

Whatever it is, it gets a bit easier to forget about it once Harry picks me up to go to his friend Annabelle's wedding on Saturday morning. He's wearing a gray pinstripe suit, the tie a bright shade of sky blue. My lime-green dress, which I'd thought was so pretty and summery in the shop a few weeks ago, clashes with it spectacularly.

"That's a lot of ruffles," Harry says, instead of *hello*, his eyebrows rising higher the longer he looks at my dress.

"I thought they were cute," I mumble, feeling like a prize idiot. I pluck at one of the layers of the skirt awkwardly. I should've known I couldn't pull this off. It always looks better on the mannequin than on an actual human.

"Very cute," he says, a bright grin belying his deadly serious tone. "You look like a very cute pile of fluorescent ruffles."

I shove him gently in the chest. "Shut up. Give me five minutes; I've got a dress I wore to a wedding last week, I can go change—"

"Absolutely not. I'd be ashamed to be seen with you in anything less garish. C'mon, hot stuff, let's go make a statement."

He all but bundles me into the low passenger seat of his Mercedes, where my hot, flushed face is immediately soothed by the AC as I sink into the soft leather seat. I might make snarky comments at Harry every so often about how he mismanages his ample funds, but I will grant him that this car is worth every penny.

"So remind me who these people are?" I ask once we're on the road to some countryside manor hotel thing. I did look up the venue briefly after Harry sent me a photo of the wedding invite, and it's *posh*. Posh enough to make Lucy's look like it was done on a shoestring budget. It makes me wonder exactly what kind of friends Harry has, what kind of world they all live in. Do they all drive cars like this, all have underfloor heating in the bathrooms of their city-center apartments, all fritter money away like it's no object because they have so much of it?

I definitely shouldn't have gone to any old high-street shop for my dress. I should've, like, looked into renting a Chanel number or something.

"Annabelle, she's one of my friends since uni, sort of? We didn't get very friendly until we ended up on the same internship, though. She's great. One of those people you might not talk to for six months but who drops everything to meet you for dinner if you're in town. Kind of like you said about your friend Frankie. You'll love her. Everyone loves her."

"Does she know about me? Or, um, I guess . . . what does she know about me?"

"I told her I was dating someone. Originally the save-the-date came addressed to me and Louisa, obviously, and . . . yeah, anyway, I messaged her to let her know your name for the place cards and stuff."

"Is—" The question is clunky, unfamiliar. "Is she going to be there? Your ex, I mean?"

Harry shakes his head with a breath of laughter, but his hands clench so tight around the steering wheel that his knuckles turn white. "No, thank god. Annabelle was my friend first, so I got to keep her in the divorce, as it were. Speaking of—the fucking *lawyers*, I swear, it's like they *want* us to fight over every little thing. Antagonizing us constantly. I mean, now I say it out loud, obviously they do—the more we fight, the longer this goes on, the more money they make . . . but seriously, we started arguing over who gets to keep *gin glasses* this week. Gin glasses! Never get married, Soph."

I can only stare at him, not knowing what to say except, "That's a great attitude to take to your friend's wedding."

Harry lets out a sudden, loud bark of laughter, the tension seeping out of his body in an instant. I relax, too, only just becoming

aware of how tense I was watching him rant about his divorce pro-
ceedings. His ex-wife is a more common topic of conversation than
his family, but he hasn't talked too much about the *actual* divorce
part beyond mentioning the occasional meeting with his lawyers.

It's on the tip of my tongue to ask him about his family again—
the brother he makes every effort not to mention, the calls from his
mum I've seen him ignore—but now he looks relaxed again, now
there's that easy, dazzling smile on his face, I don't want to spoil it.

He'll talk about it if he wants to.

But today isn't about me taking my turn to play therapist in our
weird little relationship. He's invited me along so he doesn't have to
face an empty seat at the table next to him, so that people ask about
me instead of his ex—because, really, what kind of arsehole would
dare to discuss an ongoing messy divorce when the new girlfriend
is right there? I'm a distraction, a prop, the very same way he was
for me at Jessica's wedding.

Which is A-okay with me. I like Harry, much more than I ever
expected to when I recruited him to be my fake boyfriend. He's so
infuriatingly easy to be around—to be myself around—that actually, I care about him quite a bit.

I just have to remember to keep him—keep *myself*—at arm's
length, because he's not after a real relationship anyway. Maybe
he's even going on other dates—fun flings and raunchy one-night
stands he didn't think were worth mentioning. Probably. He does
keep joking how he's on the rebound.

It's not too hard, so long as I remind myself about all the ways
we're incompatible.

But, you know. He *could* be a little bit less easy to open up to
and care about.

The realization of how I feel about Harry, even just as a friend (with harebrained-scheme benefits), trickles over me slowly, like warming up when you sink into a hot bath: that I *like* him, I care about him, I want to be around him, not just spend time with him.

I don't feel that way about Jaxon.

And I'm not saying I want to ask Harry to be my boyfriend— which, a) he isn't interested in, and, b) didn't a conversation with my mum already establish that being as fundamentally incompatible as we apparently are wouldn't work out anyway?—but I *do* know that whatever I have with him, the forced affection I have with Jaxon pales in comparison.

Harry is effortless.

And they *do* say opposites attract, right?

I try not to think too hard about it, or about Jaxon and his newest attempt at pseudo-ghosting me, for the rest of the drive. Instead, I focus only on the way Harry's laugh makes my chest feel warm, and the crinkle at the corner of his eye when he smirks at his own jokes, and the spark that fizzes through me when he puts a hand on my thigh every so often.

• • •

"There's a *seating chart* for the ceremony," I hiss at Harry in a mixture of horror and awe. "What do they think this is, New York Fashion Week?"

"It could well be," he muses, unbothered by it. "Annabelle got styling credits in *Vogue* a couple of months ago, you know."

My jaw drops, and Harry laughs before dropping a kiss at the corner of my mouth, his arm slipping around my waist to escort me to my assigned seat. I was right to wonder at what kind of friends Harry's got, and how posh this wedding is going to be. The guests look like they could be waiting for a show at New York Fashion

Week too—there's something glamorous and sophisticated and distinguished about the entire affair, which has tasteful flower arrangements and a two-piece string duet playing classical music.

The fiancé (nearly husband) is some tech guy who got rich on cryptocurrency, and Annabelle does something mysterious and glamorous at a fashion studio part-time and is also a part-time influencer. Like, a *real* one. The Gigi Hadid kind. Or at least a bargain-basement Gigi Hadid, which is still pretty fancy. She has almost three hundred thousand followers, either way. I looked her up on Instagram on the drive over after Harry mentioned it, so casually, like it was so *not a big deal*.

I'm too stunned by the entire thing to even think about feeling jealous; it's such a completely different world that I can't even begin to comprehend it. Like my mum, Annabelle clearly lives on another plane of existence that us mere mortals can only glimpse from afar.

But to be fair to Annabelle, I see lots of people here who can only be family, and Harry points out several familiar faces from their university days. Anna Wintour is nowhere in sight. It's every bit as big and busy as Lucy's wedding, but from what Harry's said, I start to think maybe Annabelle's only been so generous with the invitations because she *wanted* to see all these people and invite them to enjoy the day with her. She was certainly generous with the plus-ones, at least.

Annabelle and her soon-to-be husband, Patrick, have also got a no phones rule for the entire wedding. Not just the ceremony, but dinner afterward and then the reception tonight too. For all her influencer-ing, today will be "totally present," and there won't be so much as an Instagram story until after the fact.

Secretly, I prefer this concept of no phones to the way Lena and Johnny are trying to come up with the perfect hashtag for *their* wedding. I know it's the done thing (Jessica had one for hers: #MrCandMrsJ1906) but that doesn't mean I have to like it. Even for Lena's sake.

Annabelle and Patrick, total strangers to me until the ceremony begins, really do make a beautiful couple. He cries when he sees her coming down the aisle in a simple, fitted white gown with an intricate lace bodice and small diamond stud earrings. She snorts with laughter during his vows, which is a disgusting sound because she's also trying not to cry so it's sort of snotty.

They look at each other as if the rest of us don't exist, and it's like something out of a movie. It's a look that moves the entire assembly to tears. It's a look that punches me right in the chest and knocks all the air out of my lungs because *I want that, I want that so badly.*

My sort-of boyfriend won't even text me back, and I don't think I want to date him anymore anyway.

What if I never have anybody who looks at me like that?

Harry looks at me a little bit like that, sometimes. But maybe that's just part of his fake-boyfriend act—commitment to the role, as it were. I'm sure that's all it is.

The ceremony is, all things considered, simple and straight-forward. The cellist and violinist play something sweet and traditional as Annabelle walks down the aisle. There is a single poem from the groom's sister, and the bride's grandmother reads a short prayer; the whole thing wraps up in the time it took Lucy to just read out her vows. Everyone bursts into applause and a chorus of cheers when the bride and groom kiss, and then we all shuffle outside to throw the eco-friendly biodegradable confetti we're provided with on the way out of the building.

Then it's picture time, and drinks are provided. Seating (*actual* upholstered seating) has been arranged outdoors for everyone before dinner and a pop-up bar has been set up; a couple of catering staff circulate with dainty canapés everyone snatches up while we drink expensive champagne and various groups of people are summoned by the photographer's assistant.

I spend the entire time on Harry's arm, basking in the late-August sunshine and my own perceived novelty. Strangers fawn over me, and one particularly stunning lady wearing an *actual* Chanel suit tell me she loves my dress, which makes my day.

And because they're strangers, when they ask what I do, I'm not afraid to tell them I have a popular column online about relationships. I don't go into details, but somehow the more vague I am, the more impressed they are, which only bolsters my confidence. I dazzle them, make them laugh, make women put their hand on my arm and tell Harry, "Gosh, she's just *lovely*. Don't mess this one up!"

That happens a couple of times—well-intentioned jokes from old friends about his divorce, wishing him better luck this time around, or a jovial wagging finger and a warning not to let his eyes wander again, and each time Harry laughs a little too loudly, a little too brashly. He turns rigid at my side then tips his drink down his throat to numb the sting of it.

The fifth time it happens, I rub a hand up and down his arm and give his shoulder a squeeze, and when I've got his full attention, I lean up to give him a kiss.

"You've got this," I tell him.

"I might punch the next person who makes a joke about keeping you away from my brother."

"You know I've only got eyes for you, sweetie," I say, only half joking, and kiss him again. Drawing back, I move my hand into his, locking our fingers together and holding tight—an anchor for him this time around. "Do you want me to spill some champagne on someone and make a scene to take the heat off you?"

He laughs, the hardened edges of his face softening. "Thanks for the offer, but I'm okay."

"All right, well, just let me know if anything changes and I need to smash a piece of wedding cake into the bride's dress later."

Thankfully, though, Harry doesn't ask, because now the initial "jokes" are out of the way, nobody attempts them a second time. Which is good because I don't think I could have smashed wedding cake into the bride's dress anyway. She's so lovely, I couldn't bear it.

Dinner takes place at long tables draped in expensive white cloth and more tasteful floral arrangements; Harry and I are sitting by some of his and Annabelle's mutual friends, whom we caught up with earlier.

During the main course Annabelle flits from table to table to see the people she didn't get a chance to talk to during the photos earlier. She's waylaid constantly on her way around the room—everyone wants a piece of her today, and I can't blame them. Even though I haven't really had a conversation with Annabelle beyond one quick "Congratulations!," when I see her heading in our direction I get a flutter of excitement. Harry was right: everybody *does* love her, and her charisma and openness make it easy to see why.

She is truly the belle of the ball and, for all the extravagance of the wedding, for all her influencer-ing, she's a much more down-to-earth bride than Lucy was last week.

Annabelle greets us, blushing under the compliments that pour from all of us at the "uni friends and their other halves" section of table and telling us how glad she is that we were all able to make it today, how glad she is that we're here to celebrate with her and Patrick and that she hopes we're having a good time. She makes her way around our table, hugging each of us and having a quick catch-up in a way that makes me wonder if she's got some kind of internal alarm that prompts her to wrap up and move on every sixty seconds, or if, in her line of work, she's just so well-versed at networking that this is second nature to her now.

Still, when it's my turn, she hugs me, warm and tight, and wants to hear all about *me*. Not a single reference to the mere existence of Harry's ex passes her lips, and she talks to me like we're old friends. She clearly has a knack for making other people feel special; she's the kind of person it feels good to be around even when she's the one basking in the limelight, like she is now.

Frankie Two could do with taking a leaf out of Annabelle's book, I think. I've been too scared to message Frankie One much since her rant at the housewarming. I bet Annabelle would never do that to Patrick's friends. I'm glad she's not doing it to me, when she knew Louisa the ex-wife and probably has her opinions on Harry's whole divorce thing.

It's a nice wedding. A *great* wedding. It puts every other wedding I've ever attended to shame (sorry, Jessica) even though I know exactly one person here.

But, to Harry's credit, he's a pretty great person to know.

And I don't mind admitting to myself that I like pretending he's *my* person, at least for today.

Twenty-four

After a few more days of brief, infrequent texts, I finally manage to see Jaxon again on Wednesday, meeting him for dinner after work.

Under the circumstances, I'm not sure if this is the sort of date where we'll actually get to have dinner. I wish I could say it's because the sexual chemistry will be so intense after over a week of not seeing each other that we'll want to get out of there as soon as possible, but I have to face the reality that he might only be seeing me to dump me. There was something in the tone of his message when he finally replied, finally suggested we meet up, that set alarm bells ringing.

Can you dump someone if you haven't even asked them to be your girlfriend yet?

I feel queasy all day before the date. I keep sweating and my heart thunders sickeningly every time I think about it. My manager notices, but once I explain that I might be heading to a "breakup date" this evening, she's more interested in psyching me up than making sure I forget all about it and focus on sending emails instead.

On her advice—and Lena's, too—I make sure to put in considerable effort. Lena says it's so he knows what he's giving up if he wants to dump me; my manager Jenny says it's so I feel so bloody good about myself I won't even care if he does. Tally sees my messages in the group chat but I guess is too busy to reply.

The problem isn't that I think he's going to break up with me. It's that I don't know *why*, or what I've done wrong. It's that I think maybe we do need to call it quits but I'm still kind of apprehensive—and by "kind of apprehensive" I mean totally fucking terrified of losing my one solid chance in a while at a real relationship, because Harry doesn't count.

I get ready for the date, and hope that an epiphany will strike, and sort of hope that Jaxon *does* break up with me so that I don't have to make a decision about him.

I keep my outfit fairly casual, since it's only dinner at some chain restaurant—jeans-and-a-nice-top kind of casual—but I take time to curl my hair and put on my favorite bold lipstick and some cute jewelry to elevate the look.

Just before I get to the restaurant, I check my reflection in a shop window.

It doesn't fill me with the *oh yeah, he's making a* big *mistake, I'm amazing* vibes I hoped it would: the elasticated cuffs on my sleeves are chafing my wrists, making me fidget, and the strap on one of my sandals looks like it might break any second. Between that and the *I'm about to get dumped* premonition, my confidence is beginning to fail me now I'm almost there.

Then I hear, "Soph! Hey!"

And look up to see Jaxon a little way ahead of me, approaching from the opposite direction. He looks good: jeans and a crisp white short-sleeved shirt that he manages to pull off as smart-casual. His hair is a bit flat and his temples and nose a little shiny with sweat, but who can blame him in this heat? He pushes his round glasses up his nose and smiles broadly as he waves at me. I wait for the butterflies, but they never come.

That's not the look of a guy who never wants to see me again, right?

Do I look like a girl who never wants to see him again?

Do I *want* to look like that girl?

I wave back awkwardly, trying to rearrange my features into something more neutral in case he can read my thoughts. "Hi."

Jaxon doesn't hesitate to wrap an arm around my waist and draw me in for a short but sweet kiss.

I want to be giddy about it, but all I can think is *Oh no, my lipstick*, and *He's not as good a kisser as Harry*.

Jaxon lifts his head but doesn't move back. Someone nearby mutters under their breath, grumbling about how we're blocking the way, but if Jaxon notices he ignores it. His lips curve into a smile. "Hi."

"Hi," I say again, too confused to say anything else.

"I missed you."

That's a bit bloody rich.

But I reply, "I missed you too."

"Shall we go in?"

"Yeah."

He lets me go and moves ahead to get the door, holding it open for me. I take the opportunity to shake myself and clear my head, doing my best to get it together.

Wasn't I convinced we were over up until about thirty seconds ago? Haven't I been irritated and panicky and stressed out about "us" for the last week? Wasn't I mad at him, and didn't I plan to give him a piece of my mind about how he's treated me lately?

Oh, but he holds the door open for me and then takes my hand as we're shown to our table, and I guess I've set the bar very low because I find myself wanting to give him the benefit of the doubt. *Genuinely* wanting, not just trying to convince myself of that or telling my friends as much so I don't have to deal with the alternative.

Jaxon orders a beer; I get a Coke.

The whole thing feels surreal, like some kind of fever dream. Like I'm floating above the table looking down and seeing myself sitting here on this date with a guy who's gone from texting me *Goodnight, beautiful xxx* to hardly speaking to me, a guy I'm only dating because . . . because, what? Because on paper, he's all the right things? Because it means I'll get to tell other people I have a boyfriend, so they finally stop making me feel less than for *not* having one?

In a sudden burst of clarity, I have a vision of myself twenty, thirty, fifty years down the line, having a family and a house and a dog and a whole life with Jaxon just to shut *everyone else* up, and it feels so fucking ridiculous I don't know what I'm even still doing here.

After the drinks arrive and we've ordered food, I finally summon the willpower to cut through the polite small talk we've been exchanging.

"So what's been up with you?"

"Sorry?"

Yeah, you should be.

"You've barely texted me lately and you canceled our date. I haven't seen you. Is everything okay?"

Jaxon takes a sip of his beer and adjusts the cutlery and napkin set out on his side of the table. His brow furrows and he looks up at me from behind his glasses, all quizzical and cute.

"Yeah. Yeah, everything's fine. I'm . . . wow, I didn't . . . I'm sorry,

Sophie. I didn't even really notice. Things have just been crazy at work, and I had some plans with friends, and then you were away over the weekend again. Just life getting in the way. I'm sorry."

I grit my teeth, fighting the flare of anger that rises from the pit of my stomach, threatening to claw out of my throat in a vicious, snappy stream of words. He makes it sound so *okay*, so *reasonable*, but—

I don't want to push. I don't want to question him. I don't want to sound like the paranoid, overbearing helicopter girlfriend who doesn't let him have his own life. Maybe I'm overthinking. Maybe Tally's right and I've been demanding perfection without even realizing it. But it's not fair. It's *not fair* of me to have slept with Harry, maybe, but that doesn't make Jaxon's hot-and-cold attitude any better. It doesn't excuse *him* for acting like a flake.

It doesn't excuse me for continuing to date him just for the sake of saying I'm seeing someone. I'm not just stringing him along; I'm stringing myself along too.

After his apology, Jaxon reaches across the table to take my hand, brushing his thumb across my skin and giving me an easygoing sort of smile. The same smile I liked so much in his Hookd profile originally.

The words spill out before I let myself get drawn in by the promise of his hand on mine, the potential in that smile, the comfort of everyone else's relief when I can tell them I officially have a boyfriend.

"I think we need to call it quits, Jaxon." I look him in the eyes, unashamed and unflinching. "I don't think this is working out between us. You text all day, then you don't text for days, you say you can't wait to see me again but then you cancel our plans . . . It's like you only want to date me when it's convenient for you. And I don't *know* what I'm looking for, but I know it's not fair to either of us to try to use you to figure that out."

"Sophie . . . "

He sounds shocked. He *looks* shocked. Eyes wide, mouth hanging open, all kicked-puppy.

But he doesn't look exactly upset either. Maybe he's not.

I try to gather my thoughts after my impromptu monologue, try to figure out how to explain it to him without sounding like a total bitch. I could easily use Harry as an excuse, say I've met someone else, say I just don't think there's a spark, but I know how hurt I was by the mere idea Jaxon had replaced me with someone else, and I don't want to do that to him.

In the end, I don't know what else to say, so I don't say anything.

And eventually, Jaxon closes his gaping mouth, looking off somewhere behind me, and then nods. "Okay."

"Okay?"

"Okay," he repeats, and I stare at him until he says, half joking, "Was I supposed to fight for us? Make some passionate plea and beg you to stay? Give me some credit, Sophie. You're right, I think we're just in different places right now."

Part of me wants to know what kind of place he thinks I'm in—if he thinks I was too serious too quick by asking him to be my date to Jessica's wedding, or if he thinks I've been "off" with him like Tally said and kept him at arm's length.

But I don't suppose it matters either way, really.

There's an awkward silence before Jaxon gets up. He wishes me all the best, so I say, "You too. Good luck out there," and he leaves money for his half of the bill. I watch him go, too awkward to walk out with him, and then, as discreetly as I can, I beckon a waiter over and ask for the food to go.

I suddenly feel everyone else's eyes on me, like they all know Jaxon and I broke up. Like, in this alternate, self-centered reality, they all *care*.

I know they don't care. Probably, nobody's even noticed. But the thought of staying and eating dinner alone is too mortifying. I pay the bill quickly and take the little cardboard boxes of food back to the bus stop and eat both of them once I'm back home in my flat, alone again.

September

To Harry & Guest

Come celebrate

ANTHONY'S TENTH BIRTHDAY

with us!

1 p.m.—5 p.m.
Saturday, September 18

Our boy turns ten this September, and we'd love it if you could come join us to celebrate this milestone birthday!

There will be some snacks and party games, and pets are welcome!

Dress code is smart-casual.

Please inform us of any dietary requirements when you RSVP.

See you there!
Penny & Ieuan

Twenty-five

What do single people have to celebrate?

Views on the abundance of parties for couples from our
Dating & Relationships columnist

"Well, you've got to kiss a few frogs before you find your prince, haven't you?" Tally says chirpily as we queue up for coffee. So far, September has been muggy and miserable: it's rained all week but the heat hasn't broken. Tally's hair is wild in the humidity, even pulled back in a ponytail. My soaked raincoat is sticking to my bare arms and dripping onto my legs; I'm starting to regret wearing a dress today.

Costa doesn't prove much of a respite, with everybody piling in to get out of the rain on their way to work; it's steamy, the air thick, everybody a little irritable.

I'm right there along with them, but it's not the weather or the briefcase digging into the back of my leg that's bugging me—it's Tally and her *kiss a few frogs* comment.

When she doesn't react to my deadpan stare, I throw my head back and sigh loudly, letting her know exactly how much I appreciate the sentiment. "It's adding up to be a lot of frogs at this point."

And let's face it: her boyfriend Sam is hardly a prince.

Well. I mean. If you're talking the entitled, misogynistic kind, sure. He's a real Henry VIII.

But obviously I can't say that, because you never tell your friends how awful their partner is when they apparently have their reasons for loving them, so instead I tell her, "I just feel like I wasted so much time with Jaxon. Three months! I could be, like, a third of the way to having a baby in that time. And people we know are having babies now, Talls. *On purpose.* That's like, a real thing. Three months is ages to sort-of date someone I only sort-of liked."

"I don't know why you wasted so much time if you didn't really like him." She shrugs, busy perusing the drinks menu now, like we both don't know exactly what she'll order anyway.

"Why I—because . . . because . . . " I stop and take a sharp, short breath, and remind myself that Tally's happily loved up and has been for a while; she's forgotten what it's like to be single. She certainly doesn't know what it's like to be single in your midtwenties and watch everyone else moving on with their lives while you get left behind and forgotten about. She doesn't know the burden of the weight of everyone else's pity when they find out you're single, the pressure to find someone and just settle down already, even if she did love my column at the end of August about the contradiction of telling people "don't settle for just anyone!" when the whole act of *getting* a partner is literally called "settling down."

We have to stop then anyway to order our drinks. Tally pays for them both using loyalty points and when I point out a table that's free, she says, "Okay, but only for two minutes. I told you I couldn't meet up for long today."

She did, in fairness, but beyond Lucy-from-uni's wedding it's felt like so long since we've actually *seen* each other, so I came in a whole hour early just to match her commute and steal fifteen minutes in this noisy, crowded Costa with her.

I miss my best friend.

"Do you want to do something this week? Or this weekend? Get drinks or go for dinner, or . . . or you could come over and I could cook, or I could come over yours and we could get takeaway, or—"

Tally pulls a face, and it reminds me of guys who, when you say at the end of a date you've had a nice time, have already planned how to reject you. It's a knife twisting in my stomach; I breathe through it and slip on a casual, carefree mask as she starts to talk.

"I'm *so* sorry. I'd love to, but things are just a bit mad this week. Things with Sam are . . . we booked that little trip to Brighton this weekend, remember? We're both just superstressed with the mortgage and the move, and the contracts exchanging any time now in the next few weeks."

"Oh, god, no, totally," I gush. Can she tell it sounds fake, or is she willfully ignoring it the same way I am? "You did tell me. My bad. I want all the pics from there!"

"We'll find another time," she says, smiling at me a bit too earnestly. It's a warped version of her usual smile, something I'm not so used to seeing. It's like looking at her through frosted glass, and the knife in my stomach suddenly yanks up into my chest, burying itself deep. My best friend feels further away than ever, and it's worse heartbreak than any romantic breakup I've ever experienced. "I'm sure I'll have a spare evening at some point before the move, maybe if Sam's got plans with his mates or something. And if you don't have any dates. But, oh my god, yes, we were talking about Jaxon. What were you saying? About carrying on with dating him or something?"

Is she changing the subject because she can sense these fractures in our friendship too? Or because she actually wants to know?

I'd like to believe it's the latter, so I grasp it with both hands—even if I can't quite make her understand the truth, I can give her enough of it.

"He was great on paper," I explain to her. "And I had a good time on the dates; we got on well. It was . . . it wasn't like there were all these red flags or I didn't think he was a decent guy or like he was rubbish in bed, or anything."

Tally turns to squint at me, her whole face scrunching up. "So you kept seeing him because you didn't have a reason *not* to? Oh my god. Babe, you *have* to read that dating column I sent you, it'll speak to you *so much*. Don't you want sparks? Romance? Someone who makes you feel all warm and fuzzy inside?"

I stare at her. Blink. Watch her set down her coffee and wait expectantly for my answer. And I think about the date I've already got organized for this evening, a guy I matched with last night on Hookd while rewatching old episodes of *Queer Eye*.

"Tally," I tell her honestly, "at this point, I'd settle for someone to make me feel warm just because they've sat on the sofa next to me for an evening after work. I think sometimes I'd even be happy to settle for Mr. Completely Bloody Wrong For Me as long as it meant I got to have someone in my life like everybody else."

• • •

Her voice rings in my ear all morning and well into the afternoon. *Don't you want sparks?*

Don't I want sparks? Of course I bloody do. Doesn't everybody? The romance media industry isn't so consistently popular because it touts great tales of finding a partner who will phone up the internet provider for you when the router has that weird orange blinking light on it. We've all been sold on sparks, on romance and wonder and soul mates. Of course I want that. Of course I hope to find it when I meet these guys from dating apps in real life for the first time.

There are sparks with Harry. Or—maybe not *sparks* so much as chemistry.

Not just sexual chemistry, obviously, but that too. Even though we talk most days, I've seen him a bunch of times outside of weddings and Auntie Dawn's baby shower, but not since breaking up with Jaxon.

And ooh, I think. Now I've broken up with Jaxon . . . well, I at least won't have to feel guilty if we *do* hook up. I regretted not sleeping with Harry the last few times I saw him, including after Annabelle's wedding. All the casual touches that have been reined in lately can finally add up to something more, like maybe him shifting that hand on my leg up to my hip and inside my clothes while he kisses his way up my neck and . . .

Almost like he can sense I'm thinking about him—and god, if he can, *please* don't let him know I was thinking explicitly about having sex with him again—my computer pings with an email from Harry.

Is this the equivalent of Mitch adding me on LinkedIn—Harry sliding into my work inbox?

I prepare myself for something totally boring, maybe him having forwarded me an article like "Five Tips on How to Ask Your Boss for a Promotion" (which he has actually sent me already, after I talked to him about maybe speaking to Jenny about getting more responsibility when she's on maternity leave).

But the email is the forward of an invitation, to someone called

Anthony's tenth birthday party, sent to Harry from someone called Ieuan who, based on their emails, works at the same company as him. There's no accompanying message from Harry, but I already know exactly what this is—it's another summons to be his fake girlfriend for the day.

And only a few seconds later, my phone lights up with Harry's name on the screen.

"Hey," he says in a rush, "did you get—"

"Your email? Yeah, I'm just looking at it now."

I reread the invite on my computer screen again and lean back in my chair, adjusting my hold on my phone at my ear.

"So are you free?" Harry asks, pleading with me.

As if I have plans. Harry knows how vacant my social calendar is—hell, he knows how vacant my *any kind* of calendar is. I go to work, I crash out on the sofa with the TV or social media, or, if I'm feeling a little more motivated, a book or some photography vlogs, and every so often my friends or family decide to monopolize my time. The most I've had on this month was an unplanned trip to the Midlands on the weekend because Auntie Dawn went into labor a bit early and had the baby. Mum flew back and the two of us dropped everything to go visit an adorable, pink baby Poppy, but I'm not due to visit again until next month, when Mum's home again. (Less by choice this time and more simply due to the fact Auntie Dawn and Auntie Janice have a bunch of friends who want to come visit.)

Still—it's nice to be asked if I'm free, for once.

"Please?"

Voice dripping in sarcasm, I say, "You know, I'm starting to think you're just using me to show off some hot young girlfriend to your co-workers, to make yourself look good."

"Hot?" he scoffs. "Don't push it. I've seen you when you haven't washed your hair in almost a week, don't forget. Hot mess, maybe."

Oof.

He's not wrong, even if he's only joking.

And since he's not wrong—and he does only mean it as a joke—I give him a pass and answer his original question.

"Of course I'm free," I tell him. The e-vite he's forwarded me from his colleague Ieuan is marked as having been sent in August, just a few days after we went to Annabelle's wedding. Noticing it again makes me roll my eyes; the party is this weekend.

"So you'll come with me?"

As if I'm going to say no.

But my split second of silence is apparently a prompt for him to start divulging an entire backstory about how there's a group of people that work with him and even though he thinks they're boring and annoying a lot of the time, they're "convenience" friends— friends through circumstance—and they invited him along to include him and they saw his new girlfriend (me) on his Instagram at the wedding with him and obviously then he told them about me so they encouraged him to come along and bring me, too, and now he can't look rude and say *no*.

"Obviously"—but not to me. We've taken a few "couple" photos together and I know he's posted some on his Instagram and his Facebook page (on his *Facebook*, I swear, what an old man), but I guess I didn't really think of him telling people about me.

It's quite a flattering concept, actually.

"I'll come with you. You can pick me up, though."

"Yes! Oh, Soph, you're a lifesaver. Thank you for compromising all your morals and being my arm candy, a favor I obviously am too proud to ever return. God, I just . . . these people, you know?"

He lets out a long-suffering sigh that I can relate to, although I get the idea when he says "these people" he doesn't mean the kind of people who constantly ask why he's single and take him for granted.

I was totally on board until now. Wary, I swing side to side slightly in my swiveling desk chair, expending some nervous energy. A frown slips onto my face.

"When you say 'these people,' what kind of people are we talking about exactly?"

"You know. Just—" He huffs again, and I just *know* he's rolling his eyes. "You know Bridget Jones?"

"What, they all wear big knickers and make blue soup?"

"No, like . . . well, probably. I bet they'd serve up blue soup and call it gourmet. I mean like when she goes to dinner, and everyone's coupled up."

"Oh!" I say, understanding now—and then, *"Oh,"* because I understand. "Please, please tell me they're not all smug marrieds. Oh my god, is that what you were? Were you one of those haughty, self-important people who wrapped up your whole personality in being married?"

I mean it as a joke, but Harry's hesitant silence on the other end of the phone makes me instantly regret saying it. The guy I've known is a bit carefree, bordering on reckless rather than spontaneous, and a little lost, maybe, too. He loves his job (or, enough to throw himself into it and do way too much overtime) and always has some mate to call up for a drink after work, always has something new and interesting to talk about. It's hard to think of him as someone who would sit at a dinner party discussing mortgage rates and the cost of childcare, or whatever "those people" talk about.

It reminds me again that he's just looking for someone to take the edge off how lonely he feels these days, how what we have isn't real by any stretch of the imagination. And how, maybe, that's why he works so much and always has a friend to hang out with. I feel a pang of pity for him—until I realize I've been doing basically the same thing with all my Hookd dates, and I cringe.

Quickly, I go on, "Just so you know, you owe me big-time."

"Noted. And, uh, while I'm racking up a tab of IOUs . . . "

"What now?" I ask, like I don't owe *him* plenty of IOUs already.

"Could you pick up a present? It's just, you know, I'm out of town the rest of the week for this press tour, and . . . "

My eyebrows go up and I purse my lips. Harry clears his throat, sensing my irritation.

"And Louisa used to sort all that kind of stuff out," he confesses then, confirming my suspicions. I guess it's easy when there's a gift registry, like for Auntie Dawn's baby shower. It's also probably a lot easier when you don't forget about a party until the week of.

Not that I know anything about buying gifts for children either. Dawn and Nadine's babies are proof—I've agonized over endless listicles trying to decide what to buy *them*, and they're family.

"What does this kid like?"

"I don't know. They go on a lot of weekends away in the country and they're always hiking and stuff. Uh . . . Ieuan said he's always singing along to the radio. Huge Adele fan, apparently. A CD or something? Or do ten-year-olds have Spotify now?"

The sing-along comment sparks an idea, a story Lena told me once about a childhood birthday present. Well, she was a teenager, but close enough.

Tucking the phone between my cheek and shoulder, I'm already typing *eBay* into the search bar on my computer.

"How much do you like these people, exactly?"

"Why?"

"Humor me."

"Between us? Not a whole fucking lot, Soph. Like I said, they're convenience friends—and honestly, they're Louisa's friends more than mine. She used to work here, so, yeah. They were her friends first, but I guess they're feeling magnanimous. Otherwise, they want to pick you apart and mock the both of us behind our backs."

"Excellent."

I click to purchase one "gently used" children's karaoke machine.

Twenty-six

Sliding into the passenger seat of Harry's car, I once again appreciate the smooth leather, the sleek dashboard, the low and barely noticeable hum of the engine. It never gets old.

"You look nice," Harry tells me.

"My best Bridget Jones look," I joke. It's actually the same dress I wore to Lucy's wedding—luckily, the weather is still warm and the rain has finally decided to let up, so I can get away with it. I even cleaned the grass stains off my sandals; and maybe if nobody looks too closely, they'll mistake my five-quid sunglasses for Dior or something.

The invite said smart-casual, but based on the way Harry talked about these colleagues, and the friends I've met so far, I'm guessing it's a safe bet to lean into the "smart" side of that.

Harry gives a melodramatic gasp, tilting his head so I can see his eyes glittering over the top of his sunglasses as he fixes me with a smirk. "Even the big knickers? Don't tempt me, Soph, we're already running late as it is."

He reaches a hand over, fingers catching the skin of my thigh near the slit in the skirt and ghosting up my leg. Warmth pools in my stomach and I'm tempted to let him carry on, see how far he'll take this, but I push his hand away before either of us gets too carried away. Laughing, Harry puts the car in gear and pulls out onto the road, but not before winking at me and promising, "Later, then."

I know he's not my boyfriend, and this is all pretend and all for convenience, but a girl could really get used to this.

A little while into the drive, I start peppering Harry with questions about the people I'm about to meet, but he's less forthcoming with information than he was about Annabelle and their mutual friends. I keep trying, determined to wheedle things out of him until he cuts me off with a laugh.

"I was joking about the whole 'pick you apart' thing, you know. Well, mostly. They're not going to quiz you."

"But I'm your 'girlfriend'"—I add air quotes around it—"I should know these kinds of things about your friends. Even if they're just work friends."

"*I* should know these things," he says, with such a deliberate tone that I realize he's correcting me. He switches lanes on the motorway then cuts me a quick look, not quite ashamed of himself but more resigned. "Like I said, they were really Louisa's friends. I can carry a conversation with them when I need to, but mostly I don't talk to them unless it's the usual office small talk. I couldn't tell you anyone's favorite movie, where their kids go to school, or where they went on holiday this summer."

"That *is* office small talk," I say. Even I know Isaac's favorite movie. (It is, to my continual astonishment, the 2005 *Pride & Prejudice*.)

Harry inclines his head, then amends, "Then I don't like them enough to retain the information."

"If you don't like them, why are we going to their party?"

"It was kind of hard to turn down the invite. Plus . . . "

He trails off with a grumble, and a grimace I've come to recognize. *Plus*, he means, *it's something else to rub in Louisa's face.*

This is usually the point where I wait for the storm clouds gathering over his head to blow over, but this time I pounce on it, my conversation with Tally the other morning still nagging in the back of my mind. "How did you meet Louisa?"

"Huh?" Distracted by driving and caught off guard by my question, Harry shrugs. "Online. Doesn't everyone?"

Oh.

I'm kind of disappointed. I guess I was hoping for something . . . more. Something *else.*

Something to suggest that maybe my love life was only going so badly because I needed a good old-fashioned IRL meet-cute.

I try again. "How did you know she was the one?"

He snorts. "Did you have a few predrinks before I picked you up, Soph? C'mon. Obviously she wasn't, or we'd still be married."

"Well, yeah, but . . . I mean, you must've liked her enough at first to want to keep dating her. To think it was worth moving in together, getting married, all that stuff, you know? You guys were together for a long time. What was it about her that made you want to do all that?"

Harry cuts me a brief, sidelong look. "I know you're not asking me about Louisa. What's your actual question?"

Damn it.

I'm starting to think Harry might know me better than I know myself when it comes to things like this. Or he's a better listener than I give him credit for, when it comes to all the times I whine to him about how difficult dating is.

"What made you want to go on a second date with her? A third, fourth, fifth?" I huff, twisting slightly to face him. The seat belt cuts into the side of my neck. "Why are all my dates such complete failures?"

Harry gives a casual shrug and a noncommittal grunt of "I dunno," leaving me staring plaintively at him until he gives in. "I *don't* know. I'm not there, am I?"

"Tally and Lena always just say they're obviously not the right guys or it'd work out. But it's like, no matter how much I keep trying, none of them are."

"Who's to say their boyfriends are Mr. Right?" Harry says. "Maybe they're just right *enough*. Relationships are about compromise, after all. Maybe you're just not compromising. Not settling down, like you said in your last column."

"Not compromising? On what?" I don't think I've got anything left to compromise on, have I? "I already extended my radius on Hookd, *and* I set up a first date with that guy who got kicked off first on the last season of *The Apprentice* even though I thought he was a complete arsehole on the show. I gave him the benefit of the doubt, didn't I?"

"Sure. But it still didn't work out, did it?"

"We didn't click. And he took like, six phone calls during our date, only to make a snide comment when I looked at my phone to check the time. Hypocrite."

"See? So you weren't willing to compromise for him, lower your standards, or anything."

I frown. "Tally and Lena didn't lower their standards for their boyfriends. Everyone always says not to settle. Like, don't accept less than you want or deserve or whatever. Isn't that the same thing?"

Although there is the whole Lena/Helena debacle, and Tally's boyfriend is a right prat sometimes, so . . .

"Relationships are about compromise, but maybe that's not

always a good thing. I'm not saying you *should*, just maybe that's what other people are doing. Look at me and Louisa. She told me when we were splitting up that she knows her worth. I think that's what you're like too."

"Too good for anybody?"

Harry snorts. "Too good to waste your time on guys you don't actually like. Too good to settle for Mr. Right Enough. I wouldn't stress about it too much, Soph. Honestly. Look, you're good at being single—not like me, so desperate for company and the illusion of intimacy that I agreed to be some random girl's fake boyfriend for a wedding."

I try to laugh at the joke. I must do a good enough job because that's where the conversation ends.

I'd like to think he's right. I really, honestly would.

But if that was true, I wouldn't keep matching with anyone I found remotely attractive or interesting on dating apps; I wouldn't keep going on dates even when I've got low expectations for them.

I wouldn't keep hoping that this time, it might work out.

• • •

"It's Charlotte, isn't it?"

My smile freezes in place, a muscle ticking in my jaw. I'm enveloped by a cloud of expensive, floral perfume as our hostess, Penny, air-kisses my cheek and promptly gets my name wrong.

"Sophie," Harry corrects her before I can. His arm is wrapped around my waist, the weight of his touch making my skin tingle, and he tucks me a little closer into his side. I hug the carefully wrapped box with our present in it a bit tighter, afraid I'll drop it.

"Sophie! Of course. I'm so sorry." Penny gives a light, tinkling laugh and shrugs one shoulder, looking at Harry with what looks at first to be affection but which I quickly notice is thinly veiled distaste.

It's much less veiled and more open when she looks my outfit up and down. Her tailored beige linen trousers and white blouse look effortless, stylish—making me look try-hard by comparison. She looks like someone who spends summer in the Hamptons. I bet she has a copy of *Vogue* somewhere in the house; I bet she has coffee table books for the aesthetic, not dog-eared romance novels stacked haphazardly underneath a wonky IKEA TV stand.

The house is huge, all open-plan with sparkling floors, clean lines, and big windows, but we hardly have time to look before Ieuan (a fair degree friendlier than his wife) escorts us through to their sprawling garden with its neatly trimmed lawn and posh patio furniture.

I look around now, tuning out whatever Ieuan and Harry and Penny are saying—something about the drive up, something about work and the city and the commute. The sky is a strikingly bright blue, the clouds fluffy and pure white, and it makes the scene in the garden look like something out of a catalog, the trees just poised for the start of autumn but clinging to the last breath of summer. Small groups of people mill around, nursing drinks. A table is set up over on the right-hand side with snacks: a large, tiered stand of cupcakes, bowls of professionally decorated cookies in the shape of balloons and birthday cakes and the number ten. A summerhouse sits at the far end of the garden—the home office Ieuan is currently talking about, I gather—and the only sign of children are a well-worn football and a couple of tennis balls discarded on the lawn. There are blue balloons hung artfully along the fence on either side of the garden, matching the ones at the front of the house, and a large banner declaring HAPPY 10TH BIRTHDAY ANTHONY. A couple of dogs are basking in the sun; two others are play fighting with a rope toy.

Maybe this is what people like this do, I think. They invite their colleagues to their kid's birthday party so the adults can gossip and drink, and they bring their pets like some upper-class playdate. All these grown-up couples with their houses and their commutes "into the city" and their pets and their kids and—

Oh god, I think.

They're *real* grown-ups. Not whatever I am. Not adults-in-training like my friends are, all just starting to move on with their lives. They're proper grown-ups in the same way as Nadine or Dawn. Put together. Experienced. *Settled.*

It's not the convivial experience Annabelle's wedding was, all old friends catching up with ready smiles. This is very, very different.

"Where's the birthday boy?" I ask our hosts, in a desperate bid to pretend like I belong.

Penny waves a hand, smiling more fondly now. (Note to self: ask about everyone's children if I want to get on their good side.)

"Oh, he's around somewhere! Probably inside with his friends having fun, I expect."

Ieuan laughs. "He was captivated all morning by *Beauty and the Beast.* Even ignored his breakfast for it. It's his favorite film, you know."

My eyes drag toward the house longingly. I'd give anything to trade the stuffy grown-up garden party for a Disney movie. That sounds like a much better way to spend a Saturday.

But I already feel like an interloper; I don't need to make a complete fool out of myself too. Besides, Penny's already not impressed by me, and I'm supposed to be here to do Harry a favor, not humiliate him by going to hang out with some ten-year-olds.

"Here, I'll take that, put it with the others," Ieuan says then, taking the gift-wrapped box from me. "Why don't you two get a drink, go chat?"

The doorbell rings from way off across the other side of the house, and Penny excuses herself to go answer it.

"She's still good friends with Louisa," Harry mumbles in my ear. "Sorry. If it helps, she's not really very nice to anybody."

"Any more people who are besties with your ex-wife and guaranteed to hate me?"

He grins. "Just a couple."

Arm still around my waist, Harry steers me toward a group of five people, making introductions. I do my best to remember their names, making mental notes of how they know each other. It seems everyone here either works together, used to work together, or is a spouse. From what I gather, most of them have known each other for years. They've been to each other's weddings or birthdays; they go for dinner and drinks together sometimes; some of them have been on holiday together. There are a lot of comments I don't follow, and even more I struggle to keep up with as they talk about work or mutual friends or kids. Luckily, it's a clique Harry hasn't been a very enthusiastic part of, so I catch a few blank looks on his face too. It makes me feel a little less out of my depth.

For the most part, I smile and nod and "mm-hmm" and try to think of something smart to say, feeling more foolish by the minute.

Everyone seems polite enough, which I suppose is generous considering they're still friends with Harry's ex-wife. I'd joked about him showing me off as his hot young girlfriend, but he talks about my career in marketing, my work as a journalist (even calling me an established journalist, which I quite like), and doesn't make me feel like I'm just there to make him look good.

And I'm not, I realize. I'm there to be his friend, his confidant. I'm there to be his person, the way he's been mine before now. I'm there for him, not for everybody else.

After the comment about my journalism, one man sniffs and asks, "Anything we might've read?"

I think about some of the latest stats—the hits on the website, the shares on social media, the barrage of comments of people loving my column. The idea that people like Jessica and Tally and Lena read it, love it, share it with their own friends. The way people at Annabelle's wedding were so impressed when I told them a bit about it.

So I smile enigmatically and say, "Probably," with such confidence that they all look at each other, (somewhat begrudgingly) impressed.

We mingle for a while before Harry excuses us, steering me to the other side of the garden. There's a table set up by the house with a bowl of punch, so we each grab a glass, and then we drift toward the food. Harry takes a cookie and I go for a cupcake, immediately regretting it, as there's a mountain of frosting and chocolate sprinkles on the top, and with a glass of fruit punch in my other hand, it's going to be awkward to eat. It's hardly going to be delicate, I think, looking mournfully at the other guests—who look like variations on Penny, for the most part. Sophisticated but low-key. Grown-up.

I always notice the age gap between me and Duncan, but it's always felt like he's an older brother or something. We take the piss out of each other for being too young or too old too often for it to be weird.

It didn't feel weird with Harry either. Things with him were only supposed to be temporary—a means to an end—so I never really factored it in very much beyond it being something to tease him about. I certainly never felt awkward about it as we spent more time together and got to know each other.

Right now, though, I feel awkward. One of the women looks like she's my mum's age, for god's sake. Maybe I should feel cool and youthful and like *I'm* the one *they* should feel jealous of, but I don't.

I down my punch, discarding the glass for a moment, and fidget with the paper cupcake case.

"What?" Harry says, noticing.

"Nothing. Nothing. So, um, what else shall I say to everyone? Just talk up what a brilliant, amazing boyfriend you are? Pretend you're not emotionally scarred by the breakdown of your marriage and are the greatest thing to ever happen to me?"

Something flickers across Harry's face, his mouth and eyebrows twitching, his eyes darting down to the ground for a moment, but before I can figure out exactly what that look is he's rolling his eyes at me. "I *am* the greatest thing to ever happen to you."

"In bed. Specifically *in bed*. That's what I said."

"Well," he says, grinning broadly, "you could always tell them *that*."

I roll my eyes and take a bite of the cupcake. There's no way to be graceful or genteel about it, but I have this horrible idea that anyone looking over will see me unhinge my jaw like a boa constrictor to swallow it whole.

I don't swallow it whole, obviously, but I get a good mouthful of frosting and chocolate sponge cake.

No, it's not chocolate. It's . . .

What is that?

Harry has taken the opportunity to chomp down half of his snack, and pulls a face at me as he chews. "Ugh," he says, choking it down. "*Ugh*, that's so dry. And weird. Savory. Who has savory cookies? What, is this how kids eat their vegetables now?"

Savory.

Oh my god.

That's what it tastes like.

It tastes like *meat*.

Sort of beefy, sort of like gravy, sort of . . .

A throat clears near my shoulder, and a lady says, "You know those are for the dogs, don't you?"

I feel the blood drain from my face in an instant. Harry chokes on his second bite of cookie, fighting not to spray it everywhere as he coughs while simultaneously trying to swallow it faster so he can talk.

Eventually, he manages, "Amelia. Hi. Well, that explains the texture, I suppose. I thought it was a bit dry."

The woman, Amelia, clicks her tongue. "Honestly! This one, he'll eat anything you put in front of him, won't he?" she adds to me.

"Mm-hmm," I mumble, my lips clamped tightly shut. I'm still clutching the cupcake, and hastily wipe any crumbs from around my mouth. With a polite smile, Amelia takes the half-eaten cake off me, peeling off the wrapper. She whistles sharply, turning to call, "Duchess, here, darling!"

A dachshund zips into sight out of nowhere, yapping as it approaches and then immediately scoffing down the cupcake as soon as Amelia places it on the ground.

Straightening back up, she rubs my arm. "So you're Harry's new flame! The two of you looked so sweet together on his Instagram at that wedding a few weeks ago. He's been keeping you all to himself for ages; we've been dying to meet you."

"Dying to interrogate you, more like," Harry says, but he makes it sound like a joke he's in on and Amelia laughs, wagging a finger at him. I wonder if she's good friends with his ex-wife too.

Before I can find out, I ease my arm away and take a step back. "Can I get a quick rain check on that interrogation? I'm just going to nip inside to the bathroom."

"Of course! It's just on the left past the stairs."

As I make a hasty escape, narrowly avoiding tripping over a spaniel chasing a tennis ball, I overhear her telling Harry about his ex's holiday to the south of France in August. I glance back to see him looking awkward and uncomfortable, and then he looks at the dog cupcakes like he'd rather stomach one of those than this conversation.

I steel myself, remembering why I'm here.

If Harry can pretend to be my boyfriend around my family, I can help him prove to his friends and colleagues that he's moving on with his life and happier out of his marriage.

What else are friends who fake-date for?

Twenty-seven

In a miraculous twist of fate, the downstairs toilet—which is larger than the entire bathroom in my apartment—has a toothbrush and toothpaste at the sink.

Obviously, I don't use the toothbrush, but I squeeze some toothpaste onto my fingertip and scrub my teeth and tongue with it, gagging at the lingering taste of the meaty dog-food cupcake I can't believe I just ate.

I'm at this ginormous, posh house near Oxford, the kind I bet Lena and Johnny will live in one day, with people I doubt I'll ever be able to impress no matter how hard I try, for a fancy afternoon drinking fruit punch and engaging in what I don't doubt will be intelligent, interesting conversation . . .

And I just ate *dog food*.

Of all the things I tell my friends about, I don't think this will be one of them. Not yet, at any rate.

I spit and rinse, then smooth my hands over my dress and head back to the garden with everybody else. I grab a drink and join Harry, who's standing with Penny, Amelia, and a handful of people I'm introduced to so swiftly by Penny that I don't retain a single one of their names. But I smile brightly and say hello politely and lean into Harry when he puts a hand low on my back.

"I can't believe he's ten already!" someone is saying to Penny, apparently picking a conversation back up. "Gosh, it seems just like yesterday you brought him home."

"I know! We were looking at pictures this morning—when he was so small that he'd fit in your hands . . . Now, of course, it's a different story," Penny says with a pretty laugh. "Still a bundle of mischief, though, always getting into everything and making a nuisance of himself!"

"They grow up so fast," someone else says sagely, nodding.

"My auntie's just had one," I blurt, feeling the need to make up for the dog-food incident and prove myself. "A girl."

"Oh! How lovely," says Amelia. "Did she adopt?"

I stare at her, then at Harry, surprised. I can't imagine him talking so much about me to his colleagues that they'd know my aunt is a lesbian.

But, hey, I didn't pin him for one of "these people," either, so what do I know?

"No," I say. "She—"

"Of course, that's all the rage now, isn't it?" someone else butts in. "Our neighbor's just adopted, from Hungary. Took weeks to arrive."

Harry and I exchange a look, speechless, horrified.

Yeah, I can *definitely* see why he doesn't like them. They can't be serious.

Except they so obviously are, and worse, *none of them think anything of it*. It takes all my willpower not to gawp, or elbow Harry.

"So how old is she? Your auntie's," Amelia asks me, with a sweet smile, looking so genuinely interested I'm put on the back foot.

"Just a couple of weeks, but—"

"Oh, gosh! I remember those days," Penny says with another laugh, tossing her hair over her shoulder. Closer, I notice it looks dry, in need of a deep-conditioning treatment or something. Her roots are showing, too, dark, the bottle-blond presumably hiding some grays that are starting to show through again. "It's such a huge adjustment, settling into a new routine, trying to get everyone used to some sort of schedule."

"Yes," I say, nodding along like I understand completely, and not just through secondhand information from Dawn. I'm here to make Harry look good, not pick fights with total strangers. "Yes, exactly. I'm going to visit in a couple of weeks."

"Careful," one man warns me. "You'll want one of your own soon enough!"

I grimace, feeling myself close off immediately from the conversation. I physically retreat into Harry, shuffling from one foot to the other. I cradle my drink in both hands, taking a sip to try and stall.

"Do you think you do?" Penny asks me, eyes piercing into mine, unflinching, her smile polite and rigid. Her eyes dart between me and Harry as she waits for an answer.

He clears his throat, starting to try to answer for me, but I decide—just this once—to humor the nosy busybodies asking me if I want children, when I'm going to have them, what my plans are. I give my best giggle, which comes off sounding superior the way I hoped it would, and lay a hand on Harry's chest, possessively, and repeat what he said when it was me being interrogated like this at Dawn's baby shower.

"Well, *obviously*, it's still very early days with us, but we have talked about it. Enough to know we're on the same page."

Catching on, he says, "Exactly. We wanted to be clear with

each other right from the start what we were getting into—isn't that right, baby?"

I throw up a little in my mouth, which has nothing to do with the dog cupcake and everything to do with the pet name "baby," but I giggle again and say, "Absolutely."

I move up on my tiptoes to kiss him—in my flats, he's tall enough that I have to stretch up to reach his mouth with mine. Harry bends his head toward mine, smiling. Smirking, trying not to laugh.

Our lips are almost touching when he recoils, coughing, pushing me away with a firm hand suddenly splayed out flat against my sternum. "Jesus, Soph. Sorry. You just—your breath *stinks*. It must be the cupcake."

I cover my mouth with a hand, breathing onto it and trying to smell. My mouth tastes funny still, but I assume it's just because my finger was a poor substitute for a toothbrush.

"But I cleaned my teeth," I say, forgetting to be embarrassed at being rejected for having smelly breath in front of total strangers.

"No, you didn't."

"Yes, I did. There was toothpaste in the downstairs toilet and I—"

Penny's laugh is delicate, grating, and makes everyone turn their attention to her, all of us moving as one. She clears her throat just as delicately, then gives me the most patronizing smile I have ever seen in my entire life.

Which is saying something because I'm very used to condescending questions about my nonexistent love life.

"Oh, sweetie," she drawls, laying a manicured hand on my shoulder. "That was the dog's toothpaste."

"Wh—I'm sorry, *what*?"

"That's Anthony's toothpaste. Ieuan must have left it out after we brushed his teeth earlier. It's liver flavored."

Harry snorts, the sound catching in his throat as he tries to muffle it, and it's followed by a smattering of laughter from everybody else. I don't receive any pity in that moment, not a hint of sympathy.

I'd glare at Harry, or maybe burst into tears, but I'm too stuck on what Penny has just said.

"I'm sorry," I say, raising my voice a little over the laughter. "Did you say that was *Anthony's* toothpaste? *The dog's* toothpaste?"

"Well, yes. Obviously. Didn't you look before you used it?"

Oh my god.

Oh, *my god*.

I look around at the banner and balloons again, the fancy cookies and cupcakes that aren't for humans, the other dogs around the garden.

Oh. My. *God*.

I'm still reeling when Penny, apparently taking pity on me at last, says, "Why don't you pop upstairs? There's a guest room on the far right, I'm sure there's toothpaste and a new toothbrush in the en suite."

"Thanks," I say, numb, and grab Harry's sleeve. "Excuse us a minute, won't you?"

I don't offer anybody the chance to respond, my fingers snatching the fabric like a claw and yanking Harry along after me. I hear a wave of murmurs and laughter in our wake.

"You're not planning to show me those giant knickers, are you?" Harry asks as we get near the door, and when he starts to laugh, I turn on him, the toothpaste momentarily forgotten now that we're out of anybody's immediate earshot.

"You cannot be serious."

"I was joking! Obviously! God, give me some credit, Sophie, I'm hardly about to shag you in my friend's guest bedroom at their—"

"Their dog's birthday party," I interrupt, my hands balling into tight, shaking fists in the air between us. "Harry, this is a birthday party for their fucking *dog*."

"No, it's—it's . . ."

But then it dawns on him. I watch his face go slack with realization as he replays what Penny said just now, as he looks around the garden for signs of ten-year-old children, as he goes back over conversations with Penny or Ieuan about Anthony.

Their dog.

"Oh my god," he mumbles. "Oh my god. It's their fucking dog."

"How could you not know it was their dog?" I hiss. My shoulders tense and my jaw is clenched.

"You heard them talk about him, Soph!" he hisses back, gesturing so wildly he slops punch out of his glass and onto the patio. "He's got a favorite movie! They buy him outfits! Bow ties! Shoes!"

"He likes going on *walks*, Harry. *Walks*. Because he's a *dog*."

"But—"

"How could you not realize they were talking about a dog? Haven't you known them for ages?"

"Yeah, but they're, you know, *work friends*. We've been over this. I don't know. They always talk about him going on playdates or, I mean, who calls their dog Anthony, anyway? That's a person name. Dogs are called . . . they're called things like Fenton! Things like Scout or Cinnamon or Pongo, or Sandwich—"

"Who calls their dog Sandwich!" I exclaim, much louder than I mean to. A few heads turn in our direction. People are staring openly, I realize, watching us bicker. To them, I'm sure it looks like a more serious fight than what is actually going on. I flush, but only half of them look away when they notice I've caught them staring.

Harry is oblivious, his back to them. He runs a hand through his hair and downs his punch, looking like he wishes it was something much stronger than fruit juice.

"Who calls their dog Anthony?" he shoots back, more quietly.

I stare at him, mouth agape, hands hanging uselessly between us now. Defeated, knowing that today is a complete shambles and there is no coming back from this, I press one hand to my forehead, close my eyes, and then drop my hands to my sides before I bite my lip and look back up at him.

"Harry," I say slowly. "We bought their dog a karaoke machine."

He stares at me, every bit as confused and helpless as I feel, before his lips press into a thin line. I think for a second he's angry—with himself, I guess, because I don't know how this is in any way *my* fault—but then his eyebrow quirks up and his mouth starts to twitch, and then a laugh sputters out of him.

A hysterical giggle bursts out of my own lips and I clap a hand to my mouth to stop it, but it's too late. Harry is laughing loudly, heartily, his smile stretched across his face and eyes shining silver. It's so infectious I can't help but keep giggling too.

We're both still laughing when Harry says, "Oh, Soph," and takes hold of my elbow, pulling me abruptly into him and planting a swift, firm kiss on my lips that leaves me so surprised I don't have a chance to wish it was something more. My laughter fades into a small smile and I feel a blush creeping over my cheeks.

"Go brush your teeth with people toothpaste, will you?" Harry tells me. "You really stink."

"Like you're any better, biscuit breath," I mutter, shoving him gently in the chest.

He rocks back, catching my wrist and leaning closer, lips brushing at my cheek as he pauses near my ear. "I could always follow you upstairs . . . "

"What about your friends?"

"What friends?"

He slips a hand around my waist, his lips starting to drag along my jaw, and every nerve in my body feels like a live wire.

A dog barks, and I gather the last fragment of rational thought left in my mind to push him away. Harry gives a breath of laughter, looking unsurprised by my rebuff but still a little bit sorry about it. He plants another kiss on my lips before pushing me toward the door and spanking me lightly, playfully.

"Go on. I'll have found some people food for you by the time you get back."

I fake a swoon before heading inside. "My knight in shining Burberry. You have dog-food crumbs on your shirt."

October

MY BIRTHDAY

Twenty-eight

Start taking up more space in your own life.

Views on avoiding relationship complications from our
Dating & Relationships columnist

It is a truth universally acknowledged that any woman turning twenty-six and in want of a boyfriend is destined to have an absolutely fucking miserable birthday.

What are you doing for your birthday? I always ask my friends. *Are you doing anything nice?*

And boy oh boy, do they have plans.

My boyfriend's taking me to dinner.

My girlfriend's booked us a weekend away.

We're going home to see my family over the weekend.

We've got plans with his family but I'm sure we'll all have some cake!

"Just a quiet one" is still always "something." Always, without fail. Because their version of a quiet one involves this other person, and for that reason alone it'll be different from an average evening because this other person is bound to make at least a *little* bit of fuss.

So when people at work or my friends know my birthday is

coming up and ask me what I'm doing, if I'm doing anything nice, I don't know what to tell them except, *Oh, nothing special, I don't think.*

I can't tell them the truth: *I'm going to spend the day by myself. I'll probably have to put some laundry on. Maybe I'll treat myself to ordering a takeaway for one. I'll scroll through social media and say thank you to the people who have messaged to wish me a happy birthday.*

How sad does that sound?

I know the stereotype is that Valentine's Day is the worst day to be single, but I have to disagree. Christmas is probably a close second on the list, but I have to disagree with that one too. Valentine's Day is nice if you've got someone to spend it with—it gives you an excuse for, like, a special date night, or whatever—but it's also just another day, and even my friends in long-term relationships don't seem massively bothered by it. And as for Christmas, well, there's always family to spend the day with, so that's fine too.

But your birthday?

I have never felt so alone.

It's always a bit of a struggle to make plans with my friends: they live far away, we all have jobs and plans on the weekends to juggle, and they tend to have *more* plans because theirs have to include another person—their partner—and a whole other family.

But clearly, I've left it too late to try and plan anything with them for my birthday.

The last month has passed in a blur. Things have felt like all systems go at work (and blissfully, with no more disasters on my part), Lena wanted us to go look at some wedding dresses with her in Bath, and then I went to visit my new baby cousin again . . . And I've had a few not-dates with Harry to keep me busy.

Now the end of October is suddenly looming and it's my birthday, and I am doing nothing at all to celebrate.

I should have tried to pin people down earlier to do something. My birthday falls on a Thursday this year and nobody really makes plans for a Thursday anyway, but at least I might have had something to look forward to this weekend instead. But Tally has plans with Sam, Lena is off doing some wedding planning stuff again, and I'm still too scared of Frankie Two after the housewarming to ask my Frankie if he wants to hang out and do something. Jessica and Conor are still "enjoying their post-wedding bubble" (like it hasn't already been long enough) and Nadine is on bed rest before the baby comes. I can't even rely on the rest of my family: Auntie Dawn and Janine are taking baby Poppy to see some of Janine's family this weekend, Mum's out of the country again, and even Dad and Camilla each have their own plans. Camilla I'll forgive, as she's over at Nadine's to look after her a bit, but Dad has a sodding *date*. I'm twenty-six and alone on my birthday and even my dad is too busy to see me because he has a date. And Duncan's no better—he's actually *seeing* someone now, so there goes my last resort of plans with work friends.

The nail in the coffin was when Harry told me he was going to be out of town again for work. Some fake boyfriend he is, abandoning me at my most needy.

It really is a sorry state of affairs.

To make things worse, I have the day off work.

And I have nothing to do.

In theory, I know I should be glad for the day. One of the (so-called) perks of working for the local paper is that they offer you an extra day off work for your birthday—or the nearest Friday, if it falls on a weekend. Objectively, that's great. But right now I think I'd rather take the day off work literally any other time, or even be in the office today.

After all, it's a Thursday. What the hell am I supposed to do on a Thursday? What does anybody do on a random Thursday? It's not even like it's near enough to Christmas that I can go out and busy myself with Christmas shopping or anything. It's *useless*.

It's worse than useless, though, because all it does is instill this deep, desperate reminder of just how alone I am.

. . .

So it's no surprise that I wake up on October 21, a cloudy, drizzling Thursday, feeling miserable as sin. I wake up groggy and grumpy, and I'm scowling even as I reach for my phone because I'm sure there are already a couple of messages wishing me a nice day.

And I'm right, but even that doesn't do much to lift my mood. There's an email from Camilla with a voucher for Lush, and Tally and Frankie have both texted me to wish me happy birthday. Jessica's friend Lydia from the hen do has written on my Facebook wall and so has Frankie Two. Siobhan sends me some enthusiastic, all-caps *HAPPY BIRTHDAY!!!!* messages on Instagram with GIFs to match.

It's only eight in the morning—I never turned off my usual work alarm—and with nowhere to go and nothing to do, I should just go back to sleep. At least then I wouldn't have to face this aching loneliness or the fact that I have nobody to celebrate today with.

I know it's not their fault everyone is busy. I know that. And I know most of them are a bit far away, too, and that's a factor, but right now it feels like a lot more than physical distance between me and them.

Wide awake, I stretch out in the bed and slump against the

pillows, sprawled in a starfish shape under the sheets, arms thrown out either side of my head.

I wonder what it's like . . . Waking up every morning next to somebody. Waking up and just knowing there's someone *there*, that they're always there, and not just the occasional night you stay over each at other's place before the whole thing fizzles out again. I wonder what it's like to wake up and know that you're just *with* someone.

Before I can stop it, a little daydream filters into my mind—the idea of waking up this morning, even with no plans and nothing to do, but to have someone next to me saying *Good morning*, and *Hey, happy birthday, Sophie*, and the warmth of their body on the sheets and their smell on the pillow next to mine before they get up to go about their day and leave me to my own devices, but not before they bring me a cup of tea, or maybe call out to see if I want them to put some toast on for me.

God, I want that. That closeness, that familiarity, that dependency.

I bet it's beautiful.

But it's just me, slouched under the duvet, wondering if the bagels I bought have gone moldy yet because I forgot to freeze the extras, my phone pinging again but this time just with some junk mail.

I don't even have a birthday cake. Who wants to buy themselves a birthday cake when they don't even have someone to share it with? It's such a small silly thing that doesn't even *matter*, but suddenly it feels so huge and horrible that it actually makes me cry. Of course I don't have a cake. What am I going to do, put some candles in a Colin the Caterpillar and sing "Happy Birthday" to myself and then make a wish and have a single, solitary slice? Yeah, right.

I burrow into the pillows and close my eyes for a while, trying to will myself back to sleep.

It doesn't come, though, and eventually my phone goes off again. This time it's a nice message from Mum wishing me a lovely day and then saying she's sent me some money for me to treat myself to something nice and to let her know what I buy, and she hopes I have fun with my day off.

I rewrite my reply half a dozen times before settling somewhere between brutally honest and casually optimistic.

> Thanks Mum! Looking like it might be a duvet day to be honest lol. Might push the boat out and order Chinese, maybe go round the shops and look for something to spend my birthday money on otherwise

> Now that sounds like a better plan!!! You can't mooch around the flat all day. Why don't you take yourself out shopping and for a nice lunch while you're out? Xxx

> Because all my friends round here are at work and can't just swan off for a couple of hours to come have lunch with me?

> Why do your friends have to be there? Just go have a nice lunch with yourself. Xxx

> What???
> Mum, no
> That's really weird
> I'm not doing that

> Why not? Xxx

For a while I stare at her *Why not?* text in disbelief. I can't formulate a reply because there are, like, a hundred and one reasons why not—but every time I try to pin them down, it just seems to amount to "it's weird." And I know this for a fact: it was *horrible* when I got left in the restaurant after Jaxon and I broke up; no way could I have stayed and eaten my meal alone.

It's all right for her, I think. She does stuff like that all the time. With traveling for work as much as she does, she *has* to eat by herself in hotel restaurants, or else she doesn't eat. But it's *different*. I just can't explain why.

So I don't bother texting back in the end.

I'm sure for someone like Mum, today is a gift. An entire day and nothing to do with it, a whole random weekday all to myself! I could do anything. The possibilities are endless. I can go out and spend it however I want.

But I'm not someone like that.

I text the girls as much, sending them a screenshot of my messages with Mum and knowing they'll back me up and say how weird it is. Tally replies quickly—first with an apology about how snowed under she is at work, she would have loved to see me today but she's really sorry—and by the time Lena joins in, I've got up and trudged to the kitchen to investigate the breakfast situation.

And my friends, the traitors, take Mum's side. They agree with me it feels weird to do stuff alone but then take the *Why not?* tack as well.

I must go quiet for long enough in the chat that it's clear I'm not receiving their encouragement very well, because eventually Tally volunteers to move some meetings around and leave early to meet me at the cinema and see a film we've been wanting to catch, and relief floods through me. I can't take her up on the offer quick enough—even if there is a bitter aftertaste to the relief, knowing how desperate and depressed I have to seem for her to make the effort.

But the movie isn't until just after four o'clock, so I still have the whole day and nothing to do.

I stand in the kitchen, waiting for my (thankfully not moldy) bagel to pop and staring down at Lena's last message, asking me what would I really love to do today, if I could. If people were with me.

And the honest answer is *I don't know.* I'm so used to just filling my time and fitting in around everyone else's calendars, I don't remember the last time I really took time for myself like that.

Lena says Take yourself out on a date, Soph.

And Tally tells me Yeah! You deserve it!

You know what?

Maybe I will.

• • •

Suddenly committed to the idea of "taking myself on a date," I get all dressed up, somehow dragging my entire morning out until it's almost lunchtime when I finally leave. I do a sheet mask, paint my nails, blow-dry my hair. I put my good jeans on, a cute top, and my favorite jacket and ankle boots. I spend some time doing my makeup, putting in a bit more effort than I would for a day at work. Before I can lose my nerve and talk myself out of it, I'm out of the house and on the bus to town.

For an hour or two I mooch around the shops, spending my Lush voucher and then some of my birthday money on a cute dress and a new hardcover book—a fantasy romance that TikTok has been raving about lately.

Now, with half an hour still to kill before I need to make my way to the cinema and meet Tally, I head into a small independent coffee shop I've been wanting to check out for a while and brace myself.

You can do this, Sophie. You're not a child. You're a twenty-six-year-old woman with a job and an apartment and you can buy yourself a bloody coffee.

It's not so much the getting-a-coffee part that feels hard but rather the concept of sitting down at a table, ordering it to stay in, and just hanging out, all by my lonesome. I'm scared people will think I'm waiting for someone and, worse, that I've been stood up. I'm worried it'll look like I'm hogging a table. I'm worried that I don't look interesting enough to be the kind of person who just takes themselves for a coffee and that people will stare at me and wonder what the bloody hell I think I'm doing.

It's only when I'm sitting down at a table as far into the corner as I can get and after spending a few minutes fidgeting with my pumpkin spice latte and then with my phone that I realize I have the perfect excuse—the perfect tool—to make it look like I'm here alone on purpose, and that this is all very intentional and very normal.

I slide the book I just bought out of the Waterstones bag and set it on the table. For some reason, I pause and look around, almost expecting someone to come over and tell me to stop taking the piss and be on my way, now, because I'm absolutely not this person. I'm not the main character with the romanticized, idealized life, a cut reel overlaid with a low-contrast filter and lo-fi beats. If anything, I'm the brash best friend making their occasional appearance as a side character, doing everything they can to steal the scene in the hope nobody forgets about them later.

But nobody even seems to be noticing me, so I open the book and, heart pounding, start reading.

I must read the first paragraph about eight times before my nerves finally settle down; after that, it's not long before I get sucked into the book.

It's not like I've never been out by myself before or like I always need someone to hold my hand to do things, but this feels new, and unfamiliar. It's pushing every boundary I have and going against all my better judgment, but I still can't explain to myself exactly *why* it all seems so wrong.

The girls were right—if I want to do these things anyway, then why shouldn't I?

How is it fair that they never have to worry about finding someone else to go with them to a restaurant or film they've been wanting to go to, never worry about something as simple as getting a coffee, because they always just *have* someone? It's not *fair*.

Why can't I do those things, too, even though I don't have someone?

Why do I feel so much like I can't? I mean, nobody's even giving me and my coffee and my book a second glance right now. They might not if this was a sit-down, three-course dinner either.

I always resent the things I can't do because I don't have a boyfriend, but . . . well, maybe I can do them.

I don't know that I'm *enjoying* myself exactly, but by the time I've finished my pumpkin spice latte and reached the end of a chapter, marking the page with the bookshop receipt, I do feel proud of myself.

At the cinema I collect two tickets for the period drama Tally and I have been dying to make time to see, and then go wait near the usher's stand. I take my phone out to message her and let her know where I am.

My message goes ignored, but that's okay. Tally will find me. She's probably just busy getting here and not checking her phone. The movie's not due to start for ten minutes, so there's plenty of time, and there's always another fifteen or twenty minutes of trailers anyway.

But with two minutes to go, I'm still waiting, and I start to feel queasy.

At three minutes past, the usher gives me a long look, staring hard enough that eventually I can't ignore them anymore and have to pretend to only just notice them and the sympathetic frown on their face.

"Did you get stood up?"

"No! No, it's just—it's my friend, she's just running a bit late. She'll be here."

Oh god. Worst-case scenario come to life: I *do* look like I've been stood up. What kind of best friend would do this to me? What kind of birthday present is this very singular brand of torture?

At seven minutes after the film was supposed to start, there's finally a message from Tally.

Tallulah King
Babe! I'm SO sorry, work has just been so hectic today and we're having a bit of an emergency, so I can't leave early anymore—been stuck in meetings all afternoon, things got so full-on I forgot all about the film and letting you know sooner! I'm the worst. Make it up to you soon, promise xxx

She's flaked. My best friend, my only hope of plans for the day, has stood me up.

And worse, I've already bought the tickets. My stomach knots at the wasted money, fingers pinching the little paper tickets tighter.

The usher, who's been watching me this whole time, says, "She's not coming, then?"

"No," I churn out, unable to meet their eye.

In my periphery, I see them shrug and hold out a hand for the ticket. "Might as well go on in, then. You'll probably still catch some of the trailers."

Go on in?

On my own? They can't mean that, surely. I can't . . .

I *can* do this.

It's not a big deal. It's just like sitting down for a coffee earlier. I watch films on my own all the time. Admittedly that's on my sofa in the comfort of my flat, but even so. It's just a movie. And it's all in the dark anyway. It's just a movie, and it's just a couple of hours, and—and goddammit, do I really need a *man* to be able to go and see a film? (Or, fine, in this case, Tally, who I guess has too much going on with her own life to see it with me.)

Gathering the remnants of the burst of courage I had this morning, I thrust my ticket at the usher and make for the screen before I have the chance to change my mind. I find my seat and sink down low in it, quickly glancing at the other people here—several also on their own, I note—and realizing that none of them are looking at me.

They don't care, I realize suddenly. These people, these strangers, do not give two shits about me. They don't care if I'm here alone or if it's my birthday or why I wanted to see this film or why I'm not at work on a Thursday afternoon or anything else—I'm really *not* the main character. I blend into background noise in their lives. I'm nothing to them—just like they are to me.

Maybe that should be a bit of a depressing thought, especially when I'm already feeling so bloody lonely on my birthday, but it has the complete opposite effect.

Nobody cares about me or how I'm spending my day.

That's fucking *liberating*.

So much so that on the way home I stop by the Marks & Spencer food hall and buy an entire birthday cake, just for me.

Twenty-nine

"Is this seat taken?"

Yes, obviously, you tool. I didn't order that partly drunk pint of beer just to make it look like I had some company.

The bar I'm in walks the fine line between just well-lit enough and dim, which lends it an air of intimacy. The music is a bit too loud, pushing each conversation that bit louder, making it all seem a bit busier than it really is.

I don't pay much attention to the guy leaning one hand on the vacant stool at my table except to say, "I'm here with someone, thanks."

"Oh. Sorry. Never mind."

He walks off, stopping at another table nearby where three girls are sitting talking animatedly. I scrunch up my nose in disgust. Can't he just leave well enough alone? Can't he tell—

They nod to him, and he takes the fourth stool from their table, carrying it off to the other side of the bar and his own group of friends.

Oh. Okay, my bad.

It's the Saturday after my birthday and by now the loneliness has crept back in, right along with resentment at my friends and family all having "better" plans. The empowerment I felt at taking myself out on a date (however unintentionally) has completely worn off, the sting of being stood up by my own best friend taking over instead. The loneliness leaves an ache in my stomach, although, I suppose, that could just be left over from eating an entire Colin the Caterpillar myself.

Tonight I'm on an actual, real date.

Well. Not *exactly*, I suppose, since it's only Harry. The cheating soon-to-be divorcé who lost five hundred quid this week betting on some football game (imagine having that kind of money to lose! And to think I felt bitter about wasting twenty-odd quid on cinema tickets when Tally bailed) and whom I'm not actually interested in properly *dating*. But, still, we've been out for dinner and now we're at a bar for some drinks because we're having a good time and don't want the night to end too soon.

Just because I refuse to think of seriously dating him and being his official rebound doesn't mean I don't like him and we can't have fun.

And being with Harry is a *lot* of fun.

And maybe I'm only refusing to think about seriously dating him out of a sense of self-preservation, because I know that's not what *he's* looking for and because this is just something fun and casual and mutually beneficial as far as he's concerned, but still.

He's a cat person. His favorite type of cake is carrot. He hates the smell of melted cheese. It would never work out.

"All right?"

Harry's voice floats over to me and pulls me out of my thoughts as he sits back on his stool, having returned from the bathroom. He grins at me, and it's the sort of look that sweeps away all my reservations about him.

I wonder if he always looks this good. Surely he must? Every time I've seen him, he's never been anything less than heart-stoppingly gorgeous. I wonder how many hours he puts into looking so effortlessly handsome. Did he style his hair like that on purpose, making it look just a teensy bit messy and inviting me to run my fingers through it? Did he consider which shirt he picked out, or did he just grab any old one, knowing that leaving that extra button undone managed to look just on the sexy side of trying too hard, no matter what he wore?

The tan he had when we first met, topped up by the summer sun, has faded now. I can make out the freckles on the bridge of his nose. There's a faint line around the fourth finger of his left hand where his wedding ring used to be.

We launch immediately back into conversation. There's still that feeling of no pressure and no consequences to anything we say, which really drives home for me how casual this is for him, so I've told him all about Tally's horrific betrayal and how I spent my birthday by myself, which I actually ended up sort of enjoying just a *teensy* bit, even if I can't believe it's taken me this long to do something as basic as go for coffee by myself. He tells me that his ex-wife is now trying to take the cat and the cat sort of hates him anyway so it shouldn't matter, but it kind of does, and he spent hours the other night crying over the damn cat.

I don't think it was about the cat.

Harry's so easygoing, so much fun, that most of the time we're texting or hanging out I forget he's going through his own shit too. I see his bachelor pad apartment on the twentieth floor with its minimalist clean lines, the expensive coffee machine in the kitchen, the low-backed leather sofa and glass furniture that came with the place, the heated floor in the bathroom, and I think—this guy's got it made. I don't know where he used to live but he talks about "their house" sometimes; Louisa, the ex, lives there for now. I wonder what it was like. Did they have a spare room he thought of as the bedroom for their future child? Was there a TV unit filled with their shared DVD collection? Did he mow the lawn on the weekend while she planted flowers and their cat snoozed in the sun?

It feels strange to think of this impulsive, smiling man as someone like that. Someone settled, serious. Someone so desperate for that future he dreamed of that he charged forward into a marriage he didn't really want.

I know he regrets the last year of his relationship, regrets going through with the proposal, the wedding, the cheating. I know he's not over Louisa sleeping with his brother, and I know he's still ignoring texts from his brother and calls from his mum, and sometimes I see the grief etched onto his face when he waits for the notification to disappear, and the way he switches straight into one of his betting apps instead—it's like the way I turn to dating apps when my friends aren't online to talk to. I know he's leaning into this "newfound freedom" of being "unshackled from the missus" (his own, very cringey, words) by throwing himself into work or seeing his mates for heavy drinking sessions.

Or he calls me. Whenever I hear from Harry, a thrill runs through me, and I know there's part of me that would like for these casual hangouts and hookups to be something more serious, more intentional, but as easy as it is to forget sometimes, deep down I know that most of the time he suggests hanging out it's because *he's* lonely and at loose ends. And since I'm usually in the same position, it's a no-brainer.

The idea that he spent hours crying over the cat who threw up in his shoes is baffling. I can't imagine the Harry I know doing that.

I wonder what he used to do for fun, before his life fell apart and the future he'd clung to crumbled around him.

I almost ask him about it all, but he takes a swig of his beer and says, "Guess I've got all this to look forward to soon, then."

Harry waves a hand at me, gesturing vaguely.

And even though I know he's talking about something else, I joke, "Wow, way to woo a lady. Keep on flirting like that, mister, and you'll find yourself a brand-new romance in no time."

He laughs. "You know what I mean. All *this*. The doing stuff alone, stuff."

"Oh. That."

"Birthdays and, *fuck*, Christmas. Oh my god," he groans, burying his head in his hands. "What am I going to do about Christmas?"

"Can't you spend it with your parents?"

"What, where my brother will show up with his kids? Yeah. Great. Can't wait for that to blow up in my face. Maybe I should go away for the holidays. Just, like, jet off somewhere. It can't be so miserable to be alone if you're in, like, Antigua or something, right?"

He looks at me like I have the answers.

Like I should know.

Like I am the expert on How to Be Single and Alone.

Maybe I am. I'm certainly not the expert on How to Find Love and Be Happy.

"I guess not," is all I can say.

Harry stares at me, gray eyes plaintive and another heavy sigh pouring from his lips as he reaches for his drink again.

As the resident expert on singledom, as evidenced by my popular column on the subject, I suppose I should try to cheer him up a little bit.

After all, he *did* pay for dinner.

"Maybe you should see this as an opportunity. You know, get out there and—and—and date yourself. Take up space in your own life a bit more, instead of making yourself smaller to fit in around other people. Find out what you like, who you are, without someone else in your life. Go do those things you always wanted to do. Go spend Christmas in Australia soaking up the sun and having shrimp barbies on the beach, or go see the Northern Lights in Iceland and then get some friends together and go up to Scotland for Hogmanay or something. Make a big deal of it, like you would if you were still with Louisa. Go do all these awesome things and enjoy the fact you don't have to factor in someone else or what they want to do or where they want to stay or what suits them. I mean, what's the point in it all if you're just living for someone else anyway, or waiting around? I get living your life *with* someone, but that's a different thing. Screw it, go to Antigua. Or if you want to spend the day with your parents, go to them for Christmas and let your brother be the one who's uncomfortable because *he's* the one who slept with your wife. Just . . . go be selfish. Have fun. Figure out what matters to you and—and go do it."

"Date myself," he repeats, nodding now. "Like you did on Thursday."

I start, only now going back over what I've just said to him.

Maybe I really am *the authority*, I think, because it sounds like great advice—the kind I'd put in one of my columns. But when was the last time I ever *believed* any of that stuff, or *did* any of it? I exaggerate all the time in my articles, smooth over the rough edges of my life and spill my darkest thoughts onto the page, coming up with theories and solutions I make up more or less on the spot each month. It's all amped up, some alternate—better, cooler, more out-spoken—version of myself. When was the last time I treated my life like some big adventure that was all mine and mine alone, and not like I needed someone else around to make any of it worth doing?

I think my birthday was the first time ever.

"Yeah. Yeah, like I did on Thursday. Exactly like that."

"Or, you know, I could just spend Christmas with you. As the fake boyfriend, obviously."

His blasé tone is belied by the sudden tension in his shoulders and the fact he won't look me in the eye.

I think about Christmas Day, which still feels ages away but I'm sure, before I know it, I'll be sitting around the table with my family, with my sisters' families, and feeling like another year has gone by and I've got fuck all to show for it.

"I'll get back to you on that," I tell him. I'd originally planned to have "broken up" with him by then, but—"Maybe that's not such a bad idea."

He tries—and fails—not to look too pleased at the idea. "Maybe recruiting a guy to pretend to date you is the new way forward. That could be your next article. It's certainly going well enough for you: your one-off event turned into you booty-calling some guy you enlisted to be your fake date at your sister's wedding for birthday sex."

"I did *not* booty-call you!"

"Oh, sure." His eyes crease at the corners, twinkling silver, as a slow smile stretches over his face. "This was only ever *just* dinner."

I feel like, if it was, he'd still have come to hang out. He seems just as desperate for company as I am tonight. But we've been flirting all night, just like we always do when we're together. You could start a fire off the sparks that fly when we hold eye contact for that beat too long or when our fingers graze lazily over the other's arm.

Right now, our legs are entwined beneath the table. I've been running the side of my foot up and down his calf without even noticing it.

In response to his comment, I use that foot to get a little leverage to pull myself a little tighter into the table, my torso leaning toward him and my chin lifting. His gaze flickers down to my neck, then my chest, and when he glances back at my face, I grin back at him.

"Exactly. Just dinner."

• • •

Listen, I'm not proud of it, but I *do* enjoy every second of the taxi ride back to my apartment. As soon as we left the bar, barely even tipsy but drunk on the chemistry between us, Harry and I were all over each other. In the back seat of the taxi, his hand slips underneath my top, pushing my bra aside. I sigh when he kisses a trail down my throat, and half climb into his lap.

We do manage to keep it fairly PG, but the second we're out of the taxi and by the block of flats where I live, the anticipation is killing me. I don't think my place is too messy, but I don't waste a second worrying about it either way; the only thought I spare is for the new box of condoms I bought a few days ago but don't think I actually ever put away, and where the hell they are, and the precious time we might waste having to stop to look for them.

We have to stop outside the main doors to the building so I can key in the code but then we're both stumbling through the heavy door, kissing and fumbling over each other's clothes, intoxicated by each other's touch. I giggle when he trips and we both almost fall over, and I jab blindly at the wall where the elevator button is. Inside, I press the button for the eleventh floor, and then lose myself in him all over again. Harry's hands fall from my hips to my arse, cupping it and yanking me close to him; my body arches against his and a low moan slides out of his mouth when I kiss him again.

There's the sound of the elevator pulling to a stop, the doors sliding open.

Harry and I stagger out, with him behind me now so I can lead the way. One of his arms is wrapped around my waist and he busies himself kissing the side of my face and my neck again, pushing my hair out of his way. I giggle but don't complain—I am definitely not complaining—and try to concentrate on rummaging through my handbag for my keys. My hand digs past my purse, past the loose lipstick that's probably been kissed off my mouth by now, past my phone, which I haven't even bothered to look at once all evening.

His hand slips from my waist, moving inside my jeans when I hear—

"Sophie?"

The sound of Tally's voice, *right there*, right in front of me, is like being dunked in ice water. I jolt upright and away from Harry, who has straightened up and pulled his hand back to his side quickly, both of us stopping in our tracks.

My stomach sinks, but not because I've just been caught with this guy's hand inside my underwear.

A few feet in front of me, her face puffy and eyes bloodshot, surrounded by a suitcase, a duffel bag, a handbag, and a bulging backpack, is my best friend, and I get the horrible feeling I know exactly why she's here.

Thirty

Sam and Tally got together not long after we graduated university. Sam is about two years older than us and was working in website design at the time; now he's working at a video game development company. They met at work, only overlapping there for a couple of months before he moved on; he handed in his notice a few days before she started.

She likes to think it was fate. They talk about what a charming, fairy tale–like story it is—that they were obviously destined to meet.

Tally says that Sam is thoughtful and profound, that he thinks deeply about the world and likes to draw his own conclusions about things. He likes to pursue his hobbies; she likes how dedicated he is and how pragmatic his approach to life can be.

I mean, she obviously sees *something* in him, to have dated him for the last four years or so.

But Sam is also a borderline misogynist (which is putting it *very* lightly, in my opinion, and all I mean by that is that he's the kind of arsehole who would never say the wrong thing out loud but who says just enough that you know he's thinking it). He's lazy and what I can only call a mummy's boy: it's not that he never learned to do anything for himself, but that he decided he never had to. He takes advantage of Tally's drive and the fact she likes things done *just so*, so would always rather do them herself because she likes having control; it makes her feel more comfortable. He spends too much time talking about his job and his life and his friends and only gives back the bare minimum. He'll ask you one question about yourself while giving you an entire monologue about some inane thing in his life.

I could go on for a while about why I do not like Sam.

But I've never done that. Not to Lena, not to Frankie, not to my family, not to anybody—because Tally is my best friend, and this is the man she's chosen.

Sure, he cooks a really great vegetarian lasagna and he spends a lot of money buying Tally nice things because he's (to quote him) "noticed that gifts are her love language" and he knows she'd never treat herself to these things. And he's very good at singing and playing the piano, but what is this, the Regency era, where you find someone to marry based on their proficiency at the pianoforte? Give me a break.

Of course I don't complain about him—the same way I don't complain to a single one of my friends that it sucks how expensive wedding season is, and so does the expectation that I will just do all these things and go to all these parties and events and buy all these gifts without expecting anything back because it's the done thing even if it is never going to be my turn.

Tally and Sam have had fights before, but so have Lena and Johnny. So have Jessica and Conor. Everybody fights. And when it's your best friend—hell, when it's *anybody*—you have to walk that line between being on their side and not completely bad-mouthing their partner.

I mean, jeez, what if the last time they had a fight I'd told Tally exactly what I thought of him, only for them to resolve it over the next couple of days and carry on with their life together? Then she would *know*. And she would probably tell him what I said. And then *he* would know. And then every time we saw each other we would all know exactly how much I think Sam sucks as a human and it would be this great big elephant in the room, this huge wedge that I, and I alone, had driven between me and Tally. It's exactly how my friendship with my work bestie Magda at my old job ended; I learned my lesson.

So I've kept my mouth shut, for the most part.

After all, it's not me who has to live with Sam day in, day out. I get on with him enough when we do end up hanging out together for whatever reason but I don't let him take up enough space in my brain the rest of the time to care enough about how much I don't really like him, or how I think Tally could do so, so much better—that she *deserves* better.

It's not my place, is it? Even if I am her best friend. She loves him and she chose him, and that should be enough for me. It has to be enough for me. It's just the way it is.

But right now, Tally is standing with *luggage*, having obviously been crying a lot, on my doorstep, and there's only one conclusion I can draw from that.

She and Sam have broken up.

Or, at the very least, have had some gut-wrenching, horrible fight that was bad enough she has taken it upon herself to move out of the flat they rent together and come seek refuge here instead.

For a moment we all stare at each other. I look at Tally with that sinking feeling in my stomach. She looks between me and Harry; he looks at her for a while and then at me and I look back at him, not really sure what to say.

And crap. This is *Harry*. Who I've had this weird, on-off,

fake-relationship-with-benefits thing with since June, and Tally has no idea about any of it; she probably still thinks this man with his hand inside my underwear is *Jaxon*, for god's sake, and it's gone way too far for me to explain now.

And then Tally bursts into noisy, snotty sobs.

"I'm sorry!" she wails. "I'm sorry, Sophie, it was—it was—it's just—I needed to leave, and I didn't know where to go and, and you said—you said you didn't have plans tonight, so I thought you'd be in and I thought I'd come here and . . . "

She starts crying so hard the rest of her words become a garbled mess after that.

I turn around to Harry. All the excitement and anticipation has vanished; I'm disappointed, but even that pales in comparison to the knots in my stomach over the state Tally is in.

"I'm really sorry," I say, because what else can I say?

He shakes his head, looking disappointed, too, but accepting the situation—whatever he thinks it is. "That's okay. We had a fun night anyway, huh? Go take care of your friend, looks like she needs you."

"Thanks."

He gives me a swift, and friendly, kiss on the cheek. "I'll see you soon. Maybe you can come to my place next time. I'll cook. And happy birthday for the other day, Sophie."

Which is when Tally lets out a fresh wail and cries, "Oh my god, it's your birthday weekend, I'm such a terrible excuse for a friend!"

I give Harry an awkward wave and smile goodbye before turning my back on him to run over to Tally. I find my key in my bag easily this time. She babbles away as I unlock the door and pick up her bags to move her inside, where she can cry in comfort.

"I'm sorry, Soph, I ruined your weekend and—and I spoiled

your night with whatshisface with the funny name and you brought
him home to have birthday sex and now you're stuck with me
instead and—but you weren't answering your phone and now I
know why, but . . ."

It's a good twenty minutes or so before I can get any sense out
of Tally. I dump her things in the hallway by the front door and sit
her down on the sofa. I peel her out of her coat and give her my
dressing gown instead, then make her a cup of tea.

While I'm waiting for the kettle to boil, I sneak a look at my
phone.

Missed calls from Tallulah King (17)

Tallulah King
Babe, you there?
Pick up
Please
SOS
Sophie
???????????
Emergency, where are you?
                              Sent at 8:03 p.m.

Tallulah King
I think Sam and I just broke up.
                              Sent at 8:17 p.m.

My gut twists again, the margarita I drank before leaving the
bar threatening to make a reappearance. My best friend needed me,
really *needed me*, and where was I? Drinking and flirting with my
fake boyfriend.

I'm such a terrible friend.

Wrapped up in my dressing gown and cradling a large cup
of tea, Tally stops crying long enough to give me the gist of what
happened.

They were packing up the apartment. That was their big agenda
item for the weekend, because they're expecting the exchange of

contracts to complete at the end of the month on the place that they're buying together.

There's a small, angry and bitter part of me that wonders—was that *really* so important she couldn't make the time to even meet me for a coffee or let me come over to hang out and have some pizza or something, so I didn't have to be alone for my birthday weekend? I tamp it down quickly, though; it's too late anyway, and there's bigger things to focus on right now. Besides, she's upset enough as it is without me dumping my problems on her because I'm apparently incapable of being by myself or of getting a boyfriend.

Anyway, they were packing and there were a couple of little arguments. Did he really need all those socks? Half of them were full of holes anyway. She had too many mugs, he thought. Why couldn't she get rid of that pile of old T-shirts, the free ones from various nights out or societies we joined at uni? He should realize that it was ridiculous to hold on to that stack of posters that they absolutely would *not* be hanging up in the new place either.

At some point, it all spiraled. Out of nowhere, it turned into a blazing row and then . . .

"Then," Tally says, voice wobbling and fresh tears spilling down her cheeks, "he told me he didn't even know why we were bothering to go through with all this and buy a place together when he wasn't even sure he wanted to be with me."

"Oh shit."

Up until that point I was sure she was being dramatic. I was sure that it had all just got out of hand and that by tomorrow morning she'd realize she was silly to pack her things and leave, and she'd be going right back to him and I'd be counting my blessings that I didn't say too many bad words against him.

But that . . .

Yeah, I think, sucking a breath in sharply through my teeth, I don't think there's much coming back from that.

"What do you mean, he said he wasn't even sure he wanted to be with you?"

"I mean, he said those exact words. I asked him why we were buying a flat together if he was so against it and he said that it wasn't that he was *against* it so much as he was just doing it because that's what we're supposed to do and what everyone else is doing and, you know, we've been together for almost five years so that's the next step."

"So what the fuck is he playing at, taking the 'next step' with you if he doesn't want to be with you?"

Tally sniffles, head bowing as she looks sorrowfully down at her mug. She whispers, "He said he couldn't even remember why we got together in the first place."

"Excuse me? So, what, you're just . . . convenient to him? He's just with you because he doesn't know what else to do, just *buying a flat with you* because he can't be arsed to break up with you?"

"It's not that simple, Soph," she says, sniffling again, and it stings.

It's that, *you don't get it because you're single; because you've never been in a relationship, you can't possibly understand.*

I grit my teeth and swallow the hurt that bubbles up.

"We've been together for five years. We know practically everything about each other. We're a *couple*. It's not that easy to just *break up*. Everything is so wrapped up in each other, especially on a practical level. The rental agreement, the place we're buying, the deposit, the bills—we've built our whole lives around each other and *with* each other for the last five years. Of course it's not all sunshine and rainbows all the time, and not some little rosy bubble of nonstop romance. Things have been tense for a while, we've been fighting, but I thought that was just because of the move and stuff! It's been so stressful getting everything sorted, chasing things up, you know? But we love each other, and— Or I love him, and he used to love me, I guess, and . . . "

Tally trails off, words hitching in her throat. Her hands shake and her face crumples, her whole world snatched out from right under her feet.

I will tear Sam limb from limb for doing this to her.

"Did he say that, though? That he doesn't love you anymore?"

"He may as well have. He said this is how he saw his life going so he didn't want to put a stop to it, and obviously *does* love me, but it just doesn't feel like it used to or how he expected it to. And I asked him what the hell that was supposed to mean, because I love him, and he just—he just sort of shrugged"—she shrugs, all slouched shoulders and sullen-faced in what's actually a very good impression of Sam—"and he said he didn't really know and if I didn't get it, maybe we weren't in the same place in this relationship."

"Not in the same place?" I echo, righteously outraged, as any person with a moral compass would be—and as any best friend ought to be. "You live together! You're buying an apartment and moving in at the end of the month! He's been viewing places with you for months, dealing with the solicitors for weeks, what the fuck kind of place did he think he was in if it wasn't that exact one?"

But Tally doesn't know, and I don't have the answers.

I decide it's still best not to sit here and reel off every awful thing about Sam and practically sit her down for a full PowerPoint presentation on All the Reasons Tally Deserves Better than that Scumbag, just in case.

But I do let her cry and rehash different facets of the argument over and over again. I make her more tea and find some chocolate bourbon biscuits in the cupboard for us to share and tell her she can stay as long as she wants. I hug her tight and tell her it doesn't matter that her "stupid breakup" has interrupted my birthday weekend and then pass her the tissues when she cries all over again because what if they really *are* broken up, what if that's it, now, for good?

When she tires herself out, I leave her with some spare blankets and a pillow and then take myself to bed. I lie under the duvet and listen to my best friend crying herself to sleep over the boy she's spent the last almost five years building a life with.

I don't envy her one bit.

• • •

Sunday morning dawns pale and cool and gray, and I wake up to the sound of Tally putting down the phone on Sam and sobbing again.

For a few minutes I stay in bed and debate how best to deal with all of this.

Then again, I don't think there is any "right" way to help Tally. It's not my relationship to fix, and, even if I know how happy she is—was—with Sam, I don't know that I want to fix it anyway. I guess all I have to do is be there for her.

It's not like I can give her much advice, is it?

I may have been Harry's expert on being single, but I don't think that's what Tally needs right now—so I get out of bed and head out to the living room to face my best friend and her heartbreak, ready to do what I can to help her.

"Oh." She sniffles, wiping the back of her hand across her face. "Hi. Sorry. I didn't mean to wake you up."

"'S'okay. Was that Sam?"

As if there's anybody else she'd have been shouting, "What about the mortgage application?" down the phone to.

"Yeah." She sniffles again. "He wants to put the move on hold. Indefinitely."

"What, like, postpone it?"

Tally rolls her eyes, eyelashes fluttering and forehead creasing. She leans forward, elbows propped on her knees, and buries her face in her hands.

"He wants to pull out altogether. Cancel it. And I—I said we just needed to talk this through. Sort it out, you know? Now we've both slept on it. Talk again when we've both got a clear head. And he said this is the clearest his head has been in a while. And that the best thing we can do now is back out before it's too late."

I'll give him a clear head. See how clearly he's thinking when I've knocked him over the head with his stupid PlayStation.

I will, however, grant that he's being very pragmatic, one of the things Tally loves most about him. If they are going through this fight or rocky patch or breakup, whatever it is, the best thing they can do is back out of buying a place before they're tied down together by that and have forked out their savings on a mortgage and moving vans and whatever else they have to pay to move house.

What I say out loud is, "So, what, he still wants to talk things through? Try to work it out, even if you aren't moving anymore?"

"I don't know," she whispers from behind her hands. "I think . . . god, Soph, I think he's already made up his mind. He's going to leave me. Isn't he?"

I wish I could tell her no.

I wish it was the right time to tell her she can do much better.

I sit down on the sofa next to her and put my arms around her.

"He's not going to fight for us, is he? He's already on his way out the door. He's *decided*. And—and the fucking bastard waited until we were buying somewhere together and about to move in and start the rest of our lives together to do it! That arsehole!"

She sits up abruptly then launches one of my decorative cushions at the door. Tears dribble down her cheeks, which are flushed now. She snatches another tissue to blow her nose and then wipes her face with the dressing gown sleeve.

"Do you think he's met someone else?"

"No! What? No! Sam loves— Look, Talls, he's a scumbag, and I can't believe he'd do this to you, but cheating? I just don't think it's his style."

He's too bloody lazy to make up the lies required to cheat. Tally would've seen right through him if he'd tried.

"He doesn't have the gall to cheat on you," I dare to say.

"Yeah, that's true . . . but then why? Why would he let it get this far? Why would he suggest we look for places to buy together, why was he talking just last week about contacting the internet provider to set it up for the new place if he didn't really want to go through with it? If he didn't love me anymore and didn't want to be with me, why didn't he *just say*?"

A horrifying realization dawns on me.

Because I think I know exactly why Sam let it all go this far.

What did she tell me he said during their fight? He was just "doing it because that's what they were supposed to do."

I think about some of the guys I've dated in the last few years, all the bad habits and bullshit I've put up with because, well, they seem *nice enough*, don't they? I want it to work out. I want to have someone, just like everyone else does. The bar is so low. It's so fucking low even Sam could meet it on his better days.

He stayed because it was the normal thing and because he loved her *enough*, so it was worth it.

I can understand that. After all, isn't it exactly why I kept dating Jaxon, hoping that he might be enough one day too? It's basically why Harry proposed to his ex-wife when their relationship was already rocky, isn't it?

Maybe Sam got spooked by it all when they were packing yesterday. Or maybe he never meant to say any of that stuff out loud but knows there's no point trying to take it back now.

That's not the answer Tally wants to hear, though, so I just say, "Because he's a bloody idiot, that's why. Honestly, the next time I see him, I'm giving him a piece of my mind. How dare he? How fucking dare he?"

I make us breakfast while she spirals, bemoaning all the ways their lives are entangled. The rent agreement, the joint bank account, their Amazon Prime subscription . . . it's an endless list, and I realize she was right: I don't understand. Until I have a relationship like that, I will never understand.

This is her *whole life*. This is everything. Every boring, ordinary nook and cranny is tied up with Sam, involves him somehow. And after five years, I can only imagine how long it's going to take to unpick all of that.

Hearing her panic and despair over separating their lives and the impact on her finances makes me feel awful for all the times I've wanted to complain about wedding season bleeding me dry. Dad and Camilla always made sure we knew how to budget and manage our money, so things like buying a used car and paying rent by myself just felt sort of par for the course. But for Tally, it's unthinkable. It's devastating to even contemplate.

Tally circles back to sadness soon enough: What is she going to do without him? She loves him so much. This hurts so much. How could he do this to her? Why doesn't he love her and what's wrong with her and where did she go wrong to make him stop loving her? How is she supposed to just go back to work and carry on as normal and do *everything* with this huge chunk of her life suddenly *gone*?

She talks like she's grieving; I guess I can't blame her for that, even if it's something else I can't fully understand.

As I'm plating our fry-ups, though, she says, "Oh god, and I'm such a terrible friend. You're the best, Soph, honestly. Thanks for letting me stay and just rant at you, all this time. Oh my god! No, and there was that fit guy last night too! Jaxon! Ohmigod, and after you broke up with him! Shit. What was that all about? I didn't know you were back together? *Please*. Tell me everything. I need the distraction."

"No, I'm not— That wasn't— We're not back together. That was just, um . . . "

I can't tell her the whole backstory now. It's too many secrets; it'll make me sound selfish and cruel. And Tally's too emotionally fragile right now. I need to be a rock for her, not another earthquake she has to deal with.

"It's not serious. We're just . . . having fun."

Tally gives a long sigh. I can't tell if it's wistful or dejected. "I suppose that'll be me soon, won't it? Going off having sex with random guys I met on dating apps."

"You say that like I'm sleeping with someone new every couple of days. Jeez. He's only the second guy I've slept with all year."

"Oh. Well, yeah. The dates, then." Her nose wrinkles, and she stabs a sausage with her fork. "They're not all as bad as the ones you find, are they?"

"Not at all. There are tons of great men. Loads better than the ones I date. But obviously I've set my filters to like, you know, a ten-mile radius, turns their underwear inside out rather than putting a load of washing on, only interested in stringing me along for something casual instead of a serious relationship, three inches shorter than whatever height they say they are in their bio . . . "

Tally cringes under the deadpan look I give her.

"Fair point."

And anyway, I want to snap at her, *Sam's no peach. Have you met him?*

"So, you're not after anything serious with him, then?"

"No."

"Perfect. You'll have extra time to help me find somewhere to live and be my wingwoman in bars when I'm single too."

Thirty-one

October wanes and my best friend's life falls apart.

The weekend of the fight, she got her things together and went back home to Sam sometime on Sunday afternoon. It was silly to have just gone like that, she said, and also, she'd be damned if she let *him* chase *her* out, when this was clearly all his fault.

They argued for a few more hours. He's been sleeping on the sofa since. Tally came to stay with me the next weekend, and Lena came to visit too.

A girls' night, they declared. That was exactly what we needed. We would hole ourselves up in my apartment watching films and talking, and we'd order some food in and do a sheet mask and eat Ben & Jerry's right out of the tub. We'd pull out all the stops to try and take Tally's mind off her heinous suddenly ex-boyfriend, and have some fun for a little while.

Don't get me wrong, I had a great weekend. I loved seeing them both, and hanging out with zero plans and zero pressure was so much *fun* for a change.

So is it really that bad if I feel angry and resentful, too? I can't help but notice that, once again, it's a relationship that's dictated our social lives. Sure, instead of a wedding or a baby shower or anything like that, it's a breakup, but the principle of the thing still stands.

Where were they for movies and ice cream on my birthday?

How many weekends have I spent puttering around trying to fill the time and scrolling through Instagram looking at all the fun, brilliant things my friends are doing with the other people in their lives? And yet Tally can't cope for one? And Lena feels obliged to shift everything around to accommodate that?

It's the bitter, horrible voice in the back of my mind that curdles my enjoyment of the weekend into something sour and mean, but I can't stop it. I don't know that I *want* to.

And Tally, I think, hasn't been so talkative over text since before Sam. Obviously we talk most days, but now she messages me constantly throughout the day, and I can't help but think—where has this been for the last few years? Or are you just desperately lonely and messaging everybody in the hopes that someone will reply and ease that pain for a little while? Is this all the sort of stuff that you filled Sam's day with before, and now you're telling me because you can't tell him?

And I think, *Is this what I'm like, to all my friends?*

I hope not, but I'm really not sure.

I know she needs me. I love Tally to bits; I want to be there for her and of course I'll support her, whatever she needs, even if that's just company and attention for now. I feel sorry and hurt for her, in her heartbreak, and despise Sam for doing this to her.

But there's still that resentment, churning away in the pit of my stomach and flaring up inside my chest every so often.

Why does she get to act like her life is over just because he doesn't want to be in it anymore?

Why is everyone acting like it's such a terrible, hopeless thing?

• • •

"You know you sound like a right heartless bitch there, Barker," Duncan tells me as I vent all to him, ignoring Tally's fiftieth message in the group chat today. He grins at me, though, to show me he's not seriously judging me.

"Shut up. You know what I mean. Like, I get that it's a terrible thing that they aren't together anymore and she's heartbroken. That's not the bit I'm talking about. I mean, the way everyone's acting so sorry for her because she's going to be single now. Like her life is over and she has to start it all again. I mean, she didn't get *fired*. She didn't . . . I mean, she almost sort of lost her house, but not really. Sam's moving out and she's extended the lease, she can cover the rent herself until she finds somewhere else. It's not *ideal*, sure, but it's also not impossible, or the end of the world. She's still got her amazing career. She's still got her flat. But everyone's acting like she's right back to the drawing board, like that's *it* now, *finito*, the end, just because he's not going to be around anymore."

"And when you say everyone . . . ?"

"Oh my god, who *don't* I mean? Her friends at work. Friends from school. Her parents. Her sister. Her brothers. Lena. Even Frankie Two heard about it and messaged her. Tally sent me the screenshots."

"Are you still mad at her for thinking you were screwing Frankie One?"

"No! I—I mean, yes, a bit, but that's not the point."

"So the point is that we bet the boyfriend's lot aren't saying all this stuff to him? That they're probably saying it's a shame but, ah, well, best crack on with life? No 'down with the patriarchy, off with these shackles society places on women with its expectations that we be settled down with kids and stuff by the time they're thirty when we don't do the same to men'?" Then he mutters, mostly to himself, "Oh yeah. I'd be totally qualified to write *that* article," and jots a note to himself in his phone. I ignore him.

"Not even that! Although, yeah, now you mention it . . . "

I'm so riled up, though, I have to file that one away to be angry about later. I adjust my hold on my mug so I can gesture at Duncan.

"The point," I exclaim, "is that people are treating her like being single is the worst thing that could have happened to her now. Like this is some awful, tragic thing. And like, the end of her relationship might be, sure, but just *not having a boyfriend anymore* isn't. They're acting like life is so bloody awful if you don't have one!"

"Right." Duncan smirks. "Because you're such a ray of sunshine all the bloody time. Not always moping over a boy or mooning over one or dating one or talking to one, or . . . "

I jerk back a little bit, staring at him as he trails off in a *you get the picture, need I go on* kind of way, grinning like he's just made a brilliant joke, but the punch line feels like a very literal punch in the gut.

Am I always like that?

Is my life every bit as miserable as everyone's making it out that Tally's will be?

I probably would have said yes even just last weekend. It was exactly that miserable.

And the seemingly endless attempts at dating and finding a boyfriend or a guy to spend my life with *are* kind of miserable, especially when they keep not working out for whatever reason and the whole cycle has to start again, but—

The rest of my life isn't that bad, is it?

I have a job. A job that I like, a job that I'm even quite good at most of the time. I rent my own flat, all by myself. I have . . . a *semblance* of a social life, even if it does mostly revolve around weddings and housewarmings and dates, and even if recently it does mainly consist of a guy I roped into being my fake boyfriend.

Is my life so worthless? I ask myself, and then realize that's completely the wrong question.

What I should really be asking is, do I value those things so little, just because I don't have someone to share it all with?

Duncan is staring at me like he can see the gears whirring and the spanner he just unwittingly threw into them. He frowns. "What did I say?"

"I'm not always like that, am I?"

"Not always, no!" he says, a little bit too quickly. "No! Just, you know. A normal amount."

"Oh my god. I *am*, aren't I?"

He looks at me steadily, then sighs and says, "Would you like me to be honest, or put a bit of a journalistic positive spin on it? I can do that, but you should know, I will be very biased as a fellow perpetual singleton."

I can't answer him, too shaken up by this horrific and mortifying realization. This feels infinitely more embarrassing than the Frankies' housewarming, overhearing Frankie Two insinuating I was a slut out to steal her man, and definitely more embarrassing than eating dog-food cupcakes and then using liver-flavored toothpaste; it's worse than going to the cinema on my own for my birthday after Tally canceled last-minute, and a rock bottom that makes finding a fake date for Jessica's wedding look like a totally sane, reasonable, everyday thing to have done.

Duncan seems to notice I've gone practically catatonic and my rant about Tally's breakup is over, because he claps his hand on my shoulder and says, "Look, Barker, really. Don't get too caught up about it. I'd be the same if I had everyone telling me my body clock was running out. You think I don't die a little inside every time a girl ghosts me or my gran gives me that big, disappointed sigh because I haven't found somebody yet? Or the worst one—those girls who ask me what's wrong with me, all jokey-like, because I'm thirty-eight and I've never been married and I don't have kids, and they say it like they don't mean it, but we both know they *do*. It gets all of us down. Actually, now, *that's* a good spin for an article. Hey, if I pitch this to Andy, you all right if I come to you for some quotes from the female perspective? This kind of stuff always does great on the website."

"Sure," I say, but I feel so zoned out I'm not even sure what I agree to. Duncan and I collect our now-lukewarm drinks and head back to our own desks. I open up the Word document with my column, all marked up with notes from the editorial team, but my eyes glaze over, and it all turns to fuzz on the screen.

My whole rant about Tally's breakup threatening to take over my own life had turned into "being single isn't that bad" without me even realizing that was the hill I was going to die on today. And boy, did I die on that hill. My chest feels tight all of a sudden; my palms are sweating and blood rushes in my ears.

I'm no better than all the people I'm complaining about, than Lena with her sudden obsession for wedding Pinterest boards or Tally for having total breakdowns over how to split up the Christmas decorations or if she's still supposed to send Sam's mum a birthday card next month.

I've made my whole life about someone else, too, and I don't even *have* someone else in my life to share it all with.

Maybe they're all right: being single is the real tragedy here after all.

November

Nadine Cox-Dawes
Hey, Soph, thanks for the lovely card and the elephant plushie—baby loves it! Sorry for being a bit MIA but Mum and Jess said they've been filling you in and sending pics and stuff. Just all been totally mad here! And I'm fucking knackered. Anyway, really looking forward to seeing you next weekend xx
                                                    Sent at 4:19 a.m.

Nadine Cox-Dawes
Also pls wear something you don't mind getting sick on. Dad wore that Ralph Lauren shirt I got him last Xmas and within two minutes it had sick on it.
                                                    Sent at 4:19 a.m.

Nadine Cox-Dawes
One last one, can you please bring me some mince pies? David refusing to get anything Xmasy in before December and I'm dying for one but basically chained to the house and Mum's FINALLY moving back home tomorrow. Can't ask Jess to bring any because she'll snitch to David. Ta xx
                                                    Sent at 4:22 a.m.

Thirty-two

**Just because I'm single doesn't mean
I'm at your beck and call.**

Views on establishing boundaries from our
Dating & Relationships columnist

"You want to be thinking about having your own soon, love. You don't want to end up being one of those geriatric mums—I know the doctors can work their magic these days, but I was reading in the *Daily Mail* the other week about it, and it can cause all sorts of problems for the baby as well as you."

Oh fuck off, Laura.

I mean, really. The *gall*. I might be expected to put up with such a comment from my own grandma, but not from Auntie Janine's mum. She doesn't even *like* me very much.

But now—oh, now she's interested, isn't she? The same woman who called me Sophia for about a year after Auntie Dawn and Janine got serious enough to introduce their families to each other.

I ignore her in favor of looking at the texts pinging through on my phone, surprised when I find they're from Nadine about visiting next weekend. She had the baby right at the start of the month—went into labor late on Halloween and gave birth some-where in the wee hours of November 1—but I haven't seen her yet. I FaceTimed to congratulate her, obviously, but since then she hasn't really been answering my messages or anything.

At first I thought it was because she was pissed off that I wasn't waiting around at the hospital or there to meet her and the baby when they got home, but Camilla told me it's just that Nadine is exhausted. If anything, I'm doing her a favor by staying away. I got all the gory details I didn't ask for about just how difficult the birth was, how many stitches Nadine needed, and all that stuff—appar-ently, she even told her best mate not to visit while she gets her bearings a bit, and while the parents-in-laws have visited, she made David's siblings and their kids stay away.

"She just needs some peace and quiet to rest," Camilla told me.

"But you're staying with her."

"Of course I am, love, I'm her mum."

I'm surprised but pleased to see the few texts from her now. The first one feels oddly formal, but I try not to let it get to me. My relationship with Nadine has always been a bit like that. Slightly removed, even if it's amiable enough. It's just circumstance—nothing personal.

But then I get to the text begging me for mince pies and laugh out loud.

Yup, that's my big stepsister all right.

"Ooh!" says Granny. "Is that your Harry?"

"It's just Nadine, about seeing her and the baby next weekend," I explain.

Even though Laura's geriatric mum spiel has petered out, she snaps to attention again at the mention of another baby. She nar-rows her eyes at me, lips pursing and emphasizing every wrinkle on her face. "You see? You want to be careful or you'll be the only one left. Oh dear, you're not one of those who doesn't want children, are you?"

Wow.

Mum, overhearing, waves a hand quickly before going back to cuddling the baby. "Oh, Laura, honestly. Plenty of people don't these days."

"Plenty of people didn't want them in the old days either—bet they used to wish it wasn't such a taboo and a bit more like it is these days," Granny supplies, with a dry laugh that just makes Laura purse her lips so much I think she might have an aneurism.

Auntie Janine shifts in her seat a little and I notice Auntie Dawn cut her a look, both of them aware that the mood has shifted, and an argument could be brewing. Auntie Dawn carries on pumping and doesn't say anything, though, apparently too tired to intervene; Janine pulls a face and looks uncannily like her mum and stays quiet, too, although she remains bolt upright, watching us all carefully, ready to shut it down if she has to.

Laura doesn't even seem to notice that I never answer, only nods in baby Poppy's direction, face softening as her granddaughter burbles happily away, oblivious. "It would be so nice for Poppy to grow up with cousins. Janine's father was an only child, of course, so she never had cousins on that side of the family, and I always thought it was a shame my brother never had children, but what can you do?"

Uh, I don't know, maybe you could have given him the third degree like you're doing to me right now? Maybe you would've done his head in, too, and he would've had them just to shut you up.

I make a mental note to mention this conversation to Duncan. Maybe he can use it for his article about the differing societal pressures placed on people to settle down. (I still need to decide if I'm going to let him name me or if I want to be quoted simply as everyone's favorite anonymous columnist.)

I look around at everyone else in the room as I respond to Laura. "Well, they wouldn't be cousins, though, if I had kids anyway, would they? They'd be . . . what is that, second cousins? First cousin once removed? Twice removed?"

Granddad, who has been sitting quietly with the paper, ignoring it completely in favor of pulling silly faces at Poppy, pipes up with, "First cousin once removed, I'm sure. Yes—yes, it's got to be. I had thirteen cousins, you know. Bunch of tossers, most of them. One of them's been in jail for forty-odd years."

"Was that the one with all the fraud, with the betting shop?" Granny asks.

"Eh? Oh, no, no, that was Eddy. Great guy, Eddy. Brilliant cricketer, you know, Sophie. He could've played for England," he adds as an aside. "No, he went off to Spain after all that, before they could come after him. It was, um, what was her name? It'll come back to me."

"Margaret," I supply, having heard this story and variations on it about fifty times before. "And she looked like the queen's sister, you always said."

"Aye, that's it! Yes, of course."

Laura looks both stricken and bewildered by the sudden turn of conversation. I make the mistake of catching Mum's eye; she's noticed, too, and we both have to fight not to laugh. I don't dare look at Granny, because I know she'll be the exact same, and then we'll all start laughing.

Granddad explains to Laura, "A real looker, she was. 'Course, all the blokes fancied her, and she had her pick of them—and did a damn sight more than pick their pockets. Stole money from a sheikh once, I think."

"Is that why she's in jail?"

"Oh, no."

Laura just stares at him.

"Anyway, point is, Poppy could have a whole boatload of cousins and it wouldn't make a blind bit of difference how she turns out. Your Janine's probably fared a damn sight better for having none than I did for having all of them lot."

"Well, Eddy did give us a loan for the house, don't forget," Granny reminds him.

"Oh aye." Granddad looks at me, all mock serious, pulling a funny face. "She's right, then, Sophie. You best get cracking and tie down that Harry of yours. If it's not Poppy, someone better carry on the family tradition, eh?"

"You really should!" Laura cries. "He's quite a bit older, isn't he? He must be thinking about starting a family, and—"

"Actually," I interrupt, "Harry doesn't want kids."

Which is a barefaced lie; he's said a few times about how much he'd love to be a dad, how it was part of the reason he went through with the wedding even when his relationship wasn't at its best. But it's so worth it for the shocked look on Laura's face, and it takes all my willpower not to laugh.

"Well," says Granny, smiling at me, "at least he's not a con artist."

I smile back, relaxing now—and feeling oddly triumphant.

I sort of expected my family to be on Laura's side there. They're always asking if I've found a boyfriend yet, how it's going with whichever guy I said I was seeing. I saw how happy and excited they all were when Dawn told us she was pregnant, and I knew they wondered when it would be my turn. They've *said*, to my face, that it'll be me next. It's a constant but familiar pressure by now, and I don't even think they realize they're doing it most of the time.

And maybe it's just that Laura can be a bit of an uppity bitch sometimes, or maybe it's just that they really *aren't* putting pressure on me and genuinely don't mean to when they do, but it's nice to feel like my family really are on my side, for once.

Then Granddad tosses the newspaper aside and gets up to go and make some more coffee, offering the rest of us a hot drink while he's up and in the kitchen. Mum hands me the baby and goes to help him. They're barely down the end of the hallway before I hear them laughing and shushing each other.

And, holy shit, there is a baby in my lap.

I've met the baby a couple of times now. It's been okay.

She's really cute. I know you're meant to say that about babies, but Poppy really is. She's got these round, rosy cheeks and tufts of soft yellow hair, and chubby, soft limbs, and big bright-green eyes and this great big beautiful gummy smile. She's adorable and precious, and I love her so much.

I am also completely fucking terrified of her because she's a baby, and I do not know what I'm supposed to do.

The first couple of times I'd been to visit, Poppy was mostly asleep, and mostly still. She was all bundled up in blankets so all I had to do was sit on the sofa while Auntie Janine carried this swaddled thing over and put it in my arms, and then someone else took her off me after a while. It wasn't much different the second time I came to visit, but then I could mostly stand over her cot and coo down at her as she played with a mobile.

Now she's wriggling around, her arms and legs free, in a soft moss-green outfit with a teddy bear printed on the top, and she is not still or sleeping or swaddled.

I put a hand around the back of her head because I know that's what you're supposed to do, but sheer terror sets in, and I lose all track of whatever conversation the others are having now. There is only me and this baby, and I mean it in the worst way possible.

I wonder if this happens to everyone—if my friends experience this too. I wonder if Jessica felt like this when she held Nadine's baby. Do they get all glossy-eyed and dream of the children they will have one day, and feel overcome with love?

I can't be the only person overcome with panic. I can't.

It's not like I'm holding Poppy and I'm actively repulsed or anything. And it's not like I look at her cute little face and cuddle her close and feel nothing or think about how I actually really *don't* want this for myself one day.

It's mostly just: *But what do I do with it?*

Am I supposed to know? Was I supposed to go on a course or read a book, like soon-to-be parents do, so I could understand? Did I miss something somewhere along the way that tells you how to deal with a baby for the first time when it's not even yours?

I feel like I did that time I agreed to dog-sit for someone at work, and in spite of the two-page list of instructions they left me with for the weekend, suddenly it was just me and this miniature schnauzer, both helpless and confused, just praying we made it through the weekend in one piece.

Poppy plants her sticky little hands right on my face, eyes boring into mine all serious and stern, almost like she knows I've gone into crisis mode and is trying to reassure me, and I burst out laughing.

"Yeah, you and me both, kid."

Thirty-three

Apparently, my entire November is going to revolve around babies. A bit like Tally's breakup, it feels like it's all somehow my responsibility (*problem* feels like a bit too strong a word when I'm talking about some very cute babies I already love dearly) and I'm not sure how that's happened. I don't know how I can be woefully single, and not even currently at risk of getting pregnant, and yet everything seems to be *babies*.

Even at work, I can't escape it. My boss Jenny is now fully gearing up for her maternity leave next year and brings it up when I've got a meeting with her about some ongoing work on Wednesday morning. Somehow, we'd gone from talking about sponsoring some local event to weekend plans to me going to visit Nadine and the new baby this weekend, to Jenny's own upcoming absence.

"Ideally, I don't want to bring in a replacement," she's saying. "I think it would ultimately upset the balance in the team and I think we've got everything running so smoothly at the moment it'd be a shame to go through all that upheaval for just a temporary basis."

"Totally," I say, even though Isaac at the desk opposite mine is still bugging me about the littlest things on a near-daily basis. "The last thing you want is to be stressing yourself out worrying about coming back to a bit of a mess or anything."

"Exactly!" Her eyes bug out and she gestures widely, looking relieved. I wonder if she's already run this by other people in the office, or maybe her husband, and they've told her it's a stupid idea. "I'm so glad we're on the same page."

"So have you got someone in mind?"

Come on, Jenny. You know what I'm asking here. Come on . . .

I don't think I'd be considering asking at all if I hadn't accidentally put the idea in my own head while arguing with Mum—and definitely not without Duncan, Harry, and even Siobhan egging me on.

I've ended up confiding in them not just because they know about the anonymous column but because they all seem to *get it*, somehow. I don't feel like I'm just "their single friend" clutching a career to fill a void, and, given they all also know about the lows I sank to with recruiting Harry to pretend to be my boyfriend, it's easy to tell them all the ways I've screwed up at work that I think might hold me back from any kind of promotion. Their encouragement feels more genuine than any enthusiastic *You've got this!* from Tally or Lena or Jessica.

Now all I can do is hold my breath and wait.

"Well." Jenny places both palms flat on her desk, leans back in her chair, and fixes me with a smile. "I was actually hoping, Sophie, that you might want to step up and take on a little bit more responsibility."

Yes!!!

I keep my cool and try to look pleasantly surprised and flattered, but also completely capable and grown-up while she carries on talking—sounding almost like she's pitching me the job, when I've been mentally preparing to pitch myself to *her* for this, planning how to "sell myself" with Siobhan, Harry, or Duncan's help.

"You've really gone from strength to strength since joining us, and I know you've seen quite a few changes in the team already, what with the push on brand promotions and deals, and a few people coming and going . . . Even with your column, I know that was a big step outside of your comfort zone, but it's a huge responsibility and you took it right on the chin. Plus"—she lowers her voice slightly, looking a bit guilty—"people around the rest of the office like you and you get on with pretty much anybody. I can't exactly say the same for the rest of the team. That's a quality that goes a *very* long way in leadership roles, you know. And I know I can trust you to speak up in the interdepartmental meetings."

I'm bursting with pride. I never understood that phrase until right now when I feel like I could quite literally burst. It's like I can feel this huge, joyful scream building in my lungs, swelling up from right in the pit of my stomach. I want to leap over the table and hug Jenny and thank her for saying all these lovely things about me and my job and making it all sound so much bigger and more important than it feels day-to-day. It's an unexpected and massive confidence boost; I want to message everyone I know and brag to them.

She carries on, telling me that she'll pass the news on to the rest of the managerial team—she'd like them to just check in from time to time, offer me a bit of extra support as and when I might need it—and says she'll set up some meeting for the two of us so she can show me the ropes.

"Thanks, Jenny. I really appreciate it. Really. This is—" I swallow the lump of raw emotion in my throat before I dissolve into excited babbling, or cry. "I know you're putting your trust in me here and it—it really means a lot. I promise I won't let you down."

To my surprise, Jenny laughs.

"Soph, don't make promises you can't keep. 'I won't let you down.' Honestly, who says things like that?"

"Uh . . . "

"One thing I really admire about you," my boss tells me earnestly, smiling broadly, "is how much you fuck up."

"I'm—I'm sorry?"

Alarm flits over her face. "Oh no, please don't take that the wrong way! Honestly, it's a good thing. You've lost a few of the brand deals you negotiated for us because you pushed too hard or misunderstood what they were looking for. You pitched us that designer last year, do you remember? To do all those street art–style ads around town. And it totally backfired, and we ended up paying that one shop owner a few grand in compensation. And like with the pub contract earlier this year . . . "

My cheeks flush hot. I've wasted a lot of time feeling guilty about those things—and would've wasted a lot more with a different sort of manager, I know—but whenever they have happened, Jenny always sweeps it under the rug and I think, *I just* have *to try again.* Do something better, do something *good*, before someone decides to sack me.

Jenny smiles at me, like these things are reasons to promote me, not fire me.

"You're quite a natural when it comes to failure."

"Right . . . um . . . thank you? I think?"

"What I mean is, you never let it get you down when something doesn't quite go to plan or if it turns out you've messed up a bit. You just crack on. If this was your annual review, I'd be telling you that maybe you could spend a bit more time *living* with those failures, doing more of a 'lessons learned' exercise, but"—she cracks another smile at me—"I'm not worried about you taking over for me while

I'm gone, even if you *do* let me down, because I know you'll just keep trying. You won't throw in the towel and pitch a fit at the first sign of a struggle. Bloody hell, even in your dating life you're like that! Your column is often about how you feel you're messing up, but that's exactly what people respond to."

We chat a little bit more about these new plans for me taking over from Jenny while she's on leave next year and how she'll take a look at budgets to get me a pay rise "reflective of these new responsibilities," but once I'm back at my desk, my excitement dims considerably, and I keep turning over her comment about being "a natural" at failing.

I already know I feel like a failure—because I'm about fifty years away from scraping together anything even resembling a house deposit, because my friends are starting to get married while I can barely get a second or third date, because of my screwups at work.

I'm always paranoid that everyone else looks at me and sees a failure, but I guess I could always console myself with the idea that maybe, *maybe*, they don't, and it's all in my head.

If even my boss is calling me out on it, and especially at being a failure at *dating* . . . it's definitely not all in my head, is it?

It eats away at the back of my mind the entire rest of the day while I'm doing work, fielding messages from Tally either directly to me or in the group chat, and when Duncan comes over to show me a text from the girl he's seeing and ask me if I think she's pissed off with him and if so, what did he say and what does he need to apologize for. It's still nagging at me when I'm at home later that night, wrapped in my dressing gown, plonked on the sofa in front of the telly with Tally next to me looking for a film to watch on Netflix. (Tally's suddenly got all the time in the world to hang out now, even on a random Wednesday night for no reason and with no notice.)

I open my mouth to ask her, but I stop myself. Do I really want to know what she thinks?

What if she agrees?

"What?" she says, barely even looking at me.

"I didn't say anything."

"You were going to. Then you pulled that face like you do when you're thinking too much about something. Like when Lena told you she didn't think burgundy was a very flattering color for you."

Damn Tally for being my best friend and being able to read me so well.

So I launch into the whole thing. She already knows about my new, temporary promotion since I told the girls earlier in the group chat, but now I give her an almost word-for-word replay of the rest of my conversation with Jenny, including the whole "failing at dating" thing.

"And she's right, isn't she? I *am* a failure at it."

"So?"

"What do you mean, 'so'? *So*, I'm obviously destined to be single forever and I'm never going to find a guy who wants to be with me or who'll fall in love with me because I can't fucking do anything right, and—"

"Well, that's a bit drastic. Look, if we're going to talk failures in romance, what about me? I was literally about to buy a flat with my boyfriend. I was in love. I was wondering how long it'd be before he proposed. And now he's off down the sodding pub all the time with his mates having apparently moved on from me and our relationship long before we even broke up. How's that for failure?"

"That's different."

"Is it? Because let me tell you, Soph, it feels like a shower of shite right now. It doesn't make me feel very *successful* in the love department."

"Yeah, but—"

"But," she tells me sharply, but not unkindly, "you are a failure. And you do always get back up, dust yourself off, and carry on. It never gets you down. Well—it *did* a bit with The Gareth Who Stole Christmas. But to be fair, he did break up with you on Christmas Eve, which would be horrible for anybody. But you bounced back after a while, didn't you? God, imagine if you didn't. Imagine if you had, like, one single bad date and swore off trying to find someone for good. Now, *that* would be sad."

I shake my head, though. There were things about her breakup I didn't understand; there are things about being perpetually single that *she* doesn't understand.

"I get that, but that's not what I mean. All I do is match with guys who seem maybe halfway decent, waste my time talking to them even if I'm not sure I like them, go on dates to see if there's chemistry or if I do like them, see if I like them as much in person, and even when it goes well, it ultimately *doesn't*. Because they ghost me, or one of us calls it off, or there's just no romantic spark there, or it was just casual, or . . . "

Or they're my complete opposite in a million tiny ways, in the middle of a horrible divorce, in no way emotionally ready for a relationship even if they pine for the intimacy of one and the lifestyle that goes along with it.

Tally just stares at me, not getting it. She knows this is how it goes, because she gets all the very detailed updates about it when and as anything happens in my dating life. I take a deep breath and carry on, suddenly desperate to make her understand.

"If being a failure is a good thing because I keep trying again, then all that means here is that I've been wasting the last however many years going in circles with this and never actually, *really*, getting anywhere. You're supposed to learn something from failure, but what have I learned? I mean, seriously. What have I learned from any of this? To do a reverse Google Images search on his photos to check he isn't catfishing me, or married? Well, whoopee, consider me an expert. It's like all I do is waste my time and money and some of my very best jokes on men it just doesn't work out with, and I *keep doing it*, and I *keep not getting anywhere*.

"I know, I know, I just haven't found the right guy," I add, sensing her about to say something, but too in the flow of my tirade or monologue or whatever this is to stop now. "And I just need to keep looking, keep trying. Kiss a few frogs! Prince Charming is out there somewhere! Well, what if he's *not*? And what if I'm really fucking tired of looking and constantly getting my hopes up? It's the same thing. It's always a failure. And it's *exhausting*. What part of that isn't a shower of shite, Tally?"

For a long moment, my best friend stares at me, stunned. Then she leans over to the coffee table for the box of tissues and hands me one, which is when I realize that there are tears streaming down my cheeks, and I have no idea how long I've been crying.

She says softly, "If it makes you feel so bad, why do you keep doing it?"

And, to that, I don't have a single goddamn answer.

Thirty-four

When Harry asks if he can come with me to Nadine's to meet the baby, I agree readily and don't think anything of it. As far as my family are concerned, I'm still dating Harry, and as far as Harry is *actually* concerned . . .

Well, he's been a bit clingy lately. Eager to see me, spend time with me. Still casual, of course, and still just having fun rather than *actually* going on serious dates or anything, but honestly, I get the impression he needs the distraction, the company. I'd worry he was only using me as a rebound if we didn't always have such a good time hanging out together, if he wasn't so invested in my life as a friend—and he *is* a good friend. A great one, even. But lately, he's *needed* me as a distraction, and I guess that's my role as *his* friend; all the meetings with divorce lawyers and arguments hashing things out with his ex seem to finally be dragging him down. Even if I can't relate to that exactly, I can relate to the feeling of being overwhelmed.

And the poor guy *looks* overwhelmed. When he shows up at my apartment on Friday night with a brown paper bag of takeaway food, there are bags under his eyes and his usually pristine clothes look rumpled; he smells like beer, and it turns out he's been drinking since lunchtime. I skip the bottle of white wine I put in the fridge for us to share and hand him a big glass of water instead. He's pale, hasn't shaved in a couple of days, and the gleam in his eyes has vanished. He mutters about credit card bills and friends not having time for him, the time he lost by not ending his relationship sooner and trying to make it work, and how behind he feels when he looks at his mates and their families. I can relate, so I let him talk and get it out of his system, while I try to reconcile the carefree man I know with this husk of him, who longs for stability and home comforts.

He's too tired to even smile, and in the end falls asleep early with his head on my lap, barely even opening his eyes when I shake him awake to move to the bedroom. He falls into bed fully clothed and makes for such a pitiful sight that I hold him close, stroking his hair.

The state he's in makes me a little wary about taking him to spend the day with my family, but by the time Dad has pulled up outside to give me a lift like we planned a few days ago, Harry's a different person. A shower, some fresh clothes, and a coffee transform him into the charming, chatty guy he was at the wedding.

I can only stare at him in disbelief when he shakes my dad's hand and they share a laugh over something, and when he flashes me a big grin and takes the bag of presents off me to put in the back of the car.

As Harry does that, Dad gives me a hug. "All right, Soph? You look a bit peaky."

"Huh? Oh, no, I'm . . . yeah, all good."

"Congrats again on your promotion! Brilliant news. We're all so chuffed for you, it's really great. I know you've been feeling down about work since you missed out last time."

"What? No, I haven't."

He gives me a funny look. "Your mum said you were a few

weeks ago. Made a lot of sense, though—you hardly want to talk about work these days. Camilla and I thought you were going to quit, you know. You can't change the subject quick enough whenever anybody asks you how it's going."

Shit. *Shit*, I have been doing that, haven't I? Too terrified of them finding out about my fuckups and my anonymous column to risk talking about it for long.

I stammer while I try to work out if I should pretend to laugh it off or not.

Overhearing, Harry pipes up, "That'll be my fault, Doug. Gets a bit dreary if we bring work home with us all the time; we've got used to leaving it at the office for the most part."

God bless my fake boyfriend, my knight in shining peacoat.

During the forty-minute drive to Nadine's, the conversation is mostly dominated by my new promotion and plans for Christmas. When Dad asks Harry what he'll be doing, he coughs and says he's not sure yet. "Might just be a quiet one this year," he adds vaguely.

I feel a pang of sadness for him, remembering how I told people I was having "a quiet one" for my birthday, but how that meant something completely different for me as a singleton to someone in a relationship. I picture Harry waking up on Christmas morning in that cold, empty flat, the entire day stretching out ahead of him, lonely and desolate and so, so sad.

I can't let him do that. No way.

"You're always welcome to spend it with us," Dad says immediately, cheerfully. "Isn't he, Soph? The more the merrier!"

"Oh, no, I couldn't impose—" Harry says, all chivalrous, like he didn't suggest spending Christmas with me in order to avoid his own family just last month. I twist in my seat to cut him an unimpressed look; he returns it with a smile that's all innocence.

"'Course he's welcome," I huff, rolling my eyes. But I give Harry a smile before I turn back around, so he knows I mean it. It really is the least I can do.

• • •

Nadine is one of the most house-proud people I know, and she always has been. Even her uni housemates weren't immune: she had such a strict chore rota in place that the run-down two-story student house above a chip shop was almost in better shape than my teenage bedroom. David is pretty tight-laced, too, so they have the kind of house where, whenever I visit, I'm permanently worried that I'll mess it up with crumbs or by spilling some tea or tracking in mud.

But now, as the three of us pile into the house, the gray-and-white hallway is a mess of bags and baby carriers and just . . . *stuff*. Various piles are scattered up the stairs: folded baby onesies that I think are clean, another wadded pile of fabric that looks dirty. One abandoned mug of half-drunk coffee, and a pair of David's glasses just waiting to get stepped on.

"We're here," I call, and immediately Dad shushes me and Camilla springs out of the nearby living room to do exactly the same.

"Shit," I whisper, cringing. An immediate faux pas, and I've barely made it through the front door. "Sorry. Is the baby asleep?"

"No, but Nadine is," Camilla replies in a loud whisper.

"Nadine *was*," huffs a weary voice behind her, and my stepsister drags herself out of the living room with a tired smile for us. Her stomach is still swollen and she's doing that waddling thing rather than walking, like she did toward the end of her pregnancy. I know I shouldn't be surprised, but Auntie Dawn seemed to ping right back to how she was before the baby; I think I was expecting Nadine to be the same, even if her birth was way more difficult. There are heavy bags under her eyes, and she looks a bit gray, her pallor matching the house décor. I don't want to guess how long it's been since she washed her hair.

"Hey, Nads," I say. "You look great."

"I look like shit," she says. "I feel like it too."

"I mean, I wasn't going to say anything . . . "

"Sophie!" Camilla hisses, eyes bulging, but Nadine only laughs. I don't know if becoming a mum has mellowed her out, or if she's just too tired to care right now. Probably the latter. She gives me a big hug; she smells different. Like baby powder, not her usual perfume, and a bit stale.

In my ear, she hisses, "Did you bring the mince pies?"

"Two packs. I'll hide them under the spare tea towels?"

"You're a star." After pulling away, Nadine looks at the bags Dad and Harry have carried in and asks, "What's all this you've brought?"

I point at them both in turn. "This is my boyfriend, Harry. This is Dad."

"Oh, ha-bloody-ha," she huffs, but manages a polite nod. "Hello again, Harry. Excuse the state of us."

He tells her not to worry, tells her she looks great and has a lovely home, and I start passing over the carrier bags. I explain, "Poppy is already growing out of her newborn stuff so Dawn gave me a bunch of things they aren't really using for you. If you don't want it, we can just donate it, or recycle it, or whatever. Um, and my mum wanted to get you something to say congrats—"

"Oh, she did text me, bless her."

"She got you some clothes?" I say, holding up the large gift bag from Mum uncertainly. "It's just a bunch of tops and stuff . . . She said it's in case you get behind on laundry and things. And there's some books for the baby too."

"Oh my gosh, that is so sweet. I'll text her later but please tell her from me. God, that's so thoughtful. Mum, look." Nadine's already snatched the bag out of my hands, pawing through the fabric and pulling one or two out to show Camilla.

"Uh, and I . . . I just got you this?"

I pick up the other gift bag and pull out the blanket I bought to show her, though I'm scared it's woefully inadequate after the other gifts have had such a good reception. It's a soft knitted one in lemon yellow, maybe three square feet, and it has the baby's initials embroidered in black—*FJD*, for Finlay James Dawes.

I ordered it on Etsy after trawling through dozens and dozens of articles along the lines of "good gift ideas for new mums." I sent a toy elephant when the baby was born, only for Jessica to mention a couple of days later that basically everyone else had the same idea. Auntie Dawn didn't even use all of the hundreds of newborn baby outfits she ended up with, so I ruled that out assuming that Nadine would be in a similar situation. And you can't just show up with *nappies* or something. Knowing me, I'd somehow buy the wrong ones anyway.

The blanket seemed cute, though. A keepsake. Practical too.

"Aww, isn't that lovely! It's so soft. That's so thoughtful, Sophie, really."

She beams at me, looking more like herself, and Camilla reaches over to feel the blanket with an appreciative hum. I breathe a silent sigh of relief, grinning back.

"Right!" Dad claps his hands together, shuffling me to one side and making his way into the living room. "Where's my grandson, then? Hiya, David, all right?"

Camilla and Harry follow him in, and Nadine cuts me a look.

"*The mince pies,*" she hisses again, waiting until I fish them out of my handbag before relaxing. One of her boobs is leaking, I notice, as a stain appears on her shirt. I don't know if I should point it out to her or not.

"Make us some tea while you're out there," she says, waving me toward the kitchen. "I'm still on the decaf; it's the one in the blue Le Creuset pot."

"Oh. Okay."

I can't argue with the new mum, so I go to the kitchen, hide the mince pies in the third drawer underneath spare, clean tea towels, and then put the kettle on. I was hoping to go straight in for a cuddle with my nephew, but—well, actually, Nadine's probably done me a favor, putting me on tea duty. Dad's loving being a grandfather; it'll be a good few minutes before any of us can pry the baby away from him anyway.

By the time I've brought everyone in the living room a cup of tea, that feeling of dread and panic that I know well by now begins to settle into my bones. What if I drop him? What if I don't hold him right? What if he's not as quiet or still as Poppy, and what if he's sick on me, what do I do then? Do I sit with it or hand him over to someone else to go clean up? Is it rude if I do the latter? Why do I care so much anyway? They're my *family*.

Harry is currently standing in the middle of the room with the baby nestled in the crook of his arm. He looks like a giant in comparison to little Fin—and, more startlingly, looks completely at ease as he rocks gently from one foot to the other, gazing down at the baby with stars in his eyes.

Oh, god. He's *broody*. I hope to god that look doesn't trigger everybody asking when I'll be having a baby, like at Dawn and Janine's last week.

Then Camilla's saying, "All right, all right, enough of that, let Sophie have a cuddle with him now. Sophie, meet Finlay!" She deftly snatches him from Harry's arms to bring him across the room to me, waving me onto the sofa next to Nadine and then placing the baby very gently in my arms. Apparently sensing my apprehension and complete cluelessness when it comes to babies, she adjusts my arms slightly so I can hold him more comfortably and positions my hand just so on the back of his head.

I know you're supposed to say all babies are cute, and Finlay is, but . . . he's also kind of weird looking. Poppy is just soft and squishy and rosy. Fin looks a bit like an old man when he scrunches his face up, which he does a lot.

He smells nice, though. They say babies smell nice, and they really do.

"Hey, Fin," I say quietly, as he stares at me with squinty blue eyes, his face reddish and wrinkled. "It's me, Auntie Sophie."

I give him a little sway side to side, trying to imitate the way Harry was just holding him, since he seemed pretty happy like that. Almost immediately, Finlay starts crying. Shit. I start bouncing him because that's what people seem to do, but Nadine takes him from me quickly.

"I'm sorry," I say, not sure why I need to say it, but I'm feeling immensely guilty all of a sudden. "I don't think I'm very good with babies. Besides Dawn, you're the first person I know to have one."

"What? No, you're fine."

"But you took him off me."

Nadine gives me a flat look. "Yes. Because unless you've been hiding some secret pregnancy from us, Soph, and your boobs just happen to be full of milk, *you can't feed him.*"

I let out an audible sigh of relief, which makes Camilla laugh. "Honestly, Sophie. You don't need to look so terrified. It's not like anybody knows what they're doing at first; you were doing just fine."

"Besides, you're not getting off that easy," Nadine barks at me. "Get used to it. You're on my future babysitting rota too."

That's me: babysitter and auntie extraordinaire.

• • •

Not to be left out of such a family gathering, Jessica shows up. Dad goes to collect her from the train station—it's only about an hour's trip for her, and she can't spend enough time with her new nephew. She must've spent a fortune in the last couple of weeks on train tickets, coming here to visit.

With the two of us on cleanup duty after dinner, me washing up a few things while she loads the dishwasher and cleans the work-tops, I take the opportunity to say, "Hey, Jess? Do you ever feel a bit overwhelmed, with the baby?"

"What, like, at the thought of having my own? I did have a few second thoughts hearing about the state of Nadine's vagina afterward," she says with a laugh, "but it's just so worth it, right? Easy for me to say, I know, it's not me with all the stitches, but, god, he's just so *lovely*. I don't know," she adds softly, shrugging, and her wedding and engagement rings catch the overhead lights as she picks up some empty mugs. "Mostly I just got a bit broody. Conor and I talked about having kids the whole night, after we met Fin."

"Doesn't it feel weird, though? Holding him and just . . . being totally responsible. Like, he is completely dependent. On you. For everything. And he's . . . *small*."

"What are you on about?"

I stop scrubbing a casserole dish and frown urgently at her, lowering my voice. "Aren't you scared you're going to drop him and break him or something?"

Jessica's eyes blow wide and for a second I think, *Fuck, I shouldn't have said that.* She's going to think I'm a horrible person.

She's going to tell Nadine and I am never going to be allowed to pick Finlay up until he's like, five years old or something.

She snatches my wrist tightly, leaning right into my face.

"Oh my god, are you serious? *Yes.* Christ, Sophie, it's terrifying. Nadine's friends started having babies ages ago, so she's sort of used to all this, but I'm totally with you there. I had to get Mum to show me *exactly* how to hold him the first time. I tried to change his nappy the other day, thinking I was being helpful, and it took me like, twenty minutes. I thought I was going to have a complete breakdown; I had to google it in the end—I was too embarrassed to tell the others I didn't have a clue."

"But you look like such a natural with him. Like you know what you're doing."

She waves her hand, sweeping away the comment. "As if. I'm probably just too busy thinking about how much I love him and how adorable he is, but believe me, there's also this voice in the back of my mind saying, 'Hold his head. Don't freak out and drop him if he's suddenly sick everywhere.'"

I could weep with relief, that even broody, seriously-planning-her-pregnancy Jessica is in the same boat as me. I'm not some horrible freak of nature after all.

"Still," she muses, glancing toward the living room where the others are chatting away and Finlay is making funny noises. "It does make you really want one, doesn't it?"

Maybe not *exactly* the same boat, then.

I mean, a baby . . . a whole other human being . . . it's just so *much*. I don't think I could handle it right now.

Some days, I'm not even sure I can handle myself.

December

CALENDAR

Friday 3rd: day off —must do Christmas shopping!!!!!

Saturday 4th: *The Lion King* matinee with Mum and Dad in London

Thursday 16th: Work Christmas do (BOOK TAXI HOME!!!!!)

Sunday 19th: Granny and Granddad's for present exchange and roast dinner

Saturday 25th :Nadine's for xmas

Friday 31st: Pub with Tally??? (Do we need to book somewhere? REMEMBER TO ASK TALLY)

Thirty-five

What am I even searching for on all these dates, anyway?

Views on figuring out your self-worth from our Dating & Relationships columnist

"Being single really is a blessing," Tally says with a sigh over one of our afternoon coffees after work, which have replaced our hasty morning meetups as a more frequent occurrence now that she's no longer with Sam. "It's the perfect time to find yourself, isn't it? Get to know yourself better. Really be the best you that you can be."

We've just been reading my latest article, uploaded just a few days ago at the end of November. It was all about how my time is always being monopolized by friends and family, the assumption being that just because I'm single I'm at their beck and call, and how it'd be nice to have some boundaries—nicer still if other (nonsingle) people respected them. Tally, apparently, didn't enjoy this one quite so much, and asked me outright if that's how I've felt being single.

I almost—*almost*—told her yes, that's exactly how I feel because I wrote the fucking thing.

Last month's article was originally supposed to focus on how to get back on the horse after a string of bad dates, inspired by Jenny telling me I'm a failure at dating, but I scrapped the whole thing three days before it got uploaded and wrote this one instead. Because it's true: I *am* exhausted. Last month, between all the visits with Poppy and Fin and Tally wanting to hang out all the time and needing help looking for a new, cheaper apartment, two rubbish Hookd dates, and going with Lena to look at venues, I officially have no energy left to give. I've been sluggish at work, going to sleep almost as soon as I get home and shovel down some dinner, and I'm so behind on laundry I had to buy new underwear just to have some clean ones to wear. I've barely even seen Harry since our visit to meet Fin, and I'm kind of starting to miss him.

Last weekend, when I was harangued into another visit to Nadine's in the family group chat (and covertly asked to bring even more mince pies), I wanted to scream. I wanted to sob. I wanted to just lie in bed all day and not emerge until I felt vaguely human and could string together a coherent thought.

But I have no leg to stand on against new parents. Or against a girl still occasionally crying herself to sleep over her breakup.

I wanted to scream and sob when Tally asked if I agreed with my own article. I wanted to laugh hysterically. In the end, I just shrugged and mumbled something about, "Maybe they've got a point about boundaries."

I wish I had better boundaries.

I wish I had *any* boundaries.

Then Tally decided, sipping her mocha, maybe the writer had a bit of a point about that, and how it's important to take time for yourself . . .

"And," she goes on now, "you just have so much time on your hands to try new things, get out there and meet new people! I don't just mean men, but, like, if I wanted to suddenly take up a new hobby, I *could*. I can't get over how much free time I have now I'm not with Sam. It's really given me an opportunity to work on *myself*, you know?"

A little bit rich, given that just yesterday she was on the phone crying to me about how the toilet wouldn't flush, and I had to go over to help fix it, having learned from that time Harry helped me out with a similar issue.

I let her carry on as she starts brainstorming all the hobbies she might like to try out, all the things she could do now she's single, but I don't participate very much. I want to tell her that she's romanticizing it, and the reality is pathetic and lonely. I want to beg her to shut up, because her thinking that single equals free time equals passions and hobbies makes me feel inferior and inadequate, like I've wasted my whole single life by not learning to code or becoming a travel blogger in my spare time or something.

But I let her talk and say the bare minimum, because I'm just *so tired*.

Toffee nut latte aside, I don't have the energy for this conversation—for any conversation—with my best friend. I let my mind drift back to boundaries, wishing I had some, and start thinking about how I wish I could just take a holiday. Nobody argues with your free time when you're on holiday, do they? People at work accept the "out of office" autoreply, and friends and family accept it too. You can't be expected to smuggle mince pies to somebody or go to wedding fairs when you're *on holiday*.

With a start, I realize I haven't even had one this year. The time I've taken off work has been mainly for events like Jessica's hen party, or a random day midweek to catch up on all the life admin that suddenly piles up—like homeowner's insurance and council tax and deep cleaning your flat before the landlord comes for the annual inspection. I have plenty of time off now in December, but mainly to pack in several visits with family over the holidays and to make sure I get the present shopping done.

Maybe I should've booked myself a holiday. Gone to Antigua, like Harry joked about.

Maybe I still could.

"I think I'm going to go to London next week," I announce to Tally, talking over whatever she was just saying.

Startled, she blinks at me, green eyes wide behind her glasses. A confused frown slips onto her face. "Well . . . yeah? You're going to see a show with your parents, aren't you?"

"No, I mean, I've already got Friday off. I think I'll book myself a nice hotel and have a little staycation sort of thing. Splurge on a fancy meal, wander around the Christmas markets and see the sights and stuff."

"Oh!" Tally says, and looks at me a moment longer, still confused. "With a guy? Has something happened—is Jaxon back on the scene again?" (She still thinks Harry is Jaxon; I should probably tell her the truth soon.) "Is it someone new?"

"No. No, I think I'll just go on my own."

My voice sounds strange. Faraway, sort of. Not exactly like me. Whoever's speaking is self-assured, unafraid of judgment.

"Are you sure? I thought you hated it when you went out alone for your birthday—"

"I'm sure," I say, with a certain finality so that she doesn't question it any further—and so firmly that I don't even stop to question *myself.*

• • •

"Table for one, please," I say a couple of days later, heart thundering and palms sweating, but the waiter doesn't even bat an eyelid, simply picks up one menu and leads me to a cozy spot in the middle of the restaurant.

An unfamiliar sensation rolls through me. Confidence? No, it's not quite that . . .

Power.

That's what it is.

It feels *powerful* to be out like this, on my own. I've dumped my bags at the left luggage in the Hilton I splurged on, hopped on the Tube, and found my way to Fulham and this nondescript little Italian restaurant for some lunch. The walls are painted dark, almost black, but large Edison bulbs are scattered throughout the room—either on the walls or hanging from the ceiling—and give the place a warm, cozy glow. Red and gold ribbons and tinsel are strung around the room; there's a teeny tiny wreath around the tea light candle on each table. It smells wonderful too.

I'm glad I picked it from the hidden gems blog post I read a couple of days ago when planning my day alone.

And I'm not the only person here by myself. There are a few couples, some small groups of friends, what looks like a business meeting in one corner, but there are a handful of other people sitting by themselves too. A young guy with his nose buried in a poetry book, who I assume is probably a student. One middle-aged guy with a newspaper and a bowl of pasta. An elegant elderly lady sipping wine and enjoying her spaghetti; she sees me staring and raises her glass slightly with a polite smile. I smile back.

The waiter returns after giving me a chance to peruse the menu, as if I didn't already study it in great detail online before coming here. I order the garlic mushrooms to start (something I would never do on an actual date, because god forbid I stink of garlic all night and put my date off), the house specialty spaghetti (again, always avoided on a date in case I flick sauce all over my outfit when twirling it around my fork), and a glass of white wine, because, honestly, why not? I *am* treating myself today after all.

While I wait for my main course, I find myself scrolling through the backlog of my articles on the paper's website. Originally, I wanted to just find the one from my birthday about taking myself out on a date, but I end up reading all of them from the last year.

And it's strange because it doesn't feel like I'm reading about *me*. They don't feel like my words. I always wanted the article to sound a bit more polished, a bit cooler, than I am in real life. Aspirational, rather than downright desperate. And I know it's me, but reading it back I start to get an idea of what my friends have been seeing when they read the column.

I like the person I sound like in the articles.

And I know that the reality is much different. By comparison, I positively languish in loneliness. I don't own it: I do my very best to erase it.

I've never thought of myself as a particularly needy person, but I think I must be. I've become resentful over the scant amount of time my friends can spare to see me, bitter about the significant others in their lives who have replaced the affection and time they used to have for *me*—and the fact that I don't even take time or affection for myself.

And if I'm going to be very, brutally honest with myself, half the reason I've been dating so much is because I've been jealous of everyone else. Because I've wanted to fill that void left by my friends with the exact thing that created it in the first place: a boyfriend. If their partners are responsible for me feeling so lonely and left out and left behind—well, I'd look for one of my own.

Obviously, I know it's not just that.

But it's only just now that I'm realizing that, maybe, part of the reason it hasn't worked out is because I haven't been looking for a boyfriend because I want a partner: I've been looking for a bandage, something to ease the pain and cover it up.

Which, let's face it, is not healthy. I don't need my friends or a therapist to tell me that.

I've never understood the whole *I'm taking a break from dating to work on myself* thing before. Now I think maybe I do.

This solo getaway was originally motivated by being sick to the back teeth of everybody else and wishing I could burrow under a duvet for three days straight, but now it's become about more than that.

It's about proving to myself that I *can* do these things.

It's like I said in my October article, after my birthday: I've made myself and my life smaller just because I haven't got someone to share it with. The holidays I haven't gone on, the movies I haven't seen, the restaurants I haven't gone to, and for what? What have I gained from doing that, beyond making myself resentful? It's not anybody else's fault I didn't do these things I've *chosen* not to. The pressure and weirdness I've felt around it is all in my head.

Thinking about it like that, it feels so strangely black-and-white. It's a punch in the gut to think about this ever-growing list of things I haven't done *just because* I'm single.

Suddenly, it's not all the dates that never work out that feels pathetic: it's how much I've been holding myself back.

I've become angry with my friends for building their lives around someone else, but I've done exactly the same thing, like

Duncan said a few weeks back. The only difference is that my "someone else" is this big empty space that I've hoped the guys I date will slot right into.

The last few years, I've become so acutely aware of the fact I'm *not* in a relationship that I've made it the center of gravity for my entire life. Everything revolves around trying to get a boyfriend or not having a boyfriend or dating someone; it's what I always come back to, the main topic of the thoughts that slink into my brain to coil around me when I'm in bed trying to fall asleep, the filter that I put everyone else's comments and actions through.

Well, I think, as the waiter comes over with my spaghetti, *it's time to put an end to that.*

Or time to start *trying* to put an end to it, at least.

It's time I started putting myself first, and there's something very difficult and very important I need to do if I really want to make an honest try of that.

I need to break up with my old life.

It feels like such a huge, earth-shattering realization that for several moments I just sit staring off into space. It's a weight off my shoulders I've never known was there to begin with; an odd sense of calm washes over me.

I know it sounds ridiculous, even laughable, but it just makes sense. Sam broke up with Tally because she wasn't making him happy: Doesn't that same principle apply here? My life isn't making me happy the way I'd like it to, so it's time I break up with it and move on to something new. Something better.

The idea feels so *big*, so life-changing, that I almost expect the rest of the world to change around me to fit this new outlook and attitude.

Obviously, it doesn't work that way.

The world keeps spinning, everyone else keeps living their lives, and mine doesn't actually change all that much either.

By the time I meet Mum and Dad the next morning for our usual Christmas get-together seeing a show, a tradition for just the three of us ever since their divorce, I'm very ready to spend time with people again.

My mini solo staycation has definitely been worth it, but being totally comfortable and confident in being alone is still very much a work in progress.

Thirty-six

The day of the work Christmas party, nearly two weeks later, I'm still feeling sure of my decision to embrace this new life and shake off my old, miserable, bitter attitude—I just haven't had a lot of opportunities to really demonstrate it to myself.

Partly because I went on a date and have seen Harry a couple more times, but it's also because I've been busy in the lead-up to Christmas, getting myself—and all the presents—organized.

The date—with a lovely dental hygienist called Mark, twenty-nine, five-eleven, and interested in cryptocurrency and crime dramas—was motivated mainly by boredom, admittedly. I slipped back into feeling sad and lonely and wishing I had someone to spend the season with, and Instagram was full of everybody else cozied up with the person they loved, and Harry was out with some friends, so back to Hookd I went.

The only difference this time was that I went in *knowing* what motivated me to go on the date—and therefore, with no expectations. To some degree, I was using him, so I sort of wrote it off before we even met up for drinks.

It was maybe the best date I'd been on in ages. (Not counting Harry; I'm still determinedly not thinking of the times we hang out or sleep together as *dates*. He doesn't think of it as anything serious, I keep reminding myself, so I shouldn't either.) Like with Harry, though, I showed up with no expectations and there was no pressure.

I've always thought of myself as a fairly open person, especially when it comes to dating, but drinks with Mark proved otherwise when I realized how much I would normally stand on ceremony, that I usually would've been trying to work out what his vibe was and what he was looking for and how keen would he think was too keen, what kind of flirting was he responding to . . .

It was a great date. Amazing, actually.

He didn't think there was a spark though, and apologized over text later that night after we'd both gone home separately. He thanked me for a nice evening and wished me luck.

You too, I messaged back, but I stared at the "good luck" for a long while.

Good luck with what?

Finding love? Romance? Good luck with dating in general, because it's rough out there?

I don't need luck, I thought, and then corrected myself—I didn't *want* luck.

I was trying to put all that behind me, wasn't I? I was moving on from myself. Finding this new me. I didn't need luck for that, just some good old-fashioned grit.

I do get drunk enough at the work Christmas party that I end up spilling all of this to Duncan—the first person I've dared to tell.

He finds it hilarious.

"So, what," he says, catching his breath and hugging the stitch in his side he's got from laughing so hard. There's even a sheen of sweat on his face, though that might be more to do with the open bar. "You're dating yourself now? You're consciously self-partnering?"

"Maybe? Yes. Sort of? I mean, it's not like I'm going to swear off men and stop dating. I don't think... But maybe I should be! Dating myself, I mean. Who wouldn't want to date me? I'm amazing."

"You're bonkers," he says, like he's correcting me.

"What's going on here? What're you two gossiping about?" Isaac asks, slinking over with his bottle of beer. With a few glasses of cheap wine down me, even Isaac seems bright and friendly tonight, positively one of my favorite people in the world. Worthy of forgiveness for always leaving it to me to tidy up the merchandise pile.

(When I'm covering for Jenny on maternity leave, he won't have a choice *but* to tidy it up then.)

I'm buzzed and loose enough that I explain it all to him too—the idea that I've been so focused on a man in my life when I don't have one and that I should focus on myself, and Duncan's suggestion of dating myself while I try to let go of the old me and all those sad, sorry attitudes that were holding me back.

Isaac looks amused but doesn't laugh like Duncan does.

He just sips his beer and says, "Huh. Good for you, Sophie. I think that sounds like a really healthy choice."

"You do?"

"Yeah. I mean, you always get so depressed when you're talking about the guys you date, or the ones you almost date. No offense, but I don't know how you do it all. It sounds fucking exhausting."

"The dating?"

"The casual sex with her pretend boyfriend?" Duncan suggests, and I elbow him sharply in the side.

"Making all the effort to *go out*, talk to people, try to impress them." Isaac grimaces. "No, thank you. That's not really for me."

"But you date sometimes."

"When I can be bothered," he says, and laughs. "I'm a major introvert. One date that doesn't come to anything is enough to wipe out my social battery for, like, three months."

"Classic ISTJ," Duncan says gravely, nodding. He looks at me for a long moment, then tells Isaac, "She wouldn't understand. Total ENFP."

"And you're a P-R-A-T," I spell at him.

Isaac laughs. "It's your Myers-Briggs. You know, the personality test."

"Oh my *god*. Oh my god! That's what all the weird letters are some guys put on their profiles, isn't it! Bloody hell." I feel so stupid for never realizing before now; I'd always been a little bit wary of it being something *weird*, or straight-up dirty, that I'd never googled. "So what does my F . . . uh, the P T . . . ?"

"ENFP," Duncan reiterates. "Didn't you read my piece on it for the website in September?"

I blink. "Is this that weird quiz you sent round the entire office?"

"Yes! Anyway, it means you're very emotional. Like, building emotional connections is very important to you. And having fun."

"That sounds like me," I say, but both of them miss the sarcasm in my comment.

Building emotional connections? If I was any bloody good at that, I want to retort, I wouldn't be so bloody single.

No—no, that's an Old Sophie belief. Don't listen to her!

With a little flare of determination, I shove the thought aside and take a long gulp of wine. Duncan and Isaac are deep in discussion now about their own personality types, so I leave them to it and go hang out with some of the girls from HR, who are in fits of giggles over a toss-the-ring-onto-the-inflatable-reindeer-antlers game they've got going.

The party isn't anything fancy, it's just in the office, but everyone logged off somewhere around two o'clock after a slow, unproductive morning. Crates of booze and soft drinks were brought out and one of the managers ordered pizzas. There are packets of shortbread and crisps and mince pies lying on desks everywhere you look. A couple of other people have brought games in, and decorating the office has been a collective and chaotic effort: some people have taped tinsel around, others strung up fairy lights, and a few others brought tiny two-foot-tall trees to plonk on the end of their desks.

It's not glamorous or exciting, but the only thing louder than the music is the laughter, and everyone—me included—is having a great time.

Someone starts up karaoke as the afternoon goes on and the sky outside turns dark. It's less karaoke and more a case of a couple of people at a time taking up a spot at one end and singing very loudly along to a song. Duncan and I sing "Fairytale of New York." My team all get up to sing "Jingle Bell Rock," which is made a thousand times better when a very pregnant Jenny and, to everyone's surprise, Isaac suddenly and completely spontaneously start doing the dance from *Mean Girls* to it. Thigh slaps and all.

People start to head home as the evening gets on, needing to go home to families and whatnot. We're down to maybe half numbers, everybody starting to pick at the food again, and I go back in search of Duncan.

"All right, Barker? You're looking very serious for someone off their tits at a Christmas party."

He grabs my hand and lifts it up to twirl me around, because he thinks I'm in need of cheering up.

"I'm fine," I argue, even as I stumble to a stop in my heeled ankle boots. "What's your secret, Duncan?"

"To life? To looking this fit every day?"

"To being on your own."

His smile drops.

"Sorry. I didn't . . . "

"Is this about your conscious self-partnering schtick?"

"A bit," I say, not bothering to correct him that that's not exactly what I'm going for.

He sighs heavily, looking down at the almost empty beer in his hand. "I don't know, Sophie. After long enough, you just . . . get used to it, I suppose. Bit like you're starting to do now. You said you didn't want to keep treating dating like you have been because it gets you down, but you think it doesn't get me down, too, sometimes?

"I don't know. It's just life. Everyone's got their own shit to be dealing with. It just comes in different packages. Like, look at your mate Tally. You thought she had it all, right? But that wasn't so rosy in the end. She was probably looking at you every time her and her boyfriend argued and thinking, *God, I'm so jealous of Sophie, she must be so much happier than me because she doesn't have to deal with all of this.*"

"Are you trying to tell me it's just 'the grass is always greener'?"

"Isn't it?" He smirks and I'm transported back to that night in York sharing a cigarette with Frankie and the dry smile on his face when he told me, *All that glitters, Soph. All that glitters.*

Duncan shrugs again. "You just deal with it. You keep going. And you and me, Barker . . . You want to know my secret? I know how to pick myself back up when I'm down. You're like that, too, even if you don't know it. People like us, we know how to look out for ourselves, because we don't have someone else there all the time to do it for us. That's the secret. Now, stop getting all soft and soppy just because it's Christmas. Come on, I can see Andy eyeing up that leftover pepperoni and I really want another slice."

It's Harry who suggests we do something on Friday night, the day after my work Christmas party. I'm still feeling delicate from my hangover, having somehow managed to drag myself through the day by working from home and doing the bare minimum, glad everybody else was also winding down for the holidays. I give my next article one last proofread and submit it—it's all about not wasting time with guys just for the sake of saying I'm *trying* to find a boyfriend to appease other people, wanting to stop seeking happiness and validation from others, and how my Christmas gift to myself this year is some self-respect.

I don't normally turn in my articles this early since they're published on the last Friday of the month, but since it's Christmas the schedule is a little different. I feel good about this one, though. It feels more like *me*, more honest than anything else I've written all year. Not sharp and witty, just up-front.

I'm so pleased with it, I even show it to Harry when we're sitting on his sofa eating pizza and watching *Love Actually*. (It's only the eighth time I've seen it this year. Harry thinks it's overrated but didn't complain too much when I put it on.) I'm sure he'll appreciate my article, though. Clichéd as it is, I think it'll really speak to him; this must be how Tally and Lena feel when they send me my own articles.

Now he lowers my phone and hands it back to me with a nonchalant "Yeah, it's good," and reaches for another slice of pizza.

"But—but it's . . . "

Somehow I'm disappointed by his reaction. I'm not sure what I was hoping for or expecting, but I do know it wasn't that. I'm fizzing with energy (now that some more pizza has mopped up the last of my hangover) and shift on the sofa to tuck my feet underneath me and kneel, facing him. I want to burst with how much relief this little epiphany has brought me, how I realize maybe it's been a long time coming. I want to shake him by the shoulders and make him see, but if he didn't get it from the article, I don't know what else to tell him.

"But don't you get it?" I press, fingers tightening around my phone and my chest puffing out. "I've had a *breakthrough*, about dating. About how I've let other people dictate and influence my life. How I've just been trying to do what everyone else thinks I should want. It's about boundaries! Making space for myself! Valuing myself!"

Harry nods, a small and bemused smile on his face and his head cocked to one side. (Add to the list of things that should be a criminal offense: the way he makes confused look so enticing. I so badly want to kiss that smile.) "Sure it is. Good for you, Soph. But . . . "

"But?"

"I don't know. I guess I just think of you as being pretty self-sufficient already. Good at being on your own. Not like me, you know?" He laughs, reaching for his bottle of Peroni and taking a swig, eyes on Alan Rickman trying to buy a necklace on the TV screen.

I want to argue, thinking about how much effort it took to just get *coffee* on my own up until recently, but then I notice, once more, how sparse and impersonal his apartment feels. Aside from a couple of books and some photos, he hasn't decorated at all—and he's been here for the better part of a year. The lone string of tinsel around the TV to mark the season somehow makes the place feel more depressing than if there were no decorations at all; I know my little three-foot tree with its cheap glittery star on top and my collection of stuffed reindeer are nothing to write home about, but they feel like a Selfridges window display by comparison.

And I think, maybe he's got a point.

I always thought our single status made us kindred spirits of a sort, on the same page; now, all of a sudden, I'm not so sure. It's not the first time I've thought, *I will never understand why he thinks that or where he's coming from*, but it is the first time I've felt like it *matters*.

It occurs to me that maybe, when I think about this idea of breaking up with my old life, maybe that should include this pseudorelationship I have with Harry. He pines for a life I can't even imagine for myself; when I try to put myself in that "picture-perfect marriage and two point four kids" life he wants—not with him, necessarily, but with *anyone*—I struggle. It makes my skin itch, my heart seize. Not because I know for certain I don't want it, but because I just *don't know*. He always said this wasn't serious and I know it can't be, but that makes me think that maybe this thing we've got going . . . as much fun as it is, as much as I like spending time with him, I don't know that anybody could call it a healthy choice.

We're just covering up the cracks in each other's lives, pretending they don't exist rather than dealing with them.

I say nothing, not really sure what to say. And knowing that we've made plans to spend Christmas together, I can't spoil that now and let him down when he needs me—so when he glances over at me and smiles, I smile back. I nestle into his side to watch the rest of the movie. Later, I get an Uber home instead of spending the night.

For the first time since we met, I'm in no danger of falling in love with Harry.

Thirty-seven

December is nonstop. Even if I don't have plans, I still have plans: watch the new cheesy rom-com on Netflix with Tally, do some present shopping, spend some time with Harry, wrap presents, run to the shops after work for the presents I forgot to buy, go up to Granny and Granddad's for the weekend to see them for a bit of a pre-Christmas weekend since I'm spending the day with Dad and Camilla and my sisters this year.

As if Nadine would let us get out of baby Finlay's first Christmas.

Auntie Dawn and Auntie Janine are much happier to have a quiet one, but Laura and my grandparents will be going over on Christmas Day—again, not willing to miss baby Poppy's first. Mum's out of the country again this year.

On December 24, I get a text from a name I don't immediately recognize.

Gareth.

It doesn't ring a bell until I open it.

And oh—it's *that* Gareth. The Gareth Who Stole Christmas, the guy I dated last year who dumped me on Christmas Eve when I thought we were meeting up to exchange presents.

Hi Sophie. Hope you're doing well. Sorry for reaching out like this but I just needed to get something off my chest. I've done a lot of growing in the last year and today's got me thinking about us, and how I ended things. I know you were very upset and believe me, it wasn't my intention to break your heart–I should have noticed that you clearly had very strong feelings for me when I thought we were still quite casual, and that's on me. I should have been more considerate, and it was unfair of me to break up with you so close to Christmas the way I did. I hope you can forgive me. 'Tis the season for it, right? All best, Gareth.

PS. I am now in a relationship with a really wonderful woman so am not looking to rekindle anything, just clear my conscience. Merry Christmas!

I read the messages five, six times, in stunned silence, before I burst out laughing. Poor, deluded Gareth, I think. It was never really about *him*—that wasn't why I was so upset. It was because it was Christmas and it was so out of the blue. It was another Sophie-centric spiral of: *But what did I do wrong? What's wrong with me? Is it too late to get a refund on his Christmas present? I'm alone again, and just in time for the holidays.*

And it's a bit bloody rich, I think, that he wants to clear his conscience. That he's done "a lot of growing" and just doesn't like living with the guilt of being the person who dumped someone on Christmas Eve.

He doesn't deserve a reply, I decide immediately, already screenshotting it to send in the group chat—and to Jessica and Nadine too. I'm halfway through the first message to the girls about it when something stops me.

I've done a lot of growing in the last year.

Yeah. Maybe that makes two of us, I think, and find myself deleting the message and the screenshots. I'd like to do some growing myself.

And I think, *Good for you, Gareth*—and I mean it.

'Tis the season! You're forgiven. Glad to hear you're doing well. Merry Christmas to you too!

And maybe it's just the festive season and the fact that Disney's *The Santa Clause* is currently playing on my TV, or maybe it's that I've done some growing lately, too, but I put my phone down feeling a little lighter, and a lot better.

• • •

Christmas Day itself is pure chaos. With Harry planning to swing by his parents' place to make a cursory appearance and then join us for lunch, Dad picks me up at seven o'clock wearing his felt antlers and a gaudy elf sweatshirt. I climb into the car with my bags of (mostly) neatly wrapped presents, bleary eyed and already regretting my sequined T-shirt dress because I don't think it will be very comfortable to take a nap in later. The car is already packed to the brim. I thought I'd gone overboard with presents for a seven-week-old baby, but it's nothing compared to Dad.

At Nadine's house the chaos only increases. She's decorated, but not to her usual pristine and carefully thought-out standards. A garland is tossed around the banister and honestly, I wouldn't be surprised if she told me Finlay decorated the tree himself.

(It turns out David did it, but he's also very sleep-deprived right now, so I'll give him a pass.)

Camilla is busy in the kitchen preparing the roast dinner and I only get a few minutes of cuddles with Fin, who's dressed in the most adorable reindeer outfit I have ever seen in my entire life, before I get roped in to help with the sprouts and carrots.

Harry shows up a full hour earlier than we were expecting him—which is saying something, because I remember it was at least an hour's drive between his parents' and Nadine's; he can hardly have spent any time at all with them.

Shuffling in from the cold, Harry sets down a Santa-emblazoned gift bag and shrugs out of his coat. He looks like he's just come from a funeral, not celebrating Christmas with family. I give him a hug and, before I can think better of it, I automatically give him a kiss— not for appearance's sake, but because, after spending so much time together the last few months, that's been our default greeting ever since I broke up with Jaxon.

As soon as my lips touch his, I cringe. After realizing the other night that we should probably stop this, for both our sakes, it feels suddenly weird to be kissing him. It's not easy or electric; it's awkward, like kissing a friend.

I try to turn it into just a quick peck on the lips; I don't want to give him one more thing to feel shitty about today after all, but he slips his arms firmly around me, securing me against him as he deepens the kiss.

He tastes of mince pie and coffee, and for a moment I almost lose myself in it, but I draw away, standing in his embrace. Harry lets out a long, weary sigh, his breath washing over my face, and tips his head forward to lean against me, his eyes closed as the tension rushes out of his shoulders.

I pull a sympathetic face. "That bad, huh?"

"My brother and the kids got there early. Think my mum was trying to ambush us into being in the same room. Like it's not enough I've already agreed to see them New Year's Eve."

I wince on his behalf. New Year's Eve was Harry's compromise to his family: he could use "his new girlfriend" as an excuse to get out of Christmas Day so he didn't spoil it for his niece and nephew, but agreed to their usual family tradition of New Year's Eve at his parents' local pub. The kids won't be there, he said, and nobody will judge him half so much if he gets incredibly drunk and ignores his brother in favor of playing pool with total strangers all night.

He looks like he'd rather go ten rounds with Tyson Fury.

My heart breaks for him. Even if I think we should stop using each other to make ourselves feel better, I *do* care about him—and I also know him well enough by now to know that New Year's Eve would be a prime opportunity to be his fake plus-one.

So I find myself blurting, "I could go with you, you know. Be an extra buffer."

"You—you'd do that? I mean, really? You're already doing me a massive favor letting me spend Christmas with you lot."

"Sure. I mean, you've helped me out plenty, and it's not like I really had plans. Tally's decided to go spend New Year's with her family anyway, so we won't be doing anything now."

Harry stares at me for a moment, his expression indecipherable, his shoulders sagging with relief. Then he yanks me in close and presses a swift, enthusiastic kiss to my lips. "You're the best, Sophie Barker. A literal lifesaver."

I smile, trying to ignore the little squirm of guilt in the pit of my stomach. Note to self: do *not* sleep with Harry again tonight, or at New Year's. He needs me, and I'm happy to be there for him, but I also know one of us has to do the right thing here, as scary as it is. We can't use each other to hide from the real world forever.

We're interrupted by Camilla leaning out of the kitchen and clearing her throat pointedly.

"Okay, lovebirds, break it up, these parsnips won't glaze themselves! Hello, Harry, dear, lovely to see you again. Merry Christmas!"

I slip out of Harry's arms. "That's my cue to go. The others are all in the living room."

"You go see them," he says, hands squeezing my waist before he pushes me off in that direction. "I'll help in the kitchen. I could use the distraction."

I'm ready to argue just on principle—he's a guest, and Dad would never forgive me for making our guest slave away in the kitchen—but Harry enjoys cooking, and he definitely looks like he could use the distraction. So I simply say, "Thanks," and let him take my place as Camilla's sous-chef while I go spend some time with the rest of my family and steal a few more cuddles from little Finlay.

• • •

We're all stuffed more than the turkey was after dinner, and find spots in the living room to flop down and drowsily argue over what to watch on TV. I decide to break open a bottle of prosecco; Camilla and Conor both have a glass with me but Jessica declines, complaining about a headache. Nadine and David crash completely, both fast asleep before long, slumped against each other. It'd look sweet, if Nadine wasn't covered in gravy-stain handprints from Fin playing around at dinner and David wasn't drooling into her hair.

Actually, to be fair, even then it still looks quite sweet.

"This one needs a change," Jessica announces from the floor, where she's playing with Fin and one of his many stuffed elephant toys. She declares this with a tone of noble self-sacrifice, but glances at Dad and Camilla, waiting for one of them to volunteer instead.

But Camilla says only, "We should put him down for a nap too."

There's a brief standoff while we all wait to see if Jessica will cave or not; I'm about to start laughing over the whole thing when Harry nudges me and stands up.

"I'll sort him out. Come on, Soph, you can give me a hand."

"Oh, no, really, Harry," Camilla starts, but then she says, "Thanks, Sophie."

I roll my eyes and when Jessica gives me a smug, triumphant grin as she hands Fin to me, I poke my tongue out at her. We leave them all checking what time the *Strictly Come Dancing* special will be on and wondering if they should bring out a board game.

Upstairs, I let Harry take care of changing Fin's nappy. I stand well back (having learned my lesson after getting peed on last time Nadine showed me how to do it).

"How do you look like such a natural?" I ask him.

"Practice. Don't forget I helped out with my niece and nephew when they were born."

For ages, I didn't even know he *had* a niece and nephew. He still rarely ever mentions them, but I've noticed that of the few pictures he does have in his apartment, they're all two sweet-looking kids with his brown hair and mischievous smile.

"Do you . . . do you miss them? Now you and your brother don't talk so much?"

Harry sighs. "Yeah. But, you know, I call to talk to them. I got to see them a couple of times when they were staying with my parents and my brother wasn't around. The oldest is only eight, so it's not like we can explain the whole thing. It'll . . . I mean, you know. It just takes time, doesn't it? I guess I'll get over it eventually."

He sets Fin down in his Moses basket but as we start downstairs again, he catches my arm, his fingers tracing languidly over my skin and a cheeky smile tugging at his lips.

And *oh*, I think, *this* is why he said for me to come with him, so we could steal a few minutes alone together.

But instead of drawing me in for a kiss he says in a rush, "I completely forgot to tell you earlier. It's been a bit hectic, so I haven't had a chance to talk to you properly since, but I finally got some good news the other day! Just in time for Christmas. Go on, guess."

He grins at me, a wild excitement glittering in his eyes. They shine silver like morning frost and, god, he's just so devastatingly handsome sometimes it's a little hard to think straight, so I say the first thing that comes to mind.

"Penny and Ieuan have let go of the fact we stole their dog's karaoke machine back before they could open it and we've been invited to their next little soirée?"

But Harry shakes his head, still beaming at me, his large hands splaying out across my arms as he takes hold of me, almost like he has to brace himself. He takes a deep breath and looks so excited I think he might almost burst into song, but what comes out of his mouth is, "The divorce papers are signed. It's *done*. It's over! Six fucking months, and it's *finished*. I'm divorced!"

He whisper-shouts it, aware of my family just downstairs, but, given the opportunity, I think he'd want to run into the middle of the street to bellow it at the top of his lungs for everybody to hear.

"Oh my god! Wow. Talk about a Christmas present. That's amazing news." I wrap him in a tight hug, genuinely pleased for him. This is good for him; he'll finally be allowed to move on.

Harry squeezes me back and when we draw apart, his mouth tilts up in a sly smirk and he winks at me. "So the next time we have sex," he says, waving his index finger at me, "you officially won't be my mistress anymore."

I flinch.

Crap. This is where I tell him I think we should just keep things PG, take a step back, isn't it? It had to come at some point, but I'm so not prepared.

Stalling, I snort, not meeting his eye. "Your mistress? Way to sound like a total dick, Harry, bloody hell. You've been separated since the start of the year. Is that what you've thought all this time, that you've been getting your own back for her sleeping with your brother by having a *mistress*? Do you really just get off on the idea of cheating or something?"

He shifts away from me; I feel the tension in his hands, still holding my arms, and I still don't quite look at him. He's quiet for long enough I risk a glance, but he just looks confused—*concerned*. We know each other well enough by now that I know the mistress comment was rooted in his own self-deprecating humor, and he recognizes that my heart's not in *my* attempt at a joke. My words came out cutting, not sarcastic.

"What's up?" he asks.

"Nothing."

"*Something's* up. You've been kind of off all day. What's going on? Did you get a UTI or something?" And then, more jokingly, he says, "This isn't the part where you say you think you're pregnant or something, is it?"

I'm not, but the mere idea sends a sharp bolt of panic through me. I'd laugh it off if Harry didn't look like that might not be the worst thing, that it might even be a welcome turn of events as far as he's concerned. The breezy smile I try to give him turns into a grimace and, not buying it, Harry raises one eyebrow. Instead of it being a devastatingly sexy look that sends a little thrill through me like it usually would, it just makes me feel worse because he looks sympathetic, like whatever the problem is, he wants to help.

"Soph, c'mon. I know you too well for that. You can tell *me*. What's up?"

I didn't realize it would be this hard. Looking at him now, I see the hopeful, charming, easygoing guy I felt such an instant connection with when we first met six months ago, and I wish things had been different.

My heart feels heavy, a leaden weight in my chest. I almost

wish Fin would wake up and start bawling so I'd have an excuse to run away from this conversation. But at least, I guess, Harry never wanted anything serious, so I don't have to worry about breaking his heart.

Still, it's the worst fake breakup I've ever had to do.

Steeling myself, I blurt, "I can't sleep with you again, Harry. And—and I think we should stop this . . . whatever it is we've been doing. I can be your plus-one for New Year's, but that's it. I think . . . I think we both need to move on. Stop using each other."

"Using each other? What're you talking about?"

The excitement that was so infectious just a moment ago has now vanished entirely from Harry's face. He drops his hands from my arms but I persevere, trying to make him understand.

He'll understand. He has to.

"Yeah, you know. Like how we try to get over our own shitty lives by getting under each other." I laugh, but Harry's expression has turned rigid. "We should deal with our shit for a change. I'm finally in a place where I want to take responsibility for myself and not feel like everyone else is constantly judging me for not living up to some kind of impossible standard. I need to make better choices, and that means *not* sleeping with a guy I recruited to be my fake boyfriend so I wouldn't look like such a sad, lonely spinster to my family, and *not* wasting my time on a guy who's so hung up on the fact he didn't have the guts to end a bad relationship sooner that he's spending all his time distracting himself instead of, you know, *dealing with that.*"

Harry moves a little farther back and for a moment I think he's going to be angry, but it's worse than that. He's *hurt*. His cheeks turn pale, his mouth goes slack as he searches my face, searches for the words, and—wait, why does he look like that? This can't be that upsetting for him, can it? He *had* to have known this would end sometime.

I press on, desperately filling the silence that yawns between us all of a sudden and trying to ignore the fact my palms are sweating and my heart is racing. "Come on, Harry. We were both as bad as each other. And obviously, I'll still come along to the New Year's thing with you and help you out, but we have to draw a line under this *somewhere*. We can't keep enabling each other, you know? One of us has to be the grown-up here, and I think we both know it's not going to be the guy who's alienating himself from his whole family and who has turned running away from his mistakes into an Olympic sport."

I offer up another smile to try to lighten the mood but Harry remains mute, stunned.

His reaction doesn't make sense. I mean, I knew it'd be a surprise to him, and he'd probably be disappointed, but . . .

And in one final, last-ditch attempt, I point out, "It's not like this was ever serious. This was only ever supposed to be a one-off. It just—"

"Turned into more than that," Harry murmurs, finishing my sentence for me. He looks at me a beat longer before the wounded look on his face twists into something more familiar—his lips part, mouth stretching into an amused smile as he lets out a breath of laughter, the frown lining his forehead relaxing as he reaches up to run a hand through his hair before meeting my eyes again.

And he says, "It's been more than that for ages. I know we keep saying this is all just pretend, but it hasn't been for a while now. What we have is . . . I want that with you. I want 'serious' with you. Sophie, don't you get it by now? *I like you.*"

All I can do is stare at him, and the pieces fall into place. The way that a few texts turned into talking every day, how natural the progression of that was. How, when he's suggested hanging out, maybe they *have* been dates, after all. The way we kiss hello and spend the night at each other's place sometimes, and talk about things that are real and meaningful, and . . .

And, oh god, he *likes me*.

My mouth is dry and my heart plummets to the pit of my stomach; I shrink back just as he tries to take my hands. I'm not sure that's the way I'm supposed to react to such an ardent declaration.

If you asked me just a month ago how I'd react to a brilliant, charming, handsome guy confessing that he *likes* me, that he genuinely wants to date me, that we have something special, I'd have been floored by the idea. Over the moon. I would've given *anything* for that.

So . . .

Why *aren't* I over the moon? Why am I not leaping into his arms and kissing him deeply, my heart racing at the idea of him, a relationship, a relationship with him? This is everything rom-coms have prepared me for—the big, romantic declaration surpassing all expectations that should be the happiest moment of my life. So why do I feel . . . kind of sorry about it, actually?

I stare at him, turning cold all over as I understand that for all I've bemoaned how I'd be happy to settle for Mr. Completely Bloody Wrong For Me half the time, now there's a guy who is pretty *right* for me in all the ways that matter, however incompatible we might be on paper. There's no pressure, I never feel like I have to stand on ceremony around him or pretend to be better or cooler or more put together than I am, the sex is great, he's so easy to be my worst self around, *and* he brings out the best in me, he's utterly *gorgeous*, and yet . . .

I don't want that.

We have chemistry, sure, but as far as my feelings for Harry go, I don't think I'll ever care for him as anything more than a friend.

Don't you want sparks? Tally asked me a while ago, and I do, and I know I don't have that with Harry. Not in the way I should. Not enough. And that's not fair for either of us.

For a moment, I imagine going along with this: letting myself carry on enjoying his company, finally being able to say I have a boyfriend, willing myself to feel more romantically for him than I do. But even in that world, I see all the things I dislike about my life now—the gaps left by my distant friends, the way I need to do a better job of learning from my failures at work; the pressure to settle down, get married, have kids all before I've even considered if those are things that I actually do want for myself.

I'm starting to understand that for all I've thought I want a boyfriend, maybe that's not what's going to make me happy. Maybe that's not the secret to it all, the key to everything.

And don't I owe it to myself to find that out? Aren't I allowed to figure out what actually does make me happy, what I want?

"Harry . . . "

His name scratches out from my throat, and something flickers across his face as he senses my rejection. "I don't understand. I thought we had a good thing going here. I thought—"

"We did," I say. "But it's . . . it was different. I like you, of course I do, but not in that way. I can't. I'm sorry."

"But we have fun, don't we? We get on. We like each other. That should— Isn't that enough?"

All I can do is shake my head and shrug, knowing any kind of apology won't make this better. However hard I might try to convince myself otherwise, I can't just invent feelings for Harry that aren't there, the way I've tried to do so often with the guys I've dated. Didn't I learn that lesson well enough with Jaxon?

I watch the emotions play out over his face. The confusion and hurt and hope and conviction. And then, finally, the sour twist of his lip and the sullen look he casts into a corner as he asks, "Is this because of the divorce? The cheating and stuff?"

"No! No, it's—" I take a step toward him, reaching for his sleeve. I hate how far away he feels; I hate myself for not noticing sooner that this meant more to him than it did to me, and how badly I've handled this. I hate seeing him hurting and blaming himself—the way I do any time a guy rejects me, sure that it's always something so fundamentally wrong with *me*.

As much as I want to reassure him, I don't want to lie to him. After all, the raw honesty we've always had with each other is what's brought us so close; I can't bring myself to start sugarcoating things now.

"I know we joke about your baggage, but that's not why. But even if I *did* have feelings for you, I couldn't fix that. I can't . . . I can't make any of that better, Harry, you do realize that? Dating me isn't going to suddenly patch up your relationship with your brother, and—"

"Fucking hell, Sophie, I'm not asking you to fix me. I'm not asking you to fix anything!"

"I know that! I'm just *saying* . . . But I treat you the same way. That's why I said we should call this off! Don't you get it? Part of the reason I like hanging out with you and sleeping with you is because it makes me feel a bit less crappy about my own life. That's not fair of me, I know. But *you* miss having someone around all the time, and that intimacy. That's why you keep turning to me. It's not something we can keep doing, or a good basis for any kind of relationship, I see that now."

He shakes his head, scowling, but I see a twinge of fear creeping in around the edges of his face, stiffening his features and clouding his eyes; a small, whispering part of him that knows I'm right.

"So what," he exclaims suddenly, "you won't be with me because you think I've been using you all this time to what, make *myself* feel better?"

"You have been! You are! That's the whole fucking reason you came here today, because you're *running away*! And that's fine, because I've been using you too! We're as bad as each other, which honestly, should make it *easier*, but I can't be in a relationship right now, and I don't think you can either."

Harry scoffs, staring at me in open disbelief, his mouth hanging open. "You can't be in a relationship right now. I—Soph, the *entire* time I've known you, all you've done is talk about how badly you want a relationship! You complain *constantly* about being single, about how hard it is to find someone, how everyone else is always judging you for it. You've got a viral column online talking all about relationships and how much it sucks to be single!"

"And I was wrong! I was, I mean—"

It *does* suck, being single. I do hate the way it feels like I'm always being judged for it, and dating is exhausting. I hate the way I'm only *just* realizing lately that a lot of that is down to my own perspective on singledom, and that's something I can control, can *change*.

I don't know how to explain myself to Harry; I'm not even sure how to explain it to myself right now, other than knowing, in my gut, my heart, my head, all the ways that matter, that this isn't something I want. Ironically, the only thing that might make him understand where I am right now is the article I showed him a couple of nights ago, the one that went right over his head, and he couldn't relate to.

So what I end up saying is, "I don't want to settle for a relationship I might regret later. I'm not going to date you just to end up going through the motions of house, wedding, baby, just to make everybody else happy. I mean, it's not like that worked out well for *you*, is it?"

Harry reels back like I've just slapped him.

His cheeks turn pink and blotchy.

Silence envelops us, the air crackling with tension, every bit as alive and electric as the chemistry that had us falling into bed together after Jessica's wedding, only so, so much worse. This time it threatens to suffocate me, and, looking at his wounded expression, I want to let it.

My breath catches in my throat; after a moment, I exhale heavily, biting my lip.

"I didn't mean it like that," I whisper, cringing, desperately meeting his gaze. Far from the friendly, flirty look I'm used to seeing there, there's something sad and defeated. Harry swallows hard; the sound feels too loud in the silence still hanging between us.

"Yeah," he murmurs. "You did. I think—I think I should . . . I should go."

He shuffles past me, moving swiftly down the stairs to pull on his coat and his shoes, and I hurry down after him.

"You don't have to go. It's Christmas, just . . . I mean, you can stay, and—"

"No, I can't."

"Harry—"

"Thanks, Soph. It was nice being your fake boyfriend."

Nothing I say now will make it any better or undo what I just said, I know that, so all I can do is watch helplessly as he slips out the front door, closing it behind him.

I stare at it, wondering if I should chase after him.

And then Nadine says from the open living-room doorway, "What's going on? Where's Harry going?"

I turn to look at her, probably to make up some excuse and pretend that fight never happened.

I open my mouth and burst into tears.

Thirty-eight

There's no good way to tell your family that you felt so pressured about being single that you lied and told them you were dating someone, and there's no good way to tell them that when the guy you *were* seeing turned you down as your date for your sister's wedding, you recruited a stranger from a dating app to pretend to be your boyfriend instead. There's also no good way to tell your family that you feel like you've been fighting just to tread water at work for months, but also have a wildly successful online column about single life and dating and relationships that you've kept secret from basically everybody.

And since there's no good way to say it, all I can do is say it exactly like that, knowing with each word how much worse it sounds and what a horrible, self-centered person I sound like.

The easy thing—the cowardly thing—to do would've been to lie about why Harry left. They probably heard our raised voices, even if they didn't hear the argument itself, so I could've gotten away with *something*. Made up some excuse about him needing to go help out a friend, hide how badly I wanted to cry, and made it through the rest of Christmas Day, maintaining the ruse a little while longer. Old Sophie would definitely have chosen that option. But honestly, the whole thing with Harry has left me so emotionally wrung out that

I don't have it in me to keep up a few more white lies and, before I know it, the whole story has come spilling out, all the secrets I've kept and lies I've told just to try to spare other people's feelings.

It all suddenly feels like so *much*, and I'm exhausted, and I just want it all to stop being a thing I have to hide all the time.

Once my sobs subside from hysterical and hyperventilating, I manage to bumble through the entire story between hiccups and sniffles, squished on the sofa with Camilla's arm around me and everyone looking on, their expressions shifting from worry to shock.

There's no good way to tell your family that you kept up a fake relationship with this random guy who was going through a rough divorce to make each other look good, or that you've been dating other guys in the meantime but none of those have gone anywhere anyway—and they're all so surprised they don't interrupt me and just let me talk.

I was so, so wrong when I thought I reached rock bottom asking Harry to pretend to be my boyfriend for the wedding.

Because *this*, right now, is rock bottom.

Jessica is the first one to break the silence, leaping to her feet and crying, "Sophie! No! You have to go after him! You can't just let him leave like that!"

I don't have the energy to roll my eyes. "This isn't a rom-com, Jess. I'm not chasing after him. I'm not in love with him."

"But you . . . "

She actually looks disappointed. Like my mad tale was all just an epic love story in the end, when it's not.

And then she says, "So you brought a total stranger to my wedding."

Before I can be berated and yelled at by anybody, I say, "You were getting so wound up about changing the table plan and my plus-one, and I couldn't stomach telling you that Jaxon wouldn't come, and my friends were all too busy—"

"So you thought you'd just *pretend* you had a boyfriend all that time instead?" Nadine asks, looking at me like I've just grown a second head. It's a look I more than deserve.

Camilla takes a more gentle tact, sighing as she says, "Sweetheart, why didn't you just tell us that you weren't seeing anyone and that you didn't have a plus-one? Going through with this entire charade just because you thought we'd be upset—"

I can't help the wry laugh that rips out of my throat, the disbelieving smile that steals over my face. I feel borderline hysterical.

"You can't be serious. It's always, 'How's the love life, Sophie? Haven't you got a boyfriend yet? Aren't you dating anybody? Try harder, put yourself out there more, don't be so picky, give them a chance, kiss a few frogs, keep at it, you'll find someone when you least expect it, *why haven't you found somebody yet?*'

"Not to mention the fucking table plan—Jess, you were borderline hysterical when you thought I was going to mess that up by not having a plus-one. It just . . . it got to be too much. As soon as I told you I was dating someone, you all looked so bloody relieved, like I'd finally done something right. Like *you've* all been under pressure because *I'm* single. Of course I went along with it. Pretending to be in a relationship with Harry made everything so much easier."

Camilla sits up straighter, face slack. Dad scowls in the armchair in the corner, shifting in his seat, looking totally lost for words. Jessica and Nadine exchange a look, a silent conversation I don't quite understand, but one Nadine takes the lead on.

"We don't do that," she tells me, but she doesn't sound so sure of herself.

"Yes, you do! You all do. Mum, Dawn, Tally, and Lena. *Everyone* does it. Frankie's girlfriend assumed I was trying to steal him from her the last time I saw him just because I'm single and we're friends, so we've hardly even spoken since! It feels like it's the first thing anybody ever asks me about and the only thing anyone really cares about, and maybe that's all in my head, but—maybe it's not? And, like, it's whatever. It's *fine*. But when it came to the wedding, and the idea of telling you all that I was going to show up alone after all, I just couldn't stand it."

To my total surprise, it's quiet, reserved Conor who looks at the others and says, "We do kind of do that. After we all met Harry, *you* said you were glad she finally found someone," he points out to Jessica, and then tells Camilla, "And you're always saying it'll be nice when she's got herself a partner and settles down, and you worry about her being on her own all the time like that."

"Of course I worry!" Camilla bursts out. "I'm her—" She cuts off abruptly and looks at me, and this time it's my turn to be stunned into speechlessness when I find her eyes are filled with tears. "You might not always think of yourself as my daughter, but you *are*. Of course I worry about you being on your own all the time! You always seem so miserable if you don't have plans, saying you miss your friends and don't see them enough. I thought you *wanted* to look for a boyfriend. You were always swiping through those apps."

"I—" My voice catches, coming out wobbly. I swallow a lump in my throat, and admit, "I don't know what I want. I just . . . I just know I don't want everyone always making me feel bad for being single, acting like it's the end of the world. If I want to feel like that, then fine, but when it's coming from everybody else, it's exhausting. And I *hate* dating. Do you guys know how many dates I've been on in the last couple of years? *Tons.* I've actually—genuinely—lost count of how many. And it makes me feel like crap. I hate it."

"So why do you keep going on dates?" David asks me. My brother-in-law is wearing a look that's not dissimilar to my dad's, both of them looking steadily more concerned the more I say.

Somehow, I manage a laugh. "Fuck knows."

"Oh, *Sophie.*" Camilla sighs, and she wraps me into a brisk, tight hug. "You daft thing. You never needed to do all this for our sake, or for anybody else's! We were only worried because we thought you were unhappy! Like with work, when you wouldn't talk about that!"

She draws back, and I find myself getting pulled into a hug by Dad next, who clicks his tongue at me and says, "Bloody ridiculous little scheme. Honestly, Sophie, if that was how you felt you could've just *talked to us.* Recruiting a stranger from the internet to pretend to be your boyfriend! Who does that sort of thing?"

But he laughs a little as he says it to try to take the edge off, giving me a wobbly attempt at a smile.

"Duncan from work came to meet him with me. Make sure he wasn't a total weirdo."

"He did seem like a decent fella," Dad concedes. "Shame it was only pretend."

"It didn't *seem* very pretend," Jessica mutters, none too quietly. "It seemed like you really liked each other. If you ask me, he likes you a *lot.*"

I ignore her, but Dad asks me, "Now, what was this you were saying about work, and some blog or something? You could have talked to us if things weren't going well."

"I just . . . I felt like work was the only thing I had going for me, I guess?" I don't know why I phrase it like it's a question when it's true. I try again, sitting up a bit straighter even as I wring my hands in my lap. "Like at least if you thought everything was okay at work, it wasn't so bad if I was single or something. And the only good thing at work was my column, but that felt like the only place I could really talk about any of this without everyone judging me or hating me, so—"

Jessica interrupts me with a sudden gasp. "Oh my god. *You're* her, aren't you? You're the person behind *Single, Swipe, Repeat*."

• • •

With the worrying, awkwardness, and embarrassment—not just on my part, but *everyone's*—now put behind us, the *Strictly* special is being ignored in favor of Jess and Nadine crowding me on a sofa with Camilla perched on the arm, peering over Nadine's shoulder as the four of us look at Jessica's phone; they're entertaining themselves by rereading my articles.

"Do you really think we take up too much of your time?"

"Sort of. You always assume I'm free but you never actually ask if I am. But that's sort of my fault; I've realized I need to have better boundaries. Like, I blame everyone else for thinking the only good reason I can't do something is if I'm busy with a boyfriend, but I never actually just say *no, I'm not free*, do I? I'm equally to blame there."

"Did you really go to a dog's birthday party thinking it was for a kid? Like, a human kid? A person?"

"Yes."

"And you *actually* ate dog biscuits?"

"It was a cupcake. But yes."

"Did you actually sleep with the best man from a wedding? The LinkedIn guy? Whose wedding was that anyway? What did he look like?"

"It was Lena's engagement party, but no. I made that up."

They scroll back further.

"But your June piece, about inviting someone to a wedding and finding a guy on Hookd to go with you—that was Harry! You talk about the instant chemistry! You said he could be your *soul mate*, Soph!"

I shrug. "It made for a good article."

Jessica's nose scrunches up when she gets to the article after her hen party. "You didn't actually hook up with the guy running our cocktail class, did you? We would've noticed that, I'm sure."

"Obviously I didn't."

Nadine snatches the phone off her sister, scrolling through ones we've already read. Having all these sordid, exaggerated details of my dating life—worse, my *sex life*, both real and invented—pulled apart by my sisters and Camilla is a very particular kind of torture, but it's the articles where I vent about how society is structured around couples or the idea of settling versus settling down that really make me squirm.

"I can't believe you were behind this all this time," Jessica gushes, but far from being pissed off or upset about how I called her bachelorette the "wake at the funeral of her single life," she looks awed. Like she's just met her favorite celebrity or I announced I could transform into a unicorn at will. "Everyone *loves* this series. It's brilliant. I can't believe it was you all this time and you never told us! How did you keep it secret?"

From across the room, dropping the determined act that he can't hear any of this, Dad says, "She kept up the boyfriend ruse for long enough, Jess, I wouldn't sound so surprised."

But everyone laughs, and Dad rolls his eyes with something close enough to affection that I know I'm not actually in trouble;

they're not actually mad. Mostly, I think, everyone feels sorry for me that I felt the need to resort to such extreme lengths—and guilty for being the ones who pushed me to it. Or, at least, for being part of the reason.

As for my anonymous column, well, that brought the opposite reaction: sheer excitement and downright glee, prompting this reread of all of my work, because if the ridiculous notion of a fake date is real, *anything* goes, and they can't even begin to guess which bits are embellished if that was the true story. David looks actually very impressed, and Dad just says, "What were you so worried about work for, you silly thing? Your own column. Bloody hell. That's something, isn't it?"

"But like, seriously," Jessica presses. "Nobody knows? *Nobody?*"

"Obviously people at work know. Like, Duncan knows, and I told Harry all about it. I didn't want him stumbling across the article about him right after your wedding and thinking I'd gone head over heels for him and getting all weirded out. And Siobhan knows."

"Who?" Nadine asks, as Jessica gawps at me, looking a mixture of furious and scandalized.

"She caught me out. The title of the article about your hen party, I said it to her first and totally forgot. I made her promise at the wedding not to say anything. She's been trying to persuade me to just tell you the truth about Harry and everything since."

"I didn't know you were friends."

I shrug. I didn't, either, really, but now Jessica mentions it, I suppose we are. We message sporadically online, send each other funny or interesting videos and articles. It's the same way my online friendship with Frankie started, I guess.

Jessica mulls it over for a moment and I wonder if she's annoyed with me for keeping another secret, or maybe for stealing her friend, but then she grabs my arm and says, "So can we get a sneak peek of this month's article?"

I can't help but laugh. Camilla plucks the phone out of Nadine's hand to get a closer look for herself, squinting to see the screen better. Jessica swats at me, crying out that she's serious, she *demands* to see it—it's Christmas, the season of giving, I *have* to. Nadine starts laughing then, giggling to herself over the dog's birthday party as Camilla reads a snippet of it out loud, and within seconds I'm collapsed back into the sofa with my sisters leaning on either side of me, all three of us in stitches.

And I think, this isn't rock bottom. It can't be, surely? Not because it wasn't the fight I expected it to be, but because this is what happens in breakups—airing the things you've tried to sweep under the carpet, confronting the things you did wrong. I did want to break up with my old life, didn't I? What better way to embrace a new start?

And if it is rock bottom, that's okay too. Because I'm here to pick myself back up.

January

NEW YEAR'S EVE

Thirty-nine

"Maybe you should sign up for *Married at First Sight*," Lena says, glugging some more rosé into our glasses, trying to split it evenly as she finishes off the bottle before she flops back onto my sofa with us. "See if the experts can find you someone!"

"I think it's really sad that you're giving up on yourself like this," Tally laments.

"I'm not giving up on myself! I'm—"

"Focusing on yourself? Practicing self-love? Going to take up jam making?" Lena says, cutting such a condescending look at Tally that I can't help but giggle.

But Tally only pulls a face, offended. "I thought you liked my apricot jam!"

Once we've both reassured her that, yes, we liked the jam she made in a class she took to try to fill her time now Sam isn't around, I say, "I mean, kind of, yeah. Maybe not the jam-making part— no offense, Talls—but the focusing-on-myself bit. I'm so tired of dragging myself out on dates just for the sake of it. If I organize a date with someone, I want it to be because I think we might get on, not just because I hope they're okay enough that I might be able to make it work. You know?"

Judging by the blank looks on their faces, they don't.

But because they're my best friends, they plaster on great big grins and nod along, saying, "Absolutely! Yes! Good for you, Soph. This is great. You're too good for them, anyway. I love it."

I try to smile back, but it suddenly becomes difficult, and my mouth has turned dry. I take a big sip of wine, though that's mostly just to postpone the inevitable.

It's lunchtime on New Year's Eve, and this is something I couldn't bear putting off any longer. An impromptu get-together is something we've only managed recently because we rallied around a brokenhearted Tally, but when I told them I had to talk to them about something important, Tally showed up with a box of Quality Street and Lena with two bottles of wine, claiming she had to start early today to make up for doing Dry January next month.

I started off easy, telling them the whole story about Harry—something they find genuinely hilarious, so much so they don't even waste time being annoyed with me for not telling them sooner or for letting them think he was Jaxon. And then I tell them about our argument Christmas Day, how I realized I didn't actually want a relationship with him, or really with anybody right now. I told the about how sick and tired I am of dating just for the sake of da^g and . . .

And now I just have to tell them about my column. *move*

If I'm really going to break up with my old life and *ing my* on, I need a completely fresh start, which includ *bite my* biggest secret to the girls. I've hated every time I'm *turning* tongue about it around them, but I hated the i

their backs on me even more.

I take a deep breath and just as the girls start chattering again, I blurt, "I've been writing an anonymous column about dating and you guys have been reading it and please don't hate me I promise I didn't really mean all the things I said. I mean, I kind of did mean them, that's why I wrote them, but—"

"Hang on." Tally holds up her hands to stop me. "What?"

At first, they take it well, with all the same excitement Jessica and Nadine had a few days ago; they don't dissect all my old articles, though, and they take my word for it that most of the stories about guys I've dated or slept with are exaggerated. But then they start to remember some of the other things I wrote about—not the footloose and fancy-free tales of a single gal but the irritable musings of someone feeling shut out by those closest to her, feeling left behind.

I do my best to explain myself honestly while still being conscious of their feelings. I'm better prepared for this conversation than I was for the one with Harry on Christmas Day. I tell them about how it felt like they never had time for me anymore now they were settling down and that I couldn't keep up. That when Frankie Two said we didn't need to bring anything to the housewarming, I felt like an idiot for not understanding she meant the opposite. That ·ried on my birthday because they weren't even around to share a s of cake with me.

either of them really know what to say. I keep talking— bat in the end—trying to make them understand, discouraged by tl ietness. The more I say, the more I see them withdraw.

fab is y promise me, "It's fine, Sophie. A column! Wow! How Th course we're not pissed off, no."

they app und so convincing, but they're trying, and I know t I'm trying too. Eventually, after we finish our wine and the *Princess Switch* movie we were half watching, the girls head off, making excuses about needing to get ready for their evening plans.

I let them go, feeling sick and on the verge of tears, but I know this is what's best. It's what I needed to do—and what they, as my best friends, deserved from me.

Then I pick myself back up, and, faced with an evening alone, I know there's only one person I want to be spending it with.

• • •

For the last few days, Harry hasn't been answering my calls.

I tried him twice on Boxing Day and left him an apologetic text asking him to call me back, but it goes ignored. For all his recklessness, his inclination to put fun first and enjoy himself, it turns out he's also completely bullheaded and painfully proud. Or, more likely, he's genuinely hurt by my rejection and didn't see it coming in a million years, and he really, really liked me, far more than I ever realized.

But I remember how reluctant Harry was to spend New Year's with his family, how much he helped me out, how much I care about him, and I scroll back through his Instagram to find a post from last year where he's geotagged the location of the pub he and his family usually go to for the night.

Desperate times, and all that.

I figure it's the very least I can do. I definitely owe him an apology for what I said Christmas Day too.

But more than that—I can't bear to leave things the way we did. I can't let that be our last conversation, and I can't bear the idea of him feeling so alone and miserable at midnight tonight. He's become one of my closest friends; he deserves better than that.

Plus, I'm convinced he won't have told his family about our fight on Christmas or that we "broke up." He'll have kept quiet to save face, so it won't be too weird when I show up out of the blue—not for his family, at least.

All dolled up in my favorite little black dress—a strappy one with a tulle skirt—and after taking the time to swipe on some shimmering gold eyeliner and curl my hair, I get a train, a bus, and finally one very expensive taxi to The Fox and Fen.

It's a huge pub, made to look bigger by the sprawling collection of wooden benches out front and the terrace on the left-hand side lit up by golden fairy lights. Lanterns are dotted around each table and the pub's doors are wide open, light streaming out of them and the windows. A cacophony of revelry pours across the grounds: bawdy laughter and the chatter of the throngs of people packed into the pub, music turned up loud, the clack of pool balls colliding, and the clink of glasses.

New Year's Eve is well and truly in full swing.

Harry said they've been coming here since his parents moved about fifteen years ago, so rather than trying to find him in the huge crowd, I head straight for the bar, asking if they've seen him anywhere yet.

"I'm his girlfriend," I lie, "and I tried calling him, but . . . "

"No chance hearing your phone in this place, love," the elderly bartender shouts back with a gruff laugh. "Aye, they'll all be over that way."

He points off to one corner, and I order a large white wine and a pint of beer before gingerly picking my way across the pub. And, as promised, Harry and his family are there, having claimed a low, round table and some very worn, squashy velvet chairs.

There's a slightly rounder, plumper version of Harry with a

spray of silver around his temples and a receding hairline—a guy I can only assume is his brother. They're with their parents and a small handful of family friends—and an uncle, I remember Harry saying—all drinking and chatting cheerfully.

Almost all.

Harry sits sunk low in his seat, sullen, jaw clenched, fidgeting with a mostly empty glass. He looks nothing like the guy I'm used to seeing, and my heart bleeds for him. My half-baked plan to come help him out and do him a favor suddenly strikes me as a horrible idea: the mood he's in right now, maybe it'll just cause another argument.

But I at least owe it to him to try.

And bloody hell, if I can create a whole fake boyfriend for my sister's wedding, I can commit to the charade for a few more hours, right? And if I can take myself to the cinema and dinner by myself, I can do this.

I plaster on a bright smile and stride over, calling out, "Hi! Hi, everyone! I'm so sorry I'm late! Harry, babe, I've been calling for ages. Can't you hear your phone? Hi! I'm Sophie! It's so nice to meet you all! Harry's told me loads about you!"

I'm met, mostly, by confusion.

Harry sits bolt upright, looking like he's just seen a ghost, but before he can say anything a woman I assume must be his mum jumps up, narrowly avoiding knocking the table with all their drinks on.

"Sophie! Hello! We didn't think you were coming! Harry said you had other plans." She gives me a quick once-over, a rapid but thorough assessment. She doesn't look massively impressed by what she finds; for once, I don't care. I just smile back, looking so superthrilled to be here. His mum returns it with a polite smile, making a quick round of introductions to everybody and saying, "Well, it's lovely of you to join us. Maybe you can get this one to lighten up a bit, hmm?"

She nods in Harry's direction, a flicker of pain crossing her face, and I feel a pang of sympathy for her. I hadn't exactly been endeared by her attempt at Christmas to get Harry and his brother to spend some time together and sort things out, but she's obviously just someone trying to hold her family together.

"I'll do my best!" I say, and because there aren't any free chairs around, I perch on Harry's leg instead, like any good fake girlfriend would. I pop my wine down, exchange his empty glass for the beer I've brought him, then pick my drink back up and kiss him on the cheek.

He turns his head as if to kiss me, but just says low enough for only me to hear, "What the hell are you doing?"

"I said I'd be here, didn't I?"

His eyebrows contort, uncertain, and for a second I think he'll tell me, categorically, to fuck off—but then his arm wraps around my waist and he murmurs, "Thanks, Sophie."

We share a smile—not the flirty, teasing ones we normally share, but something softer, something much more meaningful—and he gives my waist an affectionate squeeze before I turn to his family and ask them cheerfully how their Christmas has been.

• • •

As midnight approaches we all move outside, ready for the count-down and the fireworks display in a nearby field we'll be able to see from the pub. The general atmosphere is incredible: boisterous and jovial and friendly.

It's a total contrast to the vibe with Harry's family. His mum is obviously trying hard to draw both her sons into conversation, and his brother strikes me as unapologetic and arrogant. The rest of them are obviously trying hard to ignore the awkwardness, which somehow only exacerbates it.

Harry and I end up standing a little away from everyone else; outside, it's a little easier to hear yourself think. And, more importantly, hear each other without having to yell to have a conversation.

And we really need to have a conversation.

I catch his arm in my free hand, drawing him around to face me. "Listen, what I said at Christmas . . . I really didn't mean it that way. I just meant, you've made it so clear that you made mistakes, and I didn't want to make those same ones. You deserve better than for me to pretend I like you more than I do; I deserve better than that too. I didn't mean that I think you'll make the same mistakes again. It wasn't supposed to be a dig at you, I promise."

"Yeah, I . . . I know that. *Now*. I didn't mean to lose it with you like that. You just hit a nerve."

I give him a gentle smile. "I sort of figured."

"Plus," he says, with more of his usual self-deprecating humor, "my fragile ego couldn't handle you rejecting me. Was a real insult to me, you know."

"You'll get over it," I say, and squeeze his arm.

But as I let go, Harry catches my hand. His fingers are warm, familiar, as they slot between mine and stroke my skin. He leans in close, his breath ghosting over my cheek and his lips grazing my ear. Instinctively, my lips part and my head tips back.

"Are you really sure you don't want to just see where this goes? For real this time, not just to make each other look good?"

His voice is low, husky, and so tempting.

But I edge away just enough to look him in the eye better, and nod. "I'm sure. I meant it, Harry. As much as I like you, I just . . . I'm not in love with you, and I don't think that's going to change. Besides, I know what kind of thing you're looking for from a relationship, and I can't give that to you right now. Maybe not ever. I owe it to myself to figure that out, and I owe it to you not to waste your time while I do. You've got your own stuff to work through—you know that, you don't need me to tell you—and so have I."

"What," he scoffs, "like a messy divorce?"

In my own way, I guess.

"I'm starting to realize I wanted a relationship for all the wrong reasons. Just because everybody else is in one. Just because I feel like being myself isn't enough—and it should be. It is. I *want* it to be enough," I tell him, and I startle myself with the passion in my words, the tremble in my voice, the tears that suddenly spring to my eyes. "I don't want to date someone just to try and fill a void that I don't think is even really there to begin with, that I've just convinced myself is there. Does that make sense?"

Harry doesn't respond immediately, but I can tell instantly that he gets it—much more than Lena and Tally did when I tried to talk to them about it, and much more than he did when I showed him a preview of my December article. Harry bows his head, sighing, and a small, resigned smile tugs at his lips.

"Yeah. It makes sense."

Someone shouts across the pub terrace, and then there's an uproar as everyone begins to chant the countdown.

Then there's Harry's voice, soft and sincere at my ear, saying, "For what it's worth, Sophie, I think you're more than enough. Don't ever let anybody convince you otherwise."

"*Three!*" chorus the crowd. "*Two!*"

"You're enough too," I tell Harry.

And when the countdown ends and midnight hits, I go on my tiptoes and kiss Harry on the cheek. I feel him smile, and we stand side by side, my head resting on his shoulder as we watch the firework display heralding the new year.

EDIT PROFILE

**ARE YOU SURE YOU WANT TO DELETE
YOUR HOOKD PROFILE?**

PROFILE DELETED.

February

~~VALENTINE'S DAY~~

GALENTINE'S DAY!

Epilogue

So long, farewell, and thanks for all the love.

Final Words from our Dating & Relationships columnist,
Sophie Barker

For all I'd like to think of January as a clean slate, especially after confessing all to my family and friends at Christmas and after everything that happened with Harry, the reality isn't so easy.

But by the time February rolls around, I see that time really does heal all wounds.

And today, February 13, I'm celebrating my new favorite holiday, Galentine's Day, surrounded by the people I love.

Tally and Lena sit to my right, looking at some guy's profile on Tally's Hookd and in peals of laughter over mimosas at bottomless brunch. (Because, honestly, what kind of Galentine's, or Sunday get-together, is complete without bottomless brunch?) They catch my eye and grin at me, shoving the phone under my nose for me to join in the laughter at this guy's awful attempts to sound impressive and cool when all his photos are of him pouting at the camera from his bed and look cringey as anything.

It's nice to have things back to normal with us after a few weeks of them feeling so distant while they got their heads around everything I told them at New Year's. By the time the three of us met up a few days ago to help Tally pack up the apartment she used to share with Sam, ready to move into a smaller, more affordable place, we were back to normal. Or this new, more honest normal, which is nice too.

Tally swipes the Hookd app closed and sets her phone down on the table before sighing and sweeping her hair back. "I know I keep swiping through, but I don't think I'm ready to actually meet anybody just yet. It's so intimidating to even message a total stranger! I don't know how you've done it, Soph. I'm in awe."

"You'll get used to it."

"Maybe sometime. I think it'll be nice to just be by myself for a while, though, like you're doing."

I smile back at her. "Maybe I'll come to jam-making class with you next week."

"Oh, no, I sacked that off. I'm doing an art class, though. Watercolor painting. That could be fun?"

"Count me in."

She gives my hand a squeeze and goes back to her food, the conversation turning to how Lena saw videos about having painters instead of photographers at the wedding to capture the first dance and how cool it looks, how she's trying to find one to get an idea of costs. Something warm and happy blooms in my chest.

I've missed my friends so much. Not just over the last couple of weeks, but the last few months. Years, even. They even apologized when we were packing up Tally's flat, like some preplanned intervention—they said they realized that as hurt as they might be because of all the secrets I kept from them, I was hurting too. Lena even said she was sorry for taking me for granted; Tally apologized for not being there for me enough.

It feels like a new phase of our friendship. And it feels good.

Jessica and Nadine didn't need the time to get over it the way Tally and Lena did, at least. They're on the other side of the girls, bickering about something, both drinking lemonade—Nadine because she's breastfeeding and Jessica because she announced to us last week that she's pregnant, which explains the booze she never drank on Christmas Day.

She told Nadine and me over a group FaceTime last week, and, even though the signs were there if I looked hard enough (or, you know, at all), my jaw hit the floor.

"No, you're not," I gasped. "Ohmigod. Does your mum know? Does Dad know? Was it planned?"

Shit, I thought. Are you supposed to ask people if their pregnancy was planned? Is it rude? Do I care, when it's only Jess?

And oh my god, it's Jessica. She's not even a full year younger than me, and in the space of the last year—the last six months!— she's gotten married *and* pregnant. And all I've done is, what? Decided to stop sleeping with my fake boyfriend because we both need some space?

I waited for that usual sting, the twist of a knife in my gut, the flare of jealousy I'm so used to. The nagging fear that it's not me, and what if it never is? The desire to suddenly cry and beg them not to leave me all behind while their own lives charge full steam ahead.

But it never arrived.

I just felt happy for her. A little surprised at the news, but happy for her.

And that's it.

Now, Nadine stabs her poached eggs on toast mournfully and says, "I can't believe you would do this to me, Jess. You weren't supposed to get pregnant for ages yet. You were supposed to be my babysitter, but now I'm going to have to be yours when you need me."

"I can still help out. I'll need the practice! And besides, there's always Sophie . . . You can babysit for both of us, can't you, Soph?" Jessica calls over to me, grinning.

And remembering what I wrote about boundaries and my free time being monopolized, how much I blame everyone else for that when I never bother to stand up for myself anyway, I tell them, "You know I'll help out when I can."

Voice dripping with sarcasm, Nadine tells me, "I think I liked you better before you grew a spine, Soph."

And Jessica tells me, "It's a good look on you."

"Thanks. It feels pretty good too."

Siobhan, sitting opposite me, doesn't miss the conversation. Smirking, she raises her mimosa to toast me. I clink my glass to hers, beaming, brimming with pride in myself.

"I'm still disappointed you're giving up the column," she tells me. "I was looking forward to reading about more of your wildly exaggerated exploits. My friend's having a party next week to celebrate the fact her cat's had a litter of kittens. I was going to invite you, see if you think dog biscuits or cat-food cupcakes taste better." She sighs, but before I can ask her if she's serious or not, she winks.

"It was just time to say goodbye to it," I say, and, while it was a little bittersweet to hand in my final piece, I know it's the right thing. Besides, my plate at work will be a little fuller now I'm taking over from Jenny while she's on maternity leave for the next few months.

"Good for you, Soph. I mean it."

"Thanks, Shiv."

On my other side, the table is occupied by Frankie and Jordan: Frankie because I bloody well miss him, and Jordan because he's cool, too, and also because I didn't want Frankie Two to get pissy about the fact that I invited her boyfriend to a group hang at brunch, even if she's busy herself all weekend with a hen party. Just because it's Galentine's doesn't mean my invitation to brunch was exclusively for girls—the whole point of it was to get my friends together, and that includes these two.

They're deep in an intense conversation about the best way to cook eggs, something so trivial rapidly turning into a heated debate.

"Are you mad? Soft-boiled eggs are *bottom tier*. I suppose I shouldn't expect anything less from someone as wet as soft-boiled egg yolk, you absolute *idiot*," Frankie is declaring in an arch tone, face wrinkled in disgust at his best friend.

I smother a giggle, sure it won't be long before they've roped all of us into their argument to get a definitive consensus on the correct ranking of ways to cook eggs, and my eyes linger on Frankie for a few moments. Things are going well with him and Frankie Two—they're adopting a dog soon. I'm happy for them. And some-how, I'm even relieved things are going so well, despite my thoughts about Frankie Two. I'm glad he's happy.

Not all that glitters, he told me, and he was right. But it's pretty golden here on my side of the fence, too, I'm realizing.

An invite to Galentine's brunch didn't extend to Harry, of course. We still talk a lot, and we've hung out a few more times, but only as friends. It's hard not to fall into old habits and flirt with each other constantly, but we're working on it. He's been on a couple of dates since New Year's, and, more importantly, he's trying to build bridges with his family again. Even if I had invited him today, he has somewhere more important to be: Sunday lunch at his parents' place, with his brother (and beloved niece and nephew) in atten-dance too. I would've offered to go as his friend to support him but he told them we broke up, so I guess it would've looked odd if I'd shown up. Besides, Harry seemed pretty determined to tackle it on his own—or to try, at least.

And honestly? Good for him.

Part of me regrets turning him down at Christmas. I look back through selfies we took together or remember how much fun he is to be with, and wonder *what if?*

But after a month of trying to figure out who I am, what I want, and not just what I'm looking for in a relationship but if I even really, truly, want one at all, I know I made the right choice. I know it wouldn't have been fair to either of us, and we would've been doomed if we'd jumped into something serious. For once, I can happily claim that I'm single.

I'm seeing him for drinks next weekend, though. So, who knows? Maybe one day, someday.

I'm glad Harry's not here today, though. I'm glad that today, it's just me and my friends.

I still feel in a bit of a daze over the simple, straightforward fact that my friends and I have all come together and we didn't even need to wait for someone to get engaged to do it. *I* didn't even need to get engaged to do it. All I had to do was ask if they were free, suggest we get together, and book a table at Slug and Lettuce—and here we all are.

Could it always have been this easy? Have I been stewing angrily over feeling neglected by my friends and like I'm not worth their time for the last couple of years for no reason?

Probably. The more I think about it, the more likely it seems.

It gives me another confidence boost, a taste of pride that's becoming gradually more familiar to me these days; a sense of power and freedom that I'm coming to enjoy, and also realizing might have been there all along if I'd only bothered to try to go after it instead of shoving it determinedly aside and trying to instead fill the void with another date, or wallowing over the fact it felt like I was losing my friends.

I know it'll still take time and practice, that it's all a work in progress. That *I'm* a work in progress.

But I'm getting there.

And I'm doing it for me, and nobody else.

Hello, world, I think, reciting the way I signed off my final article to myself one more time. I'm Sophie. I'm twenty-six, a Libra, and I'm single.

It's nice to meet you at last.

Acknowledgments

I feel like this book needs to come with a disclaimer to my friends and the brides of the weddings/hen parties I've attended—I promise I don't feel the way Sophie does in this book, even if I am your resident Single Friend. I sincerely love your dogs with their people names, and will make a joyful fool of myself dancing to "Single Ladies" any time.

As with all my books, I write what I want to read. In the case of this book, having spent almost my entire twenties so far (happily) single, I wanted to read about a fellow twentysomething singleton: the trials and tribulations, the friendships and self-love, and the solo cinema trips that go along with it.

First, to my friends: I love you, you're awesome, and thanks for always being there. To Lauren and Jen, whom I can always rely on for cheers and laughs; Amy and Katie, forever on the other end of my needy messages and the rare first-date dramas; the physics gang, because even if we only get together every few months (or years!) it's always a blast; the Gobble Gals (née Cactus Gals) who let me rope them into some Dungeons & Dragons larks and are truly excellent brunch buddies. To the folks across the pond—Iny, MC, Tyler and Ethan and Emily, Pix, Rach, Kait and Linton—y'all are awesome. To Becca, too, who was so excited for my tropey fake-dating book. I wish you could've seen it, mate. And last but not least, to Aimee:

this book is dedicated to you and all the dating-debrief Snapchats over the years, and the brilliant and bonkers stories you always have to share. Here's to finding our Prince Charmings one day, huh?

As always, thanks to my family—especially thanks for not pressuring me to "settle down" the way Sophie thinks her family do to her, and for always making swiping through Bumble a good laugh. Thanks in particular to Mum for coming up with the name for my fictional dating app, Hookd, and Gransha for always championing my books.

One more big thank-you to go and then I promise I'm done. There are so many wonderful people behind the scenes who make a book happen, but thank you to my ever-brilliant agent Clare for always being a total powerhouse; to Bec, Deanna, and Fiona for believing in this book; and everyone else who brought it to life—and to bookshelves!

About the Author

Beth Reekles is the author of bestselling YA series The Kissing Booth (now also a hit trilogy on Netflix) alongside several other rom-com novels. Her tenth book and debut adult novel, *Lockdown on London Lane*, was published in 2022. A self-confessed nerd and rom-com fan, she is now a full-time author and shares movie reviews on her Instagram.

More from Beth Reekles

FROM THE INTERNATIONALLY BESTSELLING AUTHOR OF
THE KISSING BOOTH

Beth Reekles

LOCKDOWN
on
LONDON
LANE

Chapter One

It's starting to get light out; the venetian blinds are a pale-gray color that does nothing to keep the sunshine away. The entire window seems to glow, and pale shadows fall across the rest of the room, obscuring the organized cluster of hair products and cologne on the dresser, playing tricks on the hoodie hanging in front of the wardrobe doors. There's a knee digging into my thigh. I rub a hand over my face, feeling last night's mascara congealing around the edges of my eyes, and start to peel myself out of the bed, hissing when I discover an arm is pinning down my hair. I bunch it up into a ponytail, slowly, to ease it free inch by inch.

The mattress creaks when I sit up, but—Nigel? I want to say Nigel—snorts in his sleep, still totally out of it, oblivious to my being in his bed.

I glance over my shoulder at him.

Still cuter than his profile picture, even with a line of drool down his chin.

"This has been fun," I whisper, even though he's fast asleep. I blow him a kiss and creep across the bedroom to silently wriggle into my jeans. I look down at the T-shirt of his I borrowed to sleep in. It's a Ramones shirt, and it feels genuinely vintage, not just some ten-pound H&M version. Actually, it's really goddamn comfortable. And cute, I think, catching a glimpse of myself in the mirror leaning against the far wall. Oversized, but not in a way that makes me look like a little kid playing dress-up. I tuck it into the front of my jeans, admiring the effect.

Oh yeah, that's cute.

Sorry, Neil—Neil? Maybe that's it—this shirt is mine now.

My long brown hair, on the other hand, looks kind of scraggly and definitely not cute. Yesterday evening's curls have dropped out, leaving it limp, full of kinks, and looking pretty sorry for itself. I run my fingers through it, but give up. Hey, at least the smeared mascara is giving me some grunge vibes that totally match the Ramones shirt.

Collecting my own T-shirt and bra from the bedroom floor, I tiptoe into the open-plan living/dining room. Where'd I leave my bag? Wasn't it—a-ha, there it is! And my coat too. I stuff my clothes into my bag, then look around for my shoes.

Come on, Imogen, think, they've got to be around here somewhere. I can't have lost them. I wasn't even drunk last night! Where did I leave my damn shoes?

Oh my God, no. I remember. He made me leave them outside, saying they looked muddy. Like it was my fault it rained last night and the pathway up to the apartment block was covered in mud from the flower beds. And I joked that they were Prada and if someone stole them this had better be worth it, even though I'd only bought them on sale from Zara.

I do a final sweep just to make sure I've got everything. Phone—check. House key—yep, in my bag.

I hesitate, then do a quick dash back to the tiny two-seater dining table near the living-room door to nab a slice of leftover pepperoni pizza from our delivery late yesterday evening.

Breakfast of champions.

I step over some junk mail as I sneak out of the front door. It can't be much later than seven o'clock. Who the hell delivers junk mail that early in the morning? Who is *that* dedicated?

My shoes are exactly where I left them.

And, all right, in fairness, they do look like I trekked through a farmyard. I really can't blame him for making me take them off outside the apartment. I'm going to have to clean them up when I get home.

I hold the slice of pizza between my teeth as I wriggle my feet into them—and *ew*, they're soggy—and then I slip my coat on.

Okay, good to go!

I skip down the stairs to the ground floor, munching on my pizza and already on the Uber app to get myself a car home. These shoes are cute, but not really made for a walk of shame.

"Excuse me, miss?"

Despite there being nobody else around, I don't realize the voice is directed at me until it says, "Hey you, Ramones!"

When I turn around, I find a tired, stressed-looking guy with a handful of leaflets. Mr. Junk Mail, I'm assuming. He's wearing a blue surgical mask over his mouth and ugly brown slippers.

"Thanks, mate, but I'm not interested," I tell him, and make for the door.

Except when I push it open, it . . . doesn't.

I grab the big steel handle and yank, and push, and rattle, but the door stays firmly locked.

What the fuck?

Oh my God, this is how I die. A one-night stand and a serial killer peddling leaflets. Please, please don't let anybody put that as cause of death on my gravestone.

"Miss, you can't leave," the man tells me wearily. "Didn't you get the note?"

"What note? What are you talking about?"

I turn to him, my phone clutched in my hand. Should I call the police? My mum? The Uber driver?

The man sighs, exasperated, stepping toward me, but still maintaining a good distance. Like me, there's a rumpled look about him, but he looks more like he rushed out of the house this morning, not like he's just heading home. There's a huge ring of keys hanging from his belt. Then I clock the white latex gloves he's wearing and get a sinking feeling in my stomach.

"We got a confirmed case from one of the residents. The whole building's on lockdown. That door doesn't open except for medical needs and food deliveries."

I stare at him, all too aware that my mouth is hanging open. After a while, he shrugs in that *What can you do?* kind of way.

It's a joke, I realize.

It's got to be a joke.

I let out an awkward laugh, my lips stretching into a smile. "Right. Right, yeah, good one. Look, um, totally get it, real serious, but can you just . . . you know, use one of those keys, let me out of here? Cross my heart, I'll be *super* careful. Look, hey, I'll even cancel my Uber and walk, how about that?"

The guy frowns at me. "Miss, do you realize how serious this is?"

"Absolutely," I reassure him, but instead of sounding sincere, it comes off as fake, like I'm trying too hard. Condescending, even. Shit. I try again. "I get it. I do, but look, the thing is, I was just visiting someone. So I shouldn't really be here right now. And I kind of have to get home?"

There's a flicker of sympathy on his face, and I let myself get excited at having won him over. But then the frown returns, and he tells me sternly, "You know you're not supposed to be traveling unnecessarily, don't you?"

Damn it.

"Well, I mean . . . couldn't you just . . . "

I look longingly over my shoulder at the door. At the muddy path on the other side of the glass, the washed-out flower beds with the droopy rosebushes and brightly colored petunias. Freedom—so close I can almost taste it, and yet . . .

And yet all I can taste is my own morning breath and pepperoni pizza.

Which is not as great now as it was two minutes ago.

What are the odds I can snatch his keys off his belt and unlock the door before he catches me? Hmm, pretty nonexistent. Or what if I just run really hard and really fast at the door? Maybe I could smash the window with one of my heels? Ooh! Could I hypnotize him into letting me out of here? I could definitely give it a go. I've seen a few clips of Derren Brown on YouTube.

"Seven-day quarantine," my jailer tells me. "I've got to deep clean all the communal spaces. Anyone could be infected, and unless you're going to tell me you've got fifty-odd tests for all the residents in that bag of yours, nobody's going anywhere. Believe me, this is no fun for me either. You think I want to be playing security guard all day long just so I don't get fired by management and end up evicted?"

Okay, *fine*, well done. Congrats, Mr. Junk Mail, I officially feel sorry for you.

"But—"

"Listen, all I can suggest is you go back to your friend"—I appreciate that he says *friend* as though we're talking about an actual friend here, when it's so obvious that's not the case—"and see if you can get a grocery delivery slot, and maybe one from Topshop or whatever, see you through the next week. But unless you need to go to a hospital, you're stuck here."

*

I trudge slowly, grudgingly, back up the stairs. My shoes are pinching my toes, so I take them off, slinging the straps over my index finger to carry them. Mr. Junk Mail stays downstairs to scrub down the door I just put my grubby hands all over, almost like he's warding me off, making sure I don't try to leave again.

What the hell am I supposed to do now?

Ugh.

I know exactly what I'm supposed to do now.

But still, I hope for the teeniest bit of luck as I jiggle the handle for Apartment 14.

Locked.

Obviously.

Weighing up my options, I finally sit down on the plain tan doormat, my back against the door, and press my hands over my face.

This is what I get for ignoring all the advice.

Not so much the *stay home* stuff (although that, too) so much as the *You're not in university anymore, Immy, stop acting like it* advice—from my parents, my friends, my boss, hell, even my little brothers.

As I always say, who needs to grow up when you can have fun?

This, however, is decidedly *not* fun.

My only option is to do exactly what I would've done back in university: phone my bestie.

Despite the early hour, Lucy answers with a quiet but curt, "What have you done this time?"

"Heyyy, Luce . . ."

"How much do you need, Immy?"

"What makes you think I need money? What makes you think I've done *anything*?" I ask with mock offense, clutching a hand to my heart for dramatic effect, even though she can't see me. And even though I can't see her, I absolutely know she's rolling her eyes when she gives that long, low sigh. "Although, all right, I am in . . . the *littlest* spot of trouble."

"Did you forget to cancel a free trial?"

Lucy's so used to my shit by now that she knows how melodramatic I can be over something like that—melodramatic enough to warrant an early-morning phone call like this.

But, alas.

I open my mouth to tell her I'm stuck with Honeypot Guy, the guy I've been messaging for the last week or so, whom she specifically told me not to go see because there's maybe a pandemic, and now I'm stuck quarantined in his building and I only have the one pair of underwear and I didn't even bring a toothbrush with me and . . .

And I *hate* admitting how right Lucy always is.

Even if, technically, this is all *her* fault, because she was too busy with some stupid wedding planning party last night to answer her phone and talk me out of going to see the guy in the first place. So I decided to go, and not tell her about it until I was safely back at home, just to prove a point about how she always makes a big deal out of nothing, how she worries too much.

"Oh Jesus Christ, you went to see him, didn't you? Honeypot?"

I *cannot* tell her the truth.

At least, not yet.

"No! No, no, of course I didn't," I blurt, even though I fully expect her to see right through me. "I, um, I'm just . . . well, look, so, the thing is . . ."

I don't like lying to my best friend—to anybody, really, if I can help it. If anything, I'm a total oversharer. But I decide this is for the greater good. I mean, really, I'm just doing her a favor, right? If she knew, she'd only spend the week worrying and stressing about me. I'm just sparing her that.

Lucy cuts me off with a sigh, understanding that whatever it is, it's a bit more than the usual mischief I get myself into, and she says, "Oh, you're properly fucked this time, aren't you?"

"Thanks, Luce."

Thankfully, she doesn't push me for answers. "How's your overdraft?"

"Not great."

"Did you run up your credit card again this month?"

"A little bit."

We both know that actually means "almost completely."

"Will a hundred quid cover it, Immy?"

"I love you."

"I'll add it to your tab," she tells me, and I know she's smiling. "Are you sure you're all right?"

"Oh, you know me!" I say, laughing. I'm weirdly relieved that being quarantined with a one-night stand isn't the craziest thing that's happened to me in the last month or so. It's definitely not as bad as the night out where I climbed onstage to challenge the headlining drag queen to a lip sync battle, is it? "I'll work it out. Just . . . yeah. Thanks again, Luce. I'll tell you everything when I see you next."

"Don't you always?"

Lucy has a way of ending conversations without having to say good-bye. I know her well enough to recognize that this is one of those moments. I say good-bye and thank her again for the money she'll send me, the way she always does, which I will repay in love and affection and memes until one day in the distant future, when I have miraculously gotten my life together enough to pay off my overdraft *and* have enough left to put a dent in my ever-growing tab at the Bank of Lucy.

Feeling at least a little better, I stand back up, dust myself off, and knock on the door.

It takes a few minutes to open.

He's disconcerted and groggy and wearing only his boxer shorts. The carefully coiffed blond hair I'd admired in his pictures is now matted, sticking up at all angles. The dried line of drool is still there on the side of his mouth.

I give him my biggest, bestest grin, cocking my head to one side and twirling some hair around a finger.

"Hey there, Niall. Um . . . "

He yawns loudly and holds up a finger to shush me before covering his mouth. He shakes his head, blinking a few times, then looks at me, confused and none too impressed.

"I hate to be an imposition, but your building is kind of . . . quarantined."

"It's what?"

I look for the piece of paper I stepped over earlier and bend down to pick it up. It's a printed notice that, at a quick glance, instructs residents to stay indoors for a seven-day period. I hold it out to him, staying silent and swaying side to side, hands clasped in front of me, while he reads it, rubbing his eyes. He has to squint, holding it up close to his face.

"Oh shit."

"There's a guy downstairs, and he won't let me leave," I say. "I'm *really* sorry, but unless you want to take it up with him . . . "

I step back inside the apartment, leaving my shoes outside once more. He's speechless as I put down my bag and coat.

"I'm just going to use your bathroom. You know, wash my hands." I waggle them at him, as if to prove what a responsible grown-up I am.

When I come out he's still standing by the door, still clutching the paper.

"So, Nico, listen—"

"It's Nate."

"What?"

"My name?" He raises his eyebrows at me, looking more pissed off than tired now. "Nate. Nathan, but . . . Nate."

I bite my lip, grimacing. I'd kind of hoped if I ran through enough names, I'd hit on the right one eventually. I'd also kind of hoped if I said them quickly enough, he wouldn't notice.

"Sorry. You're . . . you're saved in my phone contacts as the honeypot emoji. You know, 'cause you . . . you said that if you were a fictional character, you'd be Winnie-the-Pooh, and you said your mum kept bees and . . . and that your favorite chocolate bar is Crunchie, which has honeycomb in it . . . I thought it was cute at the time, and funny, but then I realized I'd forgotten your name, and you deleted your profile off the dating app, so I couldn't check *that* . . . "

Nate's face has softened.

But then, as I take my coat off, he realizes what I'm wearing and lets out a loud, disbelieving laugh. "You're really something, aren't you? Talking your way over here when everyone's meant to be social distancing—"

"I didn't hear *you* complaining," I mutter, none too quietly.

"Sneaking out without so much as a good-bye, *and* you were planning to make off with my favorite shirt. Wow."

"Maybe it was just going to be a good excuse to see you again."

He laughs, rolling his eyes. "Imogen, believe me when I say I have *never* met anybody like you before."

I curtsy, even though it sounds like an insult, the way he says it. "Thank you."

That, at least, makes him laugh. Nate-Nathan-Nate runs a hand through his hair, taming it only slightly, then tells me, "There are spare towels in the bathroom cabinet if you want to take a shower. I'm going to see if I can get a food delivery slot online. Then, I guess we'll . . . I don't know. Figure this out."

I'm not exactly sure what there is to "figure out" besides maybe ordering some frozen lasagnas and a few pairs of underwear, but I nod. "Right. Totally. You got it, Nate."

So much for my swift exit.

Chapter Two

It's automatic, the way I roll over when I'm not even fully awake yet, my arm out to pull her closer. The empty space beside me startles me for a second before I wake up enough to remember where she is. I turn back over to face my bedside cabinet, rubbing the sleep out of my eyes with one hand and fumbling for my phone with the other. My hand closes on it and I yank out the charger.

There's a notification waiting for me on the screen: a text from Charlotte an hour ago.

Just about to leave—I'll see you in a couple of hours! Xxxxx

She always tells me she's not a morning person, but the honest to God truth is she absolutely is. What she is, is the kind of person who likes a *lazy* morning. She'll wake up an hour before she has to be at work just so she can spend some time curled up under the covers reading, or jotting things down in the powder-blue notebook she takes everywhere with her.

Today must be a special occasion, though, for her to have been actually up and out of bed so early. Well—either that, or after three days being home with her twin sister and parents, clearing out her childhood bedroom and the attic to get ready for her parents to sell up and downsize, she's been going stir-crazy and can't wait to get home.

Yeah, I think, it's definitely that one. She's been putting this weekend off for as long as she can; she's been living in denial of her parents selling the house since they announced it a couple of months ago, and I can't say I blame her. My parents divorced when I was ten and after that, they both moved around a couple of times. If I had to say goodbye to the kind of home Charlotte's known her whole life, I'd be pretty upset about it too.

I can only imagine how tough this weekend has been for her; it makes sense she'd be on the road before eight o'clock.

What doesn't make sense is how much I've missed her the last couple of days. It's genuinely pathetic. I can just imagine my friends telling me, *Ethan, grow a pair, any guy would give his right arm to have the place to himself for a weekend, get the girlfriend out of the way, have a break from her!*

I *did* see a couple of mates on Friday night, but that was for a Fortnite livestream for my Twitch channel. And *see* is stretching it a little—we all joined from the comfort of our own homes. Real crazy, frat-boy kinda stuff, of course. While the cat's away, and all that.

But I've missed her.

It's not like I can't *cope* without her, like I'm some mummy's boy who never learned to do the dishes or make a bed or do the laundry or anything. It's not like that. If anything, *I'm* the one who does the bulk of the cleaning around here, always tidying up after her.

It'll be good to have her back home, that's all.

I stay in bed for a while checking my other notifications—YouTube, Twitter, WhatsApp. I clear through some emails saying I've got new patrons on Patreon, which sends a thrill of excitement through me, as it always does, and finally I haul my lazy ass up to take a shower before Charlotte gets back.

We can catch up on *The Mandalorian* this afternoon, maybe, if she doesn't want to spend some time writing. Or we could watch a movie. I wonder if she'll have a bunch of stuff from her childhood bedroom we need to find the space for—old exercise books and homework projects we'll have to shove in a box under the bed, or Beanie Babies.

Maybe she'd let me put the Beanie Babies on eBay, if they're worth anything.

I can't complain too much if she does want to keep them. It's not like I don't have my fair share of action figures and collectibles in the apartment. And the giant Charizard plushie . . .

I dread the day my parents get the same idea; I hope that by the time they do, I'll at least live somewhere with enough space to store my entire collection of Neil Gaiman books, my old PlayStation, records from my vinyl phase that I can't quite bear to get rid of.

It occurs to me now that when Charlotte thinks of us moving somewhere with more space one day, she thinks about it in the context of a guest bedroom, or a potential future nursery. Or a library. Actually, I could definitely get on board with a home library.

Breakfast made, I'm sat on the sofa watching old episodes of *Parks and Rec* and daydreaming about the studio space I might have one day that *isn't* just a dedicated few square feet of the living room, when my phone rings. It's Charlotte, which is weird, and I answer with a knot in my stomach, visions of her car broken down on the side of a motorway or—

Come on, Ethan, take a breath and answer the phone.

Sliding my thumb across the screen to answer, I manage to *not* start with, "What's wrong?" and instead say, "Hey, what's up? Did you forget your key?"

"Ethan," she says. Her voice wobbles. The catastrophizing part of my brain kicks into high gear for a second, thinking I was right, her car broke down, something is horribly wrong. She sounds upset, but it's not just that—she's agitated, angry. "Ethan, you have to get down here. He's saying I'm not allowed in the building."

"What? Who?"

"Mr. Harris," she tells me, meaning the building's live-in caretaker. "He's—Ethan, can you please come down here and talk to him? And wear a mask."

Confused as hell, I can only hold the phone near my ear even after Charlotte's hung up on me, before kicking myself into gear. I leave my plate of half-eaten bagel on the sofa and root through the set of drawers in the hallway. She thought it was ridiculous when I ordered a bunch of blue surgical masks online a couple of weeks ago, before they even started using the word *pandemic* in the news; now, I can't help but feel a little smug. Anxiety: 1, Charlotte: 0.

I wash my hands and put the mask on, then snatch up my key and leave the apartment. There's a scrap of paper on the floor someone's pushed under the door, but I'll check it later. I go down the single flight of stairs in just my socks, almost tripping over my own feet in my haste.

Mr. Harris is standing near the main doors to the building with his arms crossed, wearing white latex gloves and a mask like mine. On the other side, with her bags on the floor and her hands bunched into fists on her hips, is Charlotte. My glasses steam up from the mask so I nudge them up on top of my head, where they balance on my thick blond-brown hair, and I squint at him instead; Charlotte's head becomes a fuzzy patch of orange where her hair is a mess.

"What's going on?"

"Ethan, tell him!" she yells, voice muffled by the door. She raises a hand to pound against the glass, leaving smudges on it. "He's locked me out! He can't do this!"

The caretaker sighs. It's a long-suffering sigh, like this is a conversation he's already had a thousand times. He turns to give me a frown and I can imagine his teeth grinding behind that mask.

"Ethan, please tell your girlfriend she can't enter the building. You got the note, right?"

"What note?"

"Bloody hell, what was even the point of me . . . ?" He trails off with a sharp sigh, rubbing the back of his forearm against his brow. "The whole building's on lockdown. You remember I put a notice out when all this started that said if anybody in the building got sick, if we had a confirmed case, we had to lock down for everybody's safety? Nobody in or out."

"Yeah . . . ?"

"Confirmed case last night. Someone, *not naming any names*, caught it from her *divorce lawyer*, if you can believe it. She got a test done and it turned up positive. So we're on lockdown. Nobody's getting *in*, or *out*. Including your girlfriend."

Oh shit.

I bump my glasses back down to see Charlotte's face, still scrunched up in anger, her lips in a tight little pout. They steam up again just as she gives me a look that says, *Ethan, I swear to God, if you don't open this door right now, I'll break it down myself.*

For someone so small . . . what's that Shakespeare quote again?

Charlotte has it printed on a tote bag. It's very accurate right now.

"Come on, Mr. Harris," I say, with a nervous laugh. My hand moves up like I'm going to step toward him and clap his arm, until I remember the six-foot rule and think better of it. "It's us, you know we're good. Charlotte lives here. Where's she gonna go?"

"Where's she been?"

"At her parents, but—"

"Well, she's going to have to go back there."

"But . . . "

I wouldn't exactly say I was *friends* with our caretaker, but we're on good terms. His apartment is directly below ours, and apparently he's glad to have us there, because the previous owners "might as well have been practicing tap dancing with all the noise they made." He watches my YouTube videos, too, he told me a while ago. He said he likes having "a celebrity" in the building, and we always stop for a chat if we see him.

I don't know why I think I'm going to convince him to let Charlotte in when he looks so determined, but for a second I really believe I can. We've never made any fuss. We're good neighbors, good people, he even knows us by name.

And how can he say no?

Charlotte lives here, this is her home. Of course he has to let her inside.

"I can't let her inside," he tells me sternly. "Nobody in, nobody out, no exceptions. Well. Exceptions are by emergency only, and this doesn't class as one."

"What about food?"

"Get it delivered. I'm setting up a sanitizing station, make sure every-thing's clean before it gets through."

For a second, I imagine having something like that for Charlotte, and Mr. Harris setting up a giant hose to douse her in Dettol spray before she's allowed inside.

"Unless she can show me a negative test," he says reluctantly, as though he's risking his job by even allowing us that much, "she's not getting in. Quarantine's lasting a week. Sure you two can survive being apart for that long, eh?"

He shrugs, and his scowl softens just long enough for me to see he actually *is* sorry about this whole mess; I know he doesn't have too much say on the matter, that this really is up to his bosses, the mysterious, faceless, building management we've never set eyes on but who occasionally send us threatening letters via Mr. Harris to remind us there are no pets in the building, there is no renovation work to be done without clearing it with them first, that if nobody owns up to who damaged the window on the third floor they *will* be charging an equal share of the (absolutely extortionate) cost of repairs to each resident.

I always picture them in the same way as Station Management, from the *Welcome to Night Vale* podcast—some mysterious, dark, writhing, many-headed mass of condemnation. Charlotte says they're more like Mr. Rochester's mad wife in the attic from *Jane Eyre*. Either way, I don't imagine petitioning *them* right now would make a blind bit of difference.

Mr. Harris steps back, but he doesn't leave. He's got to make sure I don't try to smuggle Charlotte indoors, I guess.

I do the only thing I can, which is to turn toward her and give her a helpless shrug, pulling a face even though she can't really see it because I'm wearing a mask. I can't see her expression clearly enough because of my fogged-up glasses, but I can guess how disappointed she is.

She gestures widely enough for me to see, though, and I get the message. I tell Mr. Harris "Thanks," even though it's really thanks for nothing, and head back upstairs. Inside, I wash my hands again, take off the mask, and pull my glasses back down so I can see the world in all its high-definition glory again. My phone is already ringing on the sofa and I grab it, answering as I head out to the balcony, leaning over it to see Charlotte standing below.

She runs a hand through her short ginger hair, shaking it out, and pouts up at me, looking so desperately sad. Through the phone, she tells me, "I thought he might listen to you."

"Because I'm a guy?" I flex a nonexistent bicep and kiss it.

"Because he likes your YouTube videos, you *idiot.*" She laughs, but it fades away quickly. "I'm going to have to go home. Just as well my parents haven't gotten rid of my old bed yet, huh?"

"Do you need your stuff? I could drop a bag down from the balcony. Clothes, or . . . ?"

She shakes her head. "Thanks, sweetie, but that's okay. I've got some stuff, and my laptop and things. I can borrow some of Maisie's clothes. She has terrible taste, but she *is* my identical twin. Give or take a few pounds." Charlotte grabs her love handles, cracking a grin.

"Didn't you both buy the same dress last Christmas?"

"Shush. Look, I'll . . . I'll just go back home. I'll see you next week, I guess."

"Providing this is all over by then." And someone else in the building hasn't contracted the virus, and then someone else, and we're not in this strict lockdown for the next several months, and Charlotte never gets to come back to our apartment, and . . . My chest constricts, and suddenly looking out at the empty common area in front of the apartment is like surveying some scene from an apocalyptic disaster movie. And *I am on my own.* I'm basically Will Smith in *I Am Legend*, except without the dog, and not half as cool, and—

"I'll be back next week when this silly lockdown thing is over. I promise. I'll scale the walls if I have to, okay? Don't spiral."

"I'm not spiraling."

She raises her eyebrows, squinting up at me, not buying it. Despite the fact that she's the one locked out of her home for the next several days, somehow she's the one comforting me.

"It'll be fine. It's—it's not a big deal, really, is it? In the grand scheme of things. We can FaceTime, and text, and you can have some peace

and quiet to film a few videos and get some work done without me walking by in the background and messing up your edits. It's fine. It's just a week."

We talk a little while longer, until Mr. Harris opens the main door long enough to tell Charlotte to please collect her bags and go, and I wave good-bye from the balcony. Charlotte blows me a kiss on her way to her car, and I catch it.

Just a week.

It'll fly by.

© 2022 Beth Reekles